Praise for Forrest Aguirre

"With imaginative vigor, Aguirre explores the fluctuating boundaries that separate human from inhuman, terrestrial from extraterrestrial, and natural from supernatural . . ."

—*Publishers Weekly* [on *Fugue XXIX*]

"*Fugue XXIX* is a selection of grotesque delicacies from the work of an enviable imagination."

—*HorrorScope*

"I was happily surprised by this truly wonderful collection of riveting stories… I know that I will be thinking about these ideas again and again, often because of how Aguirre crafted his words more than the concept itself. *Fugue XXIX* is a fine collection from one of the great stylists of our age and another work that proves genre IS literature."

—SFRevu.com

"Forrest Aguirre's beautiful stories are a set of portals that lead to the very quintessence of the ancient and noble art of the fantastic. His narrative is the contemporary prose equivalent of the wildly imaginative paintings of Hieronymus Bosch."

—Zoran Zivkovic, author of *The Fourth Circle*

Also by Forrest Aguirre

Fugue XXIX
Swans Over The Moon

Leviathan 3 (co-edited with Jeff Vandermeer)
Leviathan 4 (edited by)

HERACLIX AND POMP

HERACLIX AND POMP

A NOVEL OF
the FABRICATED
and the FEY

FORREST AGUIRRE

Underland Press

Map courtesy of The National Library of Israel, Shapell Family Digitization Project and The Hebrew University of Jerusalem, Department of Geography—Historic Cities Research Project.

This is U015, and it has an ISBN of 978-1-63023-001-2.

This book was printed in the United States of America, and it is published by Underland Press, an imprint of Resurrection House (Puyallup, WA).

Leap clear of all that is corporeal . . .

Edited by Mark Teppo
Cover Design by Claudia Noble
Book Design by Aaron Leis
Copy Edit by Darin Bradley

First hardback Underland Press edition: October 2014.

www.resurrectionhouse.com

HERACLIX AND POMP

*To Stepan Chapman, Gary Gygax, Dave Arneson, Dave Trampier,
and Ronnie James Dio for keeping this kid's dreams alive.*

"Think that you are not yet begotten, that you are in the womb, that you are young, that you are old, that you have died, that you are in the world beyond the grave; grasp in your thought all of this at once . . . then you can apprehend God."

—Hermes Trismegistus, *Hermetica*

The Golem:

He walked with the perpetual forward lean of a man forever climbing stairs. Perhaps this was because he had been resurrected in pieces and was carried forward by an instinctive, unasked-for will to live when he had awakened and risen from the dead. Or, rather, the pieces of him had. In fact, it was difficult to call him "he" at all—though this wasn't a question of gender, it was a question of pluralities. Wouldn't "they" be more appropriate, seeing that the body his amnesiac conscience now inhabited was a stitched-up mosaic of several lives that had gone before the current incarnation? At the moment, he didn't have time to think about anatomical philosophy. He had a sorcerer to kill—to murder, to be exact—for no better reason than the doddering old lich had been the one to create him. Oh, and there was the matter of the prim young lady dying on the floor—the girl with the wings.

The Fairy:

She has always been; she will always be. This is the way with her kind. Neither age, nor senescence, nor disease, nor slumber can take hold of her. Granted, there are dangers in the modernizing world, but they're nothing that her innate abilities can't handle. Instantaneous invisibility, dragonfly wings, and a quiver full of

7

potent arrows—along with a charming personality—are her assurances of everlasting life. What did she have to fear from a kindly old man who wanted merely to engage her in conversation about the beauties of the meadow beyond the woods she calls home? Now, the answers seem more evident. Can she be both gullible and immortal? Not for long, she thinks as she lays dying on the floor. Then, she thinks, "What is long?"

The Sorcerer:

The artifices of magic couldn't completely hide the sorcerer's age and its effects, not even from the man himself. He had recently celebrated his 300th birthday, if one considers stopping in the street long enough for a hearty cackle between wheezes a true celebration. He didn't have time for a full-blown party with all the niceties. He was rushing to meet a deadline, in the truest sense of the word. Three hundred years meant nothing if it was to end soon, and his falsely summoned charisma had barely held out long enough to entice the fairy out of the woods. The fairy was critical to his success, and if he continued to deteriorate, he would never get another chance to renew his contract, to hold off his creditors for another century or two, the length of the extension dependent on who or what he happened to dredge up from the underworld when he cast his bait into the depths. This time, he was lucky enough to call up Beelzebub himself, rather than the lesser fiends he had summoned before. This contract could be good for another millennium, enough time to gather the forces to carve out a comfortable place in Hell on *his* terms, rather than those of his devilish creditors. For most men, death was inevitable. For him, immortality, of a sort, was attainable, for the right price. Death was merely an obstacle.

CHAPTER 1

Heraclix's view of his own creation as a birth was much more than idle Romanticism, though this was the *zeitgeist* that had then begun to take hold of Europe. The new Romantics would have exaggerated the pathos of the event, focusing on the dramatic, under-emphasizing the cold facts and looking for a deeper meaning beyond the banal. But even an enlightened observer would have been compelled to acknowledge that the coming forth of Heraclix-qua-Heraclix was indeed a birth.

He remembered nothing of what came before the womb, though he felt intimations from that pre-existent time that he couldn't quite form into full realizations. As the will to live slowly fused with his nascent consciousness, his heart, brain, and eyes awakened. Immediately, questions led to posits that led to more questions, and his awareness grew: Who am I? I am I. Where am I? I am here. What is here? It is where I am. What is where? And so forth.

Red.

He knew the color, but he didn't know how or to what use the knowledge should be put, though he felt a need to act.

Liquid.

He floated in a sort of semisuspended animation, feet above the ground, head below the ceiling, but he knew he wasn't flying. The weight he felt on his bones would not allow him to fly.

Blood.

He knew the word, knew that blood came from bodies, knew it was not a good thing to be surrounded by it on all sides, which he was.

Air.

He needed air.

Now!

He flailed his arms above his head, seeking purchase, and found it. Each hand grasped something hard, something rough, something that he could use to pull himself up. He stretched and pulled himself through the liquid.

At first, he thought he might fly, after all. Then he found that he was falling out of whatever it was that had contained him into the open air and onto a stone floor. It was bitterly cold, and he dripped with blood, shivering like a newborn.

A large apartment full of bookshelves, beakers, small cauldrons, and musty tomes swept into his vision as he lifted his dizzy head. Behind him was a gigantic cauldron, which must have been his womb. Above him, to one side, stood a thin, trembling old man who filled him with revulsion, despite Heraclix's best efforts to withhold judgment.

"Ah, my boy, you are ready. And you live!" the geriatric said. "I am your father, boy, and your mother. You are my son, and I shall name you Heraclix."

But Heraclix, driven by an insatiable need to know all he could about the man who had named him, learned the old man's name, in time: Mattatheus Mowler. Heraclix also learned much more about the old man. Much of it he learned while his master was away on errands. Reading came naturally to Heraclix, though, like many things about himself, he could not say whence the ability came. Nevertheless, the many books and frequent correspondences that Mowler received were too rich a temptation to pass up in those nervous moments between the time the door clicked shut behind Mowler and when the door handle rattled to signal the old man's return. Heraclix was able, from the journals, letters, and ledgers that he read, to piece together a rough map of his master's life.

Mowler was very, very old. Unnaturally so. But records or notes or even hints between the lines of the man's childhood simply did not exist.

Heraclix drew his mental map of the old man, gaining finer and finer resolution the more he read and associated one letter with another. Certain themes emerged like topographical features: details of interest, emotion, and experience. Mowler was a touch insecure, but driven. Driven enough, in fact, that his ambitions and their execution were enough to bury those insecurities and mask them as strengths. His overconfidence veiled a lack of confidence. His sharp wit belied a fear of ridicule. His praise of youth obfuscated his fear of death.

It was the last of these that drove him into a study of the arcane arts. He refused to succumb to the inevitability of aging and death. Mowler's creation of Heraclix—as the golem learned from the magician's notebooks—was only an experiment in reanimating dead tissue, another insurance against the grave, though Mowler's notes made it clear that reanimation, with its attendant loss of memory, wouldn't suffice for the sorcerer. His mind had to be clear in order to successfully maneuver the Byzantine contractual obligations that he had brought on himself through deals with various devils, demons, and necromancers. He couldn't afford a legal *faux pas*.

Heraclix read further and discovered that Mowler was well-connected from top to bottom in the material world, as well as the abyss. His list of contacts and those he referred to as "clients" ranged from a local beggar who provided him with street-level information to those who had access to the secret chambers of the Holy Roman Emperor, Joseph II himself. The golem noted that the designation "client" was clearly a misnomer for the relationship that Mowler kept with others. The sorcerer's journals were filled with scorn enough for everyone mentioned, while his letters ranged between sarcastic ridicule and outright berating of the unfortunate addressee. There was ample evidence that the old man was manipulating some of his clients, pitting them against each other in a political and social chess game designed to produce one victor: Mowler. The magician's tendrils reached outward to grasp at any opportunity to seize power. Heraclix could sense in the man's writings an unquenchable desire for more, ever more.

This obsession with authority showed clearly in Mowler's maltreatment of his "boy." Despite Heraclix's gargantuan frame, he couldn't muster the attitude to fight back against his master's abuses. Whenever he thought he might lash out, a heavy sense of self-loathing held him back. He felt that he deserved the beatings as penance for some un-remembered sin he had committed before he was even aware of himself. Self-deprecation was endemic to his being. Mowler rained cane blows down on Heraclix's broad back, screamed epithets into his deformed ears, and committed shameful acts to the rest of his gigantic body. Heraclix suffered willingly those things he did not understand, like a child, all in a spirit of meek obedience for what must have been months.

Then the tiny girl came, and the abject humility began to cave into other, more base, more powerful emotions.

She had arrived like some specimen collected from the fields outside of Vienna. Heraclix had, in fact, mistaken her, at first, for an insect. One day, Mowler brought in a large jar containing something unseen—or unseeable—within it, something that weighed more than the mere jar itself. When Mowler stepped out on some errand, Heraclix plodded over to the jar and shook it, listening for what might rattle about inside, what gave it such mass.

"Eep!" the jar shouted in protest.

Heraclix dropped the jar, then caught it before it hit the ground. The fear of the beating he would have suffered had he broken the jar overcame his shock at the voice.

"Hello?" he asked.

Nothing.

He shook the jar again.

"Ow!" it shouted in a little voice.

This was a strange jar.

"I hear you, but I don't see you."

A light began to glow within the jar, brightening enough to reveal a pair of slowly flapping lacey wings.

"Are you a lightning bug? I have heard of such things existing far, far away." He could not recall where he had heard this, but he knew it to be true, like many thoughts and feelings that came to him unbidden.

"I am Pomp," a tiny voice said as the light grew, illuminating a female figure whose back was, indeed, surmounted with wings.

The voice was difficult to hear, but it was confident, even overconfident. "And you are going to free me."

The golem, for Heraclix knew he was a golem by the stitches that sutured his flesh and through his study of Mowler's books, stared down at the little fairy. "I am not going to free you," he said in a rattling, graveyard voice. "My master will decide your fate."

"You will free me!" she said.

"No, I won't," he said.

She put her hands on her hips and glared up at him. Her grass-green eyes glowed from beneath her black bob-cut hair.

"You should stand up for yourself," she said. "Don't let that old man push you around. Push back!"

"Oh, I don't have the heart for that," he said.

"You have a heart inside your chest. I can see its place."

Heraclix looked down at his chest where a massive capital X-shaped scar showed, quite clearly, that she was right.

"How do you know it wasn't just removed, that Mowler hasn't already carved it out of me?"

"Because of your eyes. I know one of them."

"You are an odd creature," he said.

"Not odd like your eyes are odd. And one of them unique!"

He looked at her quizzically, trying, unsuccessfully, to narrow both eyes. The right cooperated, the left did not. He hoped that she wouldn't think he was winking at her.

"That red right eye, him I do not know. That big blue left eye, him I know."

Heraclix brought his fingers to his face. His left eye, the one Pomp claimed was blue (he couldn't see it, after all, and had to take her word for it), was obviously an interpolation to this head, stitched to his face by the sorcerer, he guessed. It was gargantuan, out of all proportion to the socket, or what must have been the original orbital. It was nearly twice the size of the red right eye, as evinced by the raised ridge of scar tissue that gave the eye the appearance of a rictus rather than an eyelid. He found that he could not fully close the lid, only scrunch it down into a tighter circle, like a malfunctioning sphincter.

"How do you know my eye?" Heraclix asked, both intrigued and irritated by her recollection of a part of him that he could not himself recall.

A set of keys jangled outside the door. Heraclix ran to set the jar back into its place, and Pomp faded quickly into invisibility. Heraclix did his best to follow suit, tucking his bulk back into a closet. The look of fear and pleading on Pomp's little face was burned into his vision, even as he hid.

Mowler shambled into the room. The magician carried several bags of goods, which he emptied onto the floor after clearing away the sparse furniture: a rough-hewn wooden table and chair. From the bags he pulled a jar of chalk, a bag of silver shavings, several small candles in the form of little tentacles, and, most threateningly, a long, very fine, curved dagger like those the Ottoman merchants at the central market wore. Mowler looked over the collection and said aloud "Now, my buzzing friend, my buzzing fiend, we will talk. I have learned your true name since last we met. There will be no negotiations. This time, I will dictate the terms of our agreement."

Mowler spread the chalk liberally on the floor, then used a straight razor to painstakingly gather it into carefully cut piles and lines that formed two circles: one smaller, one larger; the former inside the latter, equidistant at all points. Within the ring this created, he arranged a series of occult sigils, signs of power meant to keep harm at bay, physical or otherworldly. Mowler hummed while building the magic circle. His humming was reminiscent of a funeral dirge. The magician was very much not like a maid doing her chores. But the methodological way in which he did his work called to Heraclix's mind a dim memory of someone, somewhen, making careful preparations for an event far more joyful than what he thought might take place next. But the harder the golem tried to capture the memory, the further it seemed to slip away from him.

Opposite the protective circle, Mowler carved another chalk ring, this one with an equilateral triangle touching the inside edge of the inner circle. Outside the ring, he gathered other eldritch symbols—these vaguely familiar to Heraclix—then sprinkled the whole of the area with the silver shavings he had brought in earlier.

He meticulously cleared the shavings out of the triangle, picking the remainders out with a pair of tweezers under a magnifying glass. He then placed a twisted candle at each of the three chalk line junctures of angle and arc and lit the wicks. The pungent odor of burning hair and fat bloomed into the air with thin ropes of black smoke that reached the ceiling. Mowler closed the apartment window's shutters and tacked black cloth over them. Only the light cast by the candles remained.

The old wizard gathered up the jar containing the fairy. He also took up the stinger-like dagger, and a large black tome encrypted with another magical symbol—this one in silver, composed of superimposed five-pointed stars slightly adrift from one another, each with extra flourishes and interpolations of other seemingly mystical signs, all wrapped up, as one would expect, in a perfect circle. He took these instruments with him into the protective circle where he sat himself down cross-legged on the floor with a pained grunt, jar to his left, dagger to his right, with the silver and black grimoire open on his lap. Heraclix could feel a certain intensity fill the air, as if a fire were beginning to blaze therein, a fire of cold, rather than heat. The room became decidedly more chilly as Mowler began to chant:

"Ia! Ia! Sussilient k'klee!"

This he repeated many times—so many, in fact, that Heraclix grew bored of counting. Heraclix felt certain that day had turned to night outside as the wizard continued the mantra. A loud snap seized the golem's attention. This was quickly followed by a crackling sound that filled the room. The temperature in the room plummeted—both Heraclix's and the old man's breath became visible, and frost shot through the room, veining the walls, ceiling, and floor with ice, causing some of the glass instruments in the room to crack or shatter. Heraclix's skin tightened in the cold, causing his stitches to strain against his flesh.

At this the man, with a deftness and speed that Heraclix had not seen before, set down the book, opened the jar, and grabbed the shivering fairy (whose brittle wings showed laced frost despite her natural invisibility), swept up the dagger, and stood to his full height in the circle. Heraclix could not recall ever having seen Mowler stand so tall and confident. It frightened him.

Mowler lifted the dagger in his right hand—the barely-visible fairy in his left—then brought the two together, sliding the fang of the blade into Pomp. Her yelp was not drowned out by the magician's change of chants.

"Kek kek agl agl nathrak," he said in slowly increasing volume as a form took shape from the candle smoke. A memory started to take shape in Heraclix's mind, passed into the present, then dissipated before he could fully grasp it. Still, he knew that he had seen something like this before. Somewhere. Somewhen.

Mowler removed the dagger and cast Pomp to the floor between the magic circles. A sparkling mist formed in the circle opposite the wizard. Each drop of blood that escaped from Pomp's body added to the concrescence of the apparition. A bulbous pair of multifaceted eyes appeared beneath a tall golden crown. Heraclix had seen this manifestation before in one of Mowler's books: Beelzebub, Lord of Flies. Below the neck, it was dressed sharply—all frills and gaudy lace under a dark purple riding coat. Its claws showed from under the sleeves, needle-like and dripping green venom. The insectile demonic eyes confused the onlookers, so that everyone in the room—Heraclix, Pomp, and the sorcerer—thought that the demon was looking his, her, and his way, respectively. The demon's proboscis, however, pointed directly at the sorcerer.

It spoke, like the buzzing of a thousand flies, in a tongue Heraclix had not before heard, nor could he comprehend it now. Mowler spoke, but his words were equally meaningless to the golem. The only thing that Heraclix understood at this point was that the magician's sacrifice of this entirely innocent creature had pushed his fear beyond horror, into rage. He did not have the heart to stand up for himself, he admitted, but his heart couldn't contain the anger that drove him to stand up for the girl. Enough was enough!

He stepped out of the shadows, determined to kill the old man once and for all. His left eye twitched of its own accord, eager to do the deed. One of his hands clenched open, shut, open, shut, curling into a tight fist then relaxing, slack, as if deciding whether to gently caress or to pummel the sorcerer. Mowler was oblivious, preoccupied with his shouted negotiations with the devil, Beelzebub, who was beginning to show signs of acquiescence: a tilt of the golden-crowned head, the wringing of clawed hands, a tone of measured restraint—even respect—in the buzzing voice. The old man seemed emboldened. His greedy eyes widened in triumph. A maniacal smile scarred his face. His eyes focused in condescension for the Lord of Flies.

Heraclix leaped, propelling his powerful frame at the old man's back with all the brute strength he could muster.

He might as well have tried to jump through a stone pillar.

A lightning aura around the magician's circle momentarily flashed as Heraclix hit the barrier. He vaulted backwards almost as far as he had lunged, his body shot through with hot pain that forced him, writhing, to the ground.

Mowler turned, only for a moment, to see what had happened, a mixed expression of curiosity and wicked humor on his face.

And in that split second, streams of flies, each accented with tiny licks of flame, poured into the corners of the room through the eight vertices where the walls, floor, and ceiling met. They shot out like burning black tentacles, a flaming insectoid octopus converging on the sorcerer within his circle, feeling their way to their master's nemesis. Each of the eight swarms struck at the barrier around the circle, and each was immediately repelled. Mowler, agitated by the flies and the lapse in concentration that Heraclix had caused him, turned with renewed energy and focus toward the demon, chanting again in that unknown tongue, which caused Beelzebub to cringe and cower, dropping to one knee with a weight that shook the floor.

Heraclix was surrounded by flies. His body smoked and portions of him smelled like cooked meat. The wracking pain in his body and head subsided, but the insects persisted. He noticed a few of the flaming insects burrowing between the seams of his flesh, having abandoned the wizard for easier game. The golem swatted wildly, killing dozens of the black fiends at a swing, and showers of sparks spattered across the floor. The swarm left him alone long enough for him to sweep the dead carcasses away, in preparation for the next onslaught.

But the next onslaught did not come.

The reason was as simple as this: corruption begets corruption, and nothing is quite so corrupt as a recently deceased demonic fly, especially one bred from the damned larval soul of a lecher whose acts in life were so debased that Beelzebub had made sure that the miscreant became *his* servant, rather than letting the erstwhile pervert rise through the ranks of the abyss in the service of some other, less disciplined prince of darkness. Astaroth, Belial, and Dispater were, after all, rather "untidy" with their demonic hordes.

This dead demonic carcass, its soul fled to the deep pits of larva, condemned to grow into another round of hateful and tortured physicality, *ad infinitum*, tumbled away from Heraclix's sweeping hand. It rolled right onto the chalked edge of Mowler's protective circle, breaching the hallowed barrier, corrupting it with a corpse. A rift opened in the magical protective fabric that had, heretofore, assured the sorcerer's safety. It took less than a second for the black tentacles to withdraw from Heraclix, reform, and writhe in through the opening. Soon the wizard was crawling with thousands of the fiery biting flies. With the wizard kept busy by his minions, Beelzebub knocked down the candles that anchored his temporary prison. The molten wax cascaded over the binding sigils, creating several paths of escape for the demon. Beelzebub dissolved away into a cloud of flies with the hint of a smile, if such a thing were even possible, then exited the room through a crack in the wall.

Seeing the wizard screaming on the floor, Heraclix took the opportunity to follow the demon's lead. He picked up Pomp, grabbed a pouch of gold coins that he knew the sorcerer kept near the door—along with a hooded cloak—and reached for the door. He looked back, nearly mesmerized by the cloud of flies, which flew in a vortex, carried aloft by the smoke that was quickly filling the room. Flames spread out underneath the tornado of insects, fanned by their wings. The fire spread in arcs across the floor and slashed up the sorcerer's robes. A table of broken beakers ignited into flame, setting a wall and the curtains ablaze. As he opened the door, Heraclix could feel air rushing into the room, feeding the increasing inferno.

Heraclix threw on the cloak, cradled the semi-conscious Pomp with one arm and walked out into the darkened street between tall buildings that loomed overhead like a murder of ravens. The eyes and mouths of the buildings' blue facades soon lit up yellow with lantern light at the first cries of "fire!" Alarm bells emptied the buildings of their residents. People poured out of their dwellings and ran to see the conflagration. The streets were choked with streams of people as thick as the flies in Mowler's apartment. Heraclix turned, with Pomp, into an empty alleyway to avoid the crowds.

She looked up at him, alive, but breathing shallow little breaths. "You are taking me to stay with you. Why?"

He hesitated, cradling her in his arm like a child. "I don't quite know why. I suppose I just feel like I should. It doesn't seem fair that death should take you."

"I have heard in my ears of death," she said. "Will I die?"

"No, the morning is coming. You will see another day," he said, not sure if it was true, but feeling that it was the right thing to say. He sat down in the alley with his back against a wall, still holding her close to his chest to shelter her from the cool air.

She drifted off, for the first time in her eternal existence, into sleep. Heraclix wondered what one who has never before slept might dream for the first time. He wondered, also, if he would ever sleep or dream again. Meanwhile, the rising sun illuminated the walls of Mowler's apartment building to match the glow of the flame-tongues that flickered out of the windows, one fire to cleanse the night, the other to awaken a new day.

CHAPTER 2

Morning comes, like he said it would. The sun shines and she gets up and flies, free. Tall buildings and alleyways can't hold her, not here. But she isn't leaving without a little fun. She is a fairy, after all. How else would she leave a human city?

First, the monks. They are out chanting, so early in the morning, all in a line. They must be disturbing people. She flies under the first one's robes and yanks on his loincloth. At least she thinks it's his loincloth. She doesn't have time to check closely; he is yelping like a beaten dog, and the line of monks is collapsing all around her. Time to go.

Next, the city guards, that pair leaning up against the wall. Too lazy! She slides one of the guards' daggers out of its scabbard and pokes the other in the rear. The stabbed one shouts. The dagger falls to the ground. A fight starts. Now they will be alert!

And what is this? There, a baby! Fussing in a flower-adorned basket. So high up above the dirty streets where the peasants walk. This child is clean, as clean as the shining marble patio beneath the basket.

Pomp peeks into the apartment. Beautiful paintings of beautiful women and men adorn the walls. Silver trays are strewn with fruit and Turkish Delights. A noble lady dressed in rich silks argues with a servant over a broken vase at their feet.

Maybe this is why the baby is beginning to cry.

It looks like the mother has put the child out for some fresh air, or to keep the noise of its bawling out of the house so she can hear herself yell. She won't mind if the crying stops. Besides, if she can buy such fine things as silver and silk, she can buy another baby. One that cries less, perhaps.

Pomp lifts the basket up into the air and flies away with it. The mother runs out onto the patio, but it's too late. The baby stops crying. The mother starts.

He's heavy, and she sinks, but she doesn't drop the basket. She arcs down and accelerates. Ahead of her, the air is torn like a cloth. It's always like this when she travels between the land of men and the land of fairies. The cloth is mankind's world. Through the torn holes is the land of her sisters, Faerie. She chooses a hole and takes the baby through to her homeland.

She takes care of the boy. He grows—such a strange thing—into a man. He is happy until he is a man. They give him everything he wants, the fairy folk do. Then, now that he is a man, he is unhappy. He is, in fact, very angry.

Why does such a sweet boy grow into such an angry old man? This is Pomp's question.

"Why must I grow old and die?" is his question. "You all keep on living. You don't change. I don't want to change! I don't want to die!"

The afterimage of the angry old man fades, overshadowed and replaced by Heraclix's engulfing frame above her. He is enormous. He blocks out the sun. But the sun has jumped in the sky. It's moving faster than usual, Pomp notices. Pomp must be moving faster than usual, too. She is here in the alley; she is there in Faerie; she is here in the alley. How can this be? It is almost too much to think about.

"You're back," she says.

"I'm back? I was never gone. You were," he says, amused.

"Gone where? I am here"—she touched her hands to their respective shoulders—"I am always here."

He studies her with the red right eye, the one she does not know.

"While you've been sleeping," he says, "I've been thinking, and something's come to me, an intimation, like knowledge out of nowhere," he scrunches his brows together, "but from somewhere."

She looks at him, confused.

He stares at her. "You've never slept before, have you?"

"What is 'slept?'"

He has so many words in his mouth that her ears do not know.

A smile tears his face. "That's what I thought. What did you dream about?"

"What is 'dream?'"

His smile sags back into a scar, which puckers and rolls as he thinks, concentrates, looks for the right words.

"What did you see, right before you saw me?"

"The angry old man."

"No, I mean just now, before you opened your eyes."

"I see blackness when I close my eyes. It is why I don't like to do it."

"But this time you saw something, didn't you?"

"Before I open my eyes to see you, I see the angry old man."

"That was a dream. You didn't really see Mowler, you just thought you saw him."

"I see the old man, then I see you."

"But that can't be true. Mowler, the wizard, died before you saw him in your dream. It was an illusion. How could he be there, being dead? How can you be sure it was really him?"

She pauses for a moment, thinking, then says: "You say you think I don't sleep?"

"I say you did not sleep before this time, yes," he folds his arms in self-satisfaction.

"How could you know I don't sleep?" she asks.

He tries to recall and document the source of his knowledge that fairies did not sleep. Strain as he might, he can't pull the thoughts out from the cloud that fills his head.

"I don't know," he says, finally.

"Then we agree!" she says. "I don't know, you don't know."

"Not necessarily," he holds up a finger, gesturing his disagreement. "I know fairies don't sleep—I just don't remember how I know. You, on the other hand, remember things in the wrong order because you have dreamed for the first time."

"What is 'remember?'"

He shakes his head and covers his face with his hands.

Pomp climbs off of Heraclix's lap and sits down in front of him.

"You say you saw the angry old man."

"Yes."

"What was he doing?"

"He says he doesn't want to die."

"Had you met me before the old man said that he didn't want to die?"

"No. He is with us when he says it."

"Us?"

"Pomp and her sisters. And he is not the old man. He is the boy."

"Now I'm thoroughly confused."

"Pomp brings him to our home, and he grows into the angry old man."

"Mowler?"

"I don't know if Mowler is the same man."

Heraclix stands up, blinks his eyes, makes strange grumbling noises.

"You don't like Mowler!" Pomp says.

"No, I don't."

"Me neither."

Heraclix sounds desperate: "This old man you saw—why was he angry?"

"He does not want to get old. He doesn't want to change. He wants to be like the fairies, not a man. But he is a man. He never wants to die."

"And does he hate fairies?"

Pomp begins to shiver as a cold, uncomfortable feeling trickles down her spine.

"Pomp thinks so."

"Would the angry old man ..." Heraclix pauses, "... would he kill a fairy so that he did not have to die?"

Pomp nods. She is shaking.

Heraclix is thinking, looking out into somewhere, but nowhere, looking for something Pomp cannot see.

"What do you see?" Pomp asks.

"The past. Or at least a part of it."

23

"What is 'past?'"

"It's what happened before now."

Pomp looks up at Heraclix with a skeptical squint.

"I met you in Mowler's apartment. You came there in a jar. *Before*, you were free. And I have a hunch that I might have once been free."

"But Mowler pushes you around."

"That's precisely it. What did I have to fear from him? I am physically superior to him in every way: stronger, faster. Yet I didn't fight back."

"You should."

"But I didn't. Something held me back."

"What holds you back?"

"Guilt."

"What is 'guilt?'"

"'Guilt' is feeling bad for something you've done."

"Why do you have guilt?" Pomp asks.

"I don't know, exactly. But I think it might have something to do with . . ." Heraclix stops.

"With what?"

"With whatever happened to me *before* I awoke in the cauldron of blood."

"Is this 'remember?'"

"No. I don't remember."

"But you have guilt."

"Somehow, yes." He shakes his head and forces a laugh. "You must think I'm crazy."

"It's all right," she consoles him. "I am still bound to you."

"Bound to me?" He looks around as if an answer to his question is somehow in the air, if he could only find it on the wind.

"Yes, bound. You save me. You kill the wizard. I am bound to you."

"No, really, you owe me nothing," he says.

"I do!" she yells with an unreasonable hint of desperation in her voice. "I am bound!"

"Alright, fine—you are bound. Look, be still. You are hurt."

"My body works. It is strong." She stands up, falters, rights herself again. "Look, I can fly," she flutters her wings, falls to her knees, doubles over in pain. "I will walk," she says, disappointed.

"No you won't. I'll carry you," Heraclix says, reaching down to lift her up onto his shoulder.

Pomp smiles weakly. "Where do we go?"

"Back to Mowler's apartment."

"Why?"

"Because I have a purpose, now: to gather what we can find of Mowler's papers. There are things I want to know."

"About what?" she asks.

"About myself."

"Like what?"

"Who I was. Why I am. Who I am."

Pomp has questions of her own, questions like *what happens when I die?* The prospect of the answer frightens her, mostly because she knows, somehow, that it had almost come to her.

And it could still be revealed.

CHAPTER 3

The stench of sodden ashes rarely fell on Vienna these days. It was not like the past, when rains soaked the smoldering remains of Ottoman campfires and the valleys ran with soot and blood, or when the city was a ballroom filled with Saint Vitus dancers, and stiffened heaps of spent participants vomited smoke up into the sky. Perhaps it was those communal memories—engendered by the lingering smell of the sorcerer's burned-out apartment—that drove residents to their homes and hovels to take up the morose contemplation of darker times, times before the enlightened despotism of the emperor.

Or, perhaps, it was the presence of the emperor's private guard, the secretive army within an imperial army, who stole out of the charred ruins bearing stacks of loot-cum-evidence. Their white jackets made them stand out against the black background like ash on burning charcoal or clouds against walls of battlefield smoke. Whatever the reason, the puddle-strewn cobblestone streets were devoid of people save for the soldiers.

Heraclix and Pomp looked at the apartment from an alleyway across the street.

"We don't dare just walk in," Heraclix said

"Why not?"

"Some of us can't just become invisible."

"I see," Pomp said.

"And I don't. Which means the guards won't either." Heraclix paused as the magnitude of the thought struck him. "How strong are you now, Pomp?"

She stood tall, becoming visible so that Heraclix could see her flex her biceps.

"Strong!"

"Good to see it," Heraclix smiled. "I'll bet it would be fun to fly in there and steal some things."

She returned a tiny smile. "That is fun!" She flew off, vanishing in mid-air.

"Get the documents!" he yelled.

A pair of guards turned around in response to his booming, hoarse voice, lowering their bayonets and approaching the alley in which he unsuccessfully tried to hide himself.

Beyond the guards, a man on horseback came into view—a man of some importance, given the rows of medals pinned upon the breast of his perfectly clean, perfectly pressed, perfectly white uniform. He spotted the pair and called out to them.

"What have you found?" His voice was strong with authority.

"A spy, perhaps?" one of the guards said.

"Or a fool," said the other.

"Carry on," said the horseman, turning his attention to other matters.

As the horseman turned away, Heraclix recognized the profile. He had seen an illustration of that face before, among Mowler's documents. He strained his memory to recall the labels associated with the face: "arrogant," "competent," "brave," "superstitious,"... and a name, "Graf Von Helmutter, Chief of the Imperial Guard and Minister of Defense." Heraclix recalled that this man was of particular interest to Mowler. "His lack of fear and plenitude of pride," the Sorcerer had written, "can both be exploited when the time is right."

Heraclix thought that, perhaps, Von Helmutter could provide some information on Mowler and on the golem's own past. He rose to his full height as Von Helmutter's soldiers drew closer.

"I'd like to speak with the graf," he said with as much courtesy as he could project through his gravely voice.

The pair stopped, eyes wide. One of them, a red-haired young man, barely a teenager, took a step back, jaw agape. *Such a young, inexperienced lad,* Heraclix thought. *How could he be a member of the Imperial Guard?*

"You," the other soldier said, "are as ugly as you are huge." Fear caused his voice to tremble, but he stepped forward, bayonet pointed at Heraclix's chest. "You come out real nice, okay? Don't make any false moves and you might not get hurt." The soldier's voice became more full of false bravado with each forward step that he took.

Heraclix's left hand started to clench and unclench uncontrollably. A raw energy coursed through it. The extremity was attached to him, but as he struggled to control it, it felt like it was another being, a separate sentience on the same body.

The soldier was now within *misura*, the striking range of the bayonet. His young companion had sidled up just behind him, ready to offer backup. The older soldier began circling and making tiny, hesitant jabbing motions with his bayonet, trying to move Heraclix out into the street.

The hand loosened, relaxing for a moment.

And just as quickly, it struck out, like a snake, grabbing the older soldier's wrist and pulling so hard that the sound of cracking bone echoed off the walls. The soldier's musket clattered to the street as the younger soldier fired his musket.

Heraclix's shock at his own action nearly matched that of the boy-soldier, who tried in vain to determine how his musket ball, fired at near point-blank range, could have possibly missed its target. The older soldier was in no less shock as he crab-walked backwards on two legs and one good arm toward the crowd of white coated soldiers that was rushing to his aid, muskets at the ready.

The hand shot out again, this time clamping around the boy-soldier's throat.

Pomp flies into the ruins, looking for things to steal. But the ruins don't look much like Mowler's apartment. The street-facing wall is mostly collapsed, and the door is nowhere to be seen. A semicircle of burnt roof is missing, as if a dragon had bitten off the front of the building before breathing fire into it. Most of the floor is covered in deep ash and charcoal. Everything is blackened with soot, even the remaining wall outside the apartment. There is no furniture, no unbroken glass, no Mowler. Pomp gets closer, looking for any sign of the documents. She finds a half-scorched pile of papers, along with a book, peeking out from under a fallen chimney stone and works to salvage what she can.

She is surprised by someone entering the ruins. A soldier!

His uniform is white with blue lapels, unlike the other foot soldiers Pomp has seen in the neighborhood. A saber is sheathed at his side. He carries no musket. The insignia on his high hat indicates that he is someone special, maybe an officer of mid-rank, an adjutant to someone of great importance.

He is alone and looks around furtively to make sure he stays so.

He smiles as he stoops to kneel on the ground. His smile is genuine and reflects, Pomp thinks, some inner goodness mixed with a touch of lighthearted mischief.

Pomp is instantly curious about this man.

From his pocket he withdraws a pair of dice, knucklebones, dotted black on white. He shakes them in his hand and throws the bones on a flat stone, looking at them in wonderment, as if scrying the numbers for meaning. A pair of ones results.

"Dog throw," he says, "not a good omen."

"Two ones are bad," Pomp agrees. "I will help this good man," she says, does, flipping one one to two, making three.

"Three?" he says, perplexed, "How very odd!"

He looks around, the mischievous smile slipping from his face, and squints into the ashen gloom, slowly sweeping his eyes around the ruins.

"Who's there?" he asks.

Pomp sees a touch of fear in his eyes.

He reaches down, grabs a handful of powder ash, and throws it into the air.

Pomp sneezes.

"Aha!" The good-natured smile returns. "Where are you, little spirit? I'd like to see the ghost that tempts lady luck."

Pomp hesitates, starts to say something, thinks better of it, stops, starts again. Decisions are so hard. She wants, she doesn't want, she wants, she really wants to, she will . . .

Musket shots ring out down the street.

"Major Von Graeb, come quickly!" someone cries out from just outside the ruins, "Von Helmutter's orders!"

Von Graeb picks up his knucklebones and runs toward the street. "I've got to go," he says to the air.

But Pomp has already flown.

The boy-soldier went limp, dead before Heraclix could pry his autonomous left hand free with his obedient right.

Three more guards raised their muskets and fired. One ball whirred under Heraclix's arm, tearing a hole in his cloak. The other two hit him—one on the forehead, another on the chest, and ricocheted off at odd angles, one breaking a nearby window. The three guards looked at each other, momentarily stunned, then quickly gathered themselves and reloaded.

Heraclix, holding one arm up to protect his head, lumbered toward them, emboldened by the surprising deflection of the balls that had bounced harmlessly off of him.

The guards shot again at close range, and again the balls spun off of the monster's body and into surrounding buildings. Screams rang out up and down the street.

Heraclix waded through the cloud of gunpowder smoke that blotted white the space between. He swatted at the muskets with his right hand, only wanting to disarm them.

They stabbed in unison, twisted the blades, but penetrated nothing, only succeeding in pushing Heraclix back an inch or so.

Heraclix's left hand shot out, trying to grope past the musket barricade to find a throat. He again swatted at the muskets, this time knocking them from the guards' grasp.

"Run!" he yelled, not as a threat, but as a warning. He did not want anyone else to be hurt by the renegade left hand.

The guards did not run, but they backed away, drawing their swords and making way for Graf Von Helmutter, who had dismounted his horse and drawn a short silver dagger.

"Back down," he told the guards, "Cordon off the street." He flipped the dagger around in his hand, twirling it around his fingers, savoring the prospect of one-on-one combat with a man, a beast, such as this.

"I did not mean to hurt anyone," Heraclix said to Von Helmutter, "nor do I want to fight with you."

Von Helmutter's face remained grim, determined.

"Lies," Von Helmutter said. "How can any ... thing ... so beastly speak anything but lies?"

"I am just a man," Heraclix said.

"I'll bet you almost believe that. But, no, you are a Hell-spawned demon."

Another group of soldiers a dozen strong moved around the pair to block off either end of the street. All doorways and windows, save the burned-out cavities on the ruins of Mowler's apartment, had been shut, locked, and barred. The guards' bayonets came down, turning the section of street into a coffin lined with spikes, an iron maiden in which Heraclix and Graf Von Helmutter circled each other, one looking for an opening to strike, the other trying to stop the conflict by giving ground.

"I have been trained by tutors greater than any general to handle your kind," the graf boasted. Then, quietly, only for Heraclix's ears: "I know the secrets of eldritch warfare, fiend. I know what can hurt you. You can't be harmed by mundane weapons," he shook the blade of his dagger at Heraclix, "but silver cuts on every plane of existence, earthly or demonic."

Von Helmutter lashed out, but his lunge fell short. Heraclix backed away.

"Cowardly devil!" Von Helmutter spat.

Von Helmutter stepped in foot-over-foot, *passe' avant*, cutting the distance between them so quickly that Heraclix stumbled in an effort to get out of his way. Too late! Von Helmutter stabbed underneath the golem's left arm, aiming for the torso, but Heraclix's stumble invited the blade to his lower tricep.

The silver bit deep, and Heraclix cried out in pain. From the wound, a shimmering liquid, like quicksilver, spurted forth, trickling around his arm, dripping down his side, and evaporating in an evanescent sparkle that left no evidence of wounding save the gash itself.

Still, the giant backed away, struggling to control his left hand. He only wanted to defend himself, but the hand seemed to have a will of its own. If he failed to control it, he would be responsible for the death of yet another victim.

The more experienced guards chuckled lightly, while the newer recruits watched in awe at the prowess of their commander, who could single-handedly wound this brute when eight musket balls and more bayonet stabs couldn't harm him.

"I don't want to harm you," Heraclix said, spittle whistling from between his gritted teeth.

The guards laughed, all except for a soldier in the back who wore the gold sash of an officer. This must have been the graf's major, likely the "Von Graeb," who had been summoned by the infantrymen earlier. He looked on with steady curiosity, studying the situation, walking around the perimeter behind the guards, but never taking his eye off the pair in the middle.

"Oh, but I want to hurt you," Von Helmutter said. "I've encountered your kind before."

Von Helmutter stabbed again, missing short of his target's belly, then slashed upward, opening a shallow cut across Heraclix's chest that welled up with quicksilver, glittered, and again disappeared, leaving the skin etched where the dagger had met flesh.

But, rather than following up with another thrust, the graf swatted at some invisible pest that had taken an interest in him. His hand connected with the assailant, knocking it aside.

Von Helmutter advanced, once more, toward Heraclix.

The graf's free hand suddenly shot up to his eyes. He screamed something incomprehensible, dropping the dagger to the ground as he reached up with the other hand to cover his nose, which had begun to bleed profusely.

The onlooking soldiers muttered among themselves.

Just then, the graf's breeches fell down around his ankles. His hand shot down to cover his exposed groin. He screeched out in pain and dropped to his knees, one hand trying to protect his face, the other his naked crotch.

The guards moved in, the experienced ones assisting their commander, the inexperienced ones laughing at his embarrassing plight. In the background, the one called Von Graeb seemed to be hiding a smile behind a raised hand.

Heraclix turned round and round, not knowing where to go or what to do.

"Pomp!" he cried out.

"Here I am!" she said, alighting on his arm, coming into visibility. The left hand, almost instantly, calmed itself.

"Where to?" he asked.

"That way!" she giggled, pointing east.

The pair bowled their way through a set of guards who had set themselves to receive Heraclix's charge.

Heraclix ran through the streets, bounding over carts and barrels, knocking over anything he could to create obstacles for any pursuers. Soon, he and Pomp ran across a bridge, disappearing from the guards' view.

Von Graeb stooped down to pick up the silver dagger that Von Helmutter had dropped. It was a crude weapon, rough hewn from a single silver vein, with marks on the handle that might naturally have occurred in the ore from which it was extracted, or might have been intentionally carved—a set of sigils whose purpose he could not divine. He wrapped it up in a cloth in order to return it to Von Helmutter.

"A dead giant lives. A ghost fixes the dice of chance to turn a prediction of misfortune into one of good luck, then the Chief of the Imperial Guard reveals himself as a demon-hunter trained by who-knows-who or what. Grandmother would have known what to make of this," he said to himself. "But she's gone now," he sighed, "and I am left to winnow through my own memories for enlightenment."

While the others were attending to Graf Von Helmutter, Von Graeb surreptitiously wandered over to look into Mowler's apartment. He looked back to where the men were helping the indignant Graf to gather his things. "I wonder," Von Graeb said, "If there's a connection . . ." He turned to the burned out remains one last time, then, shaking his head, he began to walk back toward his men. "How odd," he said. "How very odd, indeed."

Chapter 4

Every flash of white—every mislaid ribbon, painted door, or cloud in the sky—sent Heraclix darting for cover in an alleyway or behind a wagon. His wounds still ached with a burning pain that ebbed and flowed, though it never fully left him. He didn't want to encounter Von Helmutter or his men again, that much was certain. Nor did he want a repeat of the uncontrolled actions, *his* uncontrolled actions, that had resulted in the death of the young guard.

Mid-day burned off any remaining clouds that had lingered through the morning. Heraclix and Pomp found shelter from the sun in an abandoned stable near the outskirts of town. Insects bothered the golem's seams but kept a respectful distance from Pomp, who baffled them whenever she appeared. She was so like a bug, yet so unlike a bug. What was a tiny insect to think of her?

"You rest," Pomp said to Heraclix, who kept rubbing the sore spots of his wounds. "I need to get something."

Heraclix started to call after her, then stopped, remembering the consequences of his last outburst. Best to keep quiet.

He watched her wink out of sight and groaned as the insects that had surrounded her now flocked to him, joining the others to explore his seams and gashes. But not only did the bugs crawl over and through him, questions also buzzed through his thoughts like gnats. He swung blindly for phantom answers.

Why had Mowler created him? Why not someone or something else?

34

Why did Mowler choose Pomp to sacrifice to Beelzebub? Did it have to be her?

And why was Mowler summoning Beelzebub in the first place?

Was Von Helmutter a crony of Mowler's? He seemed to know a great deal about sorcery. Was he a customer? A patron?

Most importantly, what were the origins of the many pieces of Heraclix? He was like a puzzle to himself, an unknown being or beings, self-aware, yet unaware of the individuals from whom he had been constructed. He was familiar with himself, yet his reflection, if he dared to look at it for any length of time, was an enigma wrapped in flesh. Or, more properly, fleshes.

Reflection shifted to boredom as the paucity of answers became clear to him. He wondered when Pomp would return.

"Where is she?" he said to himself.

"She is here!" Pomp said, startling him. She appeared with sheets of folded paper and a book in her arms. "You think too much," she said.

"And you spy too much. Perhaps you are right: perhaps I think too much," he said. "But I have no other way of gaining the insight I seek."

"You talk too much, too! Here, read these," she said, dropping the book and papers to the ground. "They are Mowler's."

"I'm afraid they are no one's. They were Mowler's, but Mowler is dead."

Pomp looked at Heraclix with a puzzled expression.

"When he dies, his things, his papers, his book; they are no one's?"

Heraclix thought for a moment. "Well, no."

"So they are everybody's?"

"Yes, I suppose so."

"When you die, whose are you?"

"Me?"

Pomp nodded. "That big blue eye. Whose is it?"

"Well . . ." Heraclix stopped. "I don't know how to answer. It's part of me, of course."

"But whose is it before you are alive? And whose is it after you die?"

"I don't know," Heraclix said. "Maybe these papers will tell us."

Heraclix unfolded the papers, quickly read them, and then skimmed through the book.

Paper 1:

Good Sir,
    I agree to your terms. I will herewith surrender the goods.
Please give me two days to make arrangements.
                                In truth, I am,
                                Your servant,
                        Vladimir Porchenskivik

Paper 2:

An ink-colored diagram of a severed human hand, *sinistra*, painted indigo with death. Each digit, each nail, each nerve and blood vessel is diagrammed, called out, labeled with magical symbols and marginalia that Pomp has no hope of interpreting.

Paper 3:

A letter, scripted in handwriting so awkward and clumsy that it is almost unreadable.

Good Sir,
    I have delivered the hand via courier, a young man from the neighboring village of Bozsok. He is sickly and stooped, a runt, but a good, innocent lad. Do treat him kindly. You can trust him entirely with the necklace, so long as you do not corrupt him. I will expect to receive him at Szalko two weeks from hence with the necklace, after which the remainder of the agreed sum will be sent.
                                Again, I am, truly
                        Vladimir Porchenskivik

The Book:

A wood-covered notebook bound with black and gray locks of human hair. The wood is thin, light in weight, dark in color. The front cover is unadorned, but the back was engraved with a representation of a rectangular tray or box, viewed from above. The tray was full of writhing worms with human faces. Each face was unique—a distinctly individual person, but with the same mouth full of sharpened teeth and the same expression of seething hatred as all the others.

The frontispiece was a handwritten page bearing the simple title *The Worm*. The bottom of the page showed a stylized human-faced worm, like the ones on the back cover, but abstracted into more of a sigil than a picture. The work was signed in a large-looped, flowing script by one Octavius Heilliger.

The bulk of the book was a treatise, mostly in German with an occasional Magyar word or phrase. Heraclix saw that between these sections were indented paragraphs in Latin, Greek, or Arabic. He was surprised by how easily he understood these languages and felt confident in his ability to read and translate them all.

Among the section headings were "On the Soul of the Homunculus,""Beyond Life, Beyond Death," and "The Alchymical Basis for Tissue Restoration."

Heraclix browsed the book, flipping past such passages as this:

"Memory loss is an almost inevitable consequence of wresting the life force from beyond the veil of death, for while the subject may not have yet abandoned all hope at the gates of Hell, he is almost certain to have at least sipped from the waters of the River Lethe, due to the hot, dry exhalations that emanate from the sixth circle of Hell, parching the throat of the newly arrived soul. Thus it is that practitioners of the necromantic arts often find that the extraction of information from the dead, no matter how exquisite the tortures applied, proves frustrating and possibly fruitless. The dead can only relate what they remember. All else is fancy or deception."

In the last few pages of the book, he found several symbols, like a swarm of strange black flies, surrounding an illustration of a malproportioned human body. The individual body parts were color-coded, making the grim picture appear far more cheery than he thought it ought to be, given how badly mismatched the parts were with one another, like some awkward children's painting. It was both grim and beautiful at the same time. Heraclix thought that the cost of producing such a book must be enormous. The author was obviously willing to sacrifice a great deal to have it printed!

A feeling of familiarity overcame him as he read, not merely a sense of identification, as if he was receiving the information for the first time. Rather, he was confident that he had seen it before, though he could not recall where or when. The color-coded drawing was of him, obviously—or at least of something so much like him as to appear to be a doppelganger.

"This is me," Heraclix said.

"No, this is you," Pomp said, grabbing one of his fingers with both of her hands.

"Yes, but this picture shows . . ."

"What?"

"Plans." He paused for a moment. "But when were they made? And by whom? Who is Octavius Heilliger?"

"You know the name?"

Now it was Heraclix's turn to look perplexed. "I don't know."

Pomp began to fidget, impatient to do something other than talk. "So where do we go?"

"I have so much to learn, it's hard to say. But we need to start somewhere."

The hand, he decided, was the best place to start.

He looked more closely at the hand than ever before. It was spindly, with long, bony fingers. The color was a deathly steel blue, with dark indigo in its deepest creases. The sickly hue contrasted with the warm flesh-tones of the rest of his body, as if the hand was leeching life from the body—a parasite. Yet, it responded readily to his mental command now, despite its earlier self-actualization, like a devil had possessed it, then left again, turning control back over to the body to which it was attached. And it might be so. He feared what else it might do, who else it might hurt. It was sinister, not only in its left-handedness, but in its disposition as well.

He held the spidery hand up near his face, carefully examining each vein, the sutures connecting the thin hand to his oversized forearm. Just above the knuckles, across the top of the hand, he saw faint writing, black letters that had been tattooed into the skin so long ago that they had faded almost to invisibility. He moved about in the stable, adjusting himself so that a sliver of evening sunlight shone through onto the hand. He noticed that the letters, garbled as they seemed, resolved into two words superimposed over one another. The original tattoo read, in Serbian, "*osvetnik*"—"Avenger." The other, more recent tattoo, appearing over the top of the first, was also written in Serbian: "*mirotvorac*"—"peacemaker."

Heraclix mulled the words over, pondering the significance of their provenance. Avenger. Peacemaker. More questions.

He unfolded one of the documents that Pomp had brought with her, the letter, written in German by one Vladimir Porchenskivik. Was this the hand mentioned in the correspondence? He must assume that it was so.

He opened the illustration of the hand. Looking closely at the diagram, he saw that the artist had indicated with an arrow where the tattoo had been imprinted on the hand, labeling it "*osvetnik*," with no indication of the overwritten "*mirotvorac*."

Who was this avenger? And who had superimposed the peacemaker title over the avenger between the time the drawing had been labeled and the hand attached to Heraclix's arm?

Only Porchenskivik would know. Somehow, they had to find him.

But now it was growing dark. It was time to move under cover of the night. He tucked the book and papers in the coin pouch as best he could, put the hood of his cloak up, and they set off.

The warm glow of the harvest moon shrank into the cold lesser light of the night, causing the cobblestone streets to seem more narrow and confining.

Heraclix was not the only cloaked one on the streets at this time of night, nor was Pomp the only unseen denizen. Dark eyes peered out from beneath hooded cowls and above razor-embedded walls. All of them noted the stranger in their midst. Heraclix felt them staring at him as he passed.

A low murmur of voices threaded its way through the streets like a snare being set for prey. It was a tongue unknown to Heraclix— not German, not Magyar, not Serbian, not Turkish. A tongue of man, not of demons, he was somehow sure, though the name or origin of the language escaped him.

The threatening tone, however, spoke for itself. It prophesied, proclaiming Heraclix and Pomp's imminent demise: how the fairy would have her wings plucked off and her body used for live fish bait, how the golem would be torn apart at the seams and sold off to Ottoman magicians and trinket shops.

Even Pomp felt the fear on the air.

"I don't think they like us!" she said.

"I don't think they like anyone," Heraclix said.

The communal voice agreed, growing more bold, more edgy.

Heraclix heard a slithering sound, as of a hundred daggers drawn in succession. He looked around to see the reflection of silver-tipped knives flashing through the darkness. Slowly, they drew closer, causing Heraclix to spin backwards like a cornered dog.

"I can save us," Pomp said.

"No!" Heraclix said. "There are too many of them."

He wheeled around, the circle tightening, closer, possibly within striking distance.

"I'd rather be fighting Von Helmutter's men right now," he said.

The circle stood static.

A voice, intelligible—though heavily accented—spoke out.

"What did you say?" asked a gruff old man.

"You heard him," said another—a young woman.

"Then you must be the one ..." a young boy said.

"... The one who killed Vorbeck's son ..." said another voice.

"... the redhead ..." yet another.

A bullseye lamp opened directly into Heraclix's eyes, temporarily blinding him.

The hand twitched. Heraclix drew his right arm up to block the light, the left pulsated then calmed at the sound of another voice, that of an old woman whose age had not yet scratched away her soft alto, though her accent was harsh and strange, like the others.

"Do not be alarmed. You are safe here," she said.

At this, the hand relaxed, rubbing its thumb over its fingertips, fingertips over thumb, caressing, soothing itself.

The lantern was turned from Heraclix's eyes and partially shuttered, allowing the light to suffuse the area with a gentle glow. After a moment, he could see around himself more clearly.

He was in an alleyway, like any other alleyway in Vienna, except this one was extremely narrow, more like a cattle chute than a side street. The walls were high, very high, but incomplete. In many places, the skeletal structures of building frames were stripped of covering, rendering the area a labyrinth of timbers and joining plates, a giant, three-dimensional wooden maze full of recesses and cross-shadows.

The crowd's daggers slid back into their sheaths.

"And where is your little friend?" the old woman asked, softly touching his arm.

"Friend?"

"Who were you talking to?" came a gruff voice from somewhere in the crowd.

"Talking to . . . to myself, I suppose."

"There was another voice," someone else in the crowd said, affirming the earlier speaker's suspicions.

"Do tell the truth," the old woman said in a firm voice. "You need not try to deceive us. I know of your little friend. Please, introduce us."

"Pomp," Heraclix said, "I think it is best to show yourself."

Pomp, who had been hiding, invisible, under the drape of Heraclix's cloak, came out from under the fabric and made herself visible.

"How can you see me?" Pomp said. The scowl on her face belied her frustration.

A collective squeal of surprise and fear erupted. The crowd jumped back, some drawing their weapons again. The old woman peered closely at Pomp.

"We are always watching and listening. Always."

Then, turning to the group, she addressed her compatriots. "This child, my brothers and sisters," she said, "is different. She has seen into the abyss. It lingers in her eyes still. She struggles to learn, to understand."

"Learn what?" Pomp asked.

"The great mystery; what lies beyond the black veil."

The crowd dispersed, skulking away, slithering like serpents into the nooks and crannies of the neighborhood's woodwork labyrinth.

The old woman took Heraclix by the arm and led him through the labyrinth. He was unfamiliar with the maze-like architecture. This unfamiliarity, along with his bulky frame amidst such tight quarters, manifested itself in a wake of bangs, splinters, and broken timbers. Sighs and groans—not Heraclix's—erupted whenever he passed by, like the frustrated expressions of parents watching a child bungle through a simple task.

At length the old woman spoke again.

"You are welcome here, but you should both be very careful if you are to stay with us. My people are wary of strangers and very superstitious."

"Then why take us in?" Heraclix asked.

"You have ended the Vorbeck line."

"I did what? I did not mean . . ."

"Whether you meant to or not, you did," she said, interrupting him. "Fate moved your hands and justice was done. We will now shelter you, take care of you. It is our privilege and our obligation."

"But I don't even know your name."

"Vadoma."

"I have never heard such a name. It's not German, Magyar, or Slavic."

"You are not Romani."

"Romani? Gypsies?"

"Depending on who you ask," she smiled.

"I thought you had all gone away, after the empress had the laws changed," Heraclix said. He wondered where the memory had come from immediately after he spoke.

"Maria Theresa would have liked that. She did everything she could, short of murdering us all in cold blood, to make it so. She took away our horses and wagons—forbidden! She forced our boys into the army, took all our names into their books and lists. They thought they owned us, like pets. They even forbid us to marry each other! What is next? Her death did not even stop the persecution. The emperor wants us all gone, too. Everyone who is not Romani loves him, but he is no better than his mother was to my people."

She paused, looking pensive, staring off into the distance, then continued.

"This is why we are taking you in. Vorbeck, the father of the young man you killed today, was Maria Theresa's favorite enforcer. The man, if I can call him that, was merciless."

Again, she looked off into the distance, remembering.

"But he is gone now. And his last son is gone now, too. Justice has been sent through you." She smiled, her tiny mouth half full of teeth.

She led Heraclix and Pomp past a beaded curtain deep within the innards of the wooden fortress. The ceiling was hung with paper lanterns in which candles burned, giving the place a ghostly radiance. In the center of what looked to be a parlor was a table surrounded by several chairs. In the middle of the table were gathered two teacups, a crystal ball on a brass stand, a small opium pipe, and a tiny animal skull of indeterminate origin bristling with horns and a mouth full of long, curved fangs. The air smelled of spices and stale tobacco. Billowing cloths and tapestries lined the room. Some of these were embroidered with symbols that Heraclix identified as having mystical significance, though whether the knowledge had come from his reading of Mowler's books or from some earlier source, he could not clearly recall.

"The Mount of Janus, the thaumaturgic triangle, Asmodeus's tail . . . You are a sorceress."

Vadoma looked around the room then laughed. "This? These are all trappings," she said, sweeping her hands to indicate the tapestries, the table, the entire room. "You forgot to ask me what my name means."

"I'm sorry?" Heraclix said, confused.

"My name. You nave not already forgotten my name, have you?"

"No, Vadoma."

"Good. 'Vadoma' is not a noun, it is a verb."

Pomp lost interest in the conversation and became distracted by the lanterns, which she flew up to so she could investigate.

"'Vadoma' means 'to know.' Some people need trappings. Some will sell their souls for information. Some of us just *know*."

"A soothsayer, then," Heraclix said.

Vadoma shook her head. "Soothsayers read the flight of birds and the casting of bones. I need neither."

"A prophetess," Heraclix said.

"That is closer to the truth. Still, it gives comfort to others to see me use some kind of object or tool—a focus—to prophesy. Sometimes it is their own bodies. Here," she said, reaching across the table, "give me your hand."

Heraclix hesitated.

"It's okay," she said. "I am not afraid. You should not be, either. Fate is fate, no?"

Heraclix let her take the hand. That left hand. He felt a wave of nervousness rise up in him as he proffered it, then a calming influence as she touched it.

It relaxed noticeably as she held the fingers back with her own hand, then traced the lines on the palm with the index finger of the other. Her face contorted, bushy eyebrows furrowed, as she examined the deep crevices that cut through the flesh like telltale caverns of destiny.

"This lifeline," she said with a touch of disbelief in her voice, "is impossibly long. It is intersected at a strange angle by a line I don't often see, a life-changing event—possibly traumatic, possibly epiphanic and wonderful—that changed the course of this life. See how the line shifts away from its original path? This person was not the same after this. He was changed forever. Looking forward, up the lifeline, is another event or decision, still forthcoming. Details after this are difficult to read: the owner was cruel, a warrior or general, but with a gentle heart buried inside. He has touched lives, for good and evil, many lives. He was never married, had troubled, confusing relationships in and out of his family. He hated other children as a child, then loved them as an adult, though he never had any of his own. Again, these relationships seem confused and vague in their quality.

"The past, then, seems clear, so far as backward divination goes. But the future is difficult to see."

She let the hand go.

"Here, let me see your other hand," she said.

Then, taking the right hand, she stopped suddenly and gagged. After regaining her composure she said, "Your hand. There is nothing there. The fingerprints, the palm prints, they have all been burned off."

Heraclix looked at his right hand, which, truth be told, he had taken for granted up to that point. He had been so fixated on the significance of the left hand that he had neither looked at nor thought much about the right. The fingerprints had, indeed, been burned off, and any creases in the palms had been cauterized, melted together as if by a flat, hot iron.

"I can learn nothing from this hand other than someone did not want it identified, did not want its past known—nor its future. Besides, reading the other has spent my gift. I have nothing more to offer this evening. Good night."

With this, she disappeared behind a curtain, leaving the pair in the parlor. Pomp, alarmed by Vadoma's sudden exit, flew down from the lanterns and stood on the table. Heraclix sat ruminating on the old gypsy's words.

He held his hands up, comparing them to one another.

"Here," he held the left hand a little higher, "a life changed forever. And here," he held up the right, "a life was meant to be forever forgotten."

He sighed deeply, then took out the papers he had earlier collected.

"We don't know where this Porchenskivik lived. Given the secretive nature of his letters, I don't believe that he actually lived at Szalko. Besides, he claimed that his messenger was from the *neighboring* village of Bozsok."

He leaned back in his chair.

"That settles it. We will travel to Bozsok soon," Heraclix told Pomp, "as soon as we can slip out quietly, without drawing attention to ourselves. We must find this man Porchenskivik."

Pomp, uncharacteristically still and focused, stared into the crystal ball on the table, enthralled.

Major Von Graeb brooded over a long wooden table. A map of Vienna's streets was spread across its top. Each corner was held by a sergeant, with a few lower-rank non-commissioned officers between them.

"We enter here," Von Graeb said in grave tones, pointing to the map. Then, pointing to another spot, "this is where the graf will be as we flush them out."

One of the sergeants spoke up: "If I may be so bold, sir?"

"Yes?" Von Graeb said.

"You do not sound very excited about this, sir."

"No," he admitted. "But we follow orders. We are loyal soldiers of the Holy Roman Empire, are we not?"

The sergeant looked to his companions, realizing that he had crossed a line. "Yes, Major. We are loyal."

"Good. I don't have to fully agree with orders to follow them. Neither do you. Now, move!"

The room cleared with military precision.

Though they marched in unison, three-dozen-plus-one strong, their boots made only a light tapping on the street. A pair of children, surprised by the sudden, almost silent appearance of a contingent of soldiers, scrambled out from the burned-out remnants of Mowler's apartment and ran off into the fading night.

"This is where the graf fought the devil," one of the soldiers said to a companion.

A sergeant responded in hushed tones, but with little restraint: "Silence, or I'll cut your tongue out!"

Silence was maintained all the way to the mouth of the gypsy quarter.

Pomp screamed, alarming Heraclix and waking Vadoma, who came running through the curtains.

"What was that about?" Heraclix asked, bewildered.

Vadoma, her face showing mixed amusement and worry, said, "I think I know the problem." She stood next to the table where Pomp sat staring into the crystal ball, transfixed.

"Your little friend has seen something. What is it, fey one?" she tapped Pomp on the back.

Pomp startled, going invisible, then flitting about the room, knocking into the little lanterns that hung from the ceiling.

"Von Helmutter! He's here!" Pomp yelled.

"No, not yet, dear. But if you saw him here, he soon will be."

"He is here!"

"He is not here yet."

"What? What is 'yet?'" Pomp asked.

Vadoma looked to Heraclix for help, but the golem merely shrugged.

"Look around, little one," Vadoma said. "Do you see Von Helmutter here?"

"No. Is he invisible?"

"No, dear, he is not invisible."

"Then he is not here," Pomp's voice relaxed considerably.

"When is he coming, Pomp?" Vadoma asked, careful to speak gently, so as not to startle the fairy.

"It is morning when he is here," Pomp said.

"Then we must hurry. They will look for you here, but they will not find you. When they do not find you, they will leave. They always do."

The sun had crested the city's outer wall of buildings but had not yet penetrated down to the streets when Heraclix and Pomp, on the incomplete rooftops of the gypsy quarter, heard the clomp and clank of Von Helmutter's men as they tried to weave through the wooden maze below. The length of the men's bayoneted muskets made the going difficult, but they dare not leave their weapons behind. They were in the midst of enemy territory, according to what Vadoma had told Heraclix and Pomp the night before.

The pair watched as the soldier's torches bounced along, bungling their way through the outer rings of the quarter.

"Torches," Heraclix said.

Pomp looked down over the edge of the rooftop.

"Still dark down there." She giggled, stretching her arms and wings out to soak up the rising sun, which was roughly parallel to their location, a good forty feet up.

"But the sun will show through soon. They have light enough to see." Heraclix said. "And why not lanterns . . . ?"

He bolted upright.

"Pomp! We're endangering Vadoma and everyone here! We must leave at once!"

Pomp saw the wisdom in this. She liked the old woman and didn't want her to be hurt.

"I will bring the soldiers with us!" she said, and flew off before Heraclix could finish saying "Pomp, no!"

Pomp doesn't think the soldiers need their torches. It's morning time! She buzzes in, bites fingers, takes one torch, then another, douses them in a bucket of water.

Soldiers shout, and so do the Romani. It's very confusing, but Pomp is able to take away and squelch two more torches before the shooting starts. The soldiers don't aim, they just shoot, and the Romani flee or fall. One, two, three of them collapse, two men and a boy-child. Another shot, a woman falls, her husband rushes at the soldiers, wielding a knife, but he is cut down by bayonets.

Von Helmutter notes the confusion, smiles, orders "throw torches to flush them out!" and the air is full of a dozen smoking brands.

Pomp can only put out a couple of them. The others set fire to the timbers, flames licking up the posts like dragon tongues.

Screaming residents throw buckets of water at the flames, some succeed at quelling them, some do not. It is not enough to stop the fires from spreading, meeting, engulfing.

Pomp pests a soldier just as a flaming section of building comes crashing down with a yell. A familiar yell.

But buildings do not have voices, she thinks.

Heraclix landed, quite awkwardly, on a large piece of roof that had become a piece of the floor. Great jets of smoke shot out from underneath, extinguishing some flames, fanning others.

Heraclix rose, then rushed a group of soldiers, screaming "It's me you want. Come and get me!"

The soldiers agreed and complied.

He barreled through them, knocking them aside, but gingerly, carefully, then continued past, away from the center of the Gypsy quarter.

Their pursuit was a bungling mess. They were not swift among the building brambles. Heraclix intentionally took face-first stumbles and pratfalls to let them keep up with him. They took the bait and closed with him as he led them toward the outer edge of the quarter, away from the bulk of the Romani.

He looked back frequently to make sure the soldiers kept him in their sights. Occasionally one of them fired a musket. Whether they missed him or the balls simply bounced off his body, Heraclix didn't know or care. They were following him, and that was all that mattered . . .

. . . until he turned around to see Von Helmutter, on his horse, silver dagger drawn, barring the path, waiting for Heraclix to come to him.

Heraclix—who didn't want to harm the soldiers but did want to draw them away—had no choice. He charged Von Helmutter.

The graf smiled, steadying his horse.

Another shot rang out behind Heraclix. In front of him, Von Helmutter's horse screamed as a red flower blossomed in its front flank. The beast reared, throwing Von Helmutter just as Heraclix overran his position. Heraclix trampled the graf. The wounded horse kept bucking, preventing further pursuit. Heraclix waited a moment to allow time for the men to clear the horse, to draw them further out. But then he realized that Von Helmutter wasn't the only one who was injured in the collision. A deep puncture in Heraclix's upper thigh gushed silver. He looked at the wound, realized its severity, and hobbled toward and through the city gate as Von Helmutter sent pursuers after the giant.

CHAPTER 5

Pomp hears cries and the cracking of burning wood, but above all else she hears shouts, in Romani accents—angry shouts, but the anger is not directed at the soldiers. The people are angry at Vadoma and "the fugitives"!

We cannot stay here, Pomp thinks. *They hate us now!*

Pomp flies above the fray, looking for Heraclix. Through the smoke she espies the giant running from the city walls toward a deep, dark forest at the foothills of the mountains. The soldiers chase after him, but he is tearing a path through the trees and leaving branches behind him. Von Helmutter's men cannot keep up with Heraclix. They shoot at him, but their bullets either miss or bounce off of him. After going into the woods only a few feet, the soldiers give up their pursuit and turn back.

"Heraclix is free," Pomp says as she watches the giant disappear into the woods where the imperial guards dare not follow without provisions.

"And now, so is Pomp!"

She flies off, directionless, heading for the portal that will lead her to her kin. She follows the contours of a hill that is not a hill, flying through a tear in the veil of the world, into a world that is not of men.

This is familiar, this place. This is home. But she can't help but feel that she has been away more than usual. However, she is not sure if this is true and is equally unsure about why she is not sure. Something is—what is the word?—*different*? Not different with here, but different with her. She dislikes the feeling and the realization. This is home, but she . . . is not. At least not completely.

She spots one of her ten thousand sisters, Gloranda, the rainbow-haired one. Gloranda is leaning around the edge of a tree, peeking at something, with her back to Pomp.

Pomp buzzes over and lays her head on Gloranda's shoulder.

Gloranda barely acknowledges Pomp, so focused is she on what she is watching.

In the distance, plump Doribell and Ilsie, twins, are saddling a large bat.

"He bucks!" Doribell says, giggling.

"And squeaks!" Ilsie says.

They jump on the bat's back, nearly crushing it. The bat squeaks, the fairies giggle.

"Hi, Gloranda!" Pomp says.

"Shh!" says Gloranda. "I'm doing a trick."

"It is good to see you," Pomp says.

"You are here," Gloranda says matter-of-factly.

"I am here . . . now," says Pomp. "There is another place where I am not here."

"That's crazy talk," says Gloranda. "You are here."

Pomp is silent, unable to explain what she means, how she has been elsewhere and has returned after an absence. The words "been" and "after" will not come to mind, and even if they do, Gloranda will not understand.

"And the twins are there," Gloranda continues. "And that bat is squeaky!"

Gloranda darts off, flying low to the ground. Then she is under the bat's shadow, flying up. She sees the strap holding the saddle to the bat and unbuckles it.

The twins start falling off the saddle. They kick and grope, each one clawing at the bat, latching on to its sensitive face. Their weight is too much, and the bat's neck snaps broken. It falls from the sky and hits the ground underneath Doribell's and Ilsie's combined crushing weight. Something pops and the bat is still.

"I do my trick!" Gloranda shouts with glee.

Pomp, from behind the tree, can't help but giggle at the prank. And yet . . . and yet . . .

What is "yet"?

One, *two*, *three*, and *four* are now, but *ten* is yet. And yet—there it is again—it is more than just numbers. It is how things happen now . . . and yet. Her mind spins, and in the midst of the swirling nausea, she cannot help but think that she would never understand, except that she had almost become not yet . . . almost, what is the word? *Dead*?

And there lays the bat. Not moving. Not breathing. Dead.

"It's broken," says Ilsie. She is bored, Pomp sees. Ilsie joins hands with Doribell and Gloranda, and the fairies fly off, leaving the broken bat behind.

Pomp is very, very confused. She walks over to the bat and tries petting it, but it does not respond.

"Get up, bat," she says. "Fly away!"

She thinks she should be happy about Gloranda's brilliant trick, but she is not happy at all.

"Wake up!" she jostles the bat, lifting a wing only to have it drop back to the ground, limp.

Her eyes are getting wet when she feels the hole open up inside her heart. She looks for the X on her chest, like Heraclix's scar, but there is nothing there.

"Why does it hurt without hurting?" she asks herself. "Why am I . . . sad?"

She has seen sad before, in the human world. But now she is sad. It is a new feeling, and she does not like it. She does not like it so much that it makes her angry! Angry!

"Sisters!" she screams. "You have made it . . . dead!"

But no one responds to her shouting and crying. She is all alone.

She is sad and angry and scared because this, this "dead" almost happens to her.

The hole inside her feels like it is growing. She has to do something, or it will swallow her up.

"Think, Pomp, think!" she says, trying to bring a word into her mind, a word she hears Heraclix say when he is sad and empty. She thinks, walks around in circles around the dead bat, then thinks some more.

"What is it, Pomp? What is it he does when he is sad and empty?" And then she remembers.

She *remembers*.

"Purpose!"

Yes, "purpose" is the word Heraclix says before they go back to Mowler's apartment to get the documents.

As her mind catches hold of this, the hole inside her gets a little smaller.

She realizes that she has changed. Things are different.

Her life isn't now about playing pranks all day every day. It isn't about not caring. All this playing pranks and not caring isn't fun any more. If she goes on like this, her life stays immortally, eternally . . . boring. Death is sad, but death makes life more worth living.

Life is precious, she thinks as she looks down at the dead bat again. Bugs have begun to crawl over the bat, just like bugs had crawled all over Heraclix.

But she won't let Heraclix become like the bat. Pomp will not let Heraclix die. She will help him.

Heraclix turned to face east, then west, then east again, standing atop the stone pillar above the tops of the trees. Bozsok, his desired destination, lay to the east. Vienna, burning, lay to the west. He was far enough away that he could not see the smoke, but he knew it was there, swirling around the soldiers and gypsies, carrying the screams and groans of the wounded and dying up into the vast, unheeding sky.

Had he reason to feel sorrow up to this point? Of course he had. But there was something in the quality of sorrow suffered at the hands of another that was different than the sorrow that one brought on others, whether through one's own stupidity and neglect or by intentional acts of hatred. The latter carried the sharpest stings of guilt, regret, self-berating, whereas the former was more easily dissociated from one's self.

"Mowler suffered for his evil actions," Heraclix said to himself. "I suffer for my ignorant acts."

He thought of the hand, looked at it, studying this thing so alien yet so much a part of him. He wondered if the same silver ichor flowed through it that had flowed, and only recently staunched, from the wound in his thigh.

"And I bring and suffer pain for those things over which I have no control. Is there no end to this pain and suffering?"

He looked down the side of the stone pillar on which he stood. Twenty feet below him, the tops of the pines scratched at the open air. Beneath their green tufts, a chlorophyll ocean whose depths he could not fathom coursed in waves. Could a dive into such a place hold salvation for him? He had been born, that he knew. And that which was born must die, was it not so? Perhaps he could end his suffering and the suffering of all those around him who had paid for his ignorance.

Yet he felt, somehow, that this would be a cheat, that, though his life might cease, suffering would continue on in the world. And who knows what suffering awaits the dead, if there is a life after?

For him, there was a life after. This was evidenced by his very existence as what he was. He had been "born," but he had been born of that which had died, which must have had an earlier birth at a time or times completely veiled to him by the bloody cauldron-womb of his inception as Heraclix. What had these men suffered or caused to be suffered before their deaths and his birth?

He could not in good conscience make a decision to end his existence without knowing all there was to know about these men—their desires, their hopes, their stories. Perhaps it was cowardly guilt, perhaps a clinical curiosity—he knew not which, but something simply drove him to know, a lust for information about those whose constituent pieces, together, made him *him*.

With great difficulty, owing to his leg, he climbed down the stone pillar and continued over the mountains, the Kőszeg Mountains, he thought he recalled from one of the many maps that he had perused in the time before the fire, toward Bozsok, the home of the once-boy who had delivered the Serb's hand to the sorcerer.

"... sickly and stooped, a runt, but a good, innocent lad ..." This is how the boy—perhaps a man now, perhaps not, Heraclix could not know—was described in the Serb's letter. He pictured a lad somewhere in his midteens, his face long, eyes sunken, bony cheeks pronounced from poverty. The boy's skin was smooth, not yet creased by age or worry, lost hope, and regret. But there was a knowing glimmer in his eyes. Innocence still held sway, but cruel experience camped around the borders, sending assassins in to lie in wait, anticipating the signal to set fire to the foundations of the boy's emotions, to burn his sense of trust to the ground. Perhaps there was time, Heraclix thought, to save the lad, or at least to steel him for what life would bring him, if it hadn't already arrived.

The mountains crested not far to the east and gradually lost their elevation as they stretched southeast. Even with Heraclix's great endurance and speed, he was not out of the mountains by evening. The thickness of the trees sped the fall of night, blanketing him in darkness. Beyond the invisible leaves, clouds rolled in, and rumbling thunder heralded gentle sheets of rain that distorted—but did not completely muffle—the sound of wolves baying in the distance.

After pain-filled and uncomfortable hours of travel, the mountains settled into less-densely forested foothills, the wolves' howls decreased, and the intensity of the storm increased. Lightning, striking from all directions, led to confusion, hesitation, and bad judgment that had Heraclix heading back up into the mountains before he realized that he was going in the wrong direction. He doubled back again, frustrated at the setback. Heraclix was wet, miserable, and distraught. The agony of his leg had grown. The wound was indeed spreading beneath his stitched up skin. His time was limited.

Half the night had fled by the time he finally found the edges of the village. The rain was a torrent by this point, and the lightning only let up for short periods. The buildings all had their shutters tied with leather thongs to keep the elements outside.

One structure was larger than the others—possibly the center-piece of town, though it was difficult to judge the relative size of the buildings in the fluctuating perspective caused by the lightning. A large wooden sign swung back and forth over the front door. On it, a carved octopus wrestled with an armored unicorn over an unfamiliar constellation of stars. The engraved words above them read THE ETERNAL STRUGGLE in Gothic script.

The oaken front door was sticky, swollen in its frame from the rain that beat sideways against it. Heraclix tried to open it, but he had to push his shoulder up against it to get enough leverage. The door suddenly opened with a snap and Heraclix fell onto the floor. He gathered himself up, thinking of how his position reminded him of his birth in Mowler's apartment.

The door slammed behind him, shut and barred by a middle-aged man in an apron whose most striking feature was his bushy, tightly curled black hair and handlebar mustache.

"You're the last one!" the curly-haired man said. "Next person that tries to come in, I stab him!" he held up a corkscrew. Heraclix looked around the room and understood the man's consternation immediately. It was a tavern, and everywhere were people, some speaking in low tones, most sleeping on any flat surface they could find, be it floor, table, bar, or crate. This might have been the entire village's shelter from the storm. And the entire village, save for a trio of passed-out drunks in the corner, looked at Heraclix with wide eyes.

"Furthermore, if I have to mop . . ." the curly-haired man looked up at Heraclix's bulky frame, his speech incrementally slowing with each word ". . . one . . . more . . . drop . . ." He stopped without finishing his sentence.

"Ah, I'm afraid," the man said, apologetically, "you'll have to rest by the door."

The rest of the crowd was not inclined to take so generous a view of the giant in their midst. Those who did not immediately roll back over into sleep glowered at Heraclix and mumbled among themselves. Heraclix wondered if he had not found himself in the Gypsy quarter of Bozsok, if there was such a thing.

"Look what the storm drove in," said a muscular bearded man with a long mane of red hair. He wore an apron that branded him as a bartender, butcher, or blacksmith. Heraclix decided he must be the last, given the charcoal smudges on the man's fingers, temples, and forehead.

"You've never been here before," said a short, skinny devil of a fellow whose piercing eyes were almost as dark as the black doublet and breeches that he wore. He was decidedly ugly, but his clothes were of the finest workmanship and neatly pressed, unlike the rest of the motley villagers in the tavern. Heraclix could even catch the shine of the man's boots from across the room.

"I am only a humble traveler seeking information," Heraclix said. He winced at the hoarseness of his own voice.

He fumbled a gold coin from the pouch he had taken from Mowler's apartment, offering the thaler to the skinny, smart-dressed man.

"I am looking"—he tried, unsuccessfully, to clear his voice—"I am looking for a young man, or at least a person who was once a young man, who delivered some goods to Vienna on behalf of one Vladimir Porchenskivik."

Several of those who were sleeping stirred at the mention of the name. Heraclix suddenly felt more eyes upon him.

The short, skinny man plucked the thaler from Heraclix's grasp.

"I will tell you who you seek and where to find him," the skinny man said in a near-whisper, "if you leave and never bring mention of that name to this village again."

"I'm sorry?" Heraclix was confused about how he had caused offense.

"The Serbian fiend," the skinny man whispered. "I shall not repeat his name. Nor should you, if you value keeping your tongue in that undersized head of yours."

Heraclix nodded his agreement. This was a time for negotiation and compromise, not for the defense of one's pride, however easy such a defense would be to mount, verbally or physically, even with his bad leg.

"Good. The one you seek is Nicklaus the idiot. He lives in the hills, by himself. His little cottage is a few miles up the northern road. You will pass a pair of massive oaks—you cannot mistake them for one is the mirror image of the other. Once you pass them, you will see a faint path to your left. This path will lead you to Nicklaus. But do not venture past his little place. He is a moron—crazy, but harmless. Beyond the vale of his home, however, lies the influence of the one I will not name. It is rumored that the ghosts of . . . well, it is best not to talk of such things. Now go," the short skinny man said, holding his hand out toward the door to indicate that Heraclix should now take his leave, which he did.

CHAPTER 6

The lightning had become more distant and less frequent, the wind had died, and the rain had settled back into a fine mist that enveloped Heraclix with a layer of water. He slid over slick roots and muddy patches, unable to see as well as he would have liked in the moisture-saturated darkness. Every bump to his leg became more and more painful as the night wore on.

"Ironic, now, that I wish the lightning was flashing more often," he said.

"What is 'ironic?'" Pomp asked, appearing right in front of Heraclix's face as a flash of lightning illuminated the night.

Heraclix jumped back, slipping in the mud.

"Glad to see me?" she asked.

"Yes, but not so suddenly!"

"Don't you want me here?" she said with a pout.

"Yes, of course," Heraclix said, picking himself up from the sodden ground. "I thought that I had lost you back in Vienna, in the fires."

"Pomp went . . . home for a while."

"You sound sad," Heraclix said. "What's wrong?"

"Home is not the same!" she said. "Pomp is not the same!"

"Are you well?"

"I am well now. But . . . different. Pomp has . . . purpose."

"Good," Heraclix said, "and I have a direction: up, into the hills."

"You found the messenger boy?"

"We're about to find him. Though I don't think that he's a boy anymore."

The rain slowed down as the night wore on, until the only remnants of the storm were the sounds of water trickling from leaves to roots.

Heraclix limped ahead through the muck, up into the foothills he had earlier descended, as dawn turned the air from black to sickly grey. They passed the trees and took the path, exactly as described by the short skinny man with the immaculate clothes. A few miles up the path they found a small cabin with a hole-peppered roof and beams warped under the weight of years. Every crease was filled with abandoned spider webs. Bits of fur caught in the splinters marked the passage of animals that used the structure for a scratching post. The only living things to be seen were earwigs and centipedes, which scuttled out from under the shack, then quickly retreated into an inch-high gap between earth and wood that ran the length of one side.

Heraclix approached, knocked. Pomp, sick of riding on his shoulder, flew over to one of the misshapen windows. The glass sagged with age, distorting anything she might see inside, but she looked around this way and that, trying to discover who or what was inside.

There was no answer. Heraclix knocked again.

"I think you stop that," Pomp said. "This man is, you say, dead."

"Dead? How do you know?" Heraclix turned the door handle and started to open the door.

"He does not move. And he stinks."

They could smell alcohol on the man's breath from the doorway.

"He's not dead," Heraclix said. "He's soused."

Nicklaus was everything Heraclix had expected—gaunt, but not broken, not completely—but he was no longer the boy who delivered the hand. That event must have taken place many years ago.

Heraclix knelt down by the man's bed, carefully removing the drunk's slack hand from a bottle of vodka. He shook Nicklaus.

"Nicklaus. It is time to awaken. We must talk to you."

Nicklaus's eyes opened. He stared directly at Heraclix with not the least bit of surprise in his eyes, like it was no odd thing for a creature such as this golem to be rousting him from a hungover slumber. Perhaps he was still dreaming.

"Who are you?" he asked with more curiosity than concern. He coughed, then gagged, almost vomiting.

"I am the owner," Heraclix raised his left hand, "of this".

A look of fascination, mixed with disdain, crinkled Nicklaus's eyebrows. His expression soon became pained, though Heraclix couldn't tell if the man was feeling the effects of a hangover or something else.

"That," he said, betraying his familiarity with and knowledge of the thing in one word, "I haven't seen for a long, long time."

"That," Heraclix mimicked Nicklaus's inflection, "is exactly why we are here to talk with you."

"We?" the drunk looked around the room and outside the still-open door.

Pomp appeared, with theatrical timing, on Heraclix's shoulder. "He and me make we!" she said.

Nicklaus looked down at the vodka bottle, then up again at Pomp, then back again at the bottle. He shook his head and took a deep breath as if accepting this strange new reality, steeling himself to act in it.

Heraclix put a hand on his shoulder, and he jumped, as if he had just realized the enormity and hideousness of the giant in his room.

"It has been a long time," he said. " I have forgotten much."

Heraclix offered a gold thaler, which Nicklaus refused.

"I do not need a bribe to try to remember. I don't want to talk!"

Heraclix put the thaler back into his pouch.

"Talking helps us feel better!" Pomp said.

"What's there to talk about?" Nicklaus looked at the wall. "I have nothing left anyway."

"Things are left," Pomp said, "inside you!"

Nicklaus let the words sink in, staring at the floor for a long time. Then he sighed and nodded, as if acquiescing. "Okay. I'll give it a try. Though it's difficult. Why do you want to know, anyway?"

"I have a strong interest in learning everything I can about this hand." Heraclix held it up.

"I don't know if I can help much," Nicklaus said.

"Any information you can give will help us," said Heraclix. "And anything you can get off your chest will help you."

"Okay. It was a long time ago, back when I lived with my poor old mother, God rest her soul." He paused, as if trying to remember her face, but the fog of years and alcohol kept her from clearly revealing herself to her son.

"Mother was desti-, destit-," his face contorted as he tried to and failed to get the word out, "very poor. Father had died after a horse kicked him in the head, not many years after I was born. I had no skills, but I could run long distances, probably from being raised in the mountains where we grew stronger than the people down in the hills and meadows. 'Lungs of iron,' Mom used to say. So I delivered letters, legal documents, and small packages for whomever would pay my fee. I became a well-known messenger. Fast, strong, and, most of all, trusted."

"How did you find customers?" Heraclix asked. "Or, rather, how did they find you?"

"Since we lived out here," Nicklaus indicated the cottage around them, "we were a sort of bridge between Bozsok and Vienna and Prague and everything that lay between. We got to know strangers, travelers, people who lived on the fringes, before anyone in Bozsok met them. The man who sent that," he pointed at Heraclix's hand, "lived, still lives, I think, not far from here."

"He—that man—had a bad reputation among the villagers, but I was too young to know why, and I never really cared—never gave it any thought all these years. He paid well, that's all I cared about."

"How do you know he had a bad reputation?" Heraclix asked.

"Mothers and grandmothers warned us against going in that direction. Said he was in league with the devil himself. But what did I care? He offered a hefty sum, a bag full of gold thalers, to deliver the hand, with the promise of more when I returned. I would be secure for a very, very long time. I could pay off my mother's debts and give her a good life. She deserved that. She was so good to me."

Nicklaus sniffled, stifled a tear, looked again at the vodka bottle.

"It is good to help mother," Pomp said. "Say more about the man."

"He was good to his word. A bag full of gold thalers, and I delivered the hand. The man on the other end gave me a return package and a generous tip, as well, though I sensed he did so because he felt obligated to. He didn't seem naturally generous."

"Tell us about the other man," Heraclix pleaded.

"I hardly remember anything. He was old, well dressed. I never learned his name and was ordered specifically not to ask. In any case, I returned home but stopped at the Serbian man's home first. Upon delivering the package, the Serb was very thankful and handed me two bags of silver thalers in addition to the gold he had already paid. I had never imagined such wealth. I was eager to share the good news with my mother."

"That is good news!" Pomp said.

Nicklaus continued: "When I came back here, she wasn't outside working in the garden, as I would have expected her to be at that time of day. I called out and checked the woods outside of our garden, where we kept the firewood, but found nothing. Finally, though it was midafternoon, I entered the cabin."

He choked up again. This time he couldn't stop the tears entirely.

"And there she was." He pointed up. Heraclix and Pomp turned, puzzled, to look where he was pointing: a set of empty rafters. "She was there, hanging by a rope."

He wept.

"I am so sorry," Heraclix said, and he was. He felt a deep emptiness in his chest where his heart may or may not have been.

Pomp felt something just beyond mere curiosity, something different, something uncomfortable but strangely necessary. She wanted to do something for the man, but she wasn't sure what to do.

"She was long dead when I took her down," Nicklaus said. "There was a note that read 'Dear Nicklaus, your dealings with that man brings shame upon our house. I can no longer live with such shame.'"

"I read the note and thought about it as I buried my mother in a clearing in the woods. Here I had worked to earn the money for her freedom, and the very source of that money had caused her death. I was despondent, in a dark and troubling dream for who knows how long. It's a wonder I didn't die of starvation. I don't remember eating for a long time. I prayed aloud, apologized to God, my mother, and all the saints for what I had done, pleading for forgiveness. Alcohol, I found, dulled the pain, soothed the hurt a little. This furthered the dream-state. I was muddled and lost."

"And then, one night, clarity came to me in a flash. I remembered: mother didn't know how to write. She couldn't have written that note. It was as if a lantern had been lit in my mind. My mother had not hung herself, she had been hung!"

"Then," a mystical tone entered Nicklaus's voice, "then I heard her speak."

Heraclix's discomfort was visible. Logic told him that Nicklaus's hearing a voice from the dead was no stranger than his own undead rebirth, yet logic also told him that he was listening to the ramblings of a drunken, emotionally broken man.

"I looked up there," Nicklaus pointed, again, to the rafters, "and there she was, hanging by a noose like the day I found her. But she was alive and smiling and she spoke to me!" He giggled, sending shivers up Heraclix's spine.

"She told me that I was right, that the villagers had killed her while I was away, that they were afraid of the Serb and our business with him. So they killed her and forged the note to convince me that she had hung herself."

"She said she was happy now, beyond the veil, sharing eternity with others who had been innocent victims of violence and misunderstanding. She looked so peaceful, just hanging there, smiling down at me. She said she would visit, from time to time. And she has, she has. She will come to me in the night sometimes, and we will talk of old times and the friends she is meeting there."

He paused, and the manic smile slipped into a satisfied grin. He nodded his head, approvingly.

"I am so very glad that she is happy. That's all I ever wanted."

He stared at the floor.

Heraclix and Pomp stared at each other.

After a long moment of silence, Heraclix cleared his throat and spoke.

"Nicklaus, we don't want to dredge up old . . . problems, but we are here to gather some information."

The smile instantly dropped from Nicklaus's face, and he was the dour, depressed-looking man they had conversed with earlier. Pomp was confused and repulsed by the change.

"Yes?" he said in a businesslike tone.

"We are curious to find this Serb, this Vladimir Porchenskivik. You mentioned that he lives not far from here. Where exactly does he live?"

"Ten miles into the mountains, up this same path."

"Very good. How will we know when we have found his home?"

"You will know, trust me," the wicked hint of a smile slipped at the corner of his mouth.

"One more question before we go: what route did you take and where exactly in Vienna did you take the hand?"

"Vienna? I didn't take the hand to Vienna. I took it to Prague."

"Prague?" The emphasis with which Heraclix said the word betrayed his surprise.

Nicklaus nodded. "To a man, a mystic or philosopher or sorcerer of some type. I don't remember exactly where, and I already told you I never knew the man's name. His place was somewhere near the old castle, I think."

Heraclix was obviously intrigued. "And what did this man look like?"

Nicklaus seemed suddenly sobered. "Why, he could have been your cousin, your brother. Could have been you yourself."

"Me?" Heraclix was now thoroughly confused, as was Pomp.

"The resemblance is strong, that's all."

Heraclix squinted an eye. "That's not really all, is it?"

Nicklaus shrank back.

"I'm not going to hurt you," Heraclix said.

"And I have no wish to hurt you," Nicklaus said. "But since you ask," he paused, concentrating to dredge up a memory, "the mystic in Prague, he resembled you in the face. Though he was not as ugly, and infinitely more sad. This is all I remember."

"Very well," Heraclix said. He slowly stood up and offered a pair of gold coins to Nicklaus.

The drunk, crazy man waved his hand, indicating that he wanted no part of the money. "I don't need your money. If anything, please give it to Herr Bohren back in the village. He hates me, and I have tried to make friends with him, but he refuses. Maybe he will take a gift of goodwill from you, acting as my proxy."

"Bohren?" Heraclix asked.

"You'll know him when you see him. He is a small man, and the most sharply dressed person in Bozsok."

"I will deliver the gift," Heraclix said.

"Good. And when you see old Porchenskivik, please thank him. He did not cause my troubles, and the wealth he gave me has helped me to cope." He looked down again at the bottle, watching as Heraclix's and Pomp's distorted images became thinner in the reflecting curves of the glass, then disappeared altogether.

Major Von Graeb sat in a tall-backed chair that loomed like a cathedral tower over him. A pair of lanterns, placed on the table at which he sat, cast the chair's shadow along the floor behind him. Their brightness caused him to squint at the city map, which was pinned under the lanterns.

Past the table, to Von Graeb's left, Graf Von Helmutter stood with his back to the Major, staring out a large window. Outside, in the darkness, soldiers stood around barrel-fires warming their hands.

"Twice," Von Helmutter said. "Twice! And he slipped from my hands both times." He shouted so loud that he began coughing. "I'm surprised the emperor hasn't forced me to resign. If his mother was still in charge, I wouldn't have lasted this long."

"Perhaps the emperor is not concerned with the giant."

"If he knew what I know about such beings, he would be sure to expunge this thing from the shadows."

"Well, he won't be hiding among the gypsies again," Von Graeb said. "We've made that quite impossible."

Von Helmutter turned toward his assistant, wiping his nose with a lace handkerchief. "You sound bitter, major."

"Some orders are easier to carry out than others, Sir."

"Understandable," Von Helmutter said. "It is sometimes difficult to do what needs to be done." He walked to the table and took a seat opposite Von Graeb, where the glare of the lanterns would hide his face from the major, while clearly illuminating Von Graeb's.

Von Graeb noted that the minister looked more pale than usual. Was it the light, or something else?

"There are some tasks, even in the stoic ranks of the military," Von Helmutter began, "where one is given latitude to make decision regarding another's fate. But in a situation such as this, where the denizens of the world beyond are involved, one can give no quarter. A monster like that cannot be reasoned with. The second you begin to listen to it, you open yourself to being deceived."

Von Graeb looked at the shadow behind the lights, perplexed.

"What I am saying," Von Helmutter said, "is that there can be no detente with the beast. He, *it*, must be found and exterminated!" He coughed aloud again.

Von Graeb could see the ghostly flash of the handkerchief in the lantern light as the minister wiped his nose and mouth. Small, dark stains now appeared on the white lace.

"You are determined to slay him," Von Graeb said.

"The powers beyond the veil are not to be trifled with," Von Helmutter said. He leaned forward enough that the lantern light shone up under his chin, making him look like a disembodied face, ghostlike. There were hints of blood beneath his nose and lower lip, contrasting sharply against his sickly, pale skin. "You know this as well as I do."

"Not as well, Kommandant. You have been trained to combat the forces of darkness. I am only aware of their presence."

"Your grandmother was a medium, I hear," Von Helmutter said.

"That is the rumor, Herr Kommandant."

"You do well to keep your knowledge a secret, Major. But I know what you know."

"I am sure you know better, sir. I have had no formal training, just tales at my grandmother's knee."

"I wonder if you don't know more than you let on," Von Helmutter said. "I was trained by an old man up in Prague. To this day, I don't know his name. I was instructed to never ask his name. I'm certain he is dead and gone now. It has been many years. I was quite young at the time, and very curious to learn every aspect of the warrior's way, regardless of the opponent. He taught me so many things that it all seems, in hindsight, like a dream, a misty whirlwind of swords and spirits. But one teaching was drilled into my head: you cannot suffer a demon to stay in this world for long. It is unnatural, blasphemy. It upsets the balance of things."

"But, sir," Von Graeb said, "we use mystic ways of dealing with the powers of Hell ourselves. Are we not the blasphemers?"

"Perhaps," Von Helmutter said. "But, if so, better that Earth should hold power over Hell."

"There is a danger," Von Graeb said, "that wielding such hellish power might itself corrupt the Earth. These supernatural powers are, by their very definition, something not natural to this world. Those who reach too far beyond the veil are liable to be pulled into the void beyond."

"All the more reason that we must do all we can to find and destroy this creature before we, too, are swept up in the tide of its wickedness."

The clouds had begun to burn off by the time Heraclix and Pomp again spotted the village. Large puddles of standing water in the flat areas reflected the clouds as they broke up, causing mottled pools of blue and grey amongst the green grasses of the low hills.

Shutters and doors were now open, and the pair saw men repairing planks and women sweeping sheets of water from their house floors. A few children played among the puddles, shattering the reflected sky with their stomping feet. In front of The Eternal Struggle, Bohren and a few companions, including the blacksmith, were gathered together in a semicircle discussing some matter.

Before Heraclix could get to the group to request Bohren's attention, the semicircle had unfolded a bit to allow egress to a young man, almost a boy, dressed in the uniform of a government messenger.

"Attention citizens of Bozsok!" the boy yelled in a voice far more powerful than his little lungs should have allowed. "I bear news from Vienna, from the offices of Graf Von Helmutter, Minister of Defense. News and a request for action. A request for action with a reward."

Heraclix stopped at the mention of Von Helmutter's name, not daring to step closer.

"He is here?" Pomp asked.

"Shh! I don't think so," Heraclix said, straining to hear the messenger.

"A renegade of giant stature is at large and wanted by the graf. He has promised a reward of thirty silver thalers to the man who captures and delivers this monster to him. Be warned, the giant is dangerous, a killer! And he is known to have kidnapped small children!"

"What?" Heraclix said, careful to suppress the volume of his voice. "Kidnapped small children?"

The villagers, who had now been joined by others, talked among themselves. Bohren then addressed the messenger. "How shall we know how to identify this creature?" he asked.

The messenger reached into a large courier bag and retrieved a scroll.

"I have placed," he announced, "several posters to help you identify the renegade." He unfurled the scroll, holding it up for all to see. "Here is the man—here is the monster!"

Gasps erupted from all present, for those who had not seen Heraclix had surely heard him described. There was no doubt that the monster in the drawing was the stranger who had barged in on them last night. A young girl, no more than eight years of age, screamed out, pointing to Heraclix in the distance, "There he is!"

Heraclix didn't wait to determine which motive drove the villagers. Rather, he bolted, not the way he had come, since that would lead them back to Nicklaus and Nicklaus's certain demise at the hands of the mob. He ran at top speed, noting one of the many posters that had been attached to the trees surrounding the village. The words were clear enough—wanted, danger, reward, and a list of legal reminders to anyone who would be so foolish as to aid or harbor the criminal. But what really caught Heraclix's attention was the picture that had been drawn on the poster. It was an exaggerated drawing of him, eyes aflame like some demon, his mouth full of needle-sharp teeth like those he had seen on the skull in Vadoma's parlor. One hand held a dead soldier by the neck; the other held a bundle of swaddling clothes out of which the pudgy face of an infant peeked.

Below the picture, the caption read BABY STEALER, KILLER.

CHAPTER 7

Pomp flies up into the mountains ahead of Heraclix. She doesn't want to overburden him by sitting on his shoulder. His leg hurts more and more as they walk on. She isn't sure if he can make it to the Serb, but she doesn't say anything about this doubt. She doesn't want to worry him. Worry, she is beginning to understand, is no fun at all.

Heraclix looks bad. He grabs his wounded thigh with one hand and his wounded arm with the other. He shakes his head. His breathing sounds bad. Pomp hopes he won't die.

"It hurts," Heraclix says. His voice is not quite the same now.

"What hurts?" Pomp asks, flying backwards just ahead of him.

He stumbles, falls to a knee, then gets back up.

". . . pain . . . will I die? Can I die?" he asks.

Pomp is confused. "I can't answer. I don't know."

". . . maybe . . . go back . . . jump from the rocks . . . it hurts so bad . . ."

He starts to turn around and walk back the way he came.

"No!" Pomp yells. She slaps his face.

He looks at her. He squints, then his eyes focus.

"We are close now," Pomp says.

"Close. Yes. I have to know . . ."

Pomp shakes her head. The hole grows inside her again as she watches her friend struggle through the pain.

Heraclix nods. "Yes . . . we will go on."

"Don't worry," Pomp reassures him. "I won't leave you."

It's evening by the time the pair comes across the path that leads to Porchenskivik's home. The narrow trail grows even thinner, encroached upon by sinewy, thorned bushes and low, dark evergreens. Ferns drape across the path, causing it to disappear from time-to-time, only to reappear in some random location, so twisted is the underlying path.

Pomp spies a rabbit in the undergrowth. It's wide-eyed and trembling. She flies down to investigate.

Heraclix crashes through the brush, reenergized. He pulls down vines and swats away branches, carving a tunnel through the web-like woods.

Pomp returns and comes up behind Heraclix to avoid the flying debris he generates. She's laughing as she approaches.

"The bunny is funny! She thinks we are in her den. She says she's never seen something as big as you underground!"

"Maybe we are underground, Pomp," he says with a mischievous grin. "Have you looked up lately?"

Pomp looks up and sees only glowing green leaves. The sky is not visible.

"No sun," she says.

"We'll find it again," Heraclix says as he rips branches down. "I think we will, anyway."

Pomp flies up high, past the branches, through the trees. Even birds avoid this place, she thinks. The only things up here are spiders and bugs.

"I will go up to see where we are," she says.

But before she gets to the top and breaks through, she remembers that she has promised not to leave her friend. So she flies back down.

She can see that Heraclix is growing tired again. He makes frustrated growls as he encounters obstacles. His voice gets weaker as they wear on.

"Keep going, Heraclix," Pomp says. "We are moving through . . . you are doing great . . . here we are!"

And they were!

They spilled out of a wall of green, crashing through ivy and tree branches onto a clearing. The sky was still invisible, but the undergrowth had been cut up and the trees had been cut back from the moss-covered stone walls of a single circular tower whose top thrust above the trees, beyond their sight. The leaves created a hemispherical bubble that glowed green. At the top of the bubble, about forty feet up, the tower disappeared, shrouded from view by the upper branches of the trees.

Heraclix spotted an ivy-clutched door set into the bottom of the tower. He went over to investigate while Pomp checked out the thin, arrow-shaped windows that occasionally punctuated its sides.

Pomp flew up to one of the windows, three stories up. She peeked inside, then froze. She hurriedly flew down to where Heraclix was.

"Pomp wants to go inside, but then Pomp *remembers* that she promised to stay with Heraclix, so Pomp is here with Heraclix."

Heraclix turned to her and gave a weak smile.

"Thank you, Pomp."

He turned and looked up at the tower, which stretched up and disappeared in the canopy of leaves overhead.

"We'll go in together."

There was no knocker on the door, no bell, so Heraclix rapped on the door, gently at first, then harder when he realized that the vines were muffling the knock of his knuckles. No matter how hard he hit the door, the sound was softened, nearly silenced, as if the tower was stuffed with cotton.

He tried the door, which opened readily, albeit noisily on squeaky hinges. Dust cascaded down, rolling out from the doorway, streaking the grass and leaving clear spots only where Heraclix's feet were. Pomp sneezed once, then flitted in, followed by Heraclix.

He was taken aback by the fact that while the tower sounded full of substance from the outside, it was remarkably empty on the inside. His eyes adjusted to the dark. To say that things came into clearer focus would not be entirely accurate. The crumbling stone walls and spiral stairway resolved themselves to his view. But the air was in flux—writhing, almost, with something other than dust, many things other than dust.

Pomp immediately flew under Heraclix's cloak, trembling.

Around, above, and through—yes, even through them—flowed a gathering of spectral beings, close to a hundred strong, their ecto-plasmic strands in tatters behind them as they floated up and down the stone stairway and the great, empty, circular shaft around which it spiraled. The specters were loathsome, every one of them crippled in some way. Many were missing limbs, several sported gunshot wounds, a few were altogether decapitated. But the mere sight of the appari-tions, strangely, did little to affect Heraclix who was himself, after all, caught in some kind of state between life and death. Rather, it was the soft crying and plaintive weeping (of those who still had mouths, tongues, and heads with which to weep), the faintly echoed pleas that caused him to shiver: "Heal me, please," "take away my wounds, I beg of you!" and "make me whole again! Just make me whole again!"

Upward and down the ghosts rose, sank, ascending and descending the stairs and air, unable to stop moving, yet equally unable to leave the tower, trapped forever by the stone walls of their own misery, like ethereal birds in a cage.

Heraclix looked up and noted that the congregation of the wounded dead was greater, more concentrated, near the ceiling, some fifty feet up. The dead passed harmlessly through him, he noticed, so he ventured to climb the stairs, himself one of the wounded, if not dead at this time. The ghosts made no effort to move out of his way. Most were too caught up in their own lamentations to notice, though a few looked at him with plaintive sadness in their eyes.

Most of those in the circular procession were men of soldiering age (or would be, if they were alive). Many of them, in fact, were uniformed as mountain irregulars. Scattered throughout this contingent of troops was a smattering of peasant women and even a few small children, all of them shuffling, floating, limping along as their injuries dictated, all of them pleading for help from some unseen source.

Heraclix made his way through the thickening crowd, higher and higher up the stairs, until he came to what must be the bottom of a trapdoor set in the ceiling. He pushed up against it, careful not to look down from this height and lose his balance.

The trapdoor opened upward, and Heraclix climbed through. The dead tried to follow but couldn't. They felt, pushed, hit the invisible barrier—all to no avail. Their efforts were as silent as the grave to Heraclix, who now sat on the floor above them. No sound reached his malformed ears, not even the sounds of their begging and wailing.

He closed the door, stood up, and looked around. The sun shone through high, arched windows, draping the inside of the tower with long rays of light shimmering with dust motes. A number of large burning candles ensconced in the walls lit the room. A trio of coal braziers lent a red glow to the room, giving it a dazzling aspect that contrasted sharply with the gloom beneath.

This upper section of the tower was larger in diameter than the lower section, though not as tall. The story on which he stood was surmounted by a demilune loft atop the juncture of a pair of semi-circular staircases, which crept up along the walls, like a beetle's mandibles. Pomp, emboldened a bit now that she knew the ghosts couldn't reach them, flew up to peek over the chest-high wood banister that blocked the view of the loft from the lower floor. Heraclix investigated the lower level.

A few small tables, two large bookshelves carved into the walls, an armed chair of elegant workmanship and embroidery, and dozens of silk pillows lay atop a mishmash of skillfully woven Oriental rugs. Judging by the furnishings, Heraclix thought it might be a crusader's castle. He was not entirely sure where the Serb's loyalties lay. It was obvious that the castle's sole living inhabitant had had some contact with the Ottomans, given the Persian rugs, the Turkish motifs on the pillows, and the smattering of books with Arabic titles on their bindings. He swore to himself to avoid the subject of politics. He couldn't allow such potential divisions to get in the way of his quest to know about himself.

Heraclix yelped, then laughed as Pomp, invisible, unexpectedly flew under his cloak.

"What is it?" he asked.

"Him!" she became visible for a split-second, long enough for Heraclix to follow her pointing finger up to the head of one of the stairways.

"Good day!" said the man as he haltingly descended the stairs. He was once, Heraclix thought, very tall, the tallest man he had seen in his current sojourn. But he was now bent with age. His long black hair was peppered with white, though it must have been jet black well into middle age. His face was carved by experience, though whether it was sad or happy experience, Heraclix couldn't tell. His eyes seemed simultaneously laughing and crying, as did his mouth, a perpetual metamorphosis was taking place in the man's face. He couldn't seem to decide between his desires for Heaven and Hell.

He was dressed in a blue-gray frock and long trousers, a combination of a military uniform, prison clothes, and a priest's vestments. Around his neck hung a large necklace with a circular medallion wrought out of iron. Inside the circle was a pentacle, and inside the central pentagon of the star, a crucifix. Beads, perhaps rosaries, studded the rest of the necklace itself.

The man raised his right hand in salutation.

"I know why you are here," he said in a thick Serbian accent. "You are here to be healed."

He smiled, showing a set of remarkably well-kept teeth, then motioned for Heraclix to sit on the floor, which he did.

The old man took the last slow steps to the lower level, then approached.

"And your little friend. I've seen her. She can show herself."

Pomp became visible and peeked out, from under Heraclix's cloak.

"It's okay," the Serb said. "I have no intention of hurting you."

Pomp mumbled something unintelligible to Heraclix.

"I'm very sorry, sir," Heraclix said to him, "but I'm afraid you are mistaken. I am not here to be healed, I—"

"Oh, but you are here to be healed," the Serb said. "You are indeed. You couldn't have come in here otherwise."

"But I am here to speak with you," he held his left hand up, "about this."

The Serb turned his face away at an angle but kept his eyes locked on the hand, as if he was keeping the option to flee open, though he couldn't help but stare at the blue thing attached to Heraclix's arm. His face became momentarily vacant, as if he was mesmerized by the ghoulish appendage. All cheerfulness had left his face.

"We can talk about that soon enough," the Serb said. "But first, you do need to be healed."

He slowly walked over to Heraclix and knelt down. His knees creaked and his back popped as he situated himself. He reached out and touched the wounded leg with his right hand.

Heraclix watched as the Serb reached up with his left arm, toward the necklace that hung over his chest. A shock passed through Heraclix as it became clear that the Serb had no left hand, that it had been severed at precisely the point where Heraclix's own left hand had begun. An even greater shock overtook him as he watched the medallion move, as if it was being manipulated by a hand of flesh.

"This is yours!" Heraclix said, holding the hand up. "You didn't just send it, you severed it!"

"Patience, my friend," the Serb said. "Look, the leg begins to heal."

Heraclix had been so enamored of his own self-righteous indignation that he had failed to notice that the pain in his leg had subsided from something rather acute to merely bothersome. The Serb walked his fingers along the line of the wound that Von Helmutter had ripped up Heraclix's leg. As he did so, the seam came together, sinew and skin mending behind the Serb's fingers. Pomp gasped in surprise.

"Where else have you been wounded?" the Serb asked.

Heraclix silently pointed to the other wounds he had received from Von Helmutter's silver dagger. These the Serb also healed. Not only did the pain subside, then disappear, Heraclix also felt enervated, more optimistic, even enlightened, as if his soul had, to some extent, been healed along with his body.

"Try that," Heraclix pointed to the stitched scar tissue connecting his neck to his body.

The Serb touched the scar, and others, in exactly the same way he had caressed Heraclix's dagger wounds. He concentrated, seeming to grasp the necklace more firmly with his phantom hand, the effort showing in his gritted teeth and curled-back lips. After straining for some time, he sighed.

"I've never seen anything like this," he said.

"Neither have I," Heraclix said.

The Serb chuckled, enjoying Heraclix's glib sense of humor.

"No," he said with a smile that quickly faded, "I cannot heal these scars. I should be able to, but cannot."

"The others are much more recent," Heraclix said. "Perhaps that is why you could heal them but not the old scars."

"I wish the answers to these mysteries were so obvious," the Serb said. "One thing is obvious, though: someone doesn't like you much."

"Von Helmutter is his name. Perhaps you have heard of him?"

"No, I can't say that I have. Should I have?"

"Not necessarily," Heraclix said. He felt that the old Serb was telling the truth. A slight shot of guilt passed through him, but he was here to pursue clues and find answers. He couldn't afford to have his conscience get in the way of direct questioning.

"And what of the sorcerer Mowler? Surely you have heard of him?"

"No, I'm sorry. I'm afraid not."

"No? Then to whom did you sell this?" Heraclix held up the left hand again, as if it would magically extract answers when held aloft. It did not.

"I am not sure of the name."

"Not sure? You had dealings with a man whose name was unknown to you?"

"I don't even know if it was a man, truth be told. It was an unusual arrangement, I'll grant you that," the Serb said.

"It was, indeed. Did you ever meet the man?"

"No, never."

"And yet you trusted him?"

"I didn't know the person's, for the sake of conversation, we will say 'the man's,' intentions. But I couldn't assign evil intent to a . . . man who offered what I wanted most."

"And how did you know that he could offer you what you wanted?"

"That, my friend, was a matter of faith."

"Faith?"

"Oh, don't get me wrong. I was, first and foremost, a man of logic. I was well-studied in the art of war, which is no art at all. It is a calculated equation, but the variables are so many that the outside observer sees war as a chaotic threnody. But I assure you, it is logical, calculable, and cold. Remove variables and you simplify the equations, no?"

"I wouldn't know of such things," Heraclix said. "But the logic seems sound enough."

He paused for a moment, growing solemn, then continued.

"I was good at figuring the equation. So good that I climbed the ranks quickly after graduating from the academy. My birth assured that I would never rise too high in the courts, but my reputation became such that I did gain much responsibility in the field. I commanded irregulars on the periphery, the rabble who knew the terrain and had been raised fighting. The kind of hard, barely disciplined men that fought like wild dogs, vicious, unforgiving. We fought other irregulars in rough country, where borders aren't so clear and allegiances fluctuated wildly. You can see how such an environment would change the equation quickly."

"Yes, I could see that," Heraclix said.

"No one could have solved the equation for long out there among such people, in such places. But I was very good at one thing: I was good at systematically eliminating variables by harnessing and directing that wild-man ferocity that simmered within my men. And that is just what I did. I believed that I was doing the right thing, setting aside sentiment for the sake of order, of justice. I was the equalizer—eye for eye, tooth for tooth, hand for hand. And again, I simplified the equation, eliminated variables present *and* future, eliminating the very possibility that variables might crop up again in the next generation. I felt that I could do better than follow the rules and win the game, I could rewrite the rules themselves, change the boundaries of war, and assure my victory."

"A very bad man," Pomp said with a scowl.

"And yet," Heraclix turned to the Serb and diplomatically interceded, "here you are with us, admitting that you thought you were doing the right thing." He paused, then spoke again, this time more slowly. "By inference, your perception must have changed. What happened?"

"Clarity came to me, unbidden. I didn't ask for it. That day was like many before it: nothing special. But for reasons unknown to me, as I looked down my bloodied saber blade into the eyes of my next victim, the next variable to be eliminated, I was suddenly sick of the killing. My boots were sticky from walking through gore. I had swung my saber so much that day that I could hardly hold it up. My ears were completely deaf to the cries of the dying."

"Then *she* looked up at me. Ten years old, no more. She had seen so much death in her decade that she had no fear of it. It was common to her, banal. She simply didn't care. And now, after a career of killing, because of the emptiness I saw in her eyes that day, I did care. I understood that she was . . . another human being. One that might have felt emotion, love, happiness, joy, if war hadn't cut these things from her heart."

"But you couldn't repair her heart," Heraclix said.

"No, I couldn't. However, I resigned my commission, took my pension, and began to build this place."

"This fortress," Heraclix said.

"Yes, this stronghold. A refuge from guilt I constructed using the spoils of conquest. But it wasn't long after building it that I came to realize that some laws cannot be broken, some rules cannot change. My supposed elimination of variables was merely a shell game. I had hidden a side of the equation from myself. Eventually, the variables themselves crawled back out from under my manipulations and demanded that the rules be obeyed, that the balance be restored."

"The ghosts beneath us!" Heraclix said.

Pomp peeked around Heraclix's shoulder at the trapdoor behind him, wide eyed.

"The same," the Serb said. "I was, am, haunted by my victims. I knew that I wouldn't be left alone until I could find a way to rectify things. There was no escaping it. But this wasn't the primary reason for my next course of action. After the epiphany in the girl's eyes, I wanted to do some good in this world and in the next, to try to undo what I had done, rather than merely drown out the guilt I felt.

"I studied, night and day, because I was kept awake, for the most part, by the ghosts of the dead. I studied and read the Gnostic texts, volumes of Sufi lore, the Hermetic traditions. I wanted to learn and practice the art of healing—spiritual and physical healing. Never again did I want to see such an abyss as I saw in that little orphan girl's eyes.

"My self-teaching, however, could only go so far. Books only show, they cannot mentor. I needed help beyond my own to seize my desires. So I left here, for a time, to seek wisdom and power to set things right.

"I spent some weeks with a group of monks not far from here, then headed toward Pest. I stopped at every church along the way, but found little in the way of enlightenment. Then, on the outskirts of Pest I stayed, for a time, in a gypsy camp. There I met some fortune-tellers, one of whom suggested that I allow her to take my needs to a man she knew in Prague who might be able to help. I agreed, thinking, after I left to return to my tower, that I had wasted my time, that I would never hear from her again.

"I began to despair, thinking that I might never achieve my aims, that I would die under the burden of guilt, haunted by ten thousand souls, then join them, forever to be tormented by their pleadings."

"It is just," Pomp said, clamping her hands over her mouth, surprised that she had said the words aloud. She thought she had spoiled everything. Now Heraclix wouldn't get the help he needed.

"It *is* just, little one. But providence saw fit to bring me to my senses while there was still time left to try to balance the scales of justice. I just wasn't sure how to proceed."

"Then, a few weeks after I returned here, there was a knock at my door. It was the gypsy, with an unsigned letter that said, in substance, 'I understand your dilemma and your desires. I can help, if the price is agreeable.'"

"Of course, money was no object. I sent her back with a response asking for terms. The gypsy never returned. Nevertheless, messengers were sent and returned, back and forth, until I had negotiated an agreeable contract with my mysterious business partner."

"The exchange was this: my hand, the hand that had shuffled the shells, hidden the variables, done the evil deeds . . . in exchange for the ability to heal—to reconcile the equation."

"Your necklace," Heraclix said.

"The necklace, yes. This was the agreement. But there were some difficulties, as with any business transaction."

"Difficulties?" Heraclix asked.

"I had thought we were at the conclusion of our business. I was awaiting delivery of the necklace, when the messenger I had sent with the hand arrived back at my tower with the necklace and a note. The note informed me that while the necklace would, as promised, impart to me the gift of healing, there was a certain key-word needed to actuate it. The key-word would be given to me as soon as I provided a piece of information, a lead, as it were, that my benefactor needed in order to finish a certain project.

"It seemed so strange at the time, his request. Yet, so simple. He wanted to know where the largest soldier on the continent would be found. It so happened that in my travels, I had heard rumors of a family of near giants, goliaths, living in Prague itself. I told my business associate to look close at hand and he would find his soldier.

"Of course, it was all a lark. I didn't have firsthand knowledge of these giants, only a secondhand reference I barely recollected. Nevertheless, he gave me the word that unlocked the power of this necklace.

"I couldn't have known his intent then, but now, in you, I see it, and it is good. You are good. I can say, now, that my overwriting of tattoos was justified. You are no avenger, no destroyer. I know this because you have come here and have let me heal you."

Heraclix shifted uncomfortably. Should he let the Serb know what he had done with that hand, or what the hand itself had done to the young soldier? He thought it best to simply accept the compliment and change the subject.

"Thank you," he said. "Now please tell me: how does my allowing you to heal me prove to you that I am good. I feel, a bit contrarily, that you are good for having healed me."

The Serb smiled. "I have uncovered all the variables. But there is still much reconciling to be done with the equation. I have, through various means, sealed off the top of this tower from the spirits of the dead. But they are still outside, waiting, and it causes me great anguish to hear their cries and to know that I caused their suffering. But I have found that whenever I heal a living person, somehow, in a way I cannot understand, the wounds of a ghost are likewise healed, and the healed spirit leaves my tower. I suppose they have what they want, and they leave. But there are still many to heal, and I am old. Very old. It's difficult for me to get around, to provide healing as I wish, and no one comes here to visit except angry villagers who are eventually scared off by my ghosts. I suppose that when all the ghosts are gone, the villagers will be emboldened and burn me alive in my tower. But I am not so concerned with this, so long as I can hold out long enough to heal enough so that I can enter the eternal realms alone, without the dead clawing me down into a gulf of misery."

"I sincerely hope that you meet your goal," Heraclix said.

"You have allowed me to heal you, which, in turn, heals two more souls: my own, and that of one of my ghosts. I owe you a debt of gratitude. Thank you."

Heraclix felt like he would blush, if such a thing was possible. Then an idea struck him.

"You can fully express your thanks, perhaps, by answering a few questions?" He asked.

"About the hand, yes. What do you wish to know?"

"I have an illustration of the hand in my possession. The tattoo, as illustrated, only shows *'osvetnik'*—'avenger,' yet that tattoo is now overlaid with *'oirotvorac'*—'peacemaker.' When did you make the change and why?"

"I did a drawing before removing the arm. You are correct in that when I drew the likeness, I only had the first tattoo. Before the amputation I inked the peacemaker over the avenger. It was a new day dawning, a new birth forthcoming. I wanted to celebrate and document the celebration."

"The other party wasn't upset with your interpolation?" Heraclix asked.

"Surprisingly not. I thought, after sending the hand, that perhaps the other party might renege on the agreement. For while I hadn't violated the letter of the terms, I might have violated their spirit. Nevertheless, my offering was considered acceptable."

Heraclix brought forth the drawing and showed it to the Serb. The old man took it, studied it intently.

"Yes," he said, "this is the picture I drew, though these characters that cloud the drawing," he indicated the sigils that pointed to the hand, "these I don't understand. They had to have been added after

I sent the initial illustration to the magician."

"Magician? You've said nothing about a sorcerer to this point. How do you know he was a magician?"

"Again, I don't even know if the person was a 'he' at all. But what else than a magician could give me such power as to heal the dying and the dead? A god?"

Heraclix thought for a moment, looking, unsuccessfully, for another line of reasoning.

"This . . . magician, did you ever hear from him again?"

"Never. All I know is that he was resident, once, in Prague. I would presume that if you could find the family of giants I mentioned earlier, you might be a step closer to your . . . man."

Chapter 8

From a distance, Prague's cream walls and red roofs looked like an ember cut through by the blue-green waters of the Vltava River. As Heraclix and Pomp drew closer, they realized that the city could not be so easily categorized by color. The palettes beneath the tall, red-roofed buildings that first dominated the eye were far too rich and varied for such simplistic observations. It was a prismatic, Baroque metropolis composed of brightly painted islands of homes and shops threaded with rivers of pedestrians flowing around Prague Castle like a moat of mercantile endeavor and intrigue. The streets pulsed with pedestrians like a heartbeat, a thing alive. Heraclix felt an unexpected sense of excitement and anticipation as he approached the stone bridge.

But gray skies and the drudgery of traveling through cold mud had taken their toll on Pomp, who was particularly dour, despite the fact that the clouds were now breaking. She had been arguing with Heraclix most of the way, and wasn't about to let it rest, just because Heraclix was smiling now.

"He is bad," Pomp said.

"He is not bad now," Heraclix tried to explain, "he is making reparations".

"He kills many. Even children!" Pomp could barely hold back tears.

"And now he heals everyone he can. He has healed thousands. Is that not good?"

"It is not *just*!" Pomp said.

"But he is making it just," Heraclix said.

"Making is not made!"

"True, but he is close to having healed all those he harmed and just as many whom he hadn't harmed. At some future point, he will heal, not to pay for past mistakes, but for the sake of healing."

"But . . . they . . . are . . . dead!" Pomp shouted, trying to make him understand. "They have no 'yet!'"

Heraclix stopped and turned to face her. "Look, you're right. But there's nothing to be done about it. Your sense of injustice is making you a very grumpy fairy. Look around you! This city is beauty itself! Its spirit is alive! Let's not ruin it by brooding over those things we can't control."

Soon, Pomp felt it, too. As she let the vigor of the crowd's movement and the warmth of the rising sun course through her, she felt a little better, until it took every bit of self-control she had not to fly off and spread mischief. She felt a little, but not completely, like her old self again. She realized that she had changed, that she was still herself, but was now different.

They crossed the bridge, shuffling with the flow of people. A voice cried out "come back here with my geld, ruffian!" The river of people shifted slightly to allow a pair of city guards to give chase to some thieves, a pair of young peasant girls, twins, who used their diminutive stature and identical appearance to their advantage, confusing the guards, submerging themselves under the crowd and occasionally breaking the surface only long enough to check their progress and reassure themselves that a steadily increasing gap was spreading between them and their pursuers. One of the guards, spotting Heraclix's hood a full two heads above the crowd, stopped long enough to look at the giant before being urged on by his companion. Heraclix wrapped his hand around the neck of his pouch to prevent any would-be pickpockets from stealing his gold. Not that he needed the money to buy food, he didn't. But a thaler seemed to keep information flowing, and he had much more information he wanted to gain.

Lining the stone bridge were dozens of statues, positioned like sentries atop the guard rails, looking down on the crowd, who passed beneath their munificent gaze. The crowd didn't return the glances, save for Heraclix. He wondered at the people's ignorance, but soon attributed it to busy-ness and the desire for fulfillment of more base needs. Heraclix had the luxury of detachment from such physical needs as food, rest, and human intimacy, whereas the common peasant was utterly consumed with them to the exclusion of all else, including matters of faith, save in those momentous occasions of birth, marriage, death, love, and fear.

Above him loomed the serene figure of Saint Vitus standing atop a cave from which a pride of lions emerged and climbed to meet him. Their expressions were indeterminate. Heraclix could not tell if the beasts were hunting Saint Vitus or if, like the prophet Daniel, they were merely trying to get close enough to enjoy a blessed scratch behind the ears. Either way, the martyr looked unconcerned.

Heraclix looked up at the saint and wondered if he, who had miraculously survived being dropped into a cauldron of boiling tar and molten lead, could understand the frailties of humanity. Or had his deliverance transmuted him, through alchemical reaction, into some finer substance than mere flesh? Heraclix questioned whether such a person could truly understand what it meant to live, die, be reborn, and live again. Then he thought of how doubly prideful his questioning was. First, the saint shared with Heraclix the peculiarity of being removed from the needs of men, which made them both strangers to humanity. Second, the martyr, indeed, knew what it meant to live and die, while Heraclix knew only what it meant to be reborn and live again. He couldn't remember having died. It was, after all, his desire to know the other side of his existence's equation that drove him to Prague in the first place.

A slithering whisper, which worked its way through the lines of people on the stone bridge became a burbling of gossip and bargaining as the crowds backed up to then poured out upon the stall-lined mouth of the Lesser Quarter.

A trio of drum, krumhorn, and hurdy-gurdy buzzed out a joyful song, not the muted bourrée of the west but something lilting and playful—a tune whose seeds were imported and planted during the crusades, no doubt, in this place where the influence of the East was more strongly felt than in most of Europe. The instruments and their players accompanied the frenetic haggling, gesturing, conversing shoppers, stall owners, street urchins, soldiers, aristo-crats, merchants, travelers, and beggars that coursed throughout the city. Pomp looked out on the masses, fascinated and delighted by the variety and energy of the people.

Heraclix stopped and started, spun this way and that, completely confused and unable to decide on a direction.

"Now what?" he asked.

Pomp responded, confident that the noise of the crowds would mask her voice: "We need to find soldiers, right?"

"I suppose you're right," Heraclix said.

"There are some soldiers," she said.

Heraclix, without the benefit of seeing where exactly she meant, spun again, then, looking through an alleyway, he spotted a large group of armed and armored men gathering into some sort of parade formation in one of the main market squares. They were beginning to face the castle and cathedral, which overshadowed all else on the horizon in the distance. The rattle of drums and the brassy call of trumpets drowned out the buzzing street musicians, who became silent in deference to the display of empire.

The troops lined up, four lines, forty strong a line, with two offi-cers mounted on destriers to either side and a marshal of noble rank at their head. Their uniforms were parchment-colored with sky-blue trim outlined in a green so dark that it appeared black in all but the most direct light. The officers barked out commands, and the four lines collapsed into one, about faced, and marched out of the Lesser Quarter and over the stone bridge toward Old Town. The citizenry moved aside or rushed ahead so that the soldiers could maintain their steady pace across the bridge. As the last of the troops marched off, the void in the marketplace was quickly filled with throngs of people smiling at the spectacle, most of who, Heraclix thought, knew nothing of the horrors of war.

A small cadre of soldiers remained, however—a half dozen army regulars who sat near or on the edges of a fountain. They smoked pipes and laughed, two of the six dancing to what sounded like a Russian song that the drum, krumhorn, hurdy-gurdy trio had struck up. The two tried and failed to perform a Cossack dance, one of the ostensible dancers falling hard on his rear, to the delight and laughter of his fellows.

87

Heraclix approached the group. The laughter immediately ceased, though the buzzing of the music continued on in the background, making for an awkwardly carnivalesque scene as the giant stood before the gaping soldiers.

Heraclix inhaled to speak but was immediately interrupted by a flurry of conversation that erupted forth from the troops.

"He looks just like, well not *just* like ..."

"I'll be ... he does, he looks like Caspar from the neck down."

"But even uglier in the face."

"Poor Caspar."

"The whole family ..."

"Unfortunate lot."

"Excuse me," Heraclix said. "I am told—"

"Doesn't sound like Caspar."

"Or any of *that* family."

"I am told," Heraclix continued, "that a family of, erm, *larger* individuals lives somewhere in the city. I have reason to believe that some may be employed as soldiers."

"Um, no."

"Not now, anyway."

"Though there was ..."

"There was Caspar and his kin."

"Where is this Caspar?" Heraclix asked.

"Dead ..."

"... and gone, far gone."

"Though some of his kin still live."

"Or at least one."

"How did he die?" Heraclix asked.

The soldiers laughed, glancing at one another, each in turn, as if sharing some inside joke, slapping their own legs and each other's backs.

Five of them turned to one—the oldest, by his graying beard and balding head.

"You tell him!" they said, between the five of them, "You know it best."

The old veteran, far too pudgy and soft to be a fighter now, stood and bowed toward his companions, toward Heraclix, and toward Pomp, though ignorant of the presence of the last, invisible as she was. Heraclix could clearly smell the alcohol mixed with the stench of stale tobacco smoke on the man's breath as he spoke.

"The tale of Caspar the Idiot," he said.

The soldiers scooted in close together like children gathering to hear a nursery rhyme.

"To begin," he began, "Caspar was an idiot. Oh, no one dared tell him he was an idiot . . ."

"No, nooooo!" the soldiers heckled, shaking their heads and laughing.

"No one dared tell him so to his face. For, though he was an oaf of the lowest sort, he could sense a direct insult after the third or fourth instance. And if the giver of the series of insults made the unfortunate mistake of not running away in the time it took for the mockery to travel from Caspar's ears to his brain, the consequences were grave."

"That's a long time!" the chorus said.

"At least the insulter was brought closer to the grave by the insulted."

"Caspar's hands, those awful, gigantic hands, were easily large enough to grasp the full girth of an average man's neck. One fist was enough to lay a strong man down for days." The speaker looked down at Heraclix's hands with a puzzled expression.

"Or the end of days!" one soldier said.

"Thankfully, his nature wasn't as brutish as his body. Truth be told, he rarely fought."

"Aww!" the soldiers lamented.

"No, Caspar was more of a lover than a fighter. And this was his undoing."

"Boo hoo!" the chorus sarcastically lamented.

"Yes, love and good natured friendship. You see, while some were indeed jealous and fearful of Caspar's gargantuan size, most liked having him around for the good cheer he invited. This he did by being the unwitting brunt of sidelong jokes and subtle jabs that he could never quite understand. He was, in a way, a sort of celebrity. He rarely had to buy himself drinks."

"Must be nice!" a soldier said.

"His friends, or those who called themselves his friends, were free with their geld around him, considering any money they spent on his behalf was money well spent on entertainment.

"So the giant, through his ignorance, enjoyed some things not even enjoyed by those who subsidized his excesses."

"Dumb lucky!" the chorus yelled.

"This included the attentions, paid for by his group of companions, of course, of the whore Vatanya."

"Vatanya!" the soldierly chorus shouted.

"Aye, Vatanya!" the veteran said with the hint of a sigh. "Two feet shorter than Caspar, yet the tallest, and longest, girl in town. She intimidated most men, which was good for business when you realize how many men think upside-down and want to be intimidated by a woman."

"Cowards!" one soldier said.

"But Caspar, Caspar wasn't cowed. No, he was never smitten by her, though he was smitten by love."

"Ah, Vatanya!" the chorus said in mock girlish voices.

"Vatanya, was used to having her way, so she found something new in Caspar, a man who wanted to please her out of love, rather than out of fear or perversion. This was something so new to her that she didn't quite know how to act. She liked that he was her match, in many ways, but she knew he wouldn't be around forever and needed to maintain the appearance of dominance in order to preserve any future business."

"Business is business," a soldier said.

"Now one way in which the man was no match for the woman was in their respective wits. Vatanya was no genius, but she had more brains than Caspar, who had very little. So it was easy for her to convince the giant that he should . . . ahem, *acquire* certain gifts for her in order to keep her favor."

"That seems fair!" one of the soldiers said. The others vehemently nodded their agreement.

"Of course, Caspar was not a good burglar, but doors and locks did little to stop him. His victims could do little to stop him, either, both because he was a giant and because he wore an imperial soldier's uniform."

"Huzzah!" yelled the chorus.

"And no one argues with a soldier . . ."

"Huzzah!" again.

". . . but another soldier."

Grumbling assent bubbled up from the troops.

"And so it happened . . ."

"It was inevit-, inev-, unavoidable!" shouted one of the soldiers, more drunk than the rest. The veteran looked at the man with disgust, perturbed by the sot's interruption.

"And so it happened that one of Caspar's victims, a man who, though not a soldier, had a soldier for a brother, convinced said sibling to talk giant Caspar into stealing a gift, a most precious gift, for his sweetheart, something from the General himself."

"Hoa!" one of the soldiers yelled.

"A fair move!" shouted another.

"A soldier's a soldier!" a third.

"Of course, it was a setup, and the framed simpleton was caught red-handed."

"Or, rather, *made* red-handed!" said the chorus.

"Yes, made red-handed. For when the General learned of the theft, he had Caspar tortured by burning off the giant's palm prints and fingerprints as a lesson to all that what is the General's is the General's."

"A good lesson," the soldiers agreed, "well taught."

Heraclix folded his arms, hiding his palms underneath the fabric of his cowl.

"He also had his feet and toes ironed, to show that a common foot-soldier dare not cross the General's threshold without permission."

"Hear, hear!" the chorus heard.

Heraclix looked down at his boot-clad feet. He thought he knew what he would see if he removed the footwear.

"And then, with a full three whacks from the executioner's axe, he was beheaded."

Pomp carefully studied the seams between Heraclix's body and neck. She knelt carefully on his shoulder, shifting her weight to the outside, then flew out from under the cowl where she had been hidden.

Heraclix started at the movement.

"What? What is it?" one of the soldiers said.

The most drunk of the bunch looked at Heraclix suspiciously.

"Hey. Ain't we supposed to be looking for someone big?"

"Haw!" laughed the veteran, who walked over to the drunk and gave him a slap on the back so hard the man almost vomited. "This ain't him. No way! Lookit him. He looks just like poor old Caspar. Could be his twin! Though a touch uglier."

"You know what this giant looked like?" Heraclix asked.

"No, no." The veteran had a far-off look in his eyes. "Caspar has been dead for a long, long time. Before my time, even. He's a legend, old Caspar."

The men all solemnly nodded, lowering their eyes to show respect to Caspar's memory.

"But I thought you said—" Heraclix began.

"Look here," the veteran said, trying, unsuccessfully, to rest his arm over the giant's back. "We're supposed to take anyone who is 'unusually large,' as the orders go, in for questioning."

"But you . . . you're like one of us, I'd say. What do you say, boys?"

"Huzzah!" said all but the one who was still doubled over on the ground.

"That's right. One of us, like the ghost of old Caspar himself, heh?" he said.

Heraclix forced a chuckle.

"So you head on over to Hradčany, by the castle. There's a bright blue flat there, stuck between a red butcher store and an orange flat. That's where old Caspar lived, a long, long time ago. I'm sure his family still lives there.

"Thank you," Heraclix said.

"No need! You've brought back some good memories, friend. And you needn't worry about us ratting you out. We never saw you, did we, boys?"

"Never!" most of them said.

"Mmph!" said the drunk, shaking his head and vomiting into his own hands.

"Well then, we'd best disappear," Heraclix joked. He heard Pomp gasp in surprise.

"We?" said the veteran, looking around Heraclix's girth to see if anyone was hiding behind him.

92

"Nothing. Ah, never mind," Heraclix said, "Figure of speech."

He quickly headed off toward Prague Castle, leaving the soldiers behind. He walked mechanically through the streets, letting his body take him where it would. His thoughts were on his body, though he felt a strange separation of physical form and conscious thought. He recalled the brightly colored illustration contained in Mowler's book and stopped momentarily.

"Why have we stopped?" Pomp whispered.

"Just thinking," Heraclix said, reaching into his pouch to retrieve the book. He started walking again, slowly, while thumbing through to the illustration. "It's a map," he said.

"A map?" Pomp asked.

"Yes, a map of who I am, and who I was."

"This is good to have, right?"

"I don't know. I think I'm even more confused than before."

He closed the book, put it back in his pouch, and walked. His legs were taking him to their next destination, but his thoughts wandered off into regions unknown.

CHAPTER 9

Finding the blue house in Hradčany is like finding a specific grain in a teaspoon of salt. Blue, red, and orange houses are everywhere. Also yellow, white, lavender, and three shades of green. Windows and doors vary in shape, size, and quantity. The buildings are united by their proximity to each other, a chaining together of rain gutters like some strange airborne river, and, of course, by their utter lack of uniformity. No two neighborhoods look exactly alike, but all are part of the same organic whole, rows of homes growing out of cobblestone fields fed by rain gutter canals.

Heraclix and Pomp wander for hours looking for the flat as described by the veteran soldier. Pomp scouts ahead, identifying blue building candidates and navigating Heraclix, who soon becomes lost in the twisting streets, through the neighborhood in the shadow of Saint Vitus Cathedral. The spire's umbra has grown long, stretching toward the river like a dark dagger blade by the time they finally find the place.

Pomp peeks in the windows.

"No one home," she says.

Heraclix knocks, but there is no answer.

Pomp flies up above the building where Heraclix can't get in.

There, there is a chimney, just big enough. She goes down, wriggling, punches a large spider who tries to bite her. The spider falls to the fireplace below. Still, she has to tear her way through the webs, down the flue and into the ash pit. The spider shakes, clenches in on itself like a fist, dies. Pomp looks around, up, down. Where is the spider's ghost? Where did it go? Would it haunt her?

Pomp backs out of the fireplace, turns around and scans the apartment. It is sparse: a desk, chair, bookshelf—papers strewn about, a silver thaler on a chain and a crucifix adorn the wall. Cobwebs are everywhere.

The shimmer of the thaler catches Pomp's attention. She lifts the chain from the wall peg. The man on the coin is different from the faces on Heraclix's gold coins. Heraclix's gold shows a woman with curly hair and a double chin. This coin shows a man wearing a laurel. His hair is just like Pomp's—short, cut in a bob. She will keep this coin!

Heraclix waited outside until his presence at the door began to draw people's attention. A pair of women nudged each other and spoke in hushed tones. Their disapproval was clear on their faces. A group of young children chased each other until one of them spotted Heraclix, pointed at him, and ran away screaming. The others followed screaming, looking over their shoulders to see what it was that they were screaming about.

An old man bumped into Heraclix and let out an almost inhuman growl. He looked up into the giant's eyes and gave an evil glare.

"Excuse me," Heraclix said.

The man pursed his lips and narrowed his eyes, then carefully backed away. After making some distance between them, the old man cast a hateful glare at the giant, then turned and ran away.

Heraclix walked away from the apartment. *He's gone to fetch the constable,* Heraclix thought. *Best to clear out and find a place to hide for a while.*

He turned and walked down the street toward the river. "This has been fruitless," he said to himself. "I have no direction. I don't even know where to begin. The more I learn about my . . . self," he hesitated to use the word, "the less I know."

Heraclix entered the west doorway of Saint Vitus Cathedral and, sitting on a back pew in the nave, brought forth the papers that Pomp had acquired earlier, hoping to find some inspiration in them. The pews were empty, allowing Heraclix to meditate on the puzzles that plagued his thoughts. But as he began to read, he was surprised to see a silver thaler on a chain materialize, seemingly out of nowhere, and plop down on top of the papers.

Pomp said. "I just find this."

"Just find? Where?" he said with a tone somewhere between amused and chiding.

"I don't know."

"What do you mean you don't know? Did you take it from the apartment?"

Pomp became visible and visibly annoyed. "That man is dead. This is not his anymore. You say so!"

Heraclix sighed, then held the coin up in the colored glow of a stained-glass window.

"This coin looks old," he said. He ran a finger over the obverse, studying the face of the noble stamped there. "Ferdinand III. This is an old coin, Pomp." He flipped it to the reverse side, noting the coat of arms. "No date. This doesn't get us any closer to finding Caspar."

He looked at the coin's edge and was surprised to see tiny letters engraved there. He squinted to read them, turning the coin in the light to get a better angle on the worn lettering. "Josefov," he said. "Probably the location of the original owner . . ." He stopped suddenly.

"What?" Pomp asked.

"Josefov! The ghetto!" He stood up and left just as a parishioner, alerted by Heraclix's loud voice, came out of Saint Wenceslaus's Chapel and walked toward the source of the disturbance. The door had closed behind Heraclix and Pomp by the time he was halfway down the pews.

They went back to the bridge, Heraclix hoping that they wouldn't run into any soldiers. Luck was on their side, and they crossed the river without incident. Desire drove Heraclix. He steered by instinct. He wasn't quite sure how he was navigating his way from the Old Town to, then through, Josefov—he merely knew that he was. It felt natural to him, yet unnatural, like he knew exactly which course to take in order to reach his unknown destination, like he had taken this route a thousand times before, though he had never even been to the city, so far as he could recall. A degree of unease entered his gut, spread through his chest and crawled up his back. He skulked and stumbled through dozens of winding streets and alleyways, oblivious to his destination, yet confident that he knew the way there, his every motion an act of frisson-building faith.

This sense of belonging, cast up against the knowledge of his very lack of knowledge, gave him pause. *How can I know this place that I have never before seen? What part of me is so attuned to this area, and why?* he thought. He felt nauseated when he dwelt on such questions: *What part of my unseen past causes the city to ring such a familiar chord? Who, really, am I?*

The buildings leaned this way and that, with no particular dominant orientation, like God had played building blocks there as a child and never cleaned up his mess. The rooftops were steeper than the Alps, walls narrow and tall, but even more inaccessible. The lower windows were barred, the upper windows too high for potential burglars to reach except by way of the treacherous roofs. If one could see out the high windows, one would be rewarded with a view of yet another beige wall, which would be like no reward at all, save for those who enjoyed unending blandness. It was an open prison, a neighborhood-cum-jail. Eaves loomed, threatening to fall on the street below at the slightest disturbance. Still, Heraclix trusted that somehow he would reach and recognize his destination, though the thought did occur to him that he might prefer to be elsewhere when he finally found it.

And then, he was there. And he knew he was there, somehow, wherever "there" was.

"There" was a door off its hinges, a two-story beige flat with boarded-up windows snowing dust from between the splintered slats and a stairway on the side of the building that led nowhere. He softly pushed at the door, which teetered on one hinge for a moment, then slammed to the floor, blowing a wave of debris out in all directions. Dirt billowed out of the open doorway, causing Pomp to cough aloud in the cloud.

"I thought you had a companion with you," an old man's voice said from within the gloom. "Now I am certain of it."

"Who are you?" Heraclix asked.

"Peek-a-boo!" the voice in the darkness said. "I see you! But not your friend. Do show yourself, little one. Show yourself to this harmless codger."

From somewhere in the room, a spark erupted, followed by the light of a candle.

Pomp entered first, followed closely by Heraclix. She showed herself to the old man, who sat on a rickety chair in the center of the main room. He wore only a pair of trousers. It was the old man Heraclix had bumped into outside of Caspar's apartment in Hradčany. His bare chest and feet were more like a skeleton than a living man.

"Fair enough. You've shown yourself. Now do come forward, my enormous friend."

Heraclix walked further in. After his eyes adjusted to the low light, he scanned the room, but there was little to scan: the man, the chair, the candle, and an extremely large mirror, which was cracked and positioned on the wall behind the chair. The reflection showed the trio and the chair, but it was difficult for Heraclix to see either his own or Pomp's features. Their faces appeared like dark smudges in the mirror. As he turned his eyes away from the muddled reflection, the squalor of the place came into sharper focus. The peeling walls were spotted black with mold. There was blood on the mirror's frame.

"I had hoped you would come," the old man said. "When I saw you outside Caspar's apartment, I hoped that you would know to follow me. And now, here you are."

"What do you have to offer us?" Heraclix asked. "And how do we know we can trust you?"

"You recall Caspar Melthazaar," the old man said, ignoring Heraclix's question, "the one whose coin you stole from the apartment?"

Heraclix nodded.

"I will tell you the truth about the man Caspar Melthazaar. I am old. My time in this world is nearly at an end, and I would tell my story before I die. It is a tale I think you will want to hear," he said, pointing at Heraclix.

Heraclix sat on the floor. "Well, go ahead, then, old man," he said. "Tell your tale. We will listen."

The man laughed, "Ha, ha! It is well that you give ear, or what little ear you have left, to my story. I am an old man, very old. This tale comes from my childhood. It's one of my earliest memories, though I suspect that my age is such that I have dragged my capacity to remember along with me. My earliest memories become later and later."

Pomp looked at the man with utter confusion.

"Please get on with it," Heraclix said.

"This memory," the old man continued, "is likely from the time I was about six. Yes, six and poor. Very poor. So poor I couldn't even afford a mother or father. I lived with my dear old grandmother. I wasn't the only one. There were a few of us cousins living together in that little flat. My parents, you see, weren't the only ones who had died from the plague—there were others. In all, I think grandma lost seven or eight children or children-in-law in a short period. She buried her grief in loving and taking care of her children's children."

"And one of these is Caspar," Pomp said.

"Caspar was absolutely her favorite. I think it was because he was so stupid that she took pity on him. She always did like him better." He scowled as he spit the words out.

He sat silent, brooding for a moment "Still, he was my cousin," he sighed, "and we all love our cousins, right?"

Pomp couldn't help smiling and clapping her hands. But she quickly realized that she must have looked ridiculous, so she stopped, embarrassed.

"We were proud of him—Caspar the imperial soldier, a terror to Turk and Prussian alike. It was said that he once wrestled an enemy officer's horse to the ground and crushed the unfortunate rider with his own steed. Oh, he was a brute in both body and mind," the old man said with a hint of pride in his voice.

"I knew he would never amount to much. So I wasn't a bit surprised when I went to watch an execution only to see Caspar kneeling at the executioner's block."

"Chop, chop, chop!" he said, his eyes growing wider and redder with each repetition of the word. One eye began to twitch. Pomp shrank back.

Heraclix's left hand tensed. He forcefully held it down on his thigh with the right hand. He looked away from the old man in an effort to calm himself. A strong sense of familiarity washed over him, as if he had been in this place before. The candlelight shimmered, and, in an instant, a vision opened up to Heraclix's sight.

The walls were clothed in color, the warm glow of a fireplace on a winter's night shimmering about the room. It was more fully furnished, with another chair, a table, and an enormous bed. Beside the bed knelt a child with a surprised look on his face, a towheaded boy whose eyes were wide with shock. In his hands was a box full of coins. He looked up at Heraclix with apparent guilt.

"What is happening here?" Heraclix-not-Heraclix asked the youth.

"Nothing!" the child said in a quavering voice.

"Something, I think."

"You don't think. You are an idiot. I am smarter than you. I deserve this more than you."

"That is for grandmother."

"What? Why?"

"She has taken care of us. She is good. She deserves better than what she has. Please put it back."

"No!"

"Then, maybe you can take it to her?"

"Yes," the child said with a smile. "Yes, I'll take it to her." He looked at Heraclix-not-Heraclix, hardly believing his luck or, perhaps, his interlocutor's stupidity. He shut the box and put it under one arm. The contents jingled loudly.

The door opened behind Heraclix-not-Heraclix. The boy peeked around him.

Standing in the doorway was a beautiful woman. Simple in dress, but beautiful, tall, with soft features, raven black hair, and a pleasant smile.

"Well, Hello there, little Georg. What do you have there?"

"Something for grandma. Coz wants me to take it to her."

"You'd better do it, then. Coz wants what is best for your grandmother."

The child walked around the adults and out the door, but not before shooting a hateful look at the woman, followed by a mischievous smile.

As the door was closing, the wind gusted, blowing the door wide open and sending snow and cold into the room.

Through the open door, Heraclix-not-Heraclix could see the faintly moonlit face of Prague's astronomical clock, the Orloj, *on City Hall. The moon was in Scorpio. The clock struck midnight.*

Heraclix blinked and the room darkened again. He saw the old man staring intently at him. A mischievous smile, not unlike the child's, had spread across the old man's face.

"Georg . . ." Heraclix said, cautiously.

"Caspar," the old man said, with a hint of hopefulness in his voice. "But not Caspar," he conceded, falling back into a more depressed tone.

Heraclix sat in stunned silence.

The old man picked up where he had left off: "Chop, chop, chop," he said, this time slowly and methodically, making a chopping motion with one hand hitting the palm of the other three times.

"I stayed," he continued. "After all the crowds had left and they had rolled his headless body into a casket, I approached the executioner. I told him that I was the next of kin.

"A stranger, who had been watching from a side street, unbeknownst to me, approached the executioner at the same time. We almost bumped into each other. We three conversed, haggled, bargained, and I sold the body to the stranger for thirty silver thalers."

"The stranger had a group of assistants, all done up in Venetian masks, who carted Caspar's body away. The stranger wanted the head, too, but the executioner said that I couldn't sell it. The general, the man who had ordered Caspar's execution, wanted the head for himself."

"Opportunistic . . ." Heraclix said.

The old man shot him a cold glance. "I went home and told grandmother, who was starting to go a little senile anyway, that Caspar had fallen into a glacier in the Alps after his lover, Vatanya the whore, had sent him on a wild search for some trinket or other. It was partially the truth," he said.

"She had to think a long time about that one, grandma did. She thought about Caspar's unfortunate 'accident' in the Alps, his association with people of ill-repute, his very enlistment in the army; all these things she . . . eventually . . . over the course of time, blamed on herself."

The wicked grin spread again across the old man's face.

"It drove her mad."

"Of course," he frowned, "she had to have someone to take care of her, someone to manage her resources. Caspar had left her much, you know."

The frown swung up into a smile. "That someone would be me!"

Pomp wondered if she could somehow find a way to set his pants on fire.

"The person to whom you sold . . . the body . . . what did he look like? Do you know who he was?"

The old man stood up, laughing maniacally, as if he was privy to a joke that no one else could hear.

"Ha, ha! Why, he had your face, Okto! The man was *you!*"

Heraclix, perplexed and indignant, stood up.

"What? What does this mean?" he said.

"Oh, you really want to know, don't you, body thief? Gravedigger! Ha! Or are you really Caspar, come to exact vengeance on me? Either way, my fate in Hell is already sealed. I shall go to my torment and leave you behind. You shall not have your vengeance, Caspar! And you, gravedigger, you'll have to follow me for answers!" the old man yelled as he threw away the chair and dashed toward the mirror. "Follow me straight to Hell!"

The reflections of shattering glass looked like a conflagration of candle flames in a rain of blood. The old man's glass-embedded body, quite dead, lay at the base of what was once a mirror. There, where the mirror had been, was a long, dark tunnel, like an open maw set with jagged glass teeth.

Down the tunnel ran the shrieking ghost of the old man, his glow fading and voice echoing off the walls as he raced into the black abyss.

CHAPTER 10

Pomp watches as Heraclix picks up the candle, steps over the old man's lifeless body and gives chase down the tunnel, careful to protect the flame with his hand.

She follows, then passes him and flies ahead, reckless in her pursuit of the ghost. She plunges into the darkness, flying full speed, careening off the passage walls, leaving clumps of dirt and frightened earthworms to fall to the tunnel floor. Keeping a spirit in sight is no easy task when you're flying blind in the dark, but Pomp is persistent. She knows Heraclix needs that ghost!

The tunnel angles down, steeper and steeper. It grows colder and colder, then warmer and warmer as she travels deep, deeper. Soon she is flying almost straight down. The ghost grows more faint as a ruddy light begins to glow along the dirt walls. The light grows stronger, the ghost more faint, the air much warmer. Then the tunnel levels out beneath her, the further she travels. The ghost is out of sight for a moment, then Pomp, as she clears the bend, can see it rushing even faster, headlong, toward a sort of shimmering membrane that fills the tunnel from top to bottom.

Beyond the membrane is a yellow-orange glow. *Firelight*, she thinks. Pomp sees shadows shifting within the membrane, pulled about and stretched by dancing flames, like dark marionettes controlled by a crazed puppeteer.

The ghost flies straight into the membrane. The jelly-like barrier ripples as the ghost disappears in a flash, leaving only wisps of spirit matter that coil up into the air, then dissipate into nothingness.

She can't see him. He is on the other side somewhere. She must follow.

Pomp plunges into the membrane and is instantly slowed to a crawling pace despite her best efforts to muscle her way through the stuff. She flutters her wings as fast as she can and swims with all her strength through the jelly-matter. All around her, she sees scenes and people and places, not from now, not from yet, but from before now. Bits and pieces of . . . "then", float all around her, shining in convex distortion from the bubbles in the thick liquid.

Pomp reaches up to touch a bubble.

Mowler has seized her by the legs and is slapping her head and body on a rock like a wet rag. The world jolts, then shakes, grows blurry, then jolts again as he repeatedly slams her. She cannot resist as he stuffs her in a sack, then smashes her again. His hand reaches in to grab her. She tries to bite him, but she feels herself falling into something smooth, hard, and cold.

Looking up, she sees the top being closed on her glass prison.

The scene disappears as the bubble floats away from her fingertips. She turns just in time to see another bubble rushing toward her nose.

The happy boy is, has, grown into an unhappy man.

She sits next to him. His forearm is as big as her entire body.

"Why so gloomy?" she says with enough cheerfulness to ban gray clouds from the sky.

He glowers at her.

"You don't know?" he says with a sneer.

"Everyone is happy!" Pomp says, spreading her hands to indicate the other frolicking fairies, some of who have gathered in a ring to dance around the man.

"You are ignorant," the man says in a grumpy voice.

"We don't ignore you!" Pomp says with the flip of a hand. "You are joking with me!"

"You are also myopic," the man says, looking away from her, off into the distance toward some unseen darkness.

"My what?"

"Never mind," the man says, standing up. "You can't understand me. You know nothing of what I am suffering."

"You suffer?" Pomp says, surprised.

"Only until I die," he says. "Of course, that's something you'd know nothing about."

"I am very confused," Pomp says.

"Yes. I bet you are, you who know nothing about what it means to grow old and decay and die."

"I want to help!" Pomp says.

"I don't need your help," he says, walking away and breaking the fairy ring at his feet. "You should have never brought me to this place." His voice fades off into the distance as he calls out, "I don't belong here!"

The vision fades, but the feelings remain, only stronger. This is an intensity of emotion she that has never felt. She can no longer not longer care, though she might not have cared . . . what is that word again? "Before." Now she feels more fully the gamut of emotions: tenderness, misery, joy, fear, hope, rage, hate, love. She feels like she might burst, that she cannot contain the swellings within her own body.

She looks down at her hands and arms and is shocked to see only bones, as if the flesh has been stripped from her body. She sees her reflection in the curve of a memory-bubble, a winged skeleton. Frail, mortal. Dead? Then she is blind with fear, thrashing out with arms, wings, legs, to escape this place. Her breathing is quick, shallow. She cannot decide whether to scream or cry.

And then, suddenly, she is free.

Pomp falls to the floor covered in slime. She wipes her eyes off first to see how she is where she is.

At least her bones are clothed in skin and muscle now. She scrapes the slime from her body, wings, and hair. The air here is hot, hotter than any other place she has been. Hotter than . . .

She looks around and must immediately shield her eyes from a bright flash of flame that shoots out of the ground. Her eyes readjust, and she carefully scans her surroundings, her hand prepared to block out any sudden surprises.

Little Pomp stands on the floor of a vast cavern. Her wings are dry enough to fly, so she flits up to have a look around. The cavern contains within it mountains and mesas layered one atop another like piles of stone wedding cakes, each taller than a castle. Jagged stone curtains snake between and over the features, creating long walls and, in some places, lithic labyrinths. All of this is peppered with fumaroles from which flames and smoke erupt at irregular intervals. The smell of sulfur is on the air. Screams and groans echo off the cavern walls from distant places, slide down the walls and mountains, and disappear into the sinkholes in enforced anonymity.

The roaring of flames and pitiful screeches reach Pomp's ears from every direction. She is surrounded by danger, fear, misery. The sounds of weeping and regret-filled lamentations surround her. Though she can't see the mourners, she can tell by the sounds that no one here is happy. This is not a place of happiness. It is under a pall of smoke and sadness. She wants to leave.

She walks over to the entrance to this unfortunate place and tries to look back into the tunnel through the membrane, but the barrier has turned black, like a giant pupil. It shines, glossy in the firelight. She touches it, pushes on it. It gives a little, then bounces back like rubber. Pomp wonders if it is indeed some kind of monstrous eye set to watch over this despair-filled cavern.

Then she looks more deeply and sees, far back in the murky darkness of the eye, something moving toward her. At first it is vague, blurry, but it comes into focus more and more clearly as it approaches her side of the lens. It is a face.

The face, attached to a body, she soon realizes, smiles contentedly, as if the man who owns it is out for a leisurely walk on a pleasant afternoon, not a care in this world—nor any world, for that matter.

The man is on the plump side, rather short, balding, with pleasant blue eyes surrounded by middle-age smile lines. He is dressed plainly but not poorly, as if he has enough for his needs, but not too much. Or at least if he is wealthy, he chooses not to flaunt it. His comportment is that of a man who makes others happy by his mere presence at a gathering.

He strolls closer and closer to Pomp's location, looking about himself as if watching a meandering cloud of butterflies.

Something looks familiar about him, Pomp decides, but she's not sure what.

Closer he comes, slowing in the substance of the portal-eye until Pomp thinks he might come to a stop and never make it through. Then, in a moment, his nose peeks through, scarred and rough, where it had been wide and smooth. Then the rest of the face emerges, stitched, poorly cobbled together, disproportionate, like a calico quilt of flesh.

He stumbles out of the eye and falls to the ground.

Heraclix knelt on the ground and sobbed. Pomp helped to remove the slime from his body. After some time, he stopped crying and pulled himself up, wiping the tears and slime from his two very-different eyes.

"You are well?" Pomp asked.

"I was. Now I'm not so sure."

"Inside the eye," Pomp pointed back to the dark membrane, "I see things. I see you, but not you."

"I saw," Heraclix paused, as if he didn't believe the words he was about to say, "my daughter."

Pomp was incredulous. "Daughter? You have no daughter!"

He sighed deeply. "Apparently I did. Or the fantasies that played upon my heart and mind were some kind of cruel cosmic joke. But seeing this around me now, I have no doubt that the scene I saw was no hallucination."

"Tell me. It makes you feel better, I think. Tell me, please. Tell me what you ... saw." She was amazed that she remembered the word "saw." She muttered to herself "see, saw, see, saw."

He stared at a far-off column of fire that curled around the cone of a mountain like a flaming snake. Several explosions burst from the serpent's scales. The roaring memories of what he saw drowned out the far-off tumult. His own voice sounded, to him, as if it was coming to him from far away, down a long, twisting tunnel.

"I was surrounded by bubbles filled with distorted figures—"

"I saw them too!" Pomp said.

He continued, not hearing Pomp. "They were each significant to me, but one attracted me above all the others. I was compelled to reach out to it, to touch it. And when I touched it, I was transported into it, entirely engulfed in the memory. I was there. I was living it. And feelings that I had at that time came back to me unbidden and unrestrained. I didn't know I could feel so much. I didn't think such a thing was possible. I was totally unprepared for it. It was . . ."

"It is scary, and I do not like it," Pomp said.

"I saw her. Little Rhoda, precious Rhoda, my reason for living after her mother died in childbirth. The miracle of Rhoda's very existence had carried me through the dark clouds of love-lost depression when my dear wife Elsie was taken. And now she lay there, little Rhoda, all twisted and mangled, a nest of ropes pressing into her soft skin. She was blanched white, save for her blue lips and eyelids. The warm blush had fled her pretty little face, though I couldn't tell where it had gone. But it was gone, forever."

"The person I was in the memory, he, I, a minister and a philosopher, I thought that I knew where to turn, that God and His angels would help me through the greatest trial I could possibly face. But the more I prayed, begged for the pain to be taken away, the more distraught I became, until I lost all hope of appealing to the celestial kingdoms for understanding.

"The beating of my heart became a dirge, then a march toward darkness. If I couldn't gain solace and understanding from above with my pleadings, I would embrace the abyss and seize my desires by whatever means and force necessary. I lost my faith the day Rhoda died, but I didn't lose my desire to bring her and, if possible, my Elsie, back to life."

Heraclix stopped, then looked around, as if waking from a trance.

"Then what?" Pomp asked.

"Then . . . I don't know," he said. "The memory ended, and I entered into this place." Heraclix looked around again, listened. "This has to be Hell."

"Come." Pomp hurriedly scraped slime from him. "We find our way out."

"I wouldn't count on it, Pomp." He stood and cleared the slime from himself anyway. "We can't go back the way we came. I don't know if I want to ever reenter that ocean of memory. Though a part of me wishes I could see other memories beyond the one I saw."

"You remember nothing else?"

"Nothing. The memory seemed to start from nowhere and end nowhere, without any connection to other events. I've told you everything I remember. Anything beyond that is inference or guesswork. I can't even tell you what Elsie looked like, though I know I loved her. Rhoda I might be able to identify, but only because I clearly saw her dead body. And what exactly I did after her death, I cannot tell. But whatever I did, I was driven by a mad passion. I felt it back in there. I don't think I would have stopped at anything, *anything*, to have my Rhoda and Elsie back. I'm beginning to think that my past might have been as ugly as my present form."

"You are not ugly . . . inside."

Heraclix smiled at Pomp's tactful self-correction.

"You don't know that," he said. "*I* don't even know that. Again, we are back to inferences."

A fumarole belched out a shaft of flame near them.

"And back to the inferno," he said.

A loud scream and the rattle of chains sounded from behind a wall of rock. He drew close to the wall's edge, with his back against the barrier, then peeked around the corner.

He ducked his head back, then turned to address his fairy friend.

"Yes, we are definitely where I thought we were, Pomp."

"Hell?"

"No need to swear," he said jokingly.

He turned to look back around the corner, then jumped, completely surprised by what looked back at him from around the other side.

The creature's body was red and covered in fine bristling hairs. It stood perhaps four feet tall at the top of its horns, though the pair of lacy wings that sprouted from its back were fully eight feet high at the tips. Another, smaller pair of wings spread straight out to the creature's side, just beneath the others. It stood on two corvine feet, sharp talons scratching the ground. Four stunted arms dangled from the torso, just above the distended belly that squatted upon those skinny bird-legs. The arms that protruded from the torso were covered with bristling hairs and insectile in their segmentation, though each of the four arms ended in something like a human hand, with four fingers and an opposable thumb. But the most disturbing aspect of this insect-human-devil hybrid was the thing's bulbous head. It was ridiculously out of proportion to the rest of the body, fully two-thirds the size of the torso. Atop the head were two sharp horns that stood up with the look of small, curved daggers. The eyes looked as if they had been stolen from a giant fly and grafted to the head. They bulged like two multi-faceted black bubbles. The thing's nose was also obscenely large, a proboscis with gargantuan nostrils that crawled up the side of the sausage-like extremity. The fiercest feature of the creature, its mouth, was cut in such a way that the creature was forever smiling, an ironic mockery of being consigned to Hell and eternal torment. The fang-lined mouth, however, hinted that it could inflict torment as well as be subjected to it.

"Vizzitōrzz," the devil-fly said with something between a wheeze and a buzz. "Or new arrivalzz?" it asked. It walked around the pair, bobbing up and down as it examined the strangers.

Pomp discovered that her invisibility didn't work here. She was unable to hide from the devil, so she settled down on Heraclix's shoulder, which increased her sense of security. For a moment.

Another nose peeked around the corner and sniffed. A second devil-fly stepped out from behind the corner, this one a foot taller than the other and significantly more corpulent than its companion.

"Estok, where have you gone? It'z almost time for our whipping, and you know how duh tormentorzz get when we're late for our"—the bigger one spotted the strangers—"oh!"

"Juzt found these two zzniveling around, Salamon," the smaller one wheezed.

"Should we report dem?" Salamon asked.

"Nah! We'd juzt get an extra whipping for not reporting them sooner. Besidez, we don't want to be late for our whippingz. Juzt azz well to keep 'em around. They might be useful to uzz."

A great gong sounded from the other side of the wall.

"C'mon Estok, we gotta go!" Salamon said.

"You stay here, yezz?" Estok said to Heraclix and Pomp. "We'll be back for ya later!"

The pair of devils disappeared around the corner. The pair of non-devils, of course, peeped around the wall to see what was happening.

The wall curved some two hundred feet away from their present location, forming a semicircular arena of sorts. Atop the wall stood a variety of devils, a circus of grotesquery. A dozen of them lined the wall, like the antithesis of the saintly statues adorning Prague's stone bridge. Yet these were not statues. They were very much alive, or at least animated. One had the body of an infant and the wings and head of a dove with plucked-out eyes that shed great gouts of bloody tears. Another looked like a woman who had been skinned, save for her scalp, from which a knee-length mass of barbed wire grew. The wire's barbs continually lashed her exposed muscles and nerves, causing her to convulse maniacally. A third looked like a stout, pot-bellied human whose arms, legs, nose, mouth, and eyes grew from all the wrong places. There was no hint of gender, though Heraclix thought of it as a man. The other nine were equally bizarre, sporting a variety of strange forms.

Each of these held an instrument of torture in its hands, claws, tentacles, or whatever it happened to be equipped with. Several held bone-studded scourges, one a pitchfork, one a giant set of pincers, one a pair of red-hot pokers, one a maul, and so forth.

In the arena itself a rack had been constructed from large bones and sinew. Beneath it were gossamer bits of wing, an insectile arm, and a shattered eye. Surrounding the rack were a hundred or so of the devil-flies, most intact, though some were missing limbs or a wing or an eye. None of them claimed the pieces on the ground, however. A few of the devil-flies were adorned with headgear that differentiated them from the others: a battered crown, a soldier's helmet, a priest's mitre.

As the pair watched, a devil-fly wearing a bronze laurel, which Heraclix took to be some representation of past authority from the condemned's mortal sojourn, approached the rack where he was tied down by his companions. The surrounding flies pushed and shoved each other in their eagerness to torture the bound fly, who, as his limbs were stretched, shouted out, "My name izz Ernezt Federici. I am guilty of crimezz against my family and myself, having extorted my father'zz fortune from my widowed mother and squandering it on cheap whorezz and wine. My punishment izz just!" Whereupon one of the quorum of twelve demons descended off the wall, falling, flying, or flopping to the ground. It then approached the one on the rack. After ensuring that the victim got a good, long look at the device with which it was to be tortured, the torturer fell upon the confessor with such vengeance, lust, and brutality that Heraclix had to admit that he had never seen anything so violent, so ruthless. The other devil-flies mocked worship of the tortured, kneeling and bowing, praising the victim as it screamed and whimpered in the midst of its torment. After a time, the devil-fly was unstrapped from the rack, the torturer returned to the wall, and the cycle started over again with the next volunteer.

When the ritual ended, the swarm of devil-flies fell upon each other, kicking, biting, rending. Heraclix and Pomp headed off in a different direction, away from the orgy of rancor. The sounds of suffering were, however, present no matter how far away they walked.

They occasionally saw groups of Hellish inhabitants marching in chained-together lines or gathered in tortured groups, mostly of the devil-fly variety, though the number of mutations, maimings and surgical perversions seemed infinite. The imagination boggled not at the possibilities but at the reality of a cosmic punishment so excruciating yet so infinitely just, based on the confessions that continually filled the air.

So, this is eternal torment, Heraclix thought. *If mankind were given a glimpse of what awaited the wicked, would they cease to cause suffering to one another in mortality, or would they simply despair and surrender to all animal instincts, knowing that they would eventually have to suffer in the afterlife for their sins anyway?*

He wasn't sure of the answer, nor did he really want to know, fearing, most of all, the answer he himself might give to such a question. For he had come to doubt his own judgment and his own motives, good or bad. The more he learned, the more he worried that he was on the verge of learning many things about himself that he would rather not have known or have known by others.

Pomp stays on Heraclix's shoulder, mostly. Except when she's flying up to look over the walls, like now. The cavern is as large as a world, though this world has a black sky, a red earth, and no sun or stars—only fire and the occasional shining of some fallen angel wailing its way over the maze of walls in which they travel. She is careful not to attract their attention. There are many other things flying around here. She has seen bat-winged black mares snorting gusts of fire; great bird-winged amorphous blobs that drip acid behind them; fallen angels who shine with a bright light but whose faces look like those of hideous, pestilence-stricken old women; a floating pair of crowned babies tethered together by one umbilical cord between them; dog-sized mosquito-like things with tattered reptilian wings; and clouds of red-eyed golden flies equipped with pincers large enough to take a ten-kreuzer-sized disk of flesh out of a man or devil or anything else it might encounter. She keeps her eye on the sky, Pomp does, or else!

She stands atop a wall, next to, but above Heraclix, scanning the twists and turns of the way ahead. A skyward cry grabs her attention, and she looks up to see, in the distance, a gigantic serpent with a fanged head at either end, attempting to entwine itself around a gigantic blue gorilla. About the gorilla's neck is a necklace of skulls. The combating pair plummets toward the ground at breakneck speed. Pomp follows the fall downward, entranced. At the very moment the snake and ape disappear behind a volcano, Pomp sees teeth, then shadow, then nothing as she is enveloped from beneath by the mixed odor of bad breath and rotting meat.

Chapter 11

Heraclix looked up just in time to see Estok swallow Pomp whole. The devil-fly's momentum carried its hook of a nose over the top of the wall, enough that Heraclix could jump up and grab the great snout, hauling the creature up and over by the proboscis, breaking it in the process.

"Gnnaah!" Estok exclaimed. "You should have stayed where I said! Than thizz wouldn't have happened! Ah, my poor, beautifully nozze."

Heraclix hadn't let go. He jerked his hand this way and that, snapping the nose twice more.

"Stop! You broke it thrice!"

"Let her out, or your neck is next! I'll rip her out of you if I have to!"

The devil-fly belched up Pomp, who flew up to the area between Estok's eyes and plucked out a pair of black hairs.

"Ai, ai! Ztop it!" it said.

Heraclix let go the shattered remains of its nose. It flopped down like a certain unmentionable which, Heraclix noted, Estok did not possess.

It continued to cough and gag. "She scraped my tonzilzz!" Estok complained.

"I'll do more than that if you don't give us the help we need," Heraclix said after puzzling out what the creature had said.

"Oh will you, now?" Estok said, suddenly full of bravado now that Heraclix had let go of its nose.

The golem reached out and tore one of the devil's arms off.

"Yes I will!" Heraclix said.

"I zee," the now-humbled devil replied. "Ungh," he rubbed his new stump with one of his three remaining arms. "What can I do for you?"

"We are looking for a ghost. One that came here shortly before we did."

"Oh, that is unfortunate," the devil said.

"What is unfortunate?" Heraclix demanded, taking a step forward as if he were going to tear another arm off the devil-fly.

"I can find this ghost! I can!" Estok cried.

"Take me to him," Heraclix said.

"I was hoping you'd tear another arm off," Pomp said.

"Not just yet," Heraclix replied.

"Come with me," the devil-fly motioned for them to follow with his three remaining arms.

They walked up out of the sharp-ridged maze that they had been in since their introduction to Hell, up a smoldering mountainside, black with ash and white with smoke. An occasional burnt skeletal hand emerged, groped around, then disappeared again beneath the ash. Bones crunched under Heraclix's feet. The summit flattened out into a desolate plain, littered with sharp shards of obsidian. Scattered across the plain were gaping sinkholes that occasionally spouted flame. Estok wove a curious course among the pond-sized sinkholes, assessing each one in turn, carefully looking for some feature or criteria, the nature of which Heraclix couldn't divine.

After passing a dozen or more of the holes, Estok finally stopped at one that seemed to meet its approval. Something in the eyes above its broken nose hinted at glee as it knelt down at the edge of the flaming orifice. It reached in, heedless of the flames that burned the hairs from its arm, and tried to pick up a writhing something. It was difficult to catch, and Estok had to plunge his other two arms in to successfully retrieve the thing from the hole.

Heraclix was shocked at the sight of the wriggling grub in Estok's hand. It looked just like the creature embossed on the back of the book *The Worm*, which Pomp had found at Mowler's burned-out apartment. Heraclix took the book from his back waistband, where he had carried it, and unwrapped it from the cloth he used to protect it. The worm on the cover was pictured with a human face and a large stinger coming out of the other end. The squirming thing that Estok held was like the representation of those abominations in every way, save one: the worm's face was clearly that of the old man whose spirit had fled, leading them on the Hellish chase that ended here at this pit.

"Qurzzikacpzz!" the old man said as Estok held the worm by its stinger, dangling it in the air.

"Excuse me?" Heraclix said.

"Xtzbshzz!" the worm exclaimed, then tried to curl up to bite Estok's hand. Estok flicked its face with a finger, causing it to go limp. It peed on itself.

"He can't talk to you," Estok said.

"Well, of course not," Pomp said indignantly, "you made him dead!"

"Can't," Estok said, staring at the old man-worm with something like fondness, like a grandfather looking at his newborn grandson. "He'z already dead, izzn't he?"

"I . . . think . . . so," Pomp said with a puzzled look.

"He'z juzt a baby," Estok said with reverence. "Can't even talk yet, though he wantz to, wantz to say all kindz of nasty thingz to you."

"How long will it be before he can talk?" Heraclix asked, growing impatient.

"Four, five hundred years . . . if he stayz on top of the heap."

It dropped the unconscious worm back into the sinkhole. "He won't stay on top. Too much competition, and he'z only a newborn." Estok shook its head. Its nose slapped from side to side.

"This is hopeless," Heraclix said.

"Thizz izz Hell," Estok said.

After a short silence, Estok said, "So, I may go now?"

"No," Heraclix said. "I need you to find someone else."

Estok stomped its crow feet like a little child. "I need to get back! The demonz don't like uzz missing confessionz."

Heraclix spoke calmly, but firmly, "I need to talk to someone from Prague, someone well-connected, who died there recently."

"Prague? That'zz easy! We have a special place in Hell for thoze that lived in Prague—Jew and Gentile alike."

"Then you must take us there. Then I will release you to go enjoy your . . ." Heraclix realized his mistake too late, ". . . erm, torture."

The devil glared at the golem.

"You are truly an idiot," Estok said with disgust. Then, walking off and looking back with disdain, it said "Are you going to come along or not?"

Pomp flew in front of Estok, careful to keep out of the devil-fly's striking distance.

Estok spoke aloud, unabashed. "I have all eternity to find you again," it said. "Your brutish friend can't be with you forever. Next time, there will be too many pieces of you to rescue. Your big friend will have to sew you up like a little dolly, just like he iz all sewn up!"

The thought made the devil smile, though it really couldn't help it.

They left the desert plateau, passing through a forest of dead, charred trees before spotting a color-bleached city that exactly mimicked the form of the earthly Prague. The city was painted weary and dreary. The inhabitants of this mock-Prague were mainly of the devil-fly sort. The occasional greater demon, like the ones Heraclix and Pomp had seen in the torture arena, could be seen strolling through a market place, plundering the unpaid merchants of their wares. The goods consisted of cast-off or involuntarily removed limbs, eyes, and other assorted parts, which customers sewed, tied, or stapled on to replace members lost at the rack.

Estok led them, at Heraclix's request, to the place where Caspar might have once dwelt on the earthly plane. It knocked softly, almost daintily. The devil-fly listened carefully at the door, but its attention was soon turned to the noise of a pair of out-of-tune trumpets coming down the cobblestone street.

Estok darted behind Heraclix, where it cowered, whimpering in fear. Heraclix put his hands out to his side, trying to reassure Estok with his protection from whomever—or whatever—threatened it.

Around the bend and down the sloping street walked another devil-fly. This one's head was even larger than Estok's. Atop the newcomer's bulbous head was a floppy feathered hat, outdated by at least two centuries, with some sort of shiny coin attached to the front of it. The bigger devil was clad in a dark blue tailored coat that was so thickly studded with ribbons and medallions that it jangled as the wearer bobbed down the street. Two smaller devil-flies, dressed in black robes, walked behind him. Each one carried a beaten brass trumpet.

"The mayor!" Estok cried.

"Well, well!" the mayor exclaimed. "Estok, what have you brought uz here?"

"He ... he came here by himself!" Estok said in a quavering voice, coming out from behind Heraclix and pointing frantically at the golem.

"Interesting," the mayor said. "And you didn't report this earlier?" It shot a glance at Estok, who shrank back again, cowering.

"And what bringz you here, my fine fellow?" the mayor asked Heraclix.

"I desire to speak with Caspar Melthazaar. Do you know where we might find him? He doesn't seem to be at home."

"Oh," the mayor shook its head and looked at the ground. "I'm afraid Caspar never made it here. We had planned on him coming here, but apparently hiz planz changed."

"Changed? You knew he was coming?"

"Maybe not 'knew,' exactly. But we felt he waz a strong candidate, from the incoming reportzz we received from newcomerzz. Apparently our informantz only looked at the man'z actionz and did not know hizz heart."

"Do you get reports of others who come here or who might be ... heading this direction?"

"Of course, it happens all the time."

"What then, of the sorcerer Mowler?"

"Mowler?!" the mayor shouted the name aloud. "Mowler! I have no need of hearsay regarding that man ..."

"What do you mean?" Heraclix asked.

"I mean that I know Mowler. Or I knew him. He wazz a contemporary of mine for a time while I served in Prague."

"Please tell me what you know. It is very important to me."

"And me!" Pomp said.

The mayor fidgeted, as if nervous. Then, looking at his trumpeters and Estok, he spoke again, in a restrained voice.

"Why . . . why iz thiz knowledge of such importance to you?"

"I am seeking to know what has become of him. I think he might have answers to some questions we have."

The mayor looked up at Pomp, licked its lips, cleared its throat, and shook its head quickly, as if trying to regain its concentration after a momentary daydream.

"And what shall I gain from imparting such useful information? Only I have the knowledge you seek," it gloated at the other devils. "Such knowledge can be had, for the right price."

Heraclix thought about it a moment. He narrowed his eyes and came so close to the mayor that their faces almost touched. "I shall refrain from ripping your nose off."

"This is Hell," the mayor laughed, "Do you think that such a threat can actually frighten me? Especially after . . ."

"After what?" Heraclix asked, pouncing on the mayor's pause.

"After he killed me," the mayor admitted. It lowered its head. "Of course, I had it coming. You don't handle snakez without being bitten."

"What?" Pomp asked.

"Mowler. I made the mistake of trying to handle him. I waz young, and he waz already old and experienced when I came on the scene. I immediately recognized that he waz smart and cunning. I knew I wanted him on my side. Who would not want such an erudite, educated man in hiz cabinet?"

"Not me!" Pomp said.

"Well then you are not suited for politicz," the mayor said condescendingly. "He waz a valuable ally, able to divine information that my best spiez couldn't hope to gain. He waz charizmatic, too. The ladiez loved him, though he gave them no more than a smile and a reluctant kissz on the hand. He had a strange aversion to small, petite women, though, preferring more corpulent female friendz."

The mayor looked at Pomp meaningfully, as if expecting some kind of reaction. Not getting any, it continued.

"Mowler waz a man of great vision in some wayz and very conservative in otherz. He waz not fond of the poor and uneducated. Thiz caused some friction between uz, since I waz, I am proud to say, a champion of the unfortunate and downtrodden, a real enlightened leader. When I proposed that all of the city'z inhabitantz be taught literacy, he balked, even rebelled, though he kept hiz feelingz on the matter hidden until the last momentz before my demize. He iz a great actor, that one."

Heraclix stopped the mayor with an uplifted hand. "You don't have to recount . . ."

"Oh, but I do! I attempted to argue with him, but waz cut short. It waz a painful death, but interesting, at least. Somehow, he called down lightning right there in my office. He chanted some garbage—I thought it waz a joke, to be honest—then he said 'Now I will show the ignorant masses real power! Not political power or the holier-than-thou emptiness of the priests and practitionerz of religion, but *my* power, the power of superior intellect and discipline, the ability to control the very powerz of nature and, in time, the very powerz of Hell!'"

"'But you said it was your power,' I argued, 'not the power of nature that—'"

"My train of logic was cut short by a clap of thunder, the echoes of which I didn't hear. Some of my other counselorz told me, after they arrived here, that the spectacle waz most impressive. The citizenz were awestruck." The mayor puffed out his chest, "I waz wept for over three dayz."

"Three days?" Heraclix asked.

"Yes, three dayz, the polite amount of time over which someone of my office should be mourned. No more, no less." It held its nose in the air. "This waz a formality, you see? Etiquette demanded that every good citizen mourn me for three dayz. They didn't really love me, though I tried to at least provide them a free education, being an enlightened ruler." The mayor sighed. "No, they were more concerned with my personal life than my policiez. They would rather see me in my bedroom than in my officez. Unfortunately, some of them did.

"So, since they thought me depraved, they only mourned as much as was required, then they spread the rumor that I had been stricken down by God's own wrath at my liberal policiez and my bedroom practicez. Though I wouldn't call them practicez. They were really more like competitionz between my—"

"Back to Mowler," Heraclix said, interrupting the mayor's story.

"Ah, yes." The mayor returned to the subject, a tiny bit embarrassed. "Mowler. I later found out that he had tried to poizon me, over time. Thank goodness for tasterz! Though my taster did last a little longer than me. When he arrived here, he told me that Mowler, frustrated by the people'z continued willful ignorance and their lack of recognition at his genius, left Prague for Vienna, ranting and raving about how he would call up the very powerz of Hell and rule the world if he had to sacrifice every living soul in the Holy Roman Empire to do it." The Mayor paused for a moment. "They don't have much imagination, those sorcerers. Though they can be a bother."

"Where is Mowler?" Heraclix asked.

"How am I supposed to know?" the Mayor said.

"He is not here?" Pomp asked.

"Mowler? Ha! Well, there's no chance he made it to Heaven. And he's not here, or I would know about it. No! He iz not dead!"

"What?!" Pomp and Heraclix yelled in unison, the former shooting up into the air, the latter reeling, then stumbling backwards over a group of devil-flies who had silently sat down in a semicircle to hear the mayor's tale.

"Are you sure?" Pomp asked the Mayor.

"Of course, I'm sure. I'm the Mayor!" it said, holding his hands up exultantly.

"My people!" it called out. "This little one thinks I don't know my own city. Haz anyone seen the sorcerer Mowler among us?"

"We would know!" shouted one of the devil-flies.

"He izn't with us," said another.

"Never heard of him," said a devil wearing a wig and tiara.

"You see?" the Mayor said. "None of my subjects have seen him here."

Heraclix noticed one of the devil-flies averting his eyes from the Mayor. This one started to shuffle away from the group, while others, beckoned by the Mayor's shouts, were flowing toward their Mayor and its strange guests.

"What about him?" Heraclix asked.

"You there!" the Mayor said.

The devil-fly slowly turned around and pointed to himself, mouthing the question: "Me?"

"Yes, you!" the Mayor said. "Come here!"

The devil approached them.

"You have not seen Mowler here, have you?" the Mayor said, puffing his chest out and looking at Heraclix the whole time.

"Well," the devil-fly said. "There waz one time . . ."

"Mmm?" the Mayor looked at his subject with a squint, displeased.

"To be honest, there waz a time when a man came among us. Not a condemned soul. Not yet, at least."

"And you did not tell me?" the Mayor asked.

The devil-fly looked up at the Mayor. "I had intended to tell, in time," he turned toward Heraclix. "But I didn't think it waz time to . . ."

The devil-fly stopped suddenly. Its humungous trap of a jaw swung wide open, and it backed away from Heraclix as if facing the confessor's rack.

"You! Who are you?!" Its voice was full of terror, frantic with fear.

"I'm very sorry, I'm afraid I don't understand . . ." Heraclix tried to placate the creature, but it didn't heed him.

"You brought her here?!"

"Brought who?" Heraclix asked.

"The girl from Szentendre . . . but how, how did you know? She iz not here, iz she?" It looked from side to side, then spun around, looking beneath itself, scanning the rooftops and windows of the surrounding buildings. "Iz she? But they buried her in Szentendre and surely her soul waz not bound for *this* place! Surely not!"

The devil tried to scramble away from Heraclix, clawing its way through the crowd.

The Mayor was as confused as Heraclix. "Someone calm him down!" he said, motioning for his herald to go take care of the situation.

But the devil shook its head and said: "That eye! Where izz she? Not here! Please, not here . . . You! I know you! I know why you're here, but you can't have me! No, I am Hizz, Hizz forever!"

"What do you know about the girl?" Heraclix asked. He began to wade through the other devils to get to the speaker. "Tell me about the eye!"

"No, no, no!" the devil said, shaking. It looked from side to side, trying to find an escape. Then, as if an epiphany had struck, it wrung its four hands together and yelled at the top of its lungs: "Maaazzter! Maaazzter! Intruderzz! Intruderzz!"

The mayor, wringing his own hands with worry and looking from side to side as if expecting the arrival of an unwanted, very unpleasant guest, tried to calm it.

"Listen, calm down. No need to bring Him into this when we can handle it ourselvez."

"Maaazzter! Heeelp us! Intruderzz!" the big one continued screaming.

A low throbbing hum, like the buzz of a palace-sized insect, pulsed through the city, vibrating the walls and cobblestones. This was punctuated by a rhythmic booming like low, rumbling thunder sounding in a regular cadence, like a giant's heartbeat or . . . footsteps! Each muffled crash shook the ground. As it came closer the magnitude of each step increased until windows shattered, and cracks began to appear in the crumbling plaster.

A great light shone from the direction of the approaching entity. It started like the first slivers of the rising sun on the horizon. Then, as it came closer, the light gradually intensified to the shine of a full moon's light on fresh fallen snow. They couldn't help but look that direction, though many of the devil-flies, including the one who beckoned to its master, scattered, running for cover from falling pieces of masonry and whatever was walking toward faux-Prague. The light continued to grow with each ground-shattering step. Then it flashed like a beacon, lighting the ceiling of the miles-high cavern with white fire and temporarily blinding all those who looked in that direction.

It was practically on top of them when their eyes readjusted and they finally saw it.

It was hundreds of feet tall. The battered and dented silver crown it wore was itself twice as tall as the spires of Prague's Saint Vitus Cathedral and no less majestic. Atop the crown, nested in the bent prongs, was a star whose rays cut through the eternal night.

The demon impassively scanned his domain through two enormous, multi-faceted eyes, which bulged beneath the shining crown. Folded creases beneath its eyes frowned on mock-Prague's inhabitants.

It wore a purple velvet doublet of exquisite workmanship. Beneath it, frilled sleeves and collars puffed out, the collar nesting the demon's tremendous proboscis like a black serpent in a frilly cotton nest. Its arms and hands, all four of them, exactly mirrored those of the devil-flies. In its hands it held a great black scepter, as large as a tree. Set in the head of the scepter was a gigantic ruby the size of a horse carriage, cut long so as to make the device look more like a mace than a representation of royal authority.

Below the doublet, about its loins, it wore a vast golden kilt embroidered with imagery taken from the war in Heaven. Each act of the story was sewn into a strip of fabric, giving the girdle the appearance of a scintillating chitin-armored skirt. The topmost band showed a group of angels, stunning in their beauty, sitting around a table and colluding over a series of maps, some of which had been pinned to the table with long daggers. The second band was embroidered with an army of white-robed angels, swords held high, marching against a vast white castle whose foundation and lower walls were hidden in a bank of puffy white clouds. Below this, on the third band, was a battle scene wherein these same angels fled, bruised and bloodied, from a cascading wave of bright light. The rebellious angels, their skins now black or red or putrid green, and their features undergoing hideous transformations, were being routed from the realms of heaven on the fourth band. The fifth band replayed the story of the Garden of Eden, the serpent wrapped around the Tree of Knowledge of Good and Evil, tempting the naked Adam and Eve. Scenes of mankind's debauchery, betrayal, and backstabbing murder dominated the sixth band. The seventh band showed a series of full-length portraits of the dukes of Hell with their diabolical insignia floating over their heads like unholy halos. The demon itself was shown standing with feet planted in the midst of a burning Prague, his wings fanning the flames of the inferno, oblivious to the suffering around him, all powerful in his kingdom.

It was then that Heraclix realized that this was the true form of Beelzebub, The Lord of the Flies. This wasn't a mere avatar, as Mowler had conjured in his apartment. This was the duke of

Hell in all of his unholy glory. Heraclix looked at the embroidered Beelzebub, then the real one. Though hidden in the skirt's representation, the golem could clearly see before him Beelzebub's cloven hooves surrounded by the crumbling remains of the buildings destroyed in its wake. Entire rooftops stripped up and flew through the air as the devil-god lifted its foot to walk toward Heraclix and Pomp.

The mayor shook its head and lifted its hands heavenward in despair before a gigantic cloven hoof clomped down, destroying half of a street and all of the mayor.

Heraclix shook off the awe that had fixed him in place and ran. Pomp flew ahead of him. They headed for the equivalent of the stone bridge but found that, rather than a line of saintly statues, the persons memorialized here were traitors and base sinners: Judas Iscariot, Brutus, Cain, a number of corrupted Popes and wicked kings and despotic rulers—some of which might not yet have been born into the world, but would surely make their mark on it.

Beelzebub's cloven hoof crashed down on the bridge near the bank they had just fled, sending stones flying. A Hell-quake shook the very foundations, causing the structure to sway to and fro. Several of the stone traitors cracked off their bases and dove into the river, sending out great waves across its bubbling surface. Heraclix was knocked off his feet and onto his back. Beelzebub nearly filled his vision.

Above the head of the gargantuan fly-god-demon, a black, buzzing swarm composed of millions of dog-sized flies materialized. They flowed around their Lord like living tentacles, then shot down toward the intruders on the bridge. They flew quickly, arriving before Heraclix could stand up.

Heraclix was buffeted by the flies, barely able to crawl to the edge of the bridge and pull himself over. As he fell toward the water, he saw Pomp flitting beside him, and then he plunged into the river's black, icy depths.

CHAPTER 12

Pomp spins under water, dodging falling pieces of statuary. She doesn't like the water and uses her wings to swim up toward the surface, up toward the blinding light, up and through the water . . .

. . . and into darkness.

She looks around and sees a river below her. And treetops lit by a full moon.

But no Beelzebub, no burning city, and, best of all, no Estok!

And there is Heraclix, floating under the water.

He isn't swimming.

He isn't moving at all.

But something is moving toward him. A barge piloted by two people, one very old, and one very young.

"Steer us easy around," the old one says. "We don't want to hit him!"

The old one pokes a long pole into the water near Heraclix, while the young one steers the boat with a large rudder.

"Easy. Easy!" the old man says. "To the right, just a bit. There you are. And . . . got him!"

The weight of the giant almost pulls the old man into the river. The barge lists toward Heraclix, but the old man is able to stay on the boat. Through a series of small maneuvers, he brings Heraclix's head and shoulders up onto the deck.

The young one comes and helps the old. Inch by inch, they work to get as much of Heraclix as they can up on the boat. But

Pomp invisibly helps, though she can do little more than move her friend's finger. But every bit helps. They get everything out of the water but his feet. He is too long and just won't fit that way.

The old man listens to Heraclix's chest. He shakes his head, then presses down on the giant's chest a couple of times. He listens at Heraclix's mouth, then holds his fingers over Heraclix's wrist.

He shakes his head again.

"Well, Alva," the old man says to the younger, who has gone back to steering the barge. "There's nothing we can do to revive him. But we won't abandon him to the fish. We'll take him to the city. Everyone deserves a proper burial."

The young one nods.

"You rest now, Alva. I'll steer."

The boy, exhausted, curls up in a pile of blankets and drifts off to sleep.

Awake!

Awake?

Only upon awakening did Heraclix realize that he had been unconscious. But was that even possible? Could the undead sleep? Could the dead wake? Or had a black veil been drawn over all of his senses? He opened his eyes a bit wider and felt gravity pull him from below. *That direction*, he thought as his sight slowly focused, *must be down.*

He was on his back, but whatever he was laying on was unstable, lolling his body with a gentle rocking.

His eyesight was blurred. He reached up with heavy hands and rubbed his eyes, trying to clear a milky smudge from his vision. The smudge remained. He realized that he was looking up at the sky. The milky smudge was the moon glowing behind the clouds, like a ghost passing behind a thin, gray curtain.

A ghost.

He shivered, not from fear of spirits, but because he was wet— no, drenched—and the night air was cool.

Recollection filtered back into him as water drained off his body, a bizarre trading scheme: droplets and streams for memes and memory. He sat up, water cascading from his skin and clothing, the undead raised from a watery grave.

Looking around him, he discovered that he was sitting on a flat barge floating down a river. But this was not the River Styx. No, the river into which he had fallen was *not* this river. Though there must be some sort of passageway between the two, since he had hurled himself into one yet emerged from the other.

His feet had been dangling over the edge, in the water. Behind him stood a man, one hand holding a cowl close around him, shielding Heraclix from the cold, the other hand holding a staff from which dangled a dimly glowing spherical lamp. Only the bottom half of the face was visible under the hood. The chin was wrinkled and covered with a wispy grey beard. Behind the hooded old man a bundle of cloth rustled and yawned.

"You are alive," the old man said in a voice that squeaked ever so slightly. "You are lucky we found you when we did. You would have drowned, otherwise."

"Where are we?" Heraclix asked.

"On the Danube," the old man said, "west of Pest, heading downstream."

Finally, thought Heraclix, *a stroke of good luck.*

"And where were you headed, friend?" the old man asked.

"Szentendre."

"Ah, then you will not be far, once we arrive in Pest."

"How long until we reach Pest?" Heraclix asked.

"Mere hours, my friend. We should be there for the sunrise."

"And what compels you to travel to Pest?" Heraclix asked.

"Nothing compels us, friend. That is, in fact, the very reason we were able to stop and pull you from the drink."

The man waited for a response, a query of some sort, but Heraclix remained silent, so he carried on.

"My grandson and I, we have no home. We have lost the others in our family to the ravages of war and disease. We felt compelled, as you say it, to make a living, at first, to work for the good things in life, establish a home, and so forth. Then we realized that we had the good things, such as each other. And we found that we had a home wherever we were at the moment. So we left all that, sold what we had, and bought this little barge. We travel where we wish when we wish. We trade up and down the river for the things we need, and we are never in want, sometimes fishing, sometimes delivering goods, always in good company with each other. We have no itinerary, else you would be dead and sinking to the bottom. The captains of other boats would have paid you heed only long enough to check your pockets for money. Then they would have rolled you right back into the water. They don't have much time to meddle in the affairs of a man already dead. After all, a dead man isn't of much use to those seeking riches, unless his riches are with him."

Heraclix carefully, secretly, checked his pouch and found that it was soggy, but still full of coin. They hadn't tried to rob him, though they might have, had they wished to do so.

"A live man, however, might be of more use to those seeking riches," Heraclix said.

The old man laughed much like a mouse hiccups. "We've heard there is a reward out upstream for the capture of a giant," he said.

The old man removed his hood to show a bald scalp, save for a ring of long wispy hair falling down from above his ears. "We have no desire to turn you in. If we did, we'd be heading to Vienna. Besides, me and Alva here wouldn't be up to the task. Neither of us is strong enough to take you in, and we don't have the stomach to sell someone into slavery. No, we enjoy our freedom," he smiled, "and grant others the same privilege."

Heraclix felt movement in his cloak.

"I trust them," Pomp whispered into Heraclix's ear. "They help you, helped you. They are good."

Heraclix and Pomp disembarked several miles north and west of Pest. Heraclix slipped up the muddy embankment and waved goodbye as the pair floated downstream. He turned and walked into the woods as the glow of the rising sun creased the horizon.

"It's tempting," Heraclix said to Pomp, who had made herself visible to him there in the woods, where no strangers would see her as they traveled, "to live like that: free of worry, no schedule, no obligations, no hurry—"

"No desire," Pomp interrupted.

"What?"

"No desire. They think they want for nothing, but they want nothing. They fear nothing. They are boring."

"This is something new to you, isn't it, Pomp?"

"Being bored?"

"No, having to think about these things."

She pursed her lips shut, petulant.

"It's okay to admit that maybe you've been thinking too much," he teased, referring to her frequent jabs at him.

"They think they have everything," she said, ignoring the comment, though she caught Heraclix's intent, "so nothing can be rewarding to them. No reward without challenges. No comfort without fear. No happiness without sadness. Everything is flat."

"You have been thinking . . ." Heraclix stopped in his tracks, listening. "Wait," he whispered. "What is that?"

Pomp flies up into the topmost branches of a tall yew tree for a better view. She sees four figures spying on Heraclix. They peer out from behind a large clump of sprawling oaks, signaling one to another with a series of gestures and short, sharp grunts.

Two of them, crouched on the verge of the clump of trees, crouch, preparing to spring.

"Heraclix! To your left!" Pomp cries out.

All four look up at her and growl. They resemble boars, with blunted snouts and dangerous-looking tusks curving out like sabers from under their snarling lips. But these pigs, more massive than a man, stand on their rear hoofs, and their fore-legs end in a single sharp claw, like a stiletto. They are covered in rust-colored fur, and their eyes glow like coals in the shadows of the morning light.

Two of them climb the trees, springing up the outstretched tree limbs toward Pomp. Surely, these are demons that followed Heraclix and Pomp from the abyss to retrieve them and drag them back to Hell. She goes invisible, but she thinks the creatures can still see her, as they pursue her all the more doggedly. But Pomp isn't about to submit to them and go back through Hell. Her mind buzzes with fear at the thought.

Or is it fear? She looks around, then above, and finds the source of the buzzing that she had thought was just in her head.

Just above her, a large wasp nest is crawling with insects. She flies above the structure, much larger than herself, and tears at the paper that holds it to a thin branch. The wasps are confused, then agitated, by their invisible assailant. The nearest swine-demon is almost within arm's reach of Pomp when the nest falls into its mouth. It bites down hard, destroying the nest and unleashing a small cloud of furious wasps, which sting the pig-thing's mouth, snout, and head repeatedly. This occupies it long enough for Pomp to break off a dead branch. She drives it into the demon-swine's left eye, causing her pursuer to fall backward out of the tree. The falling body catches its companion mid-chest, and the two tumble down through crackling branches with cracking of bones onto the hard earth and roots beneath.

They can be hurt, then!

The other two tackled Heraclix, knocking him to the ground with suprising force. One pinned his shoulders to the ground while the other gored him in the side of the chest, thrusting its tusk in where a heart should have been. The pain was intense and real. Self-loathing washed over him, a sense of inadequacy at his past inability to save his daughter and his wife. He thought of the condemned in Hell, of their sufferings, and felt sure that he would be brought to that same place to suffer that same fate, no matter what he did. His utmost desire at that moment was to simply give up and give in. Then he looked up to the trees and saw Pomp repel her opponent. It fell through the trees as if in slow-motion, snapping branches, bouncing until it hit its comrade and sent them both to the ground.

Seeing this caused him a glimmer of concern for her, a ray of tentative hope. He kneed the demon-swine next to him in the jaw, knocking it off of him, then swung his feet up over his head to kick the other one in the snout, freeing himself from the demon's claws. He tore at the face of the one that had gored him, gouging great pieces of pork from its snout then grabbing a tusk and yanking it from its roots. The pig fell to the ground, then dissipated in a gaseous wisp.

The other had regained its feet by then and was circling Heraclix, looking for an opening to strike.

"Tell your master," Heraclix said, "that he won't have the pleasure of our presence in Hell today."

The demon, seeing an opening, leaped at Heraclix.

The golem, having feigned the weakness in the defense, caught the pig-man mid-air, the blue left hand clasping the demon's throat.

The demon wheezed and rasped until it caught enough breath to speak. Its voice was that of a petulant little girl, a disquieting contrast to the fierce demon's face. "Do what you will. I'll see you again in Hell, brother!" The demon tittered until Heraclix crushed the beast's trachea. The creature disolved into mist, leaving the smell of sulfur on the air.

Heraclix fell to his knees, holding his side where the tusk had penetrated.

"That took everything I had in me. I am so ... tired."

Pomp patted him on the head. She made herself visible, but he was staring at the ground, not giving her his full attention.

"You have more in you. If not, you'd stop complaining. Come, Heraclix. We are close to Szentendre. Very close," she said with a smile, hoping to encourage him. "We must go. We go through Hell, then we go to Szentendre, right? Isn't that what the fly-devil tells us?"

"And another devil just told me I was its brother."

"You don't believe it, do you?" Pomp said.

"I don't know what I believe any more."

"You are sad," Pomp said. "When you are sad, you must hope."

"For what?"

"To know who you are!" Pomp said. "Besides, this isn't just about you!"

"No one cares about me," Heraclix said. "I have no one left. I let them all die: Rhoda, Elsie, even myself."

"Then you must hope to see them again. Don't you think they would hope to see you ... again ... if you had ... died?" Pomp looked a bit puzzled, but pleased with the words she spoke.

He looked up to the sky. "I suppose they would."

"There, you see? They have hope that you can share!"

Heraclix stood, staggered for a moment, then regained his balance. "Yes, Pomp. I think you may be right."

"Listen to little Pomp! She hopes for you, too."

The golem looked at her with tired eyes, but the hint of a smile was beginning to show on his face.

"Then let's go on, Pomp. To Szentendre!"

CHAPTER 13

Heraclix's senses came back to him as they approached Szentendre. He had no idea how long he had been traveling. Vigor was slowly filtering back into his veins. He felt, as he came closer, a faint sense of familiarity punctuated by powerful impressions of déjà vu. The village was bucolic, a quaint picture of peasant life. The sun shone down, not harshly, and the skies were as blue as he could ever remember them. A gentle breeze brushed his skin.

"This place is beautiful. And I sense that my realm is close here," Pomp said to Heraclix, who absorbed her words in reverent silence.

They stopped a passing herdsman and inquired where they might find the local church. He hastily directed them to a low, long hill crowned with a semicircle of trees with a trembling finger, then ran off so quickly that his lambs had difficulty keeping pace. In the midst of the opening between the trees sat a conglomeration of five stone buildings. The central, and largest, building was surmounted by a large granite cross. The stone from which it had been hewn must have been hauled from some distance away, judging from its size and the absence of a quarry nearby. Several stone gargoyles hung from the eaves. Pomp, energized by the proximity with Faerie, playfully flew from fanged mouth to fanged mouth while Heraclix knocked at a door in one of the buildings.

"We're out of bread," a man with a dullard's voice declared.

"Not everyone who knocks wants bread," came another man's voice, this one much higher-pitched.

The door opened.

"Oh!" said the man with the high-pitched voice in a note of surprise. "You are" the man looked stunned, at a temporary loss for words "...rather tall," he said to Heraclix. This man was dressed in the simple brown robes of a monk. He wore a tonsure above his long, skinny head. "Forgive me," he said, "but I was surprised by your stature." He took a deep breath. "How may I help you today, sir?"

"I am looking for the graveyard."

"The graveyard," the man looked at him suspiciously, "Yes, it's by the old church."

"The old church?" Heraclix asked.

"Yes. This is the new church. The old church is on the other side of this hill."

"Thank you, sir," Heraclix said, turning to go.

"Ah, may I interest you in buying some of our fine bread?"

"We hain't got no more bread!" the dullard shouted from a back room.

"Perhaps tomorrow?" the monk said.

"Perhaps tomorrow," Heraclix said, then walked on.

"The old church," the monk called out, "it was burned down by a madman years ago and is not much to look at."

"Neither is he!" the dullard said.

Heraclix stopped and turned.

The thin monk sputtered out an apology "Oh, I'm very sorry, you see, he is an utter—"

"No, no," Heraclix reassured him that he had no intent to harm. "The old church, burned down by whom?"

"I don't know the name. Lost his family, lost his faith, lost his mind. Poor chap. You know the story."

"I just might," Heraclix said.

"I think his family's gravestones are in the cemetery there, but I can never remember which name goes with which story. His grave is the empty one. They put a stone there in case he ever returned."

"I see. How many years ago did this happen?"

"Oh, two, two hundred-fifty years ago. Lots of people say its haunted, so they avoid it. You'll be okay, though. You're such a big boy...sorry..."

"Apology accepted," Heraclix said, then set off again.

The other side of the hill and the little valley it overlooked was covered in golden grass as high as Heraclix's waist. A few small trees with wide black branches sprouted up here and there. At the base of the hillside was a large pile of burnt stone and timbers smoothed with years of wear. He approached the ruins, stooping down to break a small piece of charcoal off of one of the timbers. He crushed the charcoal in his fingers, then sniffed the pungent powder. As he smelled the burnt wood, an inexplicable feeling of guilt washed over him. He thought he saw a vision of flames shooting out of windows, but the phantasm passed almost as soon as it had appeared.

"This must have been the church," he said, then quickly turned away, shaken. Then a quick gust of wind blew across the hills, drawing his attention away from his thoughts. He focused his efforts on finding the graveyard.

Heraclix and Pomp combed through the tall grass until they found a low mound in the valley where the grass grew higher, greener, and darker. Tall yellow meadow wildflowers grew upon the mound, setting it apart from its surroundings even further. Here Heraclix stubbed his toe on a grave marker, so the pair did their best to mat down the grass and flowers to expose any other gravestones they might find.

Pomp flew from stone to stone, unable to read them but able to infer that the size of the stone meant something either about the interred person's age or importance in life. Most were set apart singly or in pairs.

One was a trio.

"Heraclix! Is this it?" She made herself visible so that he could see where she was.

He hastened to the spot at which she pointed: a line of three gravestones covered in lichen, each larger than the one to its left. Carefully, he scraped the lichen away to clear the weatherworn grooves that indicated faint lettering. The carving on the smaller two stones was crude, the sloppy shape of the letters suggesting a job hastily done. The third, and largest, bore no inscription at all. There were no dates on the stones. The smallest read RHODA HEILLIGER.

"Rhoda . . . and Elsie . . . Then my memory wasn't a fabrication. This," he held his immense hand to the smallest stone, then the second, "is all that remains of them." He looked at Pomp, deep pain showing in his red eye. The blue left eye twitched of its own accord, darting around like a chameleon's eye, frantically looking for . . . something.

"I am very sorry," Pomp said.

"For what?" Heraclix asked curtly.

"For your feelings."

"That's just it, Pomp," his voice was more aggressive toward her than it had ever been. "I should be devastated, disconsolate, or at least saddened. But I feel nothing, not even the self-loathing I think I ought to feel for not mourning their loss. Perhaps I should be surprised by my lack of reaction, but I'm not even surprised by that. I feel absolutely nothing. This is a day like any other day in a place like any other place. It is no different to me, and I am not different for having been here."

"My heart hurts for you," Pomp said. Her tone indicated sympathy and sincerity, but this had no effect on Heraclix.

"Maybe I have inherited the memories of another man," he said, ignoring her. "Or the old man is truly dead and gone and though I know something of his history—maybe even share a piece of his soul—I am a new man, unconnected with the old." Heraclix was smiling, almost laughing, but Pomp didn't think he was really happy. "Perhaps my very existence is moot and my quest to know my history is a buffoon's folly—running around in chronological circles to no end except a great cosmic joke for whatever power truly controls the universe."

Pomp isn't laughing. She is crying with sadness, frustration, anger, fear. "He is a good man," she whispers to herself. "He should be happy for his goodness. Mowler has caused this unhappiness." She thinks of how she had met Heraclix, the tortured servant, how he had freed her, saved her life, tended to her, been her companion, patiently tolerated her adjustment to the realization of her own mortality. She thinks of those horrible devil-flies and how, being susceptible to death, she might become one of them: stupid, loathsome, selfish—if she didn't do some good in the world. She already had the wings, after all. Was she closer to being condemned to Hell than she knew? She might be, if she didn't set some things straight. She is in no better shape than the Serb who raced against the end of his life to repent for the wrongs he had done. There was only so much time in this world, and Pomp feared that hers might run out if she didn't do some good, and quickly! Time was short.

Pomp knows that Mowler is still alive. But where is he? Wherever he is, he is surely dangerous. Pomp must be ready to face him, to help Heraclix. Perhaps she should arm herself. No, not perhaps. She will yet. She will now. Now! She flies for Faerie!

By the time Heraclix had roused himself from his vigil in the graveyard, the sky had darkened. The stars and moon shined down on the road leading back to Szentendre. Bright firelight lit up the open doorway of a tavern, inviting him in from the cooling night. He entered boldly, not caring about the whispered remarks of the locals or the murmured insults of a quartet of what appeared to be traveling dandies who glared at him as he walked in. What did it matter what they said? Had he not already been through Hell, and couldn't he break their necks like twigs, should he choose? He had nothing to fear, nothing to regret. Nothing really mattered anymore.

He spent and drank liberally and was surprised that, after a quarter cask, the alcohol began to have some slight effect, relaxing him and adding to his carefree attitude a touch of warmth and good cheer. "Huzzah!" he yelled with the crowd as a pair of mountebanks took the stage, juggling and jostling each other in an act that swiftly devolved into comedic violence before the two were removed from the stage by hook to a chorus of good-natured jeers.

A bawdy cabaret followed, which sent the bar's customers into a frenzy until the stage manager came out onto the stage to calm and shush the crowd. The manager was pelted with insults and rotting fruit. Still, he calmed the crowd and spoke in an exaggeratedly soft voice:

"My friends, I beg your indulgence for silence. You see, my next performer is up past her bedtime . . ."

"Pervert!" someone yelled.

The stage manager shot a stabbing glance at the miscreant, who slid back into the shadows.

"She is very young and sensitive," the man continued, "but I assure you that your patience will be well-rewarded. For she is a virtuoso who, it is rumored, is soon to be invited to the imperial court to perform before the Holy Roman Emperor, Joseph II, himself."

One of the dandies started to laugh, but his mirth ended in a weak chuckle under the collective glare of the audience.

Tiny footsteps sounded across the stage as a young girl with straw colored hair and blue eyes, wearing a light blue dress, entered from behind a side curtain. She looked innocent but confident, ignoring the baseness of the crowd, determined to beautify this place with her voice, despite the circumstances in which she found herself.

Any tension in the crowd melted away as the girl began her song, an old French lullaby. Heraclix was unsure who in the crowd understood the plaintive words, but they listened in a respectful silence that was only broken by the occasional sniffle. A longing sadness filled the room as she sang. Even the dandies nodded their approval.

Heraclix knew the song.

He remembered another voice singing that song, a voice from long ago, a voice arising out of the melding of his own and that of his beloved wife. Rhoda had sung that song, her voice airy and full of gladness . . . to be alive.

He held the baby close to his chest, his back to the wind, sheltering the infant from the weather. Rain blew past them toward the pall-bearers, who carried their grim cargo ahead of the funeral party to the hillside graveyard.

"Don't cry, Rhoda. I'll take good care of you."

Behind him, a light snow fell on a small, freshly-filled grave; in front of him, the church vomited flame into the night sky. Shouts came from the road at the bottom of the hill. He disappeared into the blackness before the townsfolk arrived.

Beyond the hooded figure, the man who had claimed to be able to speak with the dead writhed in a stinking alleyway, clawing at his moon and star tattooed throat with bejeweled fingers.

"That man was a charlatan," the hooded figure said, "a purveyor of parlor tricks. But I, I can teach you where real *power lies, Octavius."*

He handed over a scroll.

The writing was unlike anything the recipient had seen before, strange, alien. But a feeling of anticipation soon overpowered any fear that he might have initially felt.

"We should talk," the hooded man said.

"We should talk," Octavius repeated.

He took one last look back at Szentendre, then faced east. The road ahead of him seemed to contract as he walked. He traveled a great distance as if in a moment and soon found himself in the midst of a city of white, plaster walled buildings that reeked of incense and hookah smoke. High above the buildings, the sky was pierced by bulbous minarets. The doorways of the dwellings were laden with silk curtains and brass lamps.

The smell of the sea was on the air.

His ears tickled with the sound of a language he had never before heard, a tongue that he thought would hold the promise of being able to tease out secrets from beyond this Earth, and possibly even beyond the veil of death.

The girl's song changed keys as she broke into a light aria, and a surge of hope broke through the gloom—a brightness rang forth through her voice, a burst of climactic optimism that left the place feeling a little warmer, a little lighter, a little happier. The crowd erupted into cheers.

Heraclix could sense that Pomp was gone. But, at this time, he reasoned that it was for the better. He had business to attend to, somewhere to the east, alone.

CHAPTER 14

In the meadow beyond the graveyard, where blue and orange butterflies hover aloft on a gentle breeze, Pomp flies through the veil between realities to the realm of Faerie. A subtle change in the direction of the breeze is the only indicator that she has passed into another world. She wonders if Mowler could find his way back to Faerie and what he might do once he gets there. The Fey would have their fun for a moment after his arrival, but the sorcerer would eventually have his way. The consequences would be tragic. This thought compels her to move swiftly through the realm. She will spend time with her sisters later. For now, she has business to attend to in one of the darker corners of Faerie.

Not all parts of the fairy realm are as pleasant as the place through which she travels. Even innocence has its dark side, and this darkness manifests itself in a few small areas on the peripheries of Faerie, where the border between Pomp's realm and Heraclix's world are thin: graveyards, murder scenes, or battlefields, for instance. Pomp understands, now, the real danger of traveling through such places. Where once she playfully flew and frolicked, she knows now that her quest will be difficult. Still, she has a purpose, and she must enter one of the darkest of these areas, the place known as "The Armory."

In a land where whimsy and frivolity are perpetual, there are inevitably standing structures whose construction and purpose have long since been forgotten, not because of the passage of time, which matters little to immortals, but because the attention of the land's inhabitants is so fleeting and so easily scattered to whatever shiny thing passes by. The Armory is just such a place.

To call it a structure is misleading, though it is obvious that some guiding hand organized it at some point in what the other-worlders would call the past. The structure is a perfect circle of lofty oaks, eighty feet from root to top branch. In the wrong light, one sees skulls in the bark, tentacles in the branches, and sharp claws in the roots, a twelve-headed wooden monstrosity.

She has never been inside the Armory before, though she has heard of it. What fairy hasn't heard the tales? As she slips between a pair of giant oaks, she feels threatened, as if she does not belong here—as if she is an intruder, a profane presence in a sacred space.

She anticipates that Mowler, having once tried to take her life, will try to take the lives of many of her kin—those who raised him as a child. And, since they are too busy playing to defend them-selves, she will attack Mowler before he can come to Faerie, before he can do any more harm. She has come here to prepare for this inevitable confrontation.

"Halt!" a booming voice calls out from somewhere in the canopy above.

"State your name!" another voice cries from a slightly different direction.

"Yes," yet another says, "whooo are you?"

She looks up to see twelve pairs of yellow eyes leering down at her. The eyes flash and blink in such a confusing way that she doesn't know if they are attached to faces at all. Then her sight adjusts a bit to the gloom. She suspects that she sees some-thing . . . very odd . . . but she cannot be sure.

"I am called Pomp," she says, hoping to verify her suspicions.

"Pomp Cimbridotter, Raiser of Man," one of the twelve says. "What is your business here?"

She tries to stare at one of them, hoping to see it a bit better, but the whirling crown of eyes is so distracting that she cannot concentrate long enough to see clearly.

"I am here to arm myself."

"Who invades the realm?"

"No one . . . yet."

"Yet?"

"Mowler will invade."

"Mowler invades? The unhappy son is back?!" a chorus of voices sounds.

"Yes!" Pomp presses, taking advantage of the guardians' lack of chronological perspective. After all, if they didn't know about "yet" yet, they would never understand her and never help her. "Yes, Mowler invades!"

"Open the doors of the Armory," one says in a surprisingly calm, solemn voice.

The others grow silent.

The ground in the middle of the circle tears open into a fissure from which rays of bright light shine forth.

Pomp looks away, up into the trees. A radiant white light bathes the Armory up to the topmost branches. She sees them clearly now, twelve immense owls of different breeds, whose heads rotate to reveal that each possesses not one, but three pairs of eyes and three beaks. Their faces spin around their heads, causing Pomp to look away from the bizarre congeries and down into a white rectangular pit that has opened up before her.

A stone ramp leads down into the pit. Pomp descends slowly, allowing her eyes to adjust to the dazzling brightness of the place. The walls are composed of brilliant white dirt, pebbles, and roots; the purest she has ever seen. At the bottom of the ramp is a stone dais raised on the backs of twelve carved marble dragonflies. Atop the dais is a white bow and a quiver of exactly twelve arrows.

She had seen them used before, back then, when an army of men had invaded through a rift created by magicians at Mohenjo-daro. Cimbri, a very brave and well-renowned soldier with a keen sense of humor, as well as a close relative of Pomp's, shot a love arrow at an enemy lieutenant's horse. The beast was quickly filled with erotic desire, not for the nearest horse, but for the nearest horse's rider, who happened to be the general who had most strongly stoked the fire of war in his men. The lieutenant's horse had felt a strong sense of admiration for the man but was now inspired by something other than a courageous heart. The horse's vision was corrupted by lust. Epaulets looked like a saddle, the general's coattails looked like a . . . well, a tail, and the leader's spit-shined boots appeared rather hoof-like in the black stirrups.

The passionate beast, in trying to mount the man, dismounted the man. The general was quickly turned to pulp in the confusion of hooves. The forlorn horse, enraged, turned on his companions and a general (or general-less) chaos ensued at the front.

Cimbri then flanked the enemy and shot a pair of dancing arrows into three other officers, one on either side of the advancing army and one in the middle. These began a silly dance in which they mimicked, with great accuracy, Pomp thought, the actions of a chicken whose feet had been glued to the floor before having its tail lit on fire. The army was quickly coming to the conclusion that some madness had overtaken their leaders. Still, they were able to hold their formation together, just barely.

Cimbri's next three arrows, carefully placed sleep arrows shot into the remaining officers, precipitated a rout. The lieutenant's horse, still looking for the jellied general, was left behind and died at a ripe old age after years of aimlessly galloping around the countryside, providing entertainment for any fairy with enough patience to set up a scarecrow and clothe it as a general.

Now Pomp reaches out and takes the bow and quiver of arrows. It's her turn to take the weapons. She will yet play Cimbri's part. She looks up to the owls, each of which nods three faces in approval.

"Go forth!" the thirty-six beaks call out in unison. "Destroy Mowler! We depend on you for the defense of the realm, Pomp Cimbridotter."

She exits the Armory then immediately flies through to the world of men. Perhaps she will encounter Mowler on the other side—or at least be closer to her target than when she left Heraclix at the graveside meadow. There is only one way to find out, so she plunges on.

Upon entering the mortal's world, she is engulfed in the midst of smoke and confusion. The world spins around her, and she is battered to-and-fro by a jostling mob that is entirely heedless of her presence above their heads. She is thrown from staff to pitchfork and back again, volleyed toward a torch. She barely stops in time to avoid being singed by the flames. Then she is unceremoniously swatted out of the air by the random swing of a peasant's wheat flail. She lands in tall weeds along the path that the mob is taking toward their destination.

There is something familiar about this place. Pomp has been here before. She looks around, but it's difficult to see from the ground, here in the weeds. And where is all of this smoke coming from?

Pomp flies up—careful, this time—to avoid the farm implements and torches that bob dangerously up and down above the mob. When she clears the trees, she sees the source of the smoke down the trail: Nicklaus's little cottage is on fire! The windows have been broken out, and the flaming door is ajar. Fingers of fire shoot out of every opening, wrapping up and around the roof, embracing the structure in a churning death grip of immolation.

The mob ascends the path, under a cloud of belligerent voices, up into the hills. They are led by the immaculately dressed Bohren who shows not one sign of blood or smoke on his clothing. Pomp wonders how this could be, then turns her thoughts back to the matter at hand.

The group's tone and direction hint at their intent, then Bohren makes it explicit:

"Death to the *Auslander*! Death to the Serbian pig!" Bohren yells, goading the rabble.

Pomp deliberates. The Serb admitted to committing war crimes and atrocities. Even his severed hand carried on the work of death, causing her friend, Heraclix, to murder a soldier. Surely, the Serb's legacy of hate deserves a fitting end. It is just. However, the Serb had healed hundreds, maybe thousands of others, including Heraclix. He seemed to have become almost kindly—truly repentant. But he can never fully restore the lives he has taken. Wasn't he condemned to Hell already? Could his own death make up for the deaths he had caused, restore balance to the scales of justice? And what if it couldn't? Would Hell benefit from one more inhabitant condemned to be reborn as a maggot, grown into a devil-fly or a demon-swine to be the plaything of arch-devils and sorcerers? How would she live with herself, knowing that she had let this man—however wicked in the past, this man who helped and healed her best friend—let him die at the hands of an angry mob and let him be damned, eternally, to Hell and misery?

No. Poor Nicklaus had died today already. Pomp won't let the mob take Vladimir Porchenskivik.

Bohren presses into the forest, unnecessarily hacking down small branches and slashing tall ferns, giving his followers the false impression that he is blazing the way before them, providing egress for their collective anger and fear. Others down the line follow his example, everyone seeking glory, some veering completely off the path just to thwack at a branch, like children demonstrating their bravado on a defenseless tree. Cowards!

There are well over a hundred, all told. Impossible to stick them all with arrows, Pomp believes. Then she remembers Cimbri's example, how the great warrior used a few well-placed arrows to defeat an entire army. Pomp can do the same!

She flies ahead and perches herself on a high branch that overarches the path. After carefully selecting an arrow, she aims for Bohren, waits until he comes into range, then lets the arrow fly. The projectile hits him squarely in the neck and he instantly collapses into a heap without so much as a peep of surprise or a grunt of pain. He is on the ground in less than two seconds, sleeping and loudly snoring. The line milled to a halt around the crumpled figure of their ersatz leader. Two of the men directly try to lift him to his feet and rouse him from his slumber. But Bohren is unresponsive. A woman further back cries out: "The Serb has killed Bohren with his dark magic! Kill the Serb! For Bohren!"

"For Bohren!" the crowd responds, then chants as it marches, inexorably, to the Serb's castle.

The two men drop Bohren, who is quickly trampled by the mob. His clothes do not look so good now. The mob, enraged that their leader has fallen, speeds the pace of its march up the hills, through the forest, toward their target destination. They surge with a newfound energy, eager to find the object of their wrath.

"That didn't work so well," Pomp says.

Thankfully, she can fly straight through the trees, as the crow flies, deviating little from her course, while the coarse mob must follow the meandering path. She waits beyond the mouth of the path in the clearing. The first man through is a short, skinny man, slovenly, with light brown hair in a bowl cut. He walks with a bent spine and hunched shoulders, though he is strong enough to wield a maul. The man smiles and looks around as he comes into the open circle surrounding the castle, looking about in stupid awe, gawking as the rest of the mob starts to pour out of the woods behind him.

Pomp easily zips an arrow into his neck, and he is instantly laughing and dancing like a scarecrow in a tempest, completely unable to stop himself from looking like a fool.

The column stops to stare at the dancing fool long enough that the stationary torches catch the overhead leaves on fire, sending small wisps of flame up into the trees.

"He is possessed!" yells one of the mob.

"The Serb's magic has driven him mad!" exclaims another.

Then, when someone in the back sees flames in the trees: "The Serbian wizard casts fire down from the sky!"

A few in the back flee down the mountain. The bulk of the mob pushes on, shoving each other into the clearing where a few strong men tackle the dancing idiot and tie him up with ropes. The fool continues to try to dance within the ropes, loudly singing a bawdy song, until someone stuffs a rag in his mouth.

"I had hoped to hang the Serb with that rope," says one. "Now I'll have to strangle him with my bare hands."

"Me first!" comes a chorus of shouts.

The remainder of the mob, heads for the stronghold door.

"This really is not working," Pomp says.

She shoots the one closest to the door, who turns to embrace and kiss the man behind him. His love is requited with a fist to the mouth, a knockout punch that sends him to the floor.

"Huh!" says another. "Who thought Gerderink had such a brittle jaw?"

"Who cares?" is the response, followed by several shouts of "Kill the Serb!" and a mass rush to the door. They don't bother using the door handle, preferring entry by axes.

"No, no, no!" Pomp says. "I need to save these arrows to fight Mowler." With that realization, she goes to the top of the trees and quickly fashions several crude arrows out of sharp, relatively straight sticks. Inaccurate, but they will have to do.

By the time she is finished, the mob has broken through the splintered door. They enter, then several immediately barrel back out, clawing their way through the opposing human traffic with cries of "Ghost!"

Pomp hopes that the introduction of the undead to the living might be sufficient incentive for the mob to break and run, but more people are rushing into the castle than are rushing out. She estimates that some three dozen strongmen are ascending the staircase, any one of them capable of killing the old Serb with little effort.

She flies at full speed up through the canopy of leaves. The tower is punctuated with lanceolate windows all the way around the circumference, high above the floor of the chamber. Pomp looks for the trapdoor from the air then, after locating it, she stands on the bottom of the window opening opposite the trapdoor. She nocks one of her arrows and waits.

The Serb—the one called Porchenskivik—kneels by the trapdoor, head bowed, his whole hand grasping the end of his stump, in the aspect of prayer. Pomp notes that Porchenskivik has piled all furnishings and books into a mound in the center of the room and interspersed sticks and kindling throughout, as if he was planning to burn it all in a bonfire. Candles are lit throughout the room. Pomp isn't sure what to make of all this, though she has an uneasy feeling about it.

Her uneasy feeling is compounded by a banging that thumps up from the underside of the trapdoor. This noise, along with the sound of muffled arguing and yelling, heralds the arrival of the mob at the top of the stairs.

"'Twas a ghost, I tell you!"

"'Twas not, you idiot!"

"I saw it . . ."

"And I felt it!"

"I'll give you something to feel!"

"No, you imbecile, not on the stairs."

"I . . . aaah!"

"Aaah!" the voice fades away, down the shaft.

"Good riddance, says I."

"Now he'll really be seeing ghosts."

"Haw, he'll just have to look in a mirror."

"But I saw it, too."

147

"Shut up, you, or you'll go down, too."

The trap door bucks but doesn't give. It's secured by a large timber held to the floor by iron rungs. The mob, having to hack above their heads while keeping their balance so as to avoid tumbling over into the stairwell shaft, would take hours to break through.

Porchenskivik, breaking his prayerful pose, slowly slides the timber out of its rungs, as if to open the trap door.

"No!" shouts Pomp, allowing herself to become visible so that he can see her. He pauses, looking straight up at her.

"Well, hello, my little friend. You're back."

"Don't open that trapdoor!" she says. "They'll kill you! And you'll be sent straightway to Hell. I've seen it. You don't want to go there. I can't stop all those people. They'll kill you! Oh, please don't open that trap door!"

Porchenskivik smiles, his eyes calm and reassuring. "Don't worry, little friend. It will be okay."

He slides the bolt away from the trap door.

"No!" Pomp screams.

She can hardly see from the tears in her eyes, but she shoots an arrow blindly at the opening trap door, then another, and another. The first two elicit a simple "ouch!"—the third a scream of agony.

"Aaah! My eye! Aaah!"

Pomp sees through her tears that she has hit the first man, whose head and arms have cleared the floor, directly in the eye.

Porchenskivik reaches down, plucks out the makeshift arrow, then holds his hand to cover the eye, his ghost hand holding the necklace.

The injured man who had been frantic just a moment before relaxes, slowly turns his head toward Porchenskivik, and looks at him as if Porchenskivik's healing hand—for the man's eye had been instantly healed—held the secrets of the universe within its palm. A look of admiration, of awe, and of understanding washes over the man's face. His body relaxes as hate gives way to peace. Porchenskivik looks down at him and smiles gently, running his hand over the man's head like a mother does a sick child's.

"No!" Pomp screams again as the rest of the mob pull back the healed man, who cannot take his eyes off his benefactor, and trample over him to get to the object of their derision.

Porchenskivik never stops smiling. He is as calm as a gently rolling brook on a clear summer day in the country.

And they are upon him.

They pummel his smile into a bloody mash, then tie him up with what rope they have left after tying up the dancing madman in the courtyard. Porchenskivik offers no resistance as they fashion a noose and throw it around his neck. They search for rafters, a hook, a sconce—anything on which to hang him. Finding none, they strap him to the pile of furniture, books, and sticks in the center of the room and light it on fire.

He lays still and allows the flames to lick his body, flinching only when the searing heat becomes too much for any man to bear. His murderers keep him in the middle of the fire, using their pitchforks to prevent him from rolling off.

Pomp, in desperation, flies down and tries to pull fuel from the fire, but her efforts are in vain. It's too late. She flees from the scene. The dying cries of Porchenskivik echo in her head as she flies out the window. The mob, as if pouring their sound into Porchenskivik's death throes, has grown silent.

Pomp flies through the trees toward Szentendre, where she last left Heraclix. She will join with him and avenge all those who have died by Mowler's hand. The fire blazing all around her gives her purpose. She will be to Mowler as the fire is to the Serb. The flaming trees don't hear the faint sounds of the dying man—they know nothing of the fate that awaits him in the afterlife, and they do not care.

Chapter 15

One moment, Heraclix was immersed in his surroundings, soothed by the breeze-driven susurrus of the barley fields through which he waded, mesmerized by the golden waves under the blue sky; the next, a sharp cry snapped him out of his reverie. Comfort fled, and he, as an almost automatic reaction, ran toward the source of the interruption. A flock of white birds, flushed from his movements, rose up in a column just ahead of him, like a feathered geyser.

Barley parted like water before him as his muscular form carved through the fields. But even the hissing and popping of the grass as he passed couldn't conceal the grating of saber blades being slid out of their scabbards. He turned his head to look back over his shoulder and spied a pair of saber points bobbing up and down through the grass. The hunt, it seemed, was already on, like it or not.

The screams—clearly from women—grew louder, and more adamant with each step he took. His pace increased into a full run. He charged forward and broke into a clearing, heads of barley exploding all around him then raining down onto the road on which he suddenly found himself sprinting.

Ahead was a tangle of bodies on the road, above which stood a tall Cossack wielding a riding crop. To the right of the people was a small caravan of three brightly decorated, horse-drawn wagons, painted to attract customers. A man lay on the ground, each limb held down by the dirty hands of a grubby Cossack. The body of

150

another victim lay partially-concealed in the grass, bloodied legs out on the road as if the man had tried and failed to leave the road before being cut down by the Russians.

The men on the ground, living and dead, were dark-bronze-skinned with black, curly hair and thin, pointed beards—both likely Turks, Heraclix thought. The dead man bore a matrix of whip-scars along his back, still bleeding into the dirt and barley. The living was about to gain some scars of his own, though he struggled mightily to be free, lithe muscles straining against his captors. But the more he bucked, the harder they pressed his wrists and ankles to the ground.

The lash of the riding crop, followed by the screams and whimpers of the captive Turk elicited, again, the women's cries, though Heraclix hadn't seen the women on the road. Perhaps they were in the wagons. After all, two men could not steer three wagons, and, from somewhere in the back of his mind, he knew that Turkish culture wouldn't allow a woman to ride as anything but a passenger. Still, there must be another man somewhere, unless he was fled or hidden in the deep grass.

Seeing the tall Cossack's hand raising the threatening riding crop, Heraclix closed the distance between himself and the tormentor. The golem's left hand twitched and pumped almost uncontrollably, anticipating the throat of its victim. The Cossack was so engrossed in the torture of the Turk, who now sobbed under the weighty sting of the skin-stripped wounds on his back, that he was completely oblivious to Heraclix's bounding approach until a split-second after the giant made his final pounce.

A loud crack signified the dissolution of the man's ribs as Heraclix tackled him with a shoulder to the Cossack's side. The Russian yelped, then struggled for breath. Heraclix forced the left hand away from the man's throat, down to the Cossack's wrist. The grip was like steel. The wrist was not. After the man's wrist bones shattered, he fainted, hanging limp like a rag doll from Heraclix's grasp.

It was over in an instant.

The next moment, bedlam broke loose.

Three of the four Cossacks who had been holding the Turk to the ground drew sabers and attacked the giant. It became immediately apparent that these were not mere conscripted soldiers, but accomplished swordsmen, veterans of battle. Their blades arced through the air in a deadly whirlwind. Their swords seemed to be an extension of the men themselves. They danced, sabers and men, around and toward Heraclix, inviting him into what would be, for most men, a courtship of death.

But they didn't know that he had already entered that relationship and ended it once, maybe twice. Another pair of screams, one from the road behind him and another from beyond the wagons to his right, convinced him that it was time for hosts and guests to reverse roles.

It was a short-lived courtesy. Heraclix threw the unconscious Cossack, by the arm, at two of his attackers, knocking one to the ground and causing the other to take a slice out of what Heraclix presumed was their commander.

The third lunged for Heraclix, hacking at his outstretched arm. Much to the man's shock, the blade bounced off. Heraclix grabbed the blade and snapped it at the hilt. The wielder backed away, stumbling over the fourth Cossack, who had been kneeling on the Turk's shoulders to keep him on the ground.

This allowed the Turk to come free. He elbowed his erstwhile captor in the throat, causing the Russian to claw at his own windpipe in an effort to breathe. He did not. He slumped to his knees then sprawled on his stomach, twitching. The others fled off into the grass.

Heraclix turned around to find the source of the screaming behind him. There were two more Cossacks, no doubt the ones who were hunting him through the barley fields earlier. But they had a third person with them, namely a young Turk of perhaps sixteen years, who clung to the back of one of the men, one arm hooked around the man's neck. The other arm rose and fell rapidly, repeatedly plunging a curved Ottoman dagger in and out of the man's back and shoulder. This, then, was one of the sources of screaming, the man screaming in agony, the youth screaming a battle cry.

The Cossack's companion swung his saber, hoping to hack the youth off of his comrade's back but, instead, slashed his friend's bowels open. Realizing what he had just done, he ran off down the road, then into the grass, leaving the other man to die there on the road.

Heraclix looked down to where the Turk had been, but he was gone. Another scream rang out from behind the wagons, so Heraclix ran between them to the other side to render what aid he might.

As he cleared the wagons, he saw the half-naked Turk taking a young woman into his arms, or, rather, his arm. The other arm held a saber, taken, no doubt, from the Cossack he had killed. The bloodied saber, along with a pair of dead, de-pantsed Cossacks, gave evidence to the fact that the Russians were after more than mere plunder. The girl's torn dress, along with the similarly torn dress of her mother, who angrily pounded the dead bodies with her fists, provided further evidence of the Cossacks' ill intent.

"You are safe now," the Turk reassured the girl.

"You are safe now!" a voice called out from down the road.

The boy who had ridden and stabbed the back of the Cossack rounded the corner, the bloodied dagger still in his hand. He was panting from the fight.

"You are safe!" he said, exultantly. Then, seeing the couple in each other's arms, his countenance fell, along with the dagger, which dropped from his grasp.

"You have done well, Al'ghul," the Turkoman said to the boy. "You have killed half a man in defense of Fuskana here," he looked into the girl's eyes and smiled. "I have killed three. You are catching up!" Al'ghul disappeared, skulking off to the other side of the caravan.

A trio of elderly men emerged from the wagons, two of them tottering over to pull the older woman away from the body she was desecrating. The third walked briskly toward Heraclix, then stopped as he beheld the giant's face. The man breathed in through his nose and held his breath, composing himself for the conversation with the unsightly Heraclix.

"You have saved us this day. I have witnessed it, Allah be praised! Now, how can we reward you, large one?"

The man wore the white robes of the Hajj, a rarity here. His sharp, pointed beard, along with his dark eyes, atop a corpulent frame, gave him a sinister appearance, but his voice bespoke kindness. "We have much to give you as a gesture of our thanks, brass pots, silk, spices, incense . . ."

Heraclix held his hand up then, realizing it was covered in blood, he wiped it on his cloak. The merchant's smile faded in a brief moment of hesitation, as if he regretted having approached the stranger so openly, then the smile returned as quickly as it had left.

"I don't want your goods," Heraclix said in German-accented Turkish. "Only some companionship."

The merchant looked at the couple. The girl showed fear in her eyes, then averted her gaze from the elder and Heraclix. The young man had fire in his eyes as he placed himself between Heraclix and the girl. Heraclix understood almost immediately that there had been a misunderstanding.

"Not that kind of companionship. I only seek to share a part of my journey east."

"East!" the merchant said loudly. "Allah is smiling on you, friend. That is exactly where we are headed! To Istanbul!"

The girl gave a puzzled gasp.

The merchant shot her a harsh glance and cleared his throat. She immediately became silent.

Heraclix noticed that the wagons were facing northwest.

"I don't want to be any trouble . . ." Heraclix began. He stopped himself suddenly, realizing that Istanbul was the city to the east that he sought.

"No trouble!" the merchant said. "None at all. We will be heading to Istanbul starting tomorrow." The merchant gave the couple a suppressing stare, then called the others together. "Tonight we share. But first, we mourn. Kaleel," the merchant said to the young man who had his arm around the girl, "you and Al'ghul will bury your cousin there, in the field. It will be known as Hamad's Meadow." The young man and the boy nodded, then hurried off. The girl tended to her distraught female companion, and the merchant wheeled around and walked off on other business, leaving Heraclix alone in the midst of the people.

Heraclix observed, listened, eavesdropped, even, and learned much in the process. He was careful not to be found alone with any one member of the party, as they all grew nervous when it seemed they might be alone with the giant, all except the youngest,

Al'ghul, the teen who felled one of the Cossacks. Al'ghul was a loner. Heraclix felt that the boy was only loosely connected with the rest of the group.

Al'ghul's eldest brother, Hamad, had been killed trying to defend the caravan from the raiders. Kaleel, the other young man whose valor and strength Heraclix found commendable, was a cousin to Al'ghul and the deceased Hamad.

The object of Kaleel's affections (and those of Al'ghul, Heraclix suspected from the younger's body language), Fuskana, was somewhere in age between Al'ghul and Kaleel. She was attractive and innocent. Heraclix didn't wonder that some jealousies between the two cousins might be provoked over her.

The girl's mother, Chandra, was wed to one of the three merchants, namely Hezrah, while the other two old tradesmen, Jubal and Mehmet, were distant cousins of the wedded pair, through Hezrah. It was unclear to Heraclix how Al'ghul or Kaleel were related, if at all, to the rest. Perhaps, he thought, he would pursue the question over dinner, which Jubal had informed him would happen after they had properly buried Hamad.

That night, after hours of exaggerated, if heartfelt, weeping, the women, along with Al'ghul, prepared a dinner of spiced porridge and rabbit. Heraclix, who neither felt hunger nor had the physical need for food, still ate as a courtesy to his hosts. His taste buds were apparently still functional. He particularly enjoyed a sort of hot spiced cider or tea. He had felt a touch of autumn on the wind coming down from the mountains to the south, and the drink warmed his insides.

Conversation flowed freely around the fire, though the travelers sat across the fire from Heraclix. His appearance obviously discomfited them, but they never remarked rudely or showed open contempt. They were the hosts, and Heraclix was their guest, no matter how ugly he was.

Jubal, a consumate storyteller, related how the little caravan was traveling from Sofia to Pest to sell their wares when they were set upon by the Russian Cossacks. Hamad and Kaleel had fought well, but were outnumbered. Al'ghul had "slunk off to hide, as a coward, until he could backstab one of the highwaymen and claim victory," Jubal said with disdain.

Al'ghul retreated from the fire, glowering at the others, especially his cousin. But Kaleel was occupied with staring into the eyes of the soft and genteel Fuskana, who seemed happy to return Kaleel's attentions.

After the boy had departed, Jubal spoke in a low voice. "'Al'ghul' means 'the ghoul' or 'the demon.' It is, of course, not the boy's given name. We, the older ones, dare not tell him his true name. Nor does he know that Kaleel," he spoke quietly enough that the fawning young man wouldn't be distracted from the girl, "is not, in truth, his cousin".

"And was Hamad his brother?"

"Indeed, he was. It was Hamad, in fact, who nicknamed the boy 'Al'ghul' not long after their mother died in Erdel at the hands of a band of raiders. The younger boy was only three years old at the time, but the trauma took hold. He wasn't like other children, after the things he had seen. And he's still not like other children. He's given to outrageous fits of jealous rage. I don't know what he recalls of his parents, but it's apparent that the memories—whether of loss or otherwise—have left him scarred for life. But, though he is an orphan, he must learn to be a man, and this we . . . myself, Hezrah, and Mehmet, vowed to teach him when we found the orphaned boys on our travels. We had done well with Hamad. For Al'ghul, I hold less hope."

"The boy is dangerous, headstrong," said Hezrah.

"Still, we vowed to teach him," Mehmet said.

"You are to be commended," Heraclix said.

"We are to go to sleep," Jubal said. "It is late and tomorrow we head back past Sofia to Istanbul."

The men retired to their wagons, careful to keep Kaleel and Fuskana separated.

Heraclix lay by the dying fire, staring up at the stars. He knew that at some point in the past he had memorized all the constellations, the transits of the planets, the specific pulsations of the stars. Now, though, he couldn't recall any of the specifics nor, most importantly, why he had taken such an interest in them before his death and reanimation. It was more than a mere pleasure in their twinkling mystery or a quaint hint of nostalgia. No, he had known the stars, mapped their meanderings, and there was some deep purpose to it all, an intent that he couldn't explicitly state, but that held as its ultimate goal some sort of grim power and arcane knowledge.

Heraclix was so consumed by his brooding puzzlement that he failed to realize that he was being watched until Al'ghul appeared, like a wolf, on the edge of the dying firelight. The embers cast a red glow upon the boy, giving him the appearance of his namesake.

"Aren't you up a little late?" Heraclix asked.

"That's what Jubal and Kaleel would say," the boy said.

"You are lucky to have Kaleel with you," Heraclix said.

"Lucky? He is a curse."

"He seems very brave to me," Heraclix said.

"*I* am brave!" Al'ghul said. "I killed one of the bandits myself!"

"No one is doubting your bravery, young one."

"Jubal doubts it."

"Jubal wants what is best for you."

"He withholds what is best for me, just as he withheld it from Hamad."

"And what would that be?" Heraclix asked.

The boy hesitated a moment before answering.

"That which Kaleel has, that which he holds, without fear, without shame, in the presence of Jubal and the others."

Heraclix thought about this for a moment, then stifled a laugh only with great difficulty. Jubal's assessment of the boy had been right on.

"So, this is about Fuskana?"

"This is about *nothing!*" the boy said sulkily, "this conversation is over!" And with that, Al'ghul disappeared into the night.

Heraclix looked up at the star that shared the boy's name. He wondered if it was fiery youth that kindled Algol's flaming light. Had jealousy ever fueled his own actions in his lifetime, the life before this one? He wondered all night, to the turning of the starry sky and the sound of barley in the breeze, until the sun drove away all other pretenders, blinding the heavens and burning them all away, banishing them to outer darkness.

The men arose and hooked the horses up to the wagons. Hezrah and Kaleel guided the first, Jubal piloted the second with Heraclix as his bench-side passenger, while Mehmet and Al'ghul steered the last wagon. Fuskana and her mother must have been within the wagons, but Heraclix wasn't sure which one, or even if the mother and daughter shared the same carriage. It seemed that the men were very careful to hide the women while traveling. Heraclix could see why.

As the monotony of the grasslands stretched out in all directions, save that of the mountains on the horizon ahead of them, Heraclix took surreptitious glances behind him, watching as Mehmet lectured young Al'ghul. The old man pointed to the heavens and expanded his arms wide, as if to encompass the hemisphere of the sky. The boy seemed genuinely interested, even cracking an occasional smile at the old man's comments.

"Mehmet and Al'ghul seem to enjoy a good relationship," Heraclix remarked to Jubal.

"Mehmet was also an orphan, for a time, until my father took him in."

"Then the two have much in common."

"In terms of their familial experience, yes," Jubal clarified, "but there the similarity ends, mostly."

"Mostly?"

"Well," Jubal said with a hesitancy that indicated that he was weighing whether or not to divulge a sensitive piece of information, "Mehmet and Al'ghul do both tend more toward the morose and pessimistic," he said, with some reluctance. "But they are very different in other ways. Mehmet is exceedingly intelligent and well-read on a number of subjects, whereas Al'ghul is a bit dull. Ambition is a word that the boy wouldn't understand if Socrates himself explained it to him, while Mehmet has his sights set high. Of course, this is reflected in a third difference: Mehmet is strictly disciplined, while Al'ghul is rather lazy."

"So Mehmet is a good mentor for the boy," Heraclix said.

Jabal smiled. "Why do you think I have them ride together?"

That night, in the mountains, they hitched their horses up to the point of a long line of trees that outlined the spur of one of the ridges over which they had trekked. Clouds had formed as the evening progressed, and Heraclix, who rested outside while the merchants and their kin slept inside the covered wagons, worried that he might have to sit in the rain. His concerns were realized as a gentle mist began to blanket the place with a damp film.

The weather rumbled into a gentle storm, the sort of atmosphere that soothes those somnolescents lucky enough to be indoors as it gains a little strength. Not a tempest, but a soft, if wet, quilt falling over the land.

Heraclix sat up against one of the wagons, pulling the hood of his cloak over his head and wrapping its collar tight around his neck. Distant rolling thunder muffled the other sounds around him, except where a trill of water spilled and splashed off the roof of one of the other wagons.

But it didn't completely mask the sound of one of the carriage doors opening, specifically that of the wagon that Al'ghul and Mehmet had steered earlier that day. Heraclix leaned forward, trying to see who exited, but the rain-veiled gloom was almost impenetrable. He stood and slowly made his way over to the wagon to investigate. He listened at the door, but could not discern a sound with the rain plip-plopping on the puddles that had collected outside. He looked to the ground and thought he spied muddy footprints, but there was no way to be absolutely sure. The rain fell more quickly in larger drops, melting away any evidence of footfalls.

Suddenly, the wind picked up, as if blown into a fury by the gods, Zeus himself awakening to first lazily toss a few thunderbolts down, then becoming more and more adamant until mad with the spirit of destruction. Again Heraclix searched by lightning light, but was unable to see footprints. He had heard no unusual sounds in the wagon, so he judged all to be well, if rather noisy, in the tempest. He pushed against the ever-increasing wind and returned to his soggy seat beside his own wagon to wait out the storm, fearful of being separated from the others by the confusion of the gale.

The few trees within eyesight were struck and splintered by lightning, a separate bolt for each trunk. In the smoking after-image that burnt into Heraclix's eyes, he thought he beheld the sharp silhouette of a man, head reared back in laughter or ecstasy, with both hands raised to the sky. But the image vanished when he blinked, wiped away, as if it had never existed.

Heraclix stood up and slowly began walking to the rise on which the phantom may or may not have been standing. Lightning continued to fall all around him, cascading down on the veritable waterfall of rain that poured down from the sky. His body tingled. What hair he had stood on end. The air was full of crackling electricity.

Or was it? He soon came to the sickening realization that the crunching sound he heard hadn't come from above, in the air, but from underfoot. As a bolt of lightning again revealed his location, he saw that the ground around him was completely covered with large earthworms, each a full six inches long and as big around as a man's finger. The worms stretched as far as he could see. They each pointed toward and converged at his feet, as if he was a magnet inexorably drawing the glistening carpet directly to him, a fleshly shrine to the megadriles before which the things had come to worship. With every step he took, the worms corrected their direction, always aiming for him, the involuntary God of Wormkind.

The lightning continued flashing all about him. He noticed that the worms were hauntingly familiar and peculiarly abnormal—not your normal annelids. They were, he realized, Hellspawn larvae, *Lumbricus Hades*, the souls of the damned beginning their migration through eternal torment. He saw their visages, millions of them bearing the face of their former selves, though the condemned wouldn't recognize themselves if held to a mirror, not at this stage. And even after they had grown back into an understanding of their past lives and sins, they would be unable to recognize their own reflections, having been so twisted and mangled by the mutations and excruciating torture inflicted on them by other souls further along in their "progression" that their appearance and voices would only remain as a pathetic mockery, a caricature of the person they had chosen to become in mortality.

He picked up one of the larvae to examine it more closely and recognized the face almost immediately. The high-cheekbones, carefully waxed mustache, stiletto beard, and smoldering eyes that, with a simple squint, had commanded whole armies and condemned man, demon, and (almost) flesh golem, to death. The face, which seemed to recognize Heraclix and snarled with rage, gnashing its teeth in an effort to bite the giant's hand, was that of Graf Von Helmutter!

The giant dropped the worm, startled into a fear that soaked into his skin as a paralyzing dread. Was Mowler nearby? Who had summoned these quasi-demons? And why did they continue to surround and harangue Heraclix? What were the implications of this weird pilgrimage?

Questions stopped instantly as the lightning, which had been cast all around the giant, finally found its mark in Heraclix's head. There would be no more answers that night, only a brilliant flash of light, followed by sudden darkness.

Chapter 16

Pomp flies with haste. The air is turning cold. Autumn is coming on. The leaves are starting to change color. Good. Mowler won't want to travel so much when winter sets in, if he's like most people she has seen. Then again, Mowler is not like most people. Not at all.

Szentendre is small, compared to Prague or Vienna, and it doesn't take long to realize that Heraclix is no longer there. She searches the burned-out church and graveyard, though the smell of burnt wood has become distasteful to her. He is not there, either, so she traces their steps back to the glade where they fought the Hell-spawned pig-demons.

Pomp can see no better than a man, but, as one of the Fey, she can sense a magical aura. And here she finds her first clue as to where the pig-demons have gone. It's not much, but it might be worth pursuing. The path leads her toward Prague. If the demons followed Heraclix and Pomp here, might the trails of their magic not lead to Heraclix now? She must try to find him, though her instinct, like that of most faeries, is to return home and ignore the world, and the problems, of mankind.

But she is not like most fairies. Not now. She knows the value of patience, the value of life. Pomp lives and thinks at a different pace than Gloranda, Doribell, Ilsie, or even Cimbri. She flies to Prague with great haste. She will find Heraclix, then, together, they will have vengeance on Mowler. Along the way, she will be the golem's eyes and ears, his scout.

Even with this newfound patience, she is amazed that while so much is at stake, Prague's citizens go about their daily duties without a care for the danger that threatens society. Mowler is a hawk, and anyone who comes in contact with him, king or beggar, is in danger of losing not only their life, but their very soul. He could be anywhere, anyone, disguised as a friend, neighbor, family member. Pomp doesn't know how she will find him. But she must start somewhere.

She starts at Caspar's apartment. Not the clean, well-ordered family flat near the castle, but the derelict, squalor-ridden hole somewhere in the maze of the Jewish quarter. The home of the entrance to Hell.

She is wary as she enters. The door isn't where Heraclix left it after it fell off its one good hinge. It is propped up against the wall that was once adorned by a shattered mirror and an old man's dead body. Someone, obviously, has been here since they pursued Georg into Hell.

This thought makes her approach the door very cautiously. There is a scrap of sky blue cloth hanging from a nail, as if someone had snagged their clothing in a hurried effort to leave. It might be a shred of a soldier's coat. She approaches the door from the side, sliding along the wall, fearful to see the tunnel behind it, but knowing that she might just have to go back down to *that* place in order to find Mowler. Her bow is strung and drawn, ready to fire a sleep arrow into whatever might peek around the corner. Hopefully, it will have some effect. Can the dead, sleeping already, be put to sleep again?

She probes into the darkness behind the door with an arrow, then swings around, still aiming the arrow at the shadow behind the door, ready to contend with whatever Hell throws at her, whatever rushes up that tunnel.

But there is no tunnel. Only a brick wall and a floor littered with broken glass. Dried blood trails across some of the shards and another tatter of blue cloth lays nearby. Pomp sidles in between the door and the wall for a closer look. A sliver of sunlight peeps into the apartment, allowing her to see a little better.

The bricks are of a different color than the wall around them, and the mortar looks fresh. There is little of the dust that smothers the rest of the room. This wall was built where the tunnel once was, and built recently. But who . . . ?

The door behind her is buffeted. The air in the room goes suddenly cold. The hairs on Pomp's neck stand on end, and she shivers, whether from fear or the change in temperature, she cannot tell. She turns around, back against the wall, and draws her bowstring back again, this time sliding out from behind the door to see what caused the noise. Then another, more insistent bang shakes the door, causing the bottom to slip out away from the wall.

Pomp flies out just in time to avoid it as it slides down the wall where she stood and crashes to the floor, sending up tidal waves of dust that fill the chamber to the rafters, where she takes refuge.

She waits for the dust to settle, hoping to see whatever it is that is causing such a ruckus in this forsaken place. But the dust hasn't cleared before she hears grunts of effort and an unbridled scream of combined frustration and malice.

"Yeeargh!" screams the voice, the last syllable drug out like an angry brogue.

Then, with a clarity that she thought she wanted, but now no longer desires, she sees it. A ghost, by the milky glow, hammers its head and fists against the wall, backs up, rushes the wall, is repelled by it, backs up, repeats, repeats, repeats, screaming the same perturbed battle cry as it slams into the wall and bounces back, time after time.

Pomp cannot help but chuckle at the ridiculousness of it all. At least her sense of humor is returning, she thinks.

Her laughter is cut short when the ghost stops, momentarily, and looks straight up at her.

"Aaah!" the ghost screams, flying up to shove his face into hers.

Pomp recoils, recalls her ineffective attempts to go invisible in the land of the dead. She knows the ghost sees her.

She knows the ghost, too.

"Von Helmutter!" she says, then shoots him squarely between the eyes.

The arrow passes through him, shattering on the brick wall behind him.

"Stupid fairy," he says, in a voice dripping with disdain. "I'm already dead. You can't kill me again."

"Again?" Pomp says, confused at his inference.

"And now I can't even go to the place where I belong because of this damned . . . I mean, undamned . . . wall!"

Von Helmutter's ghost again throws itself against the brick wall, unsuccessfully trying to smash the physical barrier with spiritual substance.

"Who put the wall there?" Pomp asks.

"I did!" It howls. "Oh, stupid, stupid, stupid. Our so-called intelligence indicated that there was something going on here, maybe even a breach of security, a tunnel dug by the Ottomans."

"And now you are—"

"Dead!"

"How?"

"Don't know, now, do I? Maybe that last meal I had was bad. It did taste a little funny. Though I'd been feeling sick for a while. I suppose I may have been killed. Yes, that's it. I was murdered! But . . . Oh, does it even matter?"

"I'm sorry." She almost believes that she's telling the truth.

"And now I can't even get to the place of my eternal torment, where I so deserve to dwell." He starts to cry ectoplasmic tears. "I can't even die and go to Hell right. What is wrong with me?"

Again, with the slamming against the wall. She is getting tired of his tantrums.

"There are other places—" she starts.

"Of course!" it says, elated. "How could I have forgotten? My books! I shall go consult my books to find the quickest route. Surely the new minister of defense hasn't gotten rid of them yet."

Its eyes narrow, and it gives a mumbled, begrudging "thank you" to Pomp. Then the ghost's eyes widen in something akin to, but far removed from the innocence of glee. "Now I can get a head start on my suffering, building up all the more regret and spite waiting for the time when my murderer goes down, and he will go down. Oh, what perverse pleasure of agony shall be mine!"

It spitefully bangs its spectral head on the wall one more time. Then it wheels around and flies out of the apartment and up through the multi-level maze of Josefov's streets to the open, if smoky, air above the Old New Synagogue.

Pomp flies right behind the now-departing recently departed, following the quickly fading wake of ectoplasm.

Pursuer and pursued dart across the sky, causing many a farmer to turn head, trying to figure out just what that was they thought they saw out of the corner of their eye and just where the laughter had come from that sounded at the limit of their hearing. Birds in their path drop to the ground, astounded and confused. Dogs bark, cattle moo, cats hiss at the unseen-by-human-eyes pair that hurtle through the air faster than a musket ball.

Vienna arises on the horizon quicker than Pomp thinks possible. Travel is faster when not waiting for a six hundred pound golem. Or when chasing a ghost.

Von Helmutter's ghost knows it's being hunted. It dives down into the market square near Heitzing, weaving between merchant stalls and crowds of well-to-do customers. Pomp narrowly avoids a flying fish, thrown by one merchant at another who has bargained prices down to a loss for himself and all other would-be fishmongers. A butcher's dog snaps at her, momentarily distracting her and almost costing Pomp her prey, but she sees a knotted trail of glowing smoke disappear through the open balcony window of one particularly well-furnished apartment.

Pomp slows, draws a dancing arrow, though it will do her no good against the already-slain, and enters the window just as a finely dressed young woman, perhaps twenty years of age, reaches up to close the shutters.

The contented smile that spreads across the girl's pretty face betrays her utter ignorance of the chase playing out in the invisible world.

Pomp realizes, though, that the chase has ended.

What looked like a simple apartment window from the street is, on Pomp's closer inspection, a portal into the quarters of an aristocrat. Four open doors lead into long hallways, each lined with doors. The ghost is gone, and she won't find it in such a place.

"Frau Kretzer," the young woman turns to a plain-looking old maid, "bring me my candles."

"As you wish, Lady Adelaide," the servant responds, bowing and retreating from the chamber in obeisance.

Lady Adelaide is beautiful, contrary to the common peasants' belief that noble inbreeding inevitably causes ugliness among the aristocracy. Her long brown hair is clean and full, her alabaster skin without visible flaw, and her eyes gleam blue as the night sky. She sings a lilting song, a quavering lullaby from her childhood, as she rearranges sconces and candle holders around the room and straightens an old portrait of a stately-looking couple, who just might be her parents, judging from their features. Pomp likes her singing.

"Mum, Daddy," the woman says to the portrait, "he's back! Viktor is back from Istanbul. You would be so proud of your nephew." A hint of sadness softens her eyes. "I wish you could see him in his proper station. You would be so very proud."

Frau Kretzer returns with a large crate full of tallow candles and sets it on the floor. "I'll be back with matches," she says as Lady Adelaide, ignoring the servant, begins filling the candleholders and wall sconces with the candles.

Lady Adelaide is perhaps halfway done placing candles in the hundred or so receptacles ringing the room when the servant reenters with a box of matches. "Set them on the floor, by that door," the noblewoman orders. Frau Kretzer concedes, bows, waits at attention in the doorway.

"Viktor says that the candles aid in concentration and are a purgative for the soul," she says to the servant. "They will burn away sadness and illuminate the heart."

"The mind!" a deep voice calls out from behind Frau Kretzer, "not the heart, the mind!"

Adelaide smiles broadly. "Yes, silly me, the mind!"

The maid steps aside, and in walks a tall, thin man with a carefully preened mustache and pointed beard. He is darkly handsome and a touch foreboding, though his gleaming smile banishes any vapors of ill-intent that his swarthiness might cause. His dress doesn't help the dark appearance, for he is dressed in a black uniform with white epaulets. Long, curly hair shows underneath his hat, a black fez embroidered with a *Totenkopf* and festooned with a brilliant white tassel. Several medallions, all tastefully small and lacking the gaudiness so often displayed on military garb, are neatly lined up on his chest. About his neck is a silver chain from which hangs the double-headed eagle of the Holy Roman Empire. His cufflinks, Pomp notices as he reaches up to remove his hat, are stylized sterling *Totenkopf*. He is, in a word, charming, though Pomp cannot yet bring herself to put him in the same category of "good" as Von Graeb.

Viktor approaches Adelaide and they embrace, though it's apparent that Adelaide is more comfortable with her display of affection than he. He holds her shoulders with his hands at arm's length and smiles that charismatic smile again. "You are, indeed, beautiful," he laughs softly. "And someday soon, you, we, will bring our family back to greatness!"

"You have already done so, my cousin," she says with a slight bow. "Now that you are the Minister of Defense, Graf Von Edelweir."

"I have only regained my rightful place," he says, returning the bow. "Besides, if it weren't for you and your relationship with our distant coz, the emperor, I wouldn't be where I am today. And what have I been, but a bachelor, married to my sword? You, *you* sweet Adelaide, will bring much more to our family's glory than I could ever do alone."

Frau Kretzer rolls her eyes behind him.

"Well, my sweet . . ." Viktor stops in mid-sentence, looking about the room suspiciously.

"What is it, Viktor?" Adelaide says, her brows furrowing.

"Nothing, I think. Just a sudden unease, as if something or someone was watching . . . almost . . ." he shakes his head. "Ah, I am sensing things where there is nothing. It's time I was back to my quarters. Parade's tomorrow!"

"Excellent!" Adelaide says. "I shall watch from my window."

"Good! Then tonight, after I leave, be sure to light the candles that will illuminate your heart!"

"Mind!"

"Ah, yes . . . mind. I'm glad you caught that. You are sharp!"

Frau Kretzer rolls her eyes again, begins to shake her head until Viktor wheels about, at which point she stiffens to attention, eyes straight ahead. She follows the soldier out of the room, closing the door behind her, but not before Pomp has slipped through, unseen.

"She has so much potential," Viktor says to the stone-faced servant. "I don't think she understands just how much of a difference she will make in the world." He pauses, thoughtfully. "No, she doesn't understand at all."

Pomp follows from above and behind as the pair continues down a short hallway lined with floor-to-ceiling mirrors. Viktor continues on, speaking affectionately about the Lady Adelaide while the servant dutifully follows, silent and unemotive.

The hallway opens up into a large parlor—a music room, furnished with a harpsichord; a few dark green upholstered chairs; and a circular wooden stand that holds a cello, a viola, and a pair of violins. This room's walls alternate between floor-to-ceiling mirrors, like the ones in the hallway, and wallpapered segments of gold fleur-de-lis on a dark green field. These latter panels are hung with landscape paintings in the old Renaissance style, with careful attention to fine details such as the individual leaves on a tree or the careful representation of each blade in a tuft of grass. It all seems so overly fastidious to Pomp, too perfect.

Several doors provide exits to the room. Viktor heads to one near the far right corner, while Frau Kretzer turns immediately left. Pomp follows the stern servant, but looks back toward Viktor as he waves and bids Frau Kretzer "goodbye" without looking behind him.

He stops suddenly, however, and looks into one of the mirrored panels that he was, up to that point, passing. Pomp sees, out of the corner of her eye, a faint flash, like twice-reflected candlelight seen through a white curtain down a long hallway, enough to know that something, some movement, had taken place, though the evidence had faded almost before it began.

"Frau Kretzer!" Viktor calls out.

The servant stops, turning wordlessly to the master of the house.

"Did you see something flash just now, Frau Kretzer?" His face holds a trace of suspicion.

"Some . . . thing, Graf?" she stifles a smile.

He turns to look at her, his smile gone.

Her smile is subdued behind pursed lips. "No, milord."

"No," Viktor repeats. Then, turning his back to her, "Thank you, Frau Kretzer."

The nobleman quickly exits the chamber.

Frau Kretzer stands still, at attention, staring at the space the graf has vacated. Pomp thinks that the old woman is staring far longer than is needful. The master is gone, shouldn't the servant be attending to other duties?

Then, as if a spell had been broken, the maid wheels around and quickly walks through her destination door.

Pomp follows, taking careful note of all she sees. Von Helmutter's ghost had fled here, intentionally. What was it he had said about finding his books? Something about another entrance to the underworld?

This, then, will be Pomp's base of operations. She will watch the residents closely and learn whatever she can until Heraclix returns, when she and the golem can flush out and exact vengeance on the sorcerer. She will continue to learn more of this, what was it called? Patience?

And yet . . . and yet.

CHAPTER 17

At first, Heraclix thought that he had again lost a part of his senses. He heard voices and the trundling of wagon wheels beneath him. Somewhere nearby horses snorted and whinnied. He tried to blink his eyes, but they were stuck wide open. His vision was not completely gone, but he was confined to a tight, dark space. He strained to move, but only his eyes responded, allowing him to see his circumstance, though he could do nothing about it. He was in a leather-lined box. The box was moving. And he was very cold. He wished he could at least shiver a bit in order to warm up, but even this pitiful comfort was denied him.

He listened carefully, taking in all the sounds his scarred ears could receive. Laughter above, and a loud thump to the side of him—along with the sound of horses and wagon wheels—helped him to understand the position he was in. He was encased in a box or coffin, with Al'ghul and Mehmet and possibly another sitting atop the box. The horses were off to his right, which must have been the front of the wagon. The riders and driver would occasionally shift their feet, inadvertently kicking the right side of his box. Once in a great while, someone would intentionally kick the box hard and Heraclix would hear Mehmet shout out "How are you doing in there? Still . . . alive?"

There were surprisingly few stretches of quiet. Mehmet really liked to talk. Amidst the seeming hours of banality, Heraclix was careful to mentally note and memorize certain snippets and conversations.

"Kaleel? Ha! You needn't worry about him, young one. I have sent him on a quest, which he is compelled to fulfill by forces inside him that even he cannot understand. You see, a bit of the warrior exists in all men, even the most effeminate. You should know this. When that warrior is coaxed out into the open, willingly or otherwise, the bloodlust can be unleashed by those who know the right charms, a bloodlust that is not easily sated. Kaleel's was easy to entice. I didn't have to do much to send him off to war. Presuming he makes it to the Sahel alive, he will fight the Fulani Jihad for Sileymaani Baal, an appropriately surnamed devil, a ruthless devil rat. Oh, Kaleel will be too busy to bother you for the remainder of his short life. Ha!"

"What do you hope we shall divine from the giant?" Al'ghul asked.

"His experiment was, obviously, successful. No doubt the knowledge that he holds will be of great worth to the society at Istanbul. This is something they have been aspiring to for hundreds, thousands of years. We have exclusive access to the receptacle for the information they wish to extract. It is mine ... ours to sell for whatever price we wish."

Several hours after Heraclix awoke, the wagon stopped. Those above shuffled their feet about, scuffing the wood of the footrest.

"I would like to check him," said Al'ghul.

"Suits me," said Mehmet. "He's not going anywhere. Only don't touch the marks on his forehead. You'll regret it if you do."

Heraclix couldn't tell if this was a warning or a threat.

He heard the boy unlatch the box and watched as the lid lifted. Cold air cascaded into what Heraclix could now see was a coffin. Al'ghul's face slipped into view against a background of stars. The moon cast its light from somewhere off to the side, giving the boy a malformed glow that rendered him hideous in the night.

"He's breathing," the boy said.

"Merely a formality," Mehmet called out from somewhere below. "Breathing isn't as important when you're halfway between life and death."

"No, I suppose not," the boy mumbled while looking into Heraclix's unblinking eyes.

"You've done well, my giant friend," Al'ghul said softly. "I have what I want now. Fuskana is mine. She is bound to me. I had hoped, but never really believed, that a girl such as her, a girl so beautiful, so pure, could be mine. I'm sorry it had to come to this. But thank you."

Then, turning his face toward the direction from which Mehmet's voice had sounded, the boy asked, "Will he be okay in there?"

"Yes—for our purposes, at least. He might be a little cold, a little uncomfortable. He might even suffer a panic attack, being unable to move, but what is that to us?"

Heraclix hadn't felt, up to that point, panic. Now, though, he had to suppress the anxiety that began to swell up from his gut into his chest, throat, and head. He tried to speak aloud to himself, but whatever power gripped his body also held his tongue. Not that having a voice would help him. Judging from the lack of noise, they were in some remote location away from civilization. All he could hear were Al'ghul, Mehmet, the horses and . . . someone else. Another pair of feet, he thought, slowly shuffling around the wagon. When the wagon door below him opened, then shut with Al'ghul in plain sight and Mehmet's droning voice distant, he was sure of it. There was another person, a silent person, moving slowly, with them. Could it be Fuskana, brokenhearted by the departure of her beloved Kaleel? There was no good way to tell.

Al'ghul shut the lid. Heraclix thought he heard a whisper of weeping beneath his coffin, then a hush fell over all.

A crack of thunder (or was it an explosion?), sounded without warning. The source was so close that Heraclix could hear the sizzling of electricity as the bolt disintegrated.

"Don't be frightened," Al'ghul's muffled voice rose up through the bottom of Heraclix's coffin. "I will protect you. I love you, you know."

There was no response as the rain began pouring down in a torrent.

Heraclix soon found that his coffin wasn't watertight. There was definitely a leak at the seams. He could do nothing to stop the water as it trickled in, taking refuge from the thunder that crashed outside. This continued for what seemed like a long time. Then, thankfully—though painfully—the rain drops stopped plopping into his box, freezing into icicles instead. He thought he could hear wind-whipped snow spattering against the side of his coffin. The thunder slowed, but continued for hours.

On what must have been the next morning, grunts of effort preceded the rocking of his coffin and the crack and tinkle of shattering ice.

Al'ghul's breath came out in steamy vapors as he spoke.

"There he is, Fuskana. Do you remember? The giant who rescued us."

Over the boy's shoulder the beautiful young Fuskana's face appeared. But it was devoid of the cheerfulness she had earlier shown. Her mouth was flat, neither smiling nor frowning. And her eyes were vacant, like the eyes of one who was raised during the trauma of war, eyes that have seen too much—vacant.

She looked down at Heraclix, but her expression remained unchanged.

Al'ghul put his hand on the girl's shoulder, and she moved with him, like a puppet under the puppet master's hand.

"Come," he said with disappointment. "Get back into the wagon. You'll be warmer in there."

The lid closed, trapping a tiny cloud of the boy's breath. It disappeared in the darkness before diffusing across Heraclix's face. It was the only warmth he would feel for days.

A shot rang out near the wagons. The echo that reverberated through the air indicated that they must be in some sort of canyon or up against a range of mountains.

The wagon stopped, but the sound of hoofbeats didn't. Someone was approaching. *Many someones*, Heraclix thought Pomp might say if she was here. He couldn't tell how many, not even when their horses slowed to a trot, surrounding the wagon.

"Stand and deliver!" came a shout in a thick Russian accent.

"Again?" shouted Al'ghul.

"Again, *da*! Only this time there will be no saving you."

Heraclix thought that this might be true.

"We still owe you for what you did to poor Yuri. Or, rather, you still owe us!"

A collective shout erupted from the robbers.

"Take the girl," the lead Cossack said.

Hoofs stuttered, and bridles clanked as the Russians moved to obey their orders.

Mehmet began chanting in Arabic.

Heraclix wondered if the old man was saying his last prayers before going to meet Allah in paradise.

Al'ghul taunted the Russians. "Any closer, and I'll cut the tongues out of your mouths."

The robbers laughed.

Fuskana screamed.

A general "huh?" rippled through the ranks of the Cossacks, followed by more specific shouts:

"Ah! What is that? It stings my bones!"

"My skin ... it's ... it's falling off!"

"What is happening to me?"

The voices rose into a crescendo of shouts and screams followed by a lone voice, that of a man aged well beyond the dusk of life, that trailed off as the wagon moved on: "Can't see. Can't see. What has happened to my eyes? I am blind. No. No! I have no eyes! I can't see! Where are the rest of you? Someone please help me ..."

The voice soon faded to silence behind them.

"H-how did you do that?" Al'ghul asked.

Mehmet answered. "In order to fully understand death, one must clearly understand the transitions between states of decay in mortality. Death is merely unfettered decay. All I did was speed up the process. You've never heard of a decrepit highwayman, have you?"

"No. No sir."

"And you never will."

"But why didn't you do that to them the first time they attacked us?" Al'ghul asked.

"These things come at a price, my boy. One doesn't go about altering one bit of the universal laws without paying for the balance, with interest, in another. Besides, your brother and the giant, as our newly-old friends have inferred, were doing just fine without me."

"But my brother died!" Al'ghul said.

"Careful boy," Mehmet warned in a low voice. "There's still a bit of balance owed to me. You are the beneficiary of some of my investment. Perhaps Fuskana there . . . perhaps she would prefer my company to yours?"

Al'ghul said nothing more . . .

. . . until the increase of bustling sounds and voices indicated that they had reached a major city, though Heraclix had no way of knowing where they were or how long they had been traveling. He tried to piece his situation together by catching snippets of conversation, but the words melted into an incomprehensible babble. All he knew was that most of the voices were speaking Turkish, with a smattering of Magyar and Serb.

Al'ghul spoke only enough to receive his orders from Mehmet, and the other responded in kind.

"How far?" the boy asked.

"Just past the gate. Park the horses there."

"How long?"

"About an hour. See that the horses are fed and watered."

"And what of us?"

"You'll be fine. I'll bring some bread when I return."

The air seeping into the seams of the coffin reeked of spices he hadn't smelt since . . . since a time he couldn't remember, though the odor was familiar and warm, comforting for reasons he couldn't fathom. His mind went reeling, searching for a window into these teases of memory that he couldn't quite resolve, like mirages in the heat of the desert—yet another analogy that he somehow understood, but knew not how. Frustration rose up in his chest, neck, and the wide space between his eyes, but was held still by the immobilization of his body, the urge to scream silenced behind his paralytic tongue. Blood, or whatever it was that coursed through his veins, flushed through his temples, the noise like the sound of rushing waters heard from afar.

Only when he calmed himself, more or less resigned to his situation, did he hear something other than his own physiological manifestations of anger.

"Kaleel?" A woman's voice. Fuskana.

"No, not Kaleel. Kaleel is gone now. Probably for good," Al'ghul replied.

"But . . . why?"

"That doesn't matter right now. What matters is that you are free to go, and you need to go now, while Mehmet is away."

"Mehmet . . . can't remember . . ."

"Don't try. Mehmet is a bad man, a selfish man, a sorcerer. You need to go now, Fuskana, before he returns."

"Where?" she asked. Heraclix wondered if the girl would ever be able to make a decision by or for herself.

"Go north to Sofia. Here is a bag full of *Kuruş* coins. This will buy your passage and hold you over until you can find your family again.

"And you?" she said with more concern than Heraclix felt the boy deserved.

"I will take care of myself . . . and the giant."

"I . . . remember . . . the giant, I think."

"There is much that you won't remember. Allah is merciful to take some memories away. Now go!"

"But I can't . . ."

"Go!" the boy yelled loud enough that she jumped in her seat. She then got out of it.

The girl's crying fell away as the boy's rose above.

Two thumps and a loud crack sounded on the side of the coffin, at the seam, followed by the rush of air into the compartment.

Tears streamed from Al'ghul's eyes, falling onto Heraclix's chest before freezing.

"You would be right to kill me," the boy said to the immobile golem. "And you may. I deserve it. Better to die at your hands, though, than to suffer at the hands of a madman, or cause Fuskana to suffer further under his enchantments."

He paused, wiping tears from his cheeks before continuing the monologue. "You see, I had Fuskana. But she was not mine. I didn't earn her. I thought she would love me, if I could have all of her attentions. Only now I know that one cannot fall in love when one is forced into it. I am a fool. Kaleel is now likely dead, or soon will be. I cannot fix either of those things now. But I can, and have, set Fuskana free. And now I shall free you. Do what you will. I have betrayed you and deserve whatever you see fit to inflict upon me."

The boy reached down and touched Heraclix's forehead, scrubbing at the skin, as if to remove a mark.

"Once I clean the sigils from your head, you will be free. You will be momentarily disoriented, but balance will come to you shortly."

Al'ghul continued to rub Heraclix's forehead, becoming more frantic as time wasted away.

Then something inside Heraclix snapped. He drew in a sharp breath, his back heaving from the influx of cold air into his lungs and the instantaneous restoration of sensation to his body. He blinked, breathing heavily, flexed his fingers and rotated his ankles. He drew his knees up and a wave of nausea swept over him as the world spun uncontrollably around him.

"That should be it," Al'ghul said, putting a hand underneath the golem's shoulder. "I can't lift you. You're going to have to sit up. Mehmet will be back soon. And if we're not gone, the consequences will be bad, not just for me, but for both of us. Come, get up."

Heraclix hadn't felt so weak since his rebirth in Mowler's apartment. The sensations were much the same, though Al'ghul's explanation of the situation at least provided a context to what was happening.

He rolled onto his side and pushed himself up. The coffin lid fell clumsily on him until Al'ghul strained with both arms to lift it up off of him.

Heraclix lifted a leg over the edge and rolled out of the coffin onto the wagon's footrest. He felt vitality come to him, not to its full strength, but enough to get down from the wagon. Al'ghul jumped down beside him.

The left hand was around Al'ghul's neck before Heraclix could even think.

"No!" the giant yelled. "I won't let you do this!" Al'ghul thought his life had, indeed, ended at that moment. But he didn't realize that Heraclix wasn't talking to the boy, but to his own hand. The golem poured all of his energy into controlling the hand, willing it to release the boy. Al'ghul, thankful to be alive, massaged his own neck and gasped in shallow breaths. "Though I have every reason to kill you," Heraclix said decisively, "you are young and impressionable. I understand what it means to love deeply and the lengths to which one will go to secure the one you love. It might be too late for my own redemption, but for you, so young, there is still time to learn patience, the true measure of love. Come," Heraclix said, grabbing the boy by the scruff of his shirt. "Which direction?"

Al'ghul pointed. Heraclix walked with the boy in tow.

"Wait!" Al'ghul protested. "The horses."

Heraclix immediately saw the wisdom of what the boy was hinting. The pair unhitched the horses from the wagon. Al'ghul took some blankets out of the wagon and put them on the horses as makeshift saddles. After quickly rigging up the bits, the pair were off.

"Where are we?" Heraclix asked as they wound through the streets.

"Edirne," the boy croaked.

"What did Mehmet plan to do here?"

"I don't know what he wants here. We were headed to Istanbul. He had arranged to sell you to a group of mystics."

"The Shadow Divan," Heraclix said, the memory coming unbidden. "You spoke a part of their creed back in Sofia. I take it you learned it from Mehmet?"

"I did, I suppose," the boy said. "Though I was only parroting what Mehmet had taught me."

"Careful where you parrot, and to whom," Heraclix said. "How well can you ride a horse?"

"As well as anyone."

"Then ride fast!"

The pair galloped out through the southeast gate, toward Istanbul, nearly knocking the city guard off their feet as they passed.

"We will meet the Divan," Heraclix shouted above the rushing wind, "on our own terms! Mehmet won't like the results, I think."

Al'ghul smiled for the first time in what felt like weeks.

CHAPTER 18

Frau Kretzer goes through a door. Steam and the smell of baked bread pour out as she walks into the kitchen. Pomp has a hard time finding a perch that isn't uncomfortably hot, and she sits as far from the steaming pots as she can so that her view is unobstructed by anything but the sweat in her eyes.

The maid pulls up a stool and lights a meerschaum pipe, exhaling her exhaustion in a puff of tobacco smoke.

"Still don't like him, do you?" an old man's voice crackles from another doorway, startling the maid.

"Must you always be lurking?" she says.

The old man's soft chuckle turns to a coughing laugh. "Not always," he says, "I'm sure I won't be here much longer to lurk around anything but the cemetery and your memories."

"What makes you so sure?" Frau Kretzer asks.

"I've seen the end from the beginning. The graf is back and healthy, mentally and physically. I worked for years trying to keep this house together, teaching the young Lady Adelaide how to take care of family affairs. I feared that she would never learn, so I put all my efforts into running this house efficiently. Then, when the graf came back, I felt it leave me."

"It?"

"The desire and energy to be in charge. I'm an old man. I'm ready for my final rest. But I cannot rest. I will work myself to death and be satisfied."

"You can't leave without my permission," Frau Kretzer jokes, though a certain soft sadness has entered her voice. "Besides, I still don't know the full story behind how the graf came back, and he is a closed book."

"Very well, but the story won't make sense unless I first tell you about the boy who grew to be a man, of sorts."

"Of sorts?"

"In some ways, young Viktor Edelweir was quite mature. For instance, he was a likable boy, easy to engage in conversation—the sort of person who makes you feel important when he asks a question of you, no matter how trivial. In other ways, he was overtaken by whims and fancies far into adulthood."

"Such as?"

"Such as the sort that made his chosen avocation a trap."

Frau Kretzer's face contorts in confusion.

"Let me explain," the old man continues. "The boy, emerging into manhood, learned to read. He was quite gifted in reading and language. Of course, he knew German, a great deal of Magyar, even some Russian. But his real love was Arabic. I remember him spending hours by the fire in winter reading Arabic poetry and philosophical texts. I'm sure that, in his mind, the snow-covered hills became sand dunes; the evergreen trees, palms; and the family horses, camels."

"A dreamer, then?" Frau Kretzer asked.

"A dreamer, but one whose reality moved in accord with his dreams. This fancy had a powerful influence on him. So much so that he dared cross the border into Ottoman territory, claiming to be an emissary of good will, which he was, in his own foolhardy way. Now the Turkish guards suspected that he was a spy. And they weren't about to give him access to their empire, else they find their heads on a pole over their own guard tower. At least that was their resolve until he spoke. He recited a poem about a man's love for his camel with such passion and candor that the Turks became interested in him. Being such a gregarious young man and so knowledge-able about Ottoman culture and philosophy—not to mention Arabic literature—he soon had their favor, and they let him enter, though he was, no doubt, watched closely, given the tensions that existed back then between the Ottomans and our Holy Roman Empire."

"Still exist," Frau Kretzer says.

"Not to the same extent. Things were much more likely to ignite into open war at that point than they are now."

"So, continue," she says.

"So Viktor Edelweir disappeared into the Turkish lands. At about that time, his cousin, Lady Adelaide, was born."

"Our Lady Adelaide?"

"The same."

"Twenty some years ago," Frau Kretzer confirms.

"Twenty one, to be exact, though the number of years isn't important. What is important is that both Lord and Lady Edelweir had desires to go find the man-child, to rescue him, but they were unable to undertake such a quest due to the fact that the Lord and Lady Adelaide had died under mysterious circumstances, leaving our Lady Adelaide in their care. And, though they had servants who might have raised the young lady, the Edelweirs couldn't bear to leave her out of their direct charge until she was mature enough to run the place herself."

"They must have been very protective," Frau Kretzer says.

"Yes! Ten years they waited, until the tensions between the two countries had abated a bit, and they could leave their niece in charge of the house servants. Oh, and there was the matter of the letter, as well."

"The letter," Frau Kretzer states, as if she already knows of the document.

"The only item remaining after the Lord and Lady were killed by a wandering band of rogue Serbs. The barely-legible, barely-intelligible missive: 'Need money. Opium is killing me, keeping me alive. Owe debts to brothels and creditors. Please send money. With my love and regret, Viktor.'"

"Now why would someone write such a thing? Why admit all those things?" Frau Kretzer asks.

"Repentance? The need for frank admission that would allow forgiveness for a prodigal son? Perhaps a drugged plea for help? Or maybe Viktor didn't write it at all. Maybe it was a ruse, a ransom demand for a dead hostage. Whatever it was, it drew the couple to their doom."

"And here we are," the maid says. "Viktor Edelweir has returned, and is set to marry his cousin, the Lady Adelaide."

"And there you are," a new voice says.

Pomp looks to the outside doorway and sees a stout man in a fine black wool coat. He is short and bald and fat and wears a pair of round-lensed spectacles. He looks like a smiling, scholarly bulldog.

"Lescher! You scalawag!" says Frau Kretzer. Pomp cannot tell if she is serious or just teasing.

"Frau Kretzer! Such language! It burns my little ears!" Lescher feigns pain, covering his ears with his fists.

"I'd tear those little ears from your head if they didn't belong to your lord," she says with force. Pomp is convinced that she isn't merely teasing.

". . . who will be arriving at any moment," says Lescher.

"What?" says the old man.

"What, indeed," Frau Kretzer says. "Are you asking us or telling us?"

"I am telling you," he said, dipping his head condescendingly. "He is coming and will be here soon."

"Well, at least one of our guests will brighten our day," she says.

"Still stinging from the potato liquor incident, eh, Frau Kretzer?"

The stool screeches as she dismounts from it and stomps toward the doorway. The old man intercedes and is nearly bowled over by the maid, who obviously isn't trying to get to Lescher to congratulate him on his cleverness.

"Ahem!" an exaggerated voice says from outside, a young voice projecting from behind Lescher.

All of the action suddenly stops.

Pomp knows she has heard this voice before.

"As I said," says Lescher, "my lord."

Von Graeb enters the kitchen, which now seems entirely too small and crowded. He glances disappointingly at each of the servants. His new uniform, matching Viktor's black coats and skull-emblazoned fez, doesn't detract from his handsomeness, though it does create an aura of dissonance between his dress and his personality.

"Pardon me for intruding," he tips his hat to Frau Kretzer, gives a slight bow to the old man.

"Sir," Frau Kretzer says demurely, "forgive an old maid for asking, but oughtn't you to have come through the front door?"

Von Graeb reaches into a pouch and withdraws a pair of coins. Handing one to each of the house servants, he explains "I have business to attend to which requires a more anonymous entrance."

The two servants smile their wrecked-tooth smiles, holding the coins up for Lescher to see. Lescher merely rolls his eyes.

Pomp's attention, needless to say, has been gotten! She leaves the servants and follows Von Graeb through the inner door, into the parlor.

The soldier walks through the parlor slowly, his thoughts obviously elsewhere. A look of concern sets into his face. He stops at a stringed instrument stand that held a pair of violins, a viola, and a cello. He plucks each string of each instrument without removing them from the stand. The violins, plucked last, are badly out of tune. He winces at their awkward pizzicato. This seems to bring him out of his daze and he exits the parlor.

Pomp continues to follow him as he weaves his way through hallways, past large pillars, outdoors on a veranda, then back indoors again. It will take some time, Pomp thinks, before she will be familiar enough with this manor to negotiate its maze without having to guess at her location. She is now lost.

As Von Graeb knocks on a door, however, she seems to remember that she has been here before. This is confirmed as the door opens to reveal Lady Adelaide, backlit by a room full of enough lit candles to mimic the sunrise. The curtains are drawn to block out any light not generated by the candles, yet their flames are so numerous that they blaze like a forest fire. The lady's shadow spills onto the floor and up Von Graeb's torso, disappearing into the creases of his black uniform until it reappears to envelop him as he enters the doorway.

"The sun *is out*!" Von Graeb teases her.

"My cousin said that I should learn to concentrate better, to focus more."

"Mmm?" Von Graeb forces a smile down, but his eyes betray him.

"You're laughing at me!" she says, beginning to laugh herself.

"Not laughing, though amused, I'll admit."

"Don't make fun of my cousin," she says, pointing at Von Graeb's chest.

"Oh, I should never do such a thing, though . . ."

"Though what?"

"Never mind. Nothing. Really."

"Though what?" she says.

Von Graeb grows thoughtful, carefully articulating words in his mind before letting them out of his mouth.

"The minister of defense, your cousin, is as capable a man as any. Since the untimely death of Graf Von Helmutter, Graf Edelweir has instilled a discipline in the imperial guard that I haven't seen for some time. He is strict, but fair—an admirable combination of traits for one in his position. I have been a willing and loyal officer and have grown to trust his judgment . . ." he pauses, ". . . insofar as it regards leading the guard."

"But . . ." she prompts him.

"But I think that his choice of emphasis should be carefully considered by the emperor."

"Emphasis?"

"Graf Edelweir seems to be overly concerned with Prussia."

"And you are not?"

"I am, truth be told. And the graf has reason to be, as well. But there are other threats, as well."

"The Ottomans?"

"Yes."

"But Viktor lived among them for years. He has said that we misunderstand them, that they are eager for peace."

"In my experience, there are two reasons for peace overtures. First, to recover from war and, second, to prepare for it. They have already recovered from their most recent conflicts."

Lady Adelaide thinks on his words.

"But," he says, "we are not here to discuss war or peace, but wedding plans for you," he breathes in sharply and straightens his back, trying to maintain decorum, "and Lord Edelweir."

She smiles. "Yes. We shall have to have a dinner, of course, to officially announce the engagement."

"Of course. And who shall be invited?"

"Well, my cousin is my only living family, though there are a dozen or so friends of my parents that should attend. And, of course, you. And Joseph."

"Joseph?"

"The emperor."

"Yes, I forget that you and he . . ."

"Are friends? Since my childhood, though he is much older than me. Still, we are related, if distantly. Kinship and friendship have bound us together for many years. Ah," a look of worry crosses Lady Adelaide's face. "Of course, he will need his entourage with him, won't he?"

"Yes, ministers and their mistresses," he says.

"Felix, you are a tease!" she laughs.

"But my thoughts on the logistics of it all are serious business. This will be a big affair."

"And shouldn't it be?"

"It should. But imagine, then, how the wedding—"

"That," she interrupts, "is the bride's family's responsibility. And since I have control over my own estate, the wedding shall be as extravagant as I wish. Besides, I'm sure Joseph will want to contribute to the celebration as well."

"First things first. I will compile a guest list. Perhaps you can work with your friend, the emperor, to arrange a location?"

"Consider it done," she says.

"I dare not race you to the completion of your task. You would surely win." He nods his head in a mock bow.

"Do stop making fun of me, Felix. Make a guest list instead."

He turns away from her, toward the doorway, then stops suddenly.

Graf Viktor Von Edelweir stands in the doorway.

"Major," the graf says sternly. Then, his countenance changing, he smiles warmly. "It is good to see you."

"Thank you, mein herr," Von Graeb's voice is a mix of confidence and hesitation.

"I was just coming to confirm with Lady Adelaide that we were, indeed, preparing to make an official announcement. Forgive my eavesdropping, but it sounds like I'm right on time?"

"Yes, sir—you are indeed," the major says with a smile.

"Well, then," Viktor looks past Von Graeb's shoulder toward his cousin. "Addy, how can I help facilitate things?"

"For now, we need to keep the engagement confidential," she says.

"Of course," Viktor says. "Who knows? You, the major here, and me, obviously . . ."

"And the emperor," Lady Adelaide adds.

"Good. Four people whom I know can keep a confidence. And what of the date of the dinner?"

"We haven't yet finalized the date," Von Graeb says. "Negotiations have been stalled for the moment."

They all laugh.

The words become a drone in Pomp's ears, like the sound of her wings on a long journey. She is becoming bored of all the talking and, to tell the truth, questioning the judgment of the good Lady Adelaide who will, it seems, marry Viktor Edelweir. If anything, the Lady Adelaide should marry the good Major Von Graeb! There is something Pomp doesn't like about Von Edelweir, though she can't quite place her finger on it. It takes all she has to hold herself back from pulling a prank of some kind or another on Lady Adelaide and Graf Von Edelweir. She can hardly contain herself.

Bored, jealous. A bad combination. She decides it best to leave for a time and visit the emperor's palace, if she can find it. What could be more exciting than seeing an emperor, after all?

CHAPTER 19

Worry spread through Heraclix's veins. The young man, Al'ghul, could be baiting him into another trap. But Heraclix trusted, maybe naively, that the boy was truly repentant. He had to hope that there was some good left in his young heart. After all, Heraclix had found goodness in his own heart despite the things he knew, or suspected he knew, about his life before undeath. Maybe he should do as the boy had done when surrendering himself to the golem: submit himself to his well-deserved fate and suffer the natural consequences of wrongdoing. But another thought overrode the guilt of past misdeeds. If he merely submitted to Mowler and allowed the sorcerer to gain power unfettered, surely the world would suffer far more than whatever mayhem his own actions had engendered. No, in this instance the lesser, repentant evil would continue to fight against the greater, unrepentant one. This would require the forming of alliances with others who opposed Mowler or swaying those who did not. He feared that he couldn't fight Mowler alone, and Pomp had been gone for some time now. This was Heraclix's impetus for the present journey to Istanbul.

They traveled east and south, hoping to beat Mehmet to the city. Al'ghul, knowing that he was slowing the pair down, allowed Heraclix to lead his horse as he slept in the saddle. He slept fitfully, frequently bumped awake by the steed's uneven gait. He sometimes half-awoke to find the giant staring at him and wondered what this creature, who had seen death, saw in him—a youth of not much worth to anyone.

The air warmed as they crossed the plains between Edirne and Istanbul, thawing the latent shards of ice in Heraclix's veins. They only occasionally crossed the roads between the two cities, preferring to stay in the countryside in order to avoid frequent contact with the main artery of information that could lead Mehmet to them. All the speed in the world wouldn't help them if their nemesis determined their destination before their arrival.

They could smell Istanbul before they saw it. The aroma of spices and cooking fish was so strong that the odor reached them even before they could see the smoke rising from the city's chimneys. Their eyes and noses continued to disagree when they saw smoke on the horizon but smelled salt water. Soon, they came close enough to the city to see a group of the Sultan's soldiers loitering, bored, outside a guard post near the city gate. The sound of waves reached their ears, yet their skin felt hotter and hotter as they neared the Bosphorus Strait.

The soldiers were dressed in tan coats sewn with too many buttons. Those who kept their hats on wore red fezzes. Unlike their counterpoints in the Holy Roman Empire, their faces were unshaven, some wearing a full beard, others wearing a thin pointed mustache and chin beard only. There was no alcohol to be seen among them. It was apparent to Heraclix now that he had arrived in the heart of an entirely different empire, now, that of Mustafa, Sultan of the Ottoman Empire.

Still, empires apart, many actions and reactions remained the same. The soldiers, though they had willfully ignored dozens of people who passed their post, suddenly stiffened upon seeing the giant approach. They tugged each other's sleeves, muttered amongst themselves, grabbed their weapons and cautiously approached Heraclix and his guide. The travelers dismounted, approaching the soldiers at their own level in an effort to appear non-threatening. *This might not work*, Heraclix thought.

Al'ghul gave out some kind of greeting and explanation. Though Heraclix wasn't familiar with this dialect, he caught the words "strangers," "welcome," and "Padishah."

"No need to cover for your friend," one of the guards said. "He is obviously a foreigner."

The speaker was very thin and not very tall, a handsome man, olive-skinned, with sharply defined cheekbones and a pointy chin that seemed even more elongated by a pencil-thin black goatee and mustache. The single medal on his chest, a brass crescent moon and star, was more adornment than the other men wore.

"And where do you hail from, friend?" The soldier asked in perfect High German. The intonation and language of the question signaled a doubled inquiry, Heraclix thought, seeking answers of both geography and intent.

"Friend," Heraclix said.

The soldier walked closer. The group of guards followed behind more slowly.

"Again, where are you from?"

"I hardly know," Heraclix said.

"You have known better times, haven't you, traveler?" the soldier said, his face contorting with disgust.

"I must admit that I don't know that for sure, either."

"You must know where you just came from. Or is your amnesia complete?" the soldier asked in a decidedly accusatory tone.

"We came from Sofia," Al'ghul said.

The soldier glared at the boy. "You will speak when spoken to, whelp!"

Al'ghul shrank back. The other soldiers whispered jokes between themselves. The man didn't smile.

Heraclix could hear the clink of the man's spurs as he circled the giant. *He must be a cavalry officer*, Heraclix thought. *But where is his horse?* He looked around, but saw no animal tethered to the hitching post outside the guard shack.

The officer continued to pace, circling Heraclix two, three, four times—silent, examining, thinking. Finally, he stopped at Heraclix's left flank, just outside the giant's field of vision, though the murderous blue eye strained to see beyond the edge of his head. He dare not turn his head or move suddenly. Al'ghul was vulnerable and surrounded by the remaining troops.

Heraclix heard a sniff as the officer breathed in before pronouncing what sounded like a verdict coming from a judge.

"You shall not enter! You are too large for our streets, your memory is failing, you could be criminally insane for all I know, and your face will terrify our women. You must go back," he paused momentarily, "to Edirne."

Al'ghul gasped. Heraclix turned to face the officer, who was now smiling at his own apparently clever deduction.

"You cannot travel through the Sultan's lands without word coming around. Leave the roads, if you like. Our eyes are everywhere."

The soldiers nodded.

"I am afraid that we will need to keep an especially sharp eye on you," the officer said. "Large as you are, you can't simply go barreling in and out of our cities like you did in your flight from Edirne. No, we expect better manners here, more respect for the citizenry. I'm sorry, but we shall have to retain you."

The soldiers were already closing in on the pair.

"But we have come as brethren in the shadow of death," Al'ghul blurted.

The soldiers looked at one another with expressions of puzzlement, followed by shrugs.

The officer, however, turned to the boy and glared at him like one who has just been bested in a game of chess by a socially inferior opponent.

"Come again?" he said, cocking his head to hear the boy more clearly.

"We have come as brethren in the shadow of death . . ." the boy repeated.

". . . seeking refuge in the kingdoms of light," Heraclix finished the greeting. The words came to him reflexively, unbidden.

The soldiers muttered among themselves, conjecturing about the nature of the strangers' formulaic speech.

"Silence!" the officer shouted at his men, who jumped back and immediately formed a line, standing at attention. Their smiles fled.

The pride that had pervaded the officer's attitude slipped away into a guarded but curious respect.

"Wherein do you seek passage?" he said to Al'ghul.

The soldiers, holding stock still at attention, tried, unsuccessfully, to communicate with each other with only the movement of their eyes.

Al'ghul relaxed as he recalled Mehmet's teachings. "We seek passage to the stronghold of the Shadow Divan."

"The Shadow Divan," the officer said. "You shall receive passage."

The soldiers tried harder than ever to talk with their eyes, frantically moving them around and around, side to side, like blind lunatics.

"You! Dog!" the officer yelled at a man at the end of the line. "Fetch my horse!"

The soldier dutifully peeled away from his companions and ran, full sprint, through the city gate, plowing over a small group of civilians.

The officer, smiling at Heraclix and Al'ghul, spoke in softer, more friendly tones now. "Aye, you shall receive safe passage to the stronghold of the Shadow Divan, my brethren."

Al'ghul smiled up at the giant, proud that he had recalled the words that Mehmet had taught him. Heraclix forced a smile, trying to reassure the boy that he had done well, while at the same time trying to stifle the fear arising within him. Not a fear of what was to come, but the fear of what the Shadow Divan might reveal about what once was and what he had once been. Mercifully, the soldier that had been ordered to retrieve the officer's horse returned with the steed, interrupting the nascent chain of logic that was forming in Heraclix's head. The golem put his thoughts aside and mounted his own horse. Confirmation of his suspicions would come soon enough, he thought.

The officer and Al'ghul mounted their horses. After a curt series of orders to his men, the officer set off, bidding the travelers to follow him toward the heart of the city.

CHAPTER 20

Pomp flies through Vienna, searching for the imperial palace. Cathedral, church, cathedral, church; too many cathedrals and churches! And—the palace! There it is, no mistaking. Throngs are there, concentric circles of people growing richer and more widely recognizable (Pomp presumes) as she flies closer to the main entrance. The only exception is a pair of guards, dressed in the black uniforms and skull-emblazoned-fezzes that identify them as members of the imperial guard. Pomp doesn't remember these two guards, though she is certain she has seen most, if not all, of the elite troops since she has met Heraclix. Regardless of who they are, Pomp is confident that they don't enjoy (if that is the right word) the same social status as the civilians who ignore them. She invisibly bows to the guards and lifts her nose up at the frilly-cuffed *petty* nobles, then flies over their heads into the palace, dodging towering powdered wigs the whole way.

The choked hallway leads to a more spacious ballroom. At the head of this is an alcove. This alcove provides a shelter, of sorts, from the music and loud talking that bubbles up from the ballroom floor and its surrounding hallways. The centerpiece of the alcove, around which all else swirls, is a small, ornately carved desk. Sitting at the desk on an equally ornately carved chair, is a small man, elegantly dressed, with a steely look of determination in his eyes, as if he is forcing himself to remain focused. Pomp hasn't yet decided if she thinks he is a good man or not, but he does catch her interest. He is obviously a man of great importance—the only one seated in this mass of people. Maybe this is the emperor? But, if it weren't for his clothes, he would look so . . . ordinary. And how could an emperor, the ruler of the Holy Roman Empire, allow himself to yawn so openly in front of his subjects?

His ennui wouldn't stand out so much were it not for the parade of eccentricity that circles around the man. Courtiers like exotic animals vie for the emperor's attention either subtly or openly in a shameless dance for approval. But still he sits, bored, looking at the carnival yet seeing right through it, looking for something else, something apparently unobtainable here, despite the glittering spectacle.

The crowd is like a sea: in places roiling, in others calm. Pomp notes with great pleasure that each "wave" is different. She is drawn in by the strangeness of it all, like a child to a kaleidoscope.

The first to catch her attention is a brass-helmeted man, or is it a bird? Do men ever grow wings? And how are these wings attached to the man's back through his crisp, pressed blue uniform? It's comical how the . . . man, she must suppose it is . . . nearly knocks another guest over with every flamboyant gesture of his hands. Maybe he *does* think he is a bird, the way he flaps his arms around as he squawks words. The medals on his chest rattle and clink as he gesticulates, mimicking an imaginary sword fight. Pomp worries that he might absentmindedly draw the saber that hangs so dangerously from his belt and accidentally kill a guest as he tells his story. That is, if he doesn't accidentally kill someone with the pair of wings jutting from his back first.

"Ah, the Prussian pride! Yes, I am all too familiar with it. A Prussian officer would rather die than submit, which might seem admirable to some, imprudent to others. I know of what I speak! It wasn't many years ago. But I cannot give exact details as to dates and places, as I wish to prevent any embarrassment to the men who were my commanding officers at the time, though they are well-known hussars."

The man has a strange accent. Of course! This bird man is one of the famed Polish hussars. How exciting! She has heard of them and their bravery, how they seem to fly while charging into battle on horseback, like angels of death. But she has never seen one in person, until now.

"It would not do well for my own command if my men were to find out the circumstances surrounding the incident, for I was, admittedly, on a bit of a side venture."

He and his audience laugh. Pomp laughs too, not at the lame joke, but at the utter ridiculousness of the man. He is very tall and slender, with a hooked nose that only strengthens the impression, together with the wings on his back, of a vulture.

"We camped very close to the Prussians, at the opposite end of the valley. I suppose we could have engaged them there, but I was keen to save my men the bother of having to fight in the cold of winter without an adequate supply of wine. Besides, there was little cover, and casualties would be high on both sides. So I sent a missive to another junior commander there, challenging him to a duel. Whoever lost would, of course, arrange a retreat, while the victor would take the valley. Both I and my Prussian opponent knew, contrary to the thoughts of our so-called superiors, that the valley was of little consequence. But I knew that he wouldn't turn down the opportunity for a good duel. Besides, there was the matter of his sister and myself when I attended university at Leipzig, but that is another matter, entirely."

Again the crowd and Pomp laugh for different reasons.

"So we arranged to secretly meet: myself and the Prussian, each with a second and a doctor. I chose the time and location: sunrise over the westernmost hill, and he chose the weapons: sabers. I was delighted with his choice."

The hussar pats the hilt of his saber as if it is his favorite dog.

"Of course, he chose sabers over a thrusting weapon because of the sheer lethality of it. Prussians would rather die dueling than suffer the shame of a mere wounding." He shakes his head, then looks off into the distance, remembering. "It was a ferocious fight. He was an excellent swordsman, but I prevailed, scoring him across the left cheek. His doctor bandaged the wound, and I thought we had settled the matter when he again demanded satisfaction. So I satisfied him with another score across the opposite cheek. This was attended to by his doctor, but the stubborn Prussian wanted more. Of course, he was already fatigued from the two wounds, not to mention being distracted by the bulky bandages under his eyes. Yet he persisted. So I did, too, obliging his desires for another wound. I opened a gash across his forehead that would show in the mirror till his dying day, once the blood was washed out of his eyes. This merely elicited a laugh from him and the comment 'I'm afraid you'll have to kill me to finish this,' after which he set on me again, knocking his own doctor to the ground. He swung blindly, blood pouring into his eyes. It was ludicrous! He almost hit his own second! The companion had to put up his own sword to avoid being hit by his own man! The Prussian, thinking he had found me, swung wildly, arcing circles in the Hungarian manner. He almost succeeded in hitting everyone but me! It was silly, pitiful, really. But I am a gracious foe. I had no desire to fulfill his death wish, so I, rather inconveniently for him, stabbed through his sword arm. His second, who was also the man's sergeant, interceded on his now-unconscious superior's behalf, saying he would honor the agreement and withdraw his troops."

The crowd laughs and applauds. Pomp wonders at their collective grim sense of humor. Should nobles joke about such serious matters? It is, she admits, difficult not to laugh at such an outrageous man as the Hussar.

Pomp turns to see Viktor engaged in a conversation with an old man whose face hasn't shed its crust in a long, long time. A scowl seems to be permanently engraved on his face. Graf Von Edelweir seems warm and friendly in comparison.

"You see," says Viktor, whose skull-emblazoned-fez rests on one arm, the other hand busied with a glass of wine. "There is little, topographically speaking, that would keep Prussia from stabbing through your state toward Vienna, which will be its main target."

"Saxony is small, but not weak," the scowling one says with hardly a movement of his taut facial muscles.

"No one doubts the bravery of Saxony's armies. Your men have been tried and battlefield tested. But there are only so many of you. It's only a matter of time before a mobilized Prussian army outflanks you. We have no desire to upstage your valiant men. We sense that your needs and our needs are mutual. We only wish to help."

The man snorts, scoffing, then smiles. It's the first time Pomp has seen him smile. It isn't a pleasant smile.

"Of course it benefits you to ally with us. We would be your first line of defense."

"*Defense*," Viktor says, "is most *definitely not* our interest."

The man's wicked smile grows even wider. His shoulders relax. He cocks his head back and looks intently into the graf's eyes.

"Now you've got my attention."

Pomp's attention shifts elsewhere, to a shifty-looking woman on the outskirts of conversation.

She is dark-haired, unhealthily thin, and not particularly attractive despite the abundance of makeup she uses to cover her sickly appearance: large red lips stand out in contrast against her thin, pale, skeletal face. She wears a burgundy dress that would have been the height of trendy fashion two decades ago and shows too much, unless the onlooker prefers to see the sternum bone between her breasts. She holds a metal stick to which is attached a pair of spectacles, which she uses as a sort of masque, though the clear lenses do nothing to hide her peeping eyes.

Pomp alights atop the woman's hair. The woman pauses when she feels the added weight, then continues stalking. She goes from group to group, vacillating between attempts to interject herself into the conversation and recoiling from the groups who are having them. The reactions to her hesitant intrusions and withdrawals are all the same: after a brief interruption on the part of those conversing, the subject changes, or the speakers shift their bodies to present their backs to the intruder. At this point, the woman backs out with a sneer, then quickly regains her smile as she spies another destination nearby.

Pomp watches this strange behavior, until, at last, she is so bored with the woman's actions and the conversants' predictable reactions that she abandons the glasses and alights on the wig of an old man engaged in a conversation with two other elderly men. They are all three intently listening to one another, as if taking mental notes for later study or reference.

The first, a man of medium build with a face that, while not thin, seems to vertically stretch, speaks in a high voice that sounds far younger than his wrinkled skin and gray hairs indicate.

"Ghosts," he says to the other two, "are clearly the spirits of the departed. The scriptures are clear on the matter, and if you take any time to interview those who have recently lost a family member, they will tell you that, in their hearts, they know this to be true."

"I must disagree," says another, a man so short that he borders on dwarfism. "First of all, the scriptures are themselves ghosts of a bygone era. And the emotional testimonies of those whose spiritual encounter hinges upon the loss of a loved one are the product of grief-stricken delusion, despite their sentimental sincerity."

The third, a bushy-eyebrowed fellow of similarly diminutive stature, looks at one, then the other with large owlish eyes, his head swiveling from side to side like the wizened bird. "I suppose it is a matter of faith in the unseen versus evidence of the seen," he says, acting as intermediary.

"But faith," says the long-faced one, "by its very definition implies the unseeable—that which does not appear in the visible realm."

"Which makes it so much the weaker argument against reason," the dwarfish one says. "Reason is based on the evidence of the seen, therefore faith, not being demonstrable by means of measurable perception, might just as well be insanity."

"No doubt," the owl-eyed one says, "ghostly visitations are often mated with stories of wild fancy."

"And *no doubt*," the long-faced one says defensively, "the human mind, when exposed to a glimpse of the divine, cannot contain nor explain the glories beheld by the spiritual eyes."

The intermediary turns to him. "Indeed. No man can behold the glory of God and remain in the flesh. This is a given tenant of religious dogma."

"Then how came Moses to speak with God face-to-face?" the dwarfish one asks.

"The Lord spoke unto Moses face-to-face," his opponent says.

"It is the same," the short one says.

"It appears so," says the owl-eyed man.

"Besides," continues the short one, "I have already stated that your book is outmoded."

"But God's word is for all times."

"Poppycock!"

"You would argue with God?"

"Yes, if I could *see* him!"

"You don't have enough faith to see Him!"

"And you do?"

"Admittedly, no."

"Then how can you prove that he and your ghosts exist?"

"How can you prove that they do not?"

"I can't see them."

"Maybe because they aren't here right now. Come to think of it, you'd have to be able to see everywhere at once to prove that they don't exist. And if you could be all places at all times and see everything simultaneously, would that not make you God? You cannot prove there is no God without being God yourself."

After a short silence, the owl-eyed intermediary says "It seems—I hate to admit it, but it must be true—that there is no way to know if we know what we think we know, whether our knowledge is based on faith or reason."

"Blasphemous," says one.

"Preposterous," says the other.

All three stand in stone-faced silence, staring at the floor.

Pomp moves on.

She finds herself hovering between a pair of twins, identical save for their dress. One wears a navy blue jacket, the other a dark brown overcoat. Otherwise, they are the same in appearance and mannerisms. Curiously, neither looks the other in the eye, though they seem to speak only to one another. They turn their eyes from side to side and peer over their own and the other's shoulder, careful to avoid catching the other's gaze. Their faces are both twisted in sneers, never disappearing, only waxing and waning like a pair of snobby moons orbiting a focus of derision for the rest of the world's inhabitants.

"Ugh, that dress!" says one.

"How gaudy!" the other.

Back and forth, forth and back, but never directly, they go. Their heads are on swivels, eyes and ears always alert for weakness. *Maybe this is why they never look at each other*, Pomp thinks. *If one sees the other, he sees himself, and if all one looks for is weakness, then the observer will implode with self-loathing. So while each is aware of the mirror in front of him, neither dares to look into it.*

Rather, their co-gazes lock on one woman whom they are unwilling or unable to insult. Their heads turn in unison, faces dumbstruck, as she passes. The woman playfully runs her finger along the waist of the nearest, causing him to involuntarily look up at his companion, who returns the gaze. Their faces twist in mutual disgust as they recoil from one another.

Pomp doesn't wait to see if the planets collide. She is already following the woman.

The woman is, by head-turning consensus, the most beautiful person in the room. She is fully aware of the fact and does nothing to conceal her knowledge of this, to the delight of young men and the disapproval of elderly women.

Jealous old women, lustful young men, Pomp thinks, *and a coquette to lead them all.*

And lead them on, she does. Behind her is a short, older gentleman with as much hair in his mustache as on his balding head.

"My dear—oh, dear," he says in a barely-audible voice, as if trying to secretly plead with her in the midst of the vast crowd. She glides through the crowd, going wherever she wants to, batting her eyes and smiling at every man she walks past. He follows, jostling to keep up with her as the wake behind her collapses in on itself with sudden admirers and new enemies. She moves through the crowd like a water snake crossing a river—lithe, confident, flowing, and dangerous.

Her fiery red hair is bundled with white silk ribbons and pierced by pearl-pommeled hairpins. Abundant white makeup gives her face a porcelain luster but takes nothing away from her sharp, elfin features. In fact, her green eyes stand out even more because of the cosmetics—two sparkling emeralds that flash in the chandelier light. Her smile is broad but unforced, quite natural. Pomp thinks that the woman might be a good woman, except for the way she persistently ignores the man who appears to be her husband, favoring the adoration of strangers over domestic faithfulness. This is confusing to Pomp, who watches as the flirtatious woman reaches out with bejeweled fingers to straighten the collar of the Polish hussar, whose ardor is obviously aroused by the forward gesture. Pomp lands on top of one of the hussar's wings, her curiosity piqued.

"Dear," says the man who must be her husband as he puts his hand on her arm. "We must be going. Our children . . ."

The woman shoots him a scalding sidelong glance that almost instantaneously switches back to a smile as she turns her gaze again to the hussar.

She speaks in a low voice that only she, her husband, the hussar, and Pomp can hear. "The children, she says sweetly, "are in good hands. The nanny will watch over them . . . for the night." She continues to stare into the hussar's eyes.

He is obviously uncomfortable with the situation, but his vanity prevents him from refusing her advances.

She turns to her husband. "Of course, you are free to go be with the children yourself, if you wish."

She turns back to the hussar. "As for me, I have plans for the evening."

The husband shrinks away, deflated, spurned.

And Pomp, infuriated by her sense of justice, has been patient long enough.

She has discovered how the hussar's wings work and puts her might into flapping the feathered contraptions, much to the surprise and confusion of the hussar, who lifts his arms and peers underneath to see who is pulling this prank—and his wings. Seeing that no one is touching him, indeed a clearing has appeared around him, he begins to panic, turning this way and that, nearly knocking over all who are within reach of his wings, including the flirtatious woman. She begins laughing at the ridiculousness of it all until her hair pins fall out, pulled loose by unseen hands. (Pomp has to press her feet against the woman's head to gain the needed leverage.)

Those down the hall think that another group of musicians has started up until it becomes apparent that the screeches are not those of a violin. The emperor, amused at the ruckus, stands up and smiles when he sees the scene. Graf Von Edelweir places himself between the emperor and the action, calling two of his guards to protect his liege from whatever witchery this is.

And no one can argue that it isn't sorcery. The woman's hair ties itself in knots around her pretty face. The hussar's wings detach and fall to the ground with a clunk. The woman falls backward into a crowd of her erstwhile admirers. The hussar's pants come undone and drop to the man's ankles.

The woman swats at her own dress, screaming about gremlins tickling her ribs and armpits and laughing hysterically. The hussar's medals fly off his chest and out into the crowd. He cries out. She cries out.

The husband rushes to her side to assist his wife. She stops suddenly, as if struck by a thunderbolt of realization. She looks at her husband through the knots in her hair, then tackles him to the ground, showering him with lustful kisses, caresses, and other maneuvers not to be detailed among polite company or around children.

The couple is quickly shepherded out, while the hussar stands there in a daze, his pantaloons still about his ankles.

Pomp hovers in the air above the scene, bow in hand, a satisfied smile on her face. Her quiver is one arrow lighter. She thinks, "It was worth it!"

Then she finds herself choking in a cloud of wig powder, which has suddenly filled the air around her. The imperial guards usher the emperor out and an even more widespread panic ensues.

"Ghost!" some yell.

"A demon!" shout others.

"Gremlin!" scream a few.

She realizes, in the mayhem, that all eyes are now on her, she who is invisible ... save for the white powder that now coats her, betraying her form to the crowd. Her cover is blown, she is exposed.

But who could know she was there? Who would have guessed how to find her? Only one ... Mowler! But disguised as ... who?

Pomp flies as high as the ceiling will allow, then scans the crowd. She looks for a wrathful glimmer in the eyes, an evil smile—any indicator of Mowler-behind-the-mask. But all of the people are overflowing with fury, shouting, jumping up to snatch at the air beneath her, throwing whatever object is at hand.

All, that is, save for one, whom she catches coming up from a kneeling to a standing position with a large powder puff in his hand. He looks at her with eyes full of curiosity—a long, long stare, as if he is studying her. That one is none other than Major Felix Von Graeb.

CHAPTER 21

The arterial roads leading to the heart of Istanbul were clogged with a mass of humanity that only reluctantly gave way to Heraclix, Al'ghul, and the officer. The officer, who formally introduced himself as Agha Beyruit Al Mahdr, worked the crowd with his riding crop and horse, clearing a path for Heraclix and Al'ghul by stroke and hoof.

"Make way for an officer of the Sultan!" he ordered.

Those in the way grudgingly obliged, eyes ablaze with hatred for the gargantuan foreigner in their midst. A couple barked out insults, but were soon silenced when they saw the face of the man under the cowl. The looks of anger transformed into faces wrung with disgust. Heraclix understood then that he would not have made it thus far were it not for Mehmet's training of Al'ghul. He silently thanked whatever gods of irony might rule over the earth, if any.

Beyond the layers of pedestrians, the streets were encrusted like barnacles on a long-moored ship with shop atop shop selling bright bolts of indigo, orange, and blood red cloth; pungent spices; polished copper pots that reflected amber sunlight; and brightly feathered and furred animals in wicker cages. Above these were balconies from which woman beat intricately woven carpets or dumped pans of water down onto the eaves of the shops below. Between buildings, down long alleyways, Heraclix thought he could see glimpses of the ocean, like little blue swatches of cloth that were snatched away by the jealous city.

In time they turned off into one of those alleys and rode down it long enough for Heraclix to see the Sea of Marmara, as if through a window. He could smell the clean scent of the sea as the salt air coursed up in tendrils through the alleys from the dockside wharfs. He was disappointed when Al Mahdr turned into an alley that ran parallel to the shore, again allowing Heraclix only intermittent peeps at the waves.

The buildings grew taller and more imposing even as the streets became more and more narrow. Soon they had no choice but to travel single file—Agha Al Mahdr at the front, then Al'ghul, with Heraclix taking up the rear. Just when Heraclix wondered if his legs might become pinched and wedged between the walls and the sides of his horse, the tightly pressing buildings gave way to a circular courtyard in the midst of which stood a single white-plastered, rectangular building, five stories high and windowless, with a single, small wooden door that he knew he would have to stoop, if not crawl, to pass. There was nothing in the courtyard: no children, no chickens, not even a fly buzzed in the empty air, which suited Heraclix just fine. He had seen enough of flies.

Al Mahdr approached the door and knocked with three solid, measured raps, a code of some sort, Heraclix thought. The door opened a crack, but Heraclix could see no more than the hand of the one who held the door open. A brief conversation in hushed tones took place between Al Mahdr and the doorman. Heraclix and Al'ghul tried to approach. But Al Mahdr, without missing a word in his quiet delivery, held up his hand to stop the golem and the boy, both of whom halted in their tracks. After a few more words were exchanged, Al Mahdr's hand waved them toward him, then he disappeared into the building's interior. Heraclix, entering last, nearly crawled to fit through the doorway.

Beyond the door, they walked through heavy silk curtains of a green so dark it was almost black. The walls, ceiling, and floor of the room were also adorned with the green-black silk, as if they had walked into the silk purse of some gargantuan pagan god of wealth. The silk was cut in strips six feet wide that reached from the apex of the ceiling to the nadir of the floor. Each strip was connected to the two next to it by a series of copper circlets in the form of long, bent bones connected end-to-end so that the curtains formed a silken globe within the cube-shaped room. From each circlet dangled a two-inch-high copper skull, which reflected the dancing lights of the dozens of candles that were set atop brass candlesticks throughout the room. Smoke rose from small censors filled with pungent incense scattered about the silken bubble. Beyond one pair of silk curtains, in a far corner, something cast a strong light from above.

The one who opened the door, Heraclix saw, was a young man, probably somewhere in his twenties if the ashen veneer of weariness could be wiped from his face. He had that far-off look in his eyes common to the opium addict. His skeletal frame and a slight nervous twitch in the arms led Heraclix to further believe that the young man was, indeed, an addict.

The young man tried to gently clear his throat, but quickly slid into a coughing fit before gathering himself enough to speak properly.

"My masters bid you welcome, Agha Beyruit Al Mahdr, and our guests . . ." He held out his hand to the others, nodding in an effort to prompt them to state their names. Heraclix looked around the room but could see no one else—only piles of cushions and throw pillows scattered haphazardly around the room.

"Al'ghul," said the younger.

"Heraclix," the other.

"Al'ghul and Heraclix," the young man said.

Heraclix noted that his pronunciation of both Al'ghul's and Al Mahdr's names seemed stilted and foreign. This man wasn't from around here, though the golem couldn't quite tell where the servant was from through the drug-induced slur. There was something familiar about the man's face, but Heraclix couldn't quite place his or the Serb's finger on where or in whom he had seen that subtle something before.

His thoughts evaporated as the Shadow Divan materialized. Seven figures slipped between the curtains and into the room like columns of smoke that coalesced into the forms of men. All were dressed similarly, though not exactly the same. Most were very tall for men, one notably so, though a pair were quite short, and one of these rotund, like a bipedal toad dressed in black. In fact, all were dressed in black. Or perhaps it was the same green as the silk curtains lining the walls—it was difficult to tell in the faint light.

Many things were difficult to tell in that dimly lit room with its undulating walls and tinkling skulls like tiny bells. It didn't help matters that all seven members of the Shadow Divan wore masks that obscured their faces to one degree or another. The tallest wore a black raven's face. The short, fat one wore a veil over his nose and mouth, like the Muslim women, while the short skinny one wore a gray and white leather skull mask. Two of the tall ones wore black masks carved into demonic visages, another wore a simple black hood with a pair of eye holes, while the last wore a long-nosed black Scaramouche—the kind that was popular during the Renaissance. All wore hats, most of them tall conical hats of black, while the Demon-twins wore gold-embroidered black bishop's mitres in the Eastern Orthodox style, and Skull-face wore a blood-red fez.

The Raven stepped forward and bowed, while the others sat or lay down on the pillows piled on the floor.

"Come, sit, my guests," the man said in a voice rough in texture, smooth in delivery. His accent was neither Turkic, Germanic, nor Slavic. Spanish, perhaps, or Portuguese? Heraclix wasn't familiar enough with those tongues to know, so he could only speculate.

The guests sat. The Raven, still standing, spoke.

"You have need of our aid, else you wouldn't have come here and presented the key words that allow ingress into our stronghold," he said to Al Mahdr.

"They came from afar," the soldier said, pointing at Heraclix and Al'ghul. "They came bearing the token words. We are obliged to give aid."

"Indeed we are, but first, we are very curious about our guest," the Raven said, looking directly at Heraclix. He walked around the giant, in much the same way that Al Mahdr had done earlier, examining him up and down. His compatriots soon followed, getting up from their seats to circumambulate the golem. They moved slowly, but in a regular cadence, all eyes on Heraclix. Al'ghul was all but forgotten to them.

"We are here because I think that you might have information relevant to my search for the sorcerer Mowler." Heraclix said to the Shadow Divan, for he knew that these were they, a dark mirror image of the sultan's Divan but completely uninterested in the politics of man. They were wholly dedicated to unraveling the great mysteries of life, death, and life beyond.

At once, in the same fluid movement, each member of the Shadow Divan withdrew from his robes a parchment, a small ink pot, and a quill. Then, as they walked, they feverishly took notes, drew charts and graphs, and made scratch mathematical calculations. Their celerity and economy of motion seemed inhuman. No man he had known could ever write or draw intelligibly with such speed, especially as they walked in circles around the object of their studies. He thought they might be writing down gibberish in an effort to put pressure on him as he spoke, a tactic to cause him to reveal ulterior motives or to inadvertently catch himself in a lie. He had to admit that the pressure was intense—the sound of swirling, scratching quills was annoying to the point of distraction. He lowered his voice only to have them lean in closer, straining to hear him.

"I think I know something about you." His voice stepped down with each word until he spoke so softly that neither Al'ghul nor Al Mahdr could hear him. "And I think that something has a great deal to do with my past, which I intend to learn more about in the coming days."

He settled into a whisper. He was smoldering with anger now and the noise of the quills was almost louder than his whispered words. They crowded him now, stooping, walking in a sideways crouch like crabs, continuing to take notes, tilting their heads this way and that in order to get a better look at him, some silently pointing their quills at his eye, his hand, the wound on his chest, as if showing a thing of interest to his companions. They were like wolves stalking a wounded deer or vultures circling over a dying man—watching, waiting, seeking weakness, herding, watching, ever watching.

"Enough!" Heraclix yelled so loudly that his observers stopped in their tracks. Some fell backwards and scrambled to their pillows.

All except the Raven, who remained standing by Heraclix. "Of course," he said, unshaken. "How rude of us. I'm afraid that we aren't very good hosts. And it *is* rare, very rare, that one of your . . . makeup should venture to visit us. We will ask questions of you later and, in exchange, you may ask questions of us. That is only fair. I think we have much information that is of mutual interest. You'll find us honest and reliable, will he not, Agha Beyruit Al Mahdr?"

The soldier smiled and nodded. "Please forgive their mannerisms, Heraclix. They don't often get visitors."

Heraclix remained guardedly silent for fear of being silently interrogated again, but the other members of the Shadow Divan were too busy comparing notes and debating their observations to be of any immediate threat to him.

"Come," said the Raven. "I will show you upstairs. I think you will find this place of great interest, as one who has seen what I suppose you have seen and experienced."

He turned to the servant. "Keep Al'ghul and Agha Beyruit Al Mahdr entertained down here. I wish to show our facilities to Mister . . . Heraclix." Heraclix noted the near-error, storing it away for future use in any potential upcoming negotiations.

Heraclix followed the Raven over to a corner of the room. From there, a light glowed—far brighter than the candles. The Raven parted the curtain in that direction, and Heraclix saw clearly for the first time the embroidered scenes of heaven and hell that adorned each pillow and cushion in the room. The Norse Valhalla, Jewish Gehenna, Muslim Paradisiacal Oasis, Dante's nine circles of Hell, visions of Buddha sipping from the cup of Enlightenment, Arthur reaching for the Holy Grail, and many more scenes that he couldn't identify, all met his glance in a moment. Then he was beyond the bone-clasped, skull-guarded curtain, ascending a ladder through an opening in the ceiling, from which the light poured.

When Heraclix pulled himself up through the opening, the Raven had his back to him, hands on hips, gazing about the room as if he had just discovered a thing of wonderment. An immense cylindrical bookcase filled the center of the room from floor to ceiling. Each of the four walls was also fitted with a bookcase, peaked on the outside ends like a pair of wooden horns. These also stretched from the floor to the ceiling. Four crescent-moon-shaped tables surrounded the center bookcase, their concave edges facing the round. Were they not scooted out from the center, they would have embraced it, fitting like puzzle pieces. Eight tall, padded chairs sat empty against the convex side of the tables.

"The Eye of Knowing, that which sees all mysteries," the Raven said, quite proudly. "We know that all the mysteries of the secrets of life, death, and being are either contained in or referenced here. It is the search for the Key of Keys to those mysteries that consumes us."

This was obvious to Heraclix. The room might perfectly resemble an eye, were it not for the stacks of books and papers that were piled atop the tables and the random piles of readings and notes that lay in mounds on the floor, and this all despite the fact that every inch of space in the bookshelves was occupied by arcane volumes, whether properly standing spine-up or, in many cases, lying flat atop the other books. Pathways had been made throughout the room between the tables and at the foot of the bookcases. *Still, this place is treacherous*, Heraclix thought. Pull the wrong book and the necromancers might have to find some way of extricating themselves from the ranks of the dead, having been buried under heavy tomes and grimoires. Heraclix wasn't quite sure where the bright illumination in the room came from, but he thought it best not to ask so banal a question, given the Raven's vainglorious boasting.

"Come!" he said, beckoning Heraclix to follow him up another ladder in the far corner. Heraclix followed, stepping as carefully as his giant body would allow so as not to upset any book piles.

Heraclix stepped off the ladder into a room whose walls were lined with mirrors and candles. A fireplace burned along one wall, with two immense censers burning sandalwood and lotus incense on either side. Each was the size of a small cauldron and was mounted atop tripods wrought in iron to represent three cloven feet. Various knick-knacks lay scattered on the floor: strange metal puzzles; crystal balls of varying sizes, clarity and color; and a dozen or more kaleidoscopes made of everything from ivory to olive wood to silver.

He walked over to a waist-high (mid-thigh for him) stone circle—a well, which must have continued down through the floor into the center of the circular bookcase on the floor below.

He ran his finger over the surface of the shining liquid that filled it, confirming his suspicion that the well wasn't filled with water but with quicksilver. He stared into the mercury, watching his reflection warp and change to show him not as a patchwork of sewn-together flesh, but as a whole, unified man. His face was unscarred, his eyes both blue and healthy. A short, balding, plump man smiled warmly back at the monster staring down at him.

"This is where we come to meditate, to gain focus, in preparation for that which is above."

Heraclix turned to look at the Raven, from whom he expected further explanation. When it appeared that none was forthcoming, he turned back to the reflection, but it showed only a molten image of himself as the golem he was.

"Come," the Raven said. "I will show you that which is above."

They climbed yet another ladder, which had been hidden by a tall mirror in a corner of the room. The reek of incense grew stronger the closer they came to the opening above. Just when Heraclix thought he might choke from the excessive smoke, the air cleared and he found himself on a rooftop open to the sky, though a thick fence of tall poplars ran the perimeter of the roof. One couldn't see out, but one could see up.

In the middle of the roof a cylindrical wooden tower had been erected. Stairs wound around the outside to the top, where Heraclix followed the Raven. Even halfway up, they could look out over the treetops to every horizon, their view unobstructed by building or minaret. Heraclix thought that this must be one of the highest points in Istanbul. They could see for miles. Finally, Heraclix could see the ocean. They continued their ascent to the top as the sunlight melted into the distant mountains and the dark sea. Night fell quickly.

"We are almost there," the Raven said. "I think you will like what you see."

The stairs opened up onto the top of the cylinder. The perimeter of the circular platform was a veritable tangle of telescopes, each of different shapes, sizes, and types. There might have been a hundred of them protruding from the edges of the platform like a crown of thorns.

Heraclix looked through a nondescript refractor pointed at the southern sky. He set his sights on Aldebaran, jumped back from the sight, and turned the telescope back on the star to confirm what he saw.

There the star burned red. He could see the ball of fire, flames licking out into space. Among the flames he thought he saw figures, creatures, among the flame. He went to a bigger telescope and trained it on the same star. This time the magnification allowed him to easily see a group of serpent-tailed, bearded flame salamanders stoking the fires of the crimson star. They poked and prodded with spears and pitchforks, delighting when a jet of red flame shot upwards from the surface to dance in space for a while before dissipating in the void. Above each of the creatures' heads a burning sigil glowed.

"Those symbols above their heads," Heraclix said excitedly. "Those must be their individual names, their true names."

The Raven chuckled. "You are starting to remember, my friend."

"Remember what?" Heraclix said, swinging the telescope to another star where a ring of angels crowned with gold halos sang a chorus that intensified the bright white light of the star's surface as they increased their volume. He could hear their unearthly voices as long as he concentrated on looking through the telescope.

"We have much to talk about," said the Raven. "But before we do, look to the west."

Heraclix swung the telescope earthward, scanning the land as he did so. He could see the magic that crossed through his field of vision in the form of glowing mystical symbols that manifested themselves wherever a bit of the otherworldly shone. Fresh graves and battlefields were particularly bright; some mosques and churches gave forth a sign or two, some did not. In the distance, a regular trickle of smaller glowing symbols wafted up from the bends and turns of the Danube. The world was full of leaks into and from the world of spirits, fountainheads of magic, all unseen by most mortal eyes.

Then he saw, somehow, over the horizon, Prague, then Vienna, as if the distance between them and Istanbul had been squeezed out of space like an accordion. Prague was a steady glow, impossible to ignore for the sheer number of magical indicators that floated above it. But Vienna! Vienna was a different story entirely. Vienna throbbed with magic! If he had not known the significance of the magic aura and what it indicated, he would swear the entire city was on fire!

"Come," said the Raven. "You have seen enough. It's time we talked a bit more openly."

Chapter 22

The air is alive with shouts, hurled objects, and a fairy exposed. A poor man might think his wishes were being fulfilled, caught in the shower of silver cufflinks, fresh fruit, and diamond brooches that arc toward the ceiling and back to the floor in glittering parabolas. Pomp doesn't feel so blessed. She is frightened and confused. With one last disappointed glance at Von Graeb, she flies, flees down the corridor and out into the open air, dodging the jewelry and shoes, as well as the occasional piece of cobblestone, that is being thrown at her.

Finally, after passing through the maelstrom of gems and metal, she finds a small, hidden pond and proceeds to wash the wig powder off. A frog takes enough interest in her to try to eat her, but she stabs the pollywog in the nose with a stick until it lets go and hops away. The attack is a blessing in disguise, she discovers, as the frog's sticky tongue takes much of the wig powder with it.

Still, it's hard to be optimistic. She thought, no, she was certain that Von Graeb was a good man. But the evidence was in his hand, a wig powder puff that he must have pounded to send up the cloud that enveloped and revealed her to the crowd. But would a good man do this? Why? Something isn't adding up. Besides, Pomp isn't very good at adding—at least not in her head. She is good at collecting, though, and this is what she will do: collect more information. She is clean enough now. She will find out why Von Graeb exposed her to the crowd.

Pomp shakes herself dry, then flies back to the palace where several fights have broken out over disagreements about who threw what at whom and why. She can easily trace where she had been by following the trail of glittering litter and disgruntled guests back into the hall where it all began. It has been some time now since she left, bathed, thought, and returned, yet she finds Von Graeb meandering, still holding the wig powder puff. He looks down at the object in his hand, then up at the air, then down and up and down and up again. He looks perplexed, trying to solve a mystery that is nestled deep within his brain. Finally, he sets the powder puff down on the floor, looks at it contemplatively, then walks away.

Pomp follows.

Von Graeb waves off a pair of imperial guards acting as would-be escorts. The officer weaves his way through the still-perplexed guests, whose anger has subsided into confused speculation as to what they saw or whether they had seen anything at all. "A mass hallucination," says one man; "something in the wine," another. The three philosophers Pomp had earlier antagonized are now arguing more vociferously than ever.

Von Graeb ignores them all, making his way toward the exit with a step full of grim determination. His brow is furrowed in thought.

He leaves the palatial grounds, spurning several offers for carriage rides. "I must walk and think," he says to one group who seems particularly familiar with him.

"Oh, he's in one of those moods," one of them says—a young lady. "I don't particularly like him when he's sulking."

The words fade away behind him as he walks along darkening cobblestone streets. Pomp follows as he wanders aimlessly, taking alleys and walking through dusky gardens and parks as the sun sets. The lamplighters are making their rounds. Pomp is thoroughly confused about direction when she sees him finally turn the door handle on a small yet elegant Baroque villa surrounded by fields of flowers that close in the night.

She darts inside as he closes the door behind him.

Pomp is not exactly sure what she was expecting to find in Von Graeb's apartment. Maybe she thought the place would betray a love of war: busts of famous historical generals, suits of armor, crossed morning stars hanging on every wall. Or, possibly, some kind of love den with an overlarge canopied bed filled with heart-shaped pillows.

She finds neither of these. In fact, as Von Graeb lights a lantern, she discovers that the place is well kept but rather ordinary. The main room holds a pair of couches facing one another over a dark blue and green Persian carpet; a dining table on the other side of the room with enough chairs for Von Graeb and five guests; a rollaway writing desk closed, at the moment, with a quill, inkwell, candle-holder with candle, matches, wax, and a seal atop the desk's back. A few large urns, from which small trees grow, line the wall next to the entrance door. The only unusual items are a saber mounted to the wall over the desk and a violin in a stand near one of the sofas. Two doors, both ajar, lead out of the room, one to what looks to be a small kitchen and the other to Von Graeb's sleeping quarters.

To call it austere would be insulting. It is sparse, yes, but each piece of furniture is finely carved and filigreed, adding elegance to what would otherwise seem like an apartment far beneath the station of one such as Von Graeb.

He walks over to the desk, lights the candle, and rolls the desk open. He sets his fez down on a small pile of books and papers, reaches in, and retrieves something small—something that Pomp cannot yet see because of his obstructing hand. He walks to the wall facing the sitting area and opens a pair of curtains to reveal a large window. Just beyond the window is a white-painted lattice wrapped in vines. Moonlight pours through the open windows, casting mysterious shadows on the carpet.

He sets the candleholder down on the floor between the sofas then seats himself on the edge of one of the cushions. Leaning over toward the floor, his knees up in his chest, he shakes one hand back and forth, and Pomp realizes that he is about to throw a pair of dice.

She can hardly contain herself. There is something about dice that connects with her deep down inside. An instinct to chance. If she was human, she might have a gambling problem. But she isn't and doesn't, though she does wonder about Von Graeb, who throws the dice across the rug and watches intently as they roll to a stop.

Seven.

Von Graeb smiles, picks up the dice, and rolls them again.

Eleven.

"Ha!" he says, triumphantly, picking up the dice and casting them again.

Two.

"Dog throw," he says with great disappointment. He stands up above the dice, eying them warily: the pair of ones has spoiled his augury, clouded his soothsaying. He stoops back down, crouching low to look at them this way and that, trying to scry meaning from the way they lay.

He stands back up, folds his arms and turns his back on the dice. The moon casts milky shadows through the window on to his face.

"Not a good sign," he says, shaking his head. "Not a good sign at all."

He turns his head slightly, looking at the dice through the corner of his eye. "I should hope my luck changes," he says, turning his head just a bit more to clearly see the dice.

One of the die flips, transforming the one to a six, making seven total.

He smiles knowingly.

"Fancy that!" he says. Pomp thinks he speaks in such a kindly voice. How could she have doubted him? "My luck has turned around again. Maybe things will be all right after all."

In that moment Pomp realizes that it isn't chance itself that she finds so intoxicating. It's the ability to affect fate with such a simple thing as a nudge of the dice. She is no taller than a man's forearm. Yet at the right time, under the right circumstances, she can steer kingdoms. She can change, what is it called?

The *future*!

"This bodes well," Von Graeb says. "And I am glad to know that it is not just some old ghost that is helping me along."

Pomp freezes in place. But Von Graeb isn't looking at her. Not now. He scans the room, eyes darting from side-to-side as he slowly walks in a backward circle around the dice. He is searching but hasn't yet seen Pomp.

"No, you are no spirit, but a sprite!"

"Eep!" says Pomp.

Von Graeb hears her, turns her direction, and takes a step forward. She stays where she is, knowing he can't see her, though he is staring right at her. He kneels down on one knee and speaks very softly.

"Friend, I know you're there. You need to know that I didn't expose you at the emperor's soiree. Someone else did, though I found the powder and brush that was used to do it. But I did see you. You are a funny fairy, no doubt about it."

He chuckles, stands up, and turns his back on Pomp. She flies up in front of him, in his field of vision, but remains invisible.

"Yrzmowski, the winged hussar, is usually unflappable. Then again, so are most career soldiers . . . when their pants are on. Ha! Well done!"

"And Lady Kleist—any idiot would say she got what she deserved. Some idiots did say so. But other idiots took offense at her fall, mostly men whom she had teased to the point of distraction before . . . er . . . showering her husband with affection."

He stops, turns. Pomp flies in front of his eyes. He doesn't see her. She wants to show herself but feels she ought not to. Not yet. She has to wait for Heraclix. She can't betray her friend because of her desire to reassure Von Graeb.

"You do know you made some enemies, don't you?"

Pomp, unseen, acknowledges this with a shrug and a sideways nod.

"You might have made some very powerful enemies, indeed. To give you an idea of the crowd you were among, well, let's say if a band of stray Cossacks were to attack our borders, the army wouldn't know what to do. Or if a thief were to walk into the imperial treasury and clear it of gold, no one would be the wiser for a day or two. This is precisely *why* you created such a commotion. Those people don't hate you. Well, maybe Yrzmowski does now. What they hate is the feeling of vulnerability that overtook them, the thought that in the heart of the Holy Roman Empire someone or—pardon me for saying so—*something* could sneak in so close to their symbol of stability and security, namely the emperor himself, so as to be a real threat. Your appearance there shook them to the core."

Pomp doesn't know whether to be pleased or embarrassed.

"But I'm sure you couldn't help yourself. You're not to blame, not for acting according to your nature. You are a fairy, after all."

Pomp smiles. He is a good man, after all.

"And I know a little bit about your kind. I learned it from my nanny when I was a child. She was a gypsy, a good woman who taught me tales of the Fey, their ways and inclinations. She taught me what evidence to look for whenever I suspected one of the fairy folk were nearby."

His smile broadens.

"Mother didn't approve."

Pomp folds her arms, sulking.

"More than anything, Nanny taught me about the carefree nature of the Fey. You are mischievous at heart. And good for you!"

The smile fades from his face.

"As for me, mischief seems to find me wherever I go lately. I think it all started when a giant of a man killed one of the guard and escaped the city. Graf Von Helmutter would have demoted me for having let him get away, were it not for the illness that suddenly overtook him after the incident. Von Helmutter was too occupied with his bad health to worry about discipline. Nevertheless, I wouldn't have blamed the graf for punishing me. He wasn't an inherently evil man, after all."

Pomp, disapproving, puts her fists to her waist and glowers.

"But he did have a bit of a mean streak. He did seem a touch . . . 'ambitious' is the word I would use."

Pomp rolls her eyes and shakes her head.

"Still, he wasn't nearly as demanding as his replacement. No, Graf Von Edelweir is a harsh taskmaster. The first thing he did was to forbid me and my men from wearing silver jewelry of any type. 'The wearing of silver by a member of the imperial guard is strictly forbidden,' his orders said. 'It is unbecoming and effeminate for a servant so close to the emperor to wear anything less than gold in his royal presence.'"

Pomp's face contorts in confusion.

"I had never heard such a ridiculous thing. And the emperor never once mentioned a dislike of silver, at least not around me. It was all very strange. Though I suppose it's really immaterial."

"What is material, however, is the changes made to our uniforms. 'We will fill our enemies with fear,' he told us, though he didn't tell us which enemies he had in mind. 'They will see their fate even before they are met by it. Blackness! Death! Annihilation!' Oh, the guard cheered aloud for the defeat of their unknown foes. I would like to think that they had no choice but to cheer for their new commanding officer. But this was no forced appeal. These men were, are, more than merely compliant. They have allowed themselves to be seduced by the lure of the sword and of blood lust. Graf Von Edelweir has planted the seed of hatred in their veins, and they, feeling the first stirrings of growth, want to water it with their enemies' blood. They submit themselves to the harsh disciplines implemented by the graf, thinking they are patriotic. But that harsh discipline that, unchecked, becomes abject punishment doesn't make soldiers into good servants of the nation. It makes them slaves to hatred itself." He shakes his fist. "Such hatred might be directed, at first, at an enemy. But it soon spills over and contaminates a soldier's natural desire for recognition and glory, infecting him with such a desire for fame that he will step over the bodies of his comrades to get it. And the more bodies, the higher he climbs."

He sighs, and a look of disappointment crosses his face.

Pomp is confused. How can a good man like Von Graeb struggle with disillusionment? Must things go badly for even the best people?

"Of course, those who issue orders know this. They spend much of their time fearful that one of their men, one possessing intelligence and ambition in equal measure, might climb right up the ranks to threaten their position. Up and over the top! So, in order to be forewarned of such a gambit, the commanding officer sends out spies to watch over any would-be usurpers."

"Lescher is my spy, the one assigned to 'serve' me by Von Edelweir. I know the type, ambitious and greedy enough to whore himself as a spy, but enough of a self-loathing toady to remain loyal to his boss."

"I sometimes wonder how Von Edelweir can share even half of Lady Adelaide's traits. They are so unlike one another as to appear to be from completely different families. Not in their physical appearance. You can clearly see that they share grandparents. But their dispositions couldn't be further apart. The graf is brooding, the lady bubbly; the man dark, the woman bright; he driven, she carefree. He is clearly warlike, and she is just as surely an advocate for peace. I fear their marriage will be tumultuous, at best.

"And here I am, a soldier that would go to war in order to ensure a world at peace to share with the good Lady Adelaide. We have been friends since we were children. Oh, that I could give her the love and security she deserves.

"I have had enough of conflict," he says, then sighs heavily, weary from his thoughts. "I've seen war and bloodshed, have taken the life out of another man's heart with my own sword, and have directed hundreds of men to do the same—to kill or die for love of king and country. But in my own heart, I am no hater of men. I just happen to be a good soldier. My vocation vexes my soul. How I wish for one final conflict to ensure everlasting peace."

Pomp is surprised when he begins to chuckle to himself. She doesn't see what is so funny.

"Ah," he catches himself, "I do sound ridiculous. My dreams are no more real than you are, my imaginary friend."

He pauses, thoughtfully holding his chin between forefinger and thumb.

"I suppose that maybe I am losing my mind through all these difficulties. Perhaps all this internal stress has driven me to the point of hallucination."

Pomp clears her throat, loudly!

"Ahem!"

He smiles, turns to her and says, simply, "Thank you."

She wants to show herself, to give definite proof that she's there, to fully demonstrate her trust in him. But can she? Really? What if it's all a ruse to bring her out into the open? That smile, is it truly friendly, or merely victorious? And what if he isn't—dare she say it? she must!—under Mowler's influence? What if Von Graeb is everything he seems to be? If she shows herself to him now, one more person will know, really know, that she is not only real, but here. That knowledge might draw the hidden Mowler out. Then again, it might endanger Von Graeb. If the sorcerer found out, he would be merciless to Von Graeb, as he was to her and Heraclix. And if she caused Von Graeb's suffering, she would simply come undone. Even if her appearance didn't result in a bad situation for Von Graeb, it would definitely change their relationship. Maybe he would laugh at her smallness. Or, perhaps her looks, cute, by all means, but not Lady Adelaide beautiful, by any means. Seeing her would definitely lessen her mystique in his eyes.

But still, she feels she must. She is compelled by some inner need not only to know, but to be known. She had been good so far, hadn't she, observing on Heraclix's behalf, but not getting involved? That is, if one can excuse a very minor slip up, likely in Mowler's presence, in front of the entire ruling class of the Holy Roman Empire? This could be forgotten, couldn't it?

No, of course not.

Then what does she have to lose, showing herself to one of the few mortals who hadn't fled or frenzied at her unanticipated appearance? How else can she prove that Von Graeb is a good man, as she thinks he is. And if he is Mowler in disguise, she could escape. She did it once before . . . with Heraclix's help. But Heraclix is not here now. She must stand on her own, nudge fate like a dice-roll, and step out into the open.

She will do it.

Now.

A knock sounds at the door so swiftly that she isn't even sure if she has appeared or not.

Either way, Von Graeb doesn't seem to see her. He turns toward the knocking door.

"Enter!" he says in a firm voice.

The door opens, and Lescher enters, bowing as he walks.

"Milord, Milady Adelaide comes soon with news about the wedding arrangements."

"What news?"

"Good news, Milord. She should be here within minutes."

Von Graeb's eyes light up.

"Excellent. I shall be ready for her arrival."

As Lescher exits, Von Graeb stoops down to pick up the dice.

Pomp flies out through the closing door. She cannot wait for the Lady Adelaide to arrive, so she flies out to see her.

As soon as she clears the doorway, the moonlight and streetlamps are shut out. Darkness, in the form of a black sack, envelops her. "I have you!" someone says in an old, familiar voice.

She struggles, but her captor flails the bag at the ground once, twice, battering her before she can react.

In an injured daze, she hears a jar lid open, feels herself being stuffed, still within the bag, into the glass cylinder. The jar lid slithers shut.

CHAPTER 23

"**B**rethren," the Raven addressed the Shadow Divan atop their stronghold under the faint light of a moon sliver. "This man, this Heraclix, is in need of our help. Our friend and brother, Agha Al Mahdr has brought him and his young companion to us, seeking our aid. The youth is too young and inexperienced to counsel with us, so he sits below, awaiting word. Agha Al Mahdr has been called out on other business, which needs his attention. We are called upon by our covenants of brotherhood to come to the aid of Heraclix, our brother. Those who consent to give aid, say 'aye.'"

"Aye!" they said in unison.

"My thanks," Heraclix said, bowing.

"Your thanks is not needed, friend Heraclix," the Raven said gravely, "for our aid does not come without a price."

"Price?" Heraclix said.

"Nothing unreasonable," said one of the Demon twins.

"Only a little information," said the other.

"We promise not to harm you," said Skull-face.

"Or your companion," added the Veiled One.

"After we have helped you, we will ask a few questions of you is all," Scaramouche said.

"Nothing that will compromise you," the Hooded One said.

"We only require your honesty," Raven said.

Heraclix thought carefully about how he should answer them, what he should be willing to reveal. He hardly knew these people. He didn't yet know whether or not to trust them. Yet he did feel a faint sense of camaraderie with these acolytes of life and death. It was a connection unexplainable by his short stay here or his hosts'... "hospitality" was not the right word. Perhaps "interest"?

Still, he was hesitant to speak of the glimpses of what may or may not have been his life before rebirth. What if it was all false and his feelings betrayed themselves as only the side effect of some electrochemical reaction? Perhaps he had hallucinated those visions of Hell and before. What if everything he thought or felt regarding those dim shivers of memory were false? What if his memories were a lie?

Worse yet, what if they were true? Could he live not only with the monster he now was, but also with the monster he might have been before waking in Mowler's cauldron? His greatest fear, he found, was himself.

Still, he felt (again, those untrustworthy feelings!) that he must push forward with some modicum of faith to break through the wall of fear in order to see for himself the unknown become the known. He had no choice but to trust the Shadow Divan and trust himself to them.

"Very well," Heraclix said. "I shall tell you what I know, as I have seen it."

"Excellent. But first, we have someone else to question. I think you will find ... the subject's comments of great interest."

The necromancers produced chalk, incense, and candles from beneath their robes. Chanting as they worked, the six created a magic circle, very similar to the one Mowler had created not long before his ostensible demise. This circle was smaller than the one in Mowler's apartment, however—not even large enough for a medium-sized man to stand in, at least not without being completely rigid and still.

"Please, sit," the Raven said, pointing to the appropriate spot.

Heraclix sat down and pulled his cowl over his head against the cold night air. He looked at the ground on which he sat.

"Oh, there's no need to worry," Skull-face said. "This one is very minor. You won't need any protection for this."

Heraclix wasn't sure that he liked the way "this" sounded.

"A simple matter," said the Veiled One, taking a seat next to Heraclix. "It will only take a matter of a minute or two in order ..." The Veiled One stopped suddenly. "Shh!" he ordered the already-silent Heraclix. "Vincenzo is about to begin the summoning."

Scaramouche had taken a spot on the opposite side of the circle, facing Heraclix. He knelt, raising his hands from the floor of the roof up to the sky, palm up, then back down again palm down. His fingers fluttered like rising smoke followed by falling ash.

Heraclix looked around him to see where the sudden glow around the group had come from. Not the moon, nor the stars. Not the candles nor the incense sticks, though there were many of each. Then he looked around at the circle of telescopes that surrounded them and realized that their eyepieces reflected back the green flow of magical energy. The lenses of the telescopes also glowed brighter and brighter as Scaramouche's chanting increased in tempo and intensity. The Demon twins, the Hooded One, and Skull-face joined in the ritual, adding their voices to Scaramouche's. As their voices chimed in and grew louder, the telescopes glowed brighter until, at a point when the necromancers were nearly shouting at the un-heeding stars, green beams of light shot forth from the cylinders, piercing the night sky with a bristling array of green glowing beacons.

Then, another light shone. It was red, like the embers of a fire, and grew out in veins from the center of the magic circle, like a tree spreading its roots. The glowing crimson veins pulsed like something alive, then grew out to the edges of the circle, where they stopped spreading horizontally and began growing vertically up and up until a shape—a short, winged shape familiar to Heraclix—took shape. Its lattice wings unfolded before Heraclix's eyes. The creature apparently had its back to Heraclix, if the golem had properly gauged the orientation of the thing's bird-like taloned legs.

Heraclix soon understood the reason for the profusion of incense that the Divan was burning. As soon as the faint scent of brimstone wore off, the stench of rotting meat poured forth out of the creature.

"What iz it you want of me?" questioned the devil-fly in a pitiable buzz.

"We will ask the questions, Bozkovitch," Scaramouche said.

Heraclix barely caught a view of the thing's immense hooked nose, but noted with a touch of humor the similarity of the face of the interrogator with what he could see of the interrogated.

"How do you know my name?" the devil-fly asked.

"We extracted it from you last time we talked," Scaramouche said. "And no more questions or we will extract much more from you."

"Ah, yes. So sorry, my memory izn't what it uzed to be. My senze of time iz fled."

"Of course it is. You are a denizen of eternal damnation. Which is precisely why we want to talk to you," Scaramouche said.

"Thiz iz fine. I am glad to get away from my master for a time. He iz in an ill-humor lately."

"Is the Lord of Flies ever in a good humor?" asks Scaramouche.

"No. But he iz particularly sore with me, since I alerted him to a recent infiltration of hiz realm. I waz only trying to be helpful, but . . ."

"Infiltration?"

"Yes. To be honest, it iz not my master'z displeazure I am so glad to be away from."

"No?" Scaramouche asked.

"No. I am glad to be away from the infiltratorz."

"Why is that?"

"Becauze I knew one of them, in part."

"In part?"

"Yes, in the eye, particularly."

"I am confused," Scaramouche said, but in an attempt to not appear too soft, he snapped, "I do not like to be confused. So explain yourself, and quickly!"

"Az I said, my memory iz not so good anymore."

"Perhaps if I let information leak to your master that you let information leak to me—"

"I understand!" the devil-fly said.

"And yet, I do not," said Scaramouche. "What did you mean that you knew of one of the infiltrators in part, in the eye, particularly."

"One of the visitorz, well, he waz not all himself."

"Do make yourself clear, or I will be contacting your master. Do I make myself clear?" Scaramouche said.

"Yes sir. You see, it iz hard to explain. This . . . man?" the word dripped with doubt. "He, well, I can't say he waz one man."

"There were more than one?"

"Yes, well, one of them. The other waz no man. Az I waz saying, one of them looked like he had been patched together from pieces of other men."

Raven and the others looked at Heraclix, but the devil-fly, whose back was still to Heraclix, was too focused on Scaramouche to notice.

"And so," Scaramouche asked, "you knew one of this man's eyes?"

"In very deed, yes!"

"There are millions of eyes on the faces of men. How could you recognize one eye among so many?"

"Oh, there iz no miztaking it. You see, or perhaps you do not," the demon said, "that eye, in its former life, in my former life, waz mine!"

"You are sure of this?"

"As sure az I am of the image burned into it."

"What image is that?" Scaramouche asked.

"The face of the girl that I killed with my own hands."

Heraclix started to get up, but the Veiled One sitting next to him put a plump hand on the giant's arm, urging him to refrain from interfering. Heraclix sat back down.

"You never fail to disgust me, Bozkovitch," Scaramouche said flatly. "And this is the source of your condemnation?"

"Yes, though even in Hell my sinz follow me."

"What do you mean?" Scaramouche asked.

"Everyone knowz everyone else in Hell. It iz part of the condemnation, to know who iz and who iz not there, alzo condemned. They say absenze makes the heart grow fonder, but it also cauzez great torment to be away from thoze you loved, to be with thoze you hated and who hated you. I learned that one who hated me had come to Hell."

"And who was that?" Scaramouche asked.

"The father of the girl I had killed."

"Surely she was innocent. Could a loving father be condemned to Hell?"

"She waz innocent, but he waz far from it. He sought to betray natural law, just az you do," the devil-fly wagged its finger.

"Your impertinence will be rewarded with further tortures, Bozkovitch," Scaramouche said flatly.

The devil-fly shrank back a half step.

"Az I waz saying," it continued, "a man whom I had never met, but who hated me with all the passion he could muster, had come to Hell. I didn't know where he waz, so I did my best to avoid him, which was a kind of torture itzelf.

"He didn't find me, at least not then. But another did find me, a man from among the living. He sought my victimz father and questioned me about hiz whereaboutz."

"In Hell?" Scaramouche asked.

"In Hell. He did not summon, he visited. A rather courteous gesture, I might add, for one practicing the sorcererz' artz."

"And why did this man seek the father of your victim?" Scaramouche asked, either missing or ignoring Bozkovitch's implication.

"He said that he had come to retrieve the man'z soul from Hell, but not to save him. He said that he had a special torment reserved for the father, who had somehow wronged him. Hiz torture waz to be so exquizite and demeaning that it must take place among the living, that even the eyez of Hell would avert their gaze for the shame of it all. He said 'that man will long to sojourn among the damned. For the punishment I have in mind for him iz more powerful than anything Hell or its minionz can contrive.'"

"And what was this vengeance-hungry sorcerer's name?" Scaramouche asked.

"Why, of all people, you should know! It waz Mattatheus Mowler!"

Heraclix felt the hair on the nape of his neck rise as a numbing sensation washed over his back, then reached around to curdle his guts.

"Did this sorcerer, Mowler, find his man?"

"Yes. At least I think so. Or I thought so."

"Don't speak in riddles, Bozkovitch. You know what happened last time you played games with our time," Scaramouche said.

Bozkovitch shrank back, holding its arm up in front of its face to shield it from the memory.

"What I mean to say iz, yes. The father'z prezence waz soon gone from Hell. I felt him leave. The sorcerer had found his man. But . . ." It stopped with a sharp gasp, realizing it had made a strategic error.

"But what, Bozkovitch?" Scaramouche said

"But he, the father, not the sorcerer. Ah, it iz all so confuzing."

"What is?"

Bozkovitch breathed in heavily and exhaled with a buzzing sigh. "Not long ago, az the living reckon, another vizitor came to uz from among the living. An impossible vizitor. A man that never existed az the man he waz. I don't mean to speak in riddlez. I cannot help it. I am a devil, after all." It began to sob in a low, throbbing buzz.

"Bozkovitch, just tell us what you mean. Who was the visitor? What did he look like?"

"He waz hideous and gigantic. I thought he might be a demon of some importanz. But I sensed that he waz alive, or at least not altogether dead. He waz an abomination, a pasted-together puzzle of men. When I saw him, one thing stood out to me: that eye, *my* eye, with the Hellish image forever burned into the pupil, the image of that poor, innocent girl that I had killed with my own handz. He had brought her there to me in Hell! I sensed, I knew, that this waz the girl'z father, with flesh of my flesh sewn onto hiz own, like some reminder to both of uz of what had happened in another life. You see why it waz all so confuzing?"

"Bozkovitch!" Scaramouche raised his voice.

"Yes, master."

"Turn around."

The devil-fly slowly shuffled around and bowed its head, exposing its shoulder to an anticipated lashing.

The Veiled One reached up and slipped Heraclix's hood from his head just as Bozkovitch raised its eyes.

"Aaah! No! Not you!" the devil-fly screamed.

Heraclix recognized it as one of the devils he had seen in Hell.

"Send me back!" Bozkovitch begged. "That eye, I cannot look at it! Pleaze send me back!"

"First," Scaramouche yelled, "you must tell us the name of the man whom Mowler sought to take from Hell. What did Mowler say his name was?"

"It was him!" Bozkovitch shouted, pointing at Heraclix. "He iz the man, he iz the father!"

"His name, Bozkovitch!"

"Ah, Okto something, ah, Octavius! Octavius Heilliger!"

Heraclix's mind shot back to the memory of his own hand inscribing a book, the book that Pomp had rescued from the ashes of Mowler's apartment: *The Worm*. He reached into his pouch and took hold of the book. But the glimpse into his past evaporated with the buzzing, rattling screams of the devil-fly, Bozkovitch, the man who had killed his daughter.

"I did what you asked. Now send me back! Send me back! Send me b—"

The voice was cut off in a puff of brimstone. The circle of candles extinguished all at once as the air exploded in the vacuum where the demon had vanished.

The Shadow Divan quickly stood up, but Heraclix sat staring at the empty circle. The Veiled One and Skull-face each put a hand under Heraclix's arm to help him up. He stood, but showed no vigor, staring vacantly, as if he were weary of himself.

"These revelations are hard to take sometimes," Raven said. "How can we help you?"

Heraclix retrieved *The Worm* from his pouch and handed it to Raven. "I think that knowing something more about the author of this work will help."

The Raven took the book from Heraclix and carefully examined it, spending an uncomfortably long time staring at the title page. The others filed off downstairs.

"Come," said the Raven, "we will go down to the meditation room so you can have some time to process your thoughts."

But his thoughts were beyond his head. His mind roared like a gale through dry autumn leaves. Snippets of lucidity parted the maelstrom only long enough for him to reach out and take hold of a thought before being batted out and sucked up again into the mind-numbing whirlwind. He moved, but not consciously. He may have even spoken, but the words that left his lips and reached his ears were not his own. They were a faint shadow of what was real, a whispered lie spoken by that being on the surface of his soul, the one that interfaced with the outside world, or had done so since his rebirth. Deep inside that Hell was the real man, divided asunder between the evil that surely was and the good that he thought was his true essence, at least until now. A battle had begun within him. The standoff was over. The horsemen were making their charge. Like a mercenary bent on self-preservation, he vacillated between allowing himself to be led by the good person he thought he had been in this second life and submitting to the evil one he had been in the first. Confusion then took hold when he realized that both before and after his rebirth he had been both good and evil, that the idealistic dichotomies that would have made choosing so much easier were simply not so clear. This, then, was the fog of war that clouded his mind when he found himself standing at the edge of the quicksilver pool.

The man-slave had brought up both Al'ghul and Agha Beyruit Al Mahdr, who stood back with the Shadow Divan, behind Heraclix. Both of his compatriots were dressed differently than when Heraclix had first left them in the room downstairs, a strange fact to pick up when his mind had been so clouded. Hadn't Al Mahdr left to attend to other business? How long, Heraclix vaguely wondered, had he been up on the roof?

He stared into the molten reflection, watching his grotesque face shimmer and swirl. Soon the silvery surface became troubled, sloshing and boiling, casting blobs of mercury into the air and back down again into the roiling eddy until the dark and light patches took on a life of their own, separating from one another, disintegrating and shape-shifting until they formed visions of the past. They came in rapid succession, a series of vignettes shining up from the metallic waves.

In a small, spartan room, Octavius Heilliger sat across a desk from Mattatheus Mowler.

"You agree to the terms, then?" Mowler's voice crackled.

"Yes, of course." Heilliger sounded rushed, almost desperate.

"*Very well. Sign the paper.*"

"*But I have no ink.*"

"*You need no ink,*" *Mowler said, handing Heilliger a quill and a knife.*

Candlelight flickered, revealing Heilliger's bloodshot eyes. His lids drooped with fatigue, but he shook himself awake in order to concentrate on the papers on the desk beneath him. He took notes on a piece of parchment with a black-feathered quill, scribbling in a script unfamiliar to most human eyes. The words and symbols were almost an exact replica of those, inked in red, on the papers from which he read. Annotations in Latin, Greek, Hebrew, and Arabic filled the edges of his transcription. He copied text and wrote his own in the marginalia with equal speed. He wrote almost frantically, in bursts, then suddenly dozed off. He awoke with a start and began writing again, picking up where he had left off.

A door creaked then closed in the distance. Heilliger suddenly stood up, knocking a pile of papers down from the desk. A look of panic washed over his face. He rearranged the papers, then took his own notes up in an armful, picked up the inkwell and quill with his free hand, and quickly exited the room.

Under cover of the night, a robed, hooded figure walked hurriedly down the streets of Istanbul. The gait was that of a man burdened down with a heavy weight. A large, ragged knapsack, caked with mud, straddled his back. It was clearly a traveler's piece of equipment. The bag's condition contrasted sharply with the man's clothing. The robe and cowl were of fine, quilted black silk. A red hem bordered the button line and skirt. Strange writing was embroidered into the hem with indigo thread. Beneath the cowl one could see a simple black veil with two rough-cut eyeholes, like a highwayman might wear.

The figure looked over his shoulders with every few steps, sometimes turning completely around to get a clear look behind him.

It was during one of these turns that he back-stepped into a trio of figures, three pig-faced, cloven-hoofed demons, eyes ablaze with flames that flickered up into the night darkness.

"*Going somewhere, Heilliger?*" *one of them grunted.*

The other two laughed and squealed.

Heilliger backed away, holding his hands up as if he could stop the approaching demons with his bare hands. He fearfully muttered some gibberish, which gave the demons pause before they again walked forward, now much amused, to seize him.

Their chuckles turned to squeaking screams as the ground beneath them exploded into a fine mist of dirt. As the dust settled, one could see hundreds of long black tentacles had erupted from the ground, entangling the demons. If one looked closely enough, one would see tiny, needle-fanged mouths within each sucker.

Heilliger didn't stay to admire his handiwork. He skirted around the demons, who shouted curses and damnation on him until their larynxes were shredded or crushed, then fled into the shadows.

The quicksilver settled; the visions abruptly ceased. Heraclix turned to look at his interlocutors.

The Raven spoke. "You have seen, now, what we have known for some years now. Mowler took on an apprentice, a prodigy who sought to bring his wife and daughter back from the dead. This savant learned so quickly that Mowler grew suspicious that Heilliger had read and stolen information from his most valuable books and manuscripts, the very information that Mowler used to sustain his unnaturally long life. The apprentice fled Istanbul when he thought that Mowler had grown too suspicious."

"How do you know these things?" Heraclix asked.

"We know because both Mowler and his apprentice spent time here as members of the Shadow Divan."

"What else do you know?" Heraclix asked.

"We know some things, but only suspect others. Mowler left the Divan soon after Heilliger . . . after *you* fled. Mowler went to Prague, spending many, many years there until, we have gathered, he left due to his notion that the bulk of the citizenry there was far too idiotic to see his genius. He then returned to Istanbul. This time he returned with another young man, a slave, not an apprentice, that he had picked up in his travels."

Heraclix saw the Shadow Divan's servant standing with his hands on the edge of the pool, staring wide-eyed into its reflections. He might have been there the entire time that Heraclix was caught up in his vision or he might have just recently taken his place there. Heraclix had no way to tell. But the man was enraptured by what he saw in the pool, that much was clear. Tears streamed from his eyes.

The Shadow Divan didn't seem to take much notice. Heraclix turned to scan all of them, finally looking into the Raven's eyes. He noted that the eyes behind the mask were old, yellowed, and bloodshot. The skin around them was grooved and wrinkled, with veins embossed in relief like mountain ranges over canyons of age.

"What else . . ."

"Mowler stayed here a few months doing research in the Eye of Knowing, beneath us." The Raven pointed to the floor. "But one night, while scanning the sky with our telescopes, he saw what he called 'a fire like the midday sun' over Vienna. He left immediately. We haven't seen him since. It is presumed he found his apprentice, or at least enough of a lead as to be worth pursuing."

"When was this?"

"Around three years ago, maybe more. Then, a few months back, we heard of the immolation of Mowler's residence in Vienna. We thought that his demonic creditors had finally caught up with him."

The servant, who had stood silently up to that point, collapsed with a groan.

Heraclix instinctively tried to catch him.

The man was sobbing.

"Now I have seen the truth," the young man said. "Now I know." His eyes took on a clarity unseen by Heraclix to that point. It was as if he had woken from a dream, as if the drugs that had so infused his veins and clouded his mind were washed away in a trice.

"The man who brought me here, this Mowler you speak of, he brought me to this city, introduced me to the brothels, to the opium dens. He corrupted me. I was so young and naive then, and I followed him willingly, letting him take me away from my mother with fair promises and enticement. Ah, my poor mother!"

"Who is your mother, man?" Heraclix asked, trying to help the man unload his sorrows.

"My mother is Lady Edelweir of Vienna."

"Then your father is Lord Edelweir." Heraclix asked.

"No!" the man said. "My real father is the man who brought me here, submerged my reason in pleasure and dreams, and sold me as a slave. My father is Mattatheus Mowler!"

Heraclix glared at the members of the Shadow Divan.

"We . . . we had no idea," the Raven said. "Had we known . . . how could we not see?" The other members of the Divan broke out in an argument amongst themselves, but Heraclix had turned his attention back to the man-slave.

"What, then is your name?"

"I remember now. I am Viktor. Viktor Edelweir."

"And you think that Mowler is your father?" Heraclix asked.

"I am sure of it. What I saw in there," he nodded toward the quicksilver pool, "only confirms it."

"Impossible," said Al Mahdr, who had remained respectfully silent to that point. "Our spies in Vienna say that Viktor Edelweir is now their minister of defense."

"What of Von Helmutter?" Heraclix asked.

"Von Helmutter died unexpectedly. Viktor Edelweir was chosen as his successor."

A cry of rage erupted from a corner of the room, the corner open to the room below. All turned to see a thin, swarthy figure rushing toward Heraclix with a small silver knife in his hand.

"Mehmet!" Heraclix cried out.

Al'ghul tackled the man to the floor.

"Leave my friend alone!" Al'ghul cried out.

"Boy! How dare you! After all I did for you!"

The two struggled, wrestling for control of the weapon. Al'ghul found himself in a familiar position, riding Mehmet's back just as he had done in dispatching the Cossack whose comrades had attacked his family on the plains.

"You did nothing of lasting worth!" Al'ghul shouted.

Heraclix, Al Mahdr, and the members of the Divan dodged the brawling pair. Viktor sought to reach in to wrest the weapon from Mehmet, getting cut on the arm in the process.

"You betray me?" Mehmet gasped, running out of breath. "But I loved you. I gave you everything you wanted."

"You did *not* love me! You flattered me in my young pride, then gave me that which I hadn't yet earned." The accusation seemed to give him strength and leverage against the older man.

"You wanted the girl!"

"I wanted her to be happy, not my slave!"

"I'll make a slave of you, whelp!" Mehmet shouted.

But Al'ghul was too strong for the old man. He guided the silver blade, still in Mehmet's hand, over the sorcerer's heart, then plunged the blade once, twice into the old man's chest.

"I am tired of slavery. The world is tired of slavery." Al'ghul said in a voice wearied beyond his years. Mehmet wheezed out his dying breath.

But the noise wasn't ended for Heraclix, nor for the Shadow Divan, who heard what the other three did not: Mehmet's ghost shouting "Master, I have failed you!"

Then the spirit fled the room through the opening in the ceiling, to the roof.

Heraclix took Mehmet's silver dagger from the dead man's hand. With it, he cut the money pouch from his own belt and slipped the weapon under the belt.

"Take this," he said, proffering the gold-thaler-filled pouch to the Raven, "in exchange for the freedom of Viktor Edelweir."

"And you, my friend," he said, turning to Al'ghul, "meet me, with Graf Von Edelweir, in Vienna. Go secretly, arrive quietly, but notify me. I will send a message giving further instructions on where and when to meet me. Now I must take my leave quickly."

The giant bounded to the hole in the floor. He swung himself down through the opening, avoiding the ladder altogether, then sprinted across the room and out the door, running through the streets of Istanbul.

CHAPTER 24

The worried look that weighed down Emperor Joseph's face betrayed the gravity of the situation. He paced around his desk in an oval, like a racing horse that thought it was running to freedom but was in reality trapped by its own path. There would be no winner in this contest, only a lesser loser.

"Inevitable?" the emperor asked.

"I'm afraid so," a black-clad messenger said without a hint of regret. Von Graeb recognized the man as Rilke, one of Graf Von Edelweir's most trusted toadies, a regular army major. Not a member of the imperial guard. Because of their differing regiments, neither truly held rank over the other. "Rutowsky's spies have collected clear evidence that Prussia plans to annex Saxony within two weeks."

"But sir," Von Graeb interjected as respectfully as his growing impatience would allow, "How do we know we can trust Saxony? They vacillate between us and the Prussians on a weekly basis, it seems."

"Have they ever made threatening moves toward us?" the emperor asked.

"Directly? No, not for some time. They are too weak . . ."

"Or, perhaps," Rilke said to the emperor, "they are friendly!"

"But there are many who have not been threatening for many years. By that logic the Ottoman Empire is our chum," Von Graeb said.

"Oh, don't be silly. Everyone knows the Sultanate has modernized itself substantially since our last *disagreement*. No, they aren't our 'chums' as you so glibly put it. But there is no indication that we need fear them as an imminent threat. Our spies give no such indications. Some have even referred to the Ottomans as 'enlightened.'"

"Enlightened by what?" Von Graeb asked.

"Felix, please," the emperor said, dropping all formality. "Viktor is, after all, the Minister of Defense. We should take the Major Rilke's report for what it is." The tone of familiarity and the use of first names would have shocked the rest of the court, had they been present.

"Mind you, Major Von Graeb," Rilke said, "the Prussians are the greater threat. The Minister of Defense has ascertained this himself through spies and allies." He held up a roll of documents that ostensibly proved his point. "Your obsession with our quiet neighbors to the south, while understandable, is misplaced. Though you and he may share common interests in military matters, I hope that your disagreement with this carefully researched assessment doesn't endanger our common interest in protecting the throne."

Rilke glanced at the emperor, who then glanced at Von Graeb.

"No, of course not," Von Graeb said, barely retaining control of himself.

"There, there, Felix," the emperor said reassuringly. "Leave it alone. There's Viktor's marriage to Addy to worry about, and I understand that she has asked you to help her prepare."

"This is precisely my concern, your Majesty. There are matters of grave military importance, and, pardon my forwardness, but where is the Minister of Defense right now? Surely, he's not just off contemplating his upcoming honeymoon!"

Emperor Joseph laughed, then looked to Von Edelweir's representative. "Major, this is a legitimate concern that Herr Von Graeb brings up."

Major Rilke shot a baleful glance at Von Graeb. He shifted uncomfortably from one foot to the other, then moved his hands, with the documents behind his back. "Your Majesty, I'm not entirely sure. I was told to tell you that he was indisposed, at the moment."

"Well," Emperor Joseph said. "I should hope that he is watching the situation closely."

"Rest assured, your Majesty, that he is. I am certain that he is aware of every eventuality and has complete control of the situation."

"I sincerely hope so, Major," the emperor said. "You are dismissed."

Rilke left the room, careful not to glance back.

"Felix," the emperor said, "you have got to be more careful with your assertions."

"I'm sorry, your Majesty. But look at this—here we are receiving intelligence that indicates a pending Prussian invasion of Saxony, yet he sends one of his majors to brief you on the situation. It doesn't make sense! Where is he? I fear his miraculous return and good family name has caused us to overestimate his capabilities as a leader of men."

"Noble cousin," the emperor said, "I will assume responsibility for that decision. Surely you aren't recommending yourself as—"

"Your Majesty!" a young page, shouted running into the room holding a hastily scrawled letter aloft.

"What is it, boy?" the emperor said, stooping down to get closer to the youth's level.

"An invasion, your Majesty!"

"Prussia, then?" he asked, looking at Von Graeb.

"No, your Majesty. They are headed this way from Sofia."

"Who is, boy?"

"Your Majesty, the Ottomans are invading."

Von Graeb paced back and forth through the makeshift war room they had set up in the palace.

"Twelve hundred men," Von Graeb complained to his staff. "How am I to defend the southern flank of the Holy Roman Empire with twelve hundred men? Twelve thousand *might* be enough, seeing that we have to defend an entire mountain chain from enemy cavalry two thousand strong and footmen of three times that number. Herzog!"

"Yes, Herr Major," answered a grizzled veteran.

"Any word from the minister's representative?"

"He says that he can spare only three hundred men, sir. Those orders came to him direct from the Minister of Defense."

"Three hundred? But nothing is happening up there."

"Sir, the minister feels that if we move too many troops from Saxony, the Prussians will perceive a weakness and move to attack at their first opportunity."

"But nothing is happening up there!" Von Graeb repeated.

"Sorry, sir. I am only relaying a message."

"Understood. Have we tried sending a diplomatic envoy?"

"Of course, sir."

"And?"

"Sir, he was cut down before he reached Sofia. There were no negotiations."

"So much for the diplomatic option. How soon until the graf's three hundred reach us?"

"Two days, sir."

"Two days?"

"They are bringing in a pair of artillery pieces, sir."

"They'll be firing on the smoldering ruins of Vienna by then."

"Surely not the entire city, sir . . ."

"Maybe more!" Von Graeb shouted, then immediately regretted losing his composure. He gained control of himself and started giving orders in a measured, if certain voice.

"We send out a squadron of cavalry to cross the enemy's front in order to mask our numbers. That will slow them by at least a couple of hours as their generals discuss how to proceed next. Then all cannons to the front gate. They will have to thin out to surround us, no?"

"Correct, sir."

"Then the three hundred reinforcements can provide some harassment to the enemy's flanks and maybe provide us a narrow gauntlet for escape from the siege, should it come to that."

"Let's hope not, sir."

"Let's hope and plan, Herzog. The squadron will leave within the hour. They are only to nettle the enemy, not to fully engage, clear?"

"Clear, sir."

"Very good. Tack my horse up. I want to be ready when the enemy arrives. But first I have someone to talk to. Lescher!"

Von Graeb's assistant came out of the shadows.

"Major?"

"Lescher, you will meet me at the emperor's residence as soon as my orders have been issued."

"Of course, sir."

"And, Lescher?"

"Yes, Major."

"I want those orders given with exactness. You will not influence Sergeant Herzog on the matter. Any deviation, and I'll have you sent to the front, if I have to drive you there myself. Understood?"

Lescher shrank. "Very well, sir."

I cannot live on patriotism forever, thought Bohren. *My body can't keep up with my convictions.*

He lifted his foot off the ground and tried to rotate it, but the shattered ankle had healed funny, and he could only make a circular motion from the knee, like some drunken Russian dancer whose movements made a mockery of his age. He recalled with irony how he had awoken on the trail to the Serb's castle amidst a mud-pit of bootprints, in utter agony. His ribs, hand, and ankle had been broken in his deep sleep. As the the pain began to rush in, so did the villagers of Bozsok, trampling him a second time. This time, however, he was capable of shouting, which he did quite adamantly. The villagers were also more quiet on their return than they had been when they had originally stormed the Serb's castle, quieted, Bohren surmised, by their own guilt at what they had done, though he felt that they had no reason for remorse at having eliminated a foreigner of suspicious motivation and intent.

Now some of those same villagers stood ready not to drive another out, but prepared to keep from being themselves driven away by foreign invaders.

The Turks were approaching, though they were not sure of the invading enemy's numbers. The villagers of Bozsok capable of fighting numbered under a hundred. A few soldiers, recently garrisoned there by Major Felix Von Graeb, held the majority of the force's firepower. Twenty soldiers, well-armed with muskets and sabers, took up positions on the leeward side of the mountains leading up to Bozsok from the southeast. Of the villagers, a dozen or so had firearms available to them. They had, in fact, been loath to let the imperial forces know that they held so many, but as the magnitude of the crisis became clearer, the villagers came clean and submitted to the soldiers' pleas to "fall in." Bohren was given charge as a provisional commander of the militia, having proven an adequate leader of the people in times past.

For the first time, he felt inadequate to the task. Thirteen old, inaccurate blunderbuss rifles, eighty pitchforks and makeshift lances, not a proper sword among them outside of the old saber that Bohren now used as a crutch. This, plus twenty trained soldiers, none of who were under his command, hastily scrabbled together but not really together since the sergeant-at-arms refused to coordinate his efforts with Bohren's; this ragtag militia was to defend the mountain village from an unknown number of Ottoman foot soldiers.

Well, they had faced these circumstances before, but not for a generation. In times past the roughness of the terrain had slowed the enemy advance long enough for help to arrive, but the sergeant wasn't forthcoming regarding information on when to expect reinforcements or on how many men to expect. When pressed on the issue, the sergeant went silent, which did nothing to reassure Bohren or the other villagers, all of whom waited with grim resolve to defend their village or die trying. They knew that it was likely they would do both.

The morning sky was cloudy, which was good. Their numbers would be hidden, and they needn't worry about the sun's glare capriciously blinding them and spoiling their aim. If they were lucky, it might even rain, forcing the enemy to charge uphill on a slippery mud slope. Bohren silently prayed for the rain to come. They would need all the help they could get.

The rain came, but only as a quick misting, enough to drip down cold and discomfiting from the forest canopy, but barely enough to dampen the ground. It would do little to stop the advancing Turks.

As the noise of the rain quieted down, another sound arose from the slopes below. It had its own rhythm, more regular than the uneven rain: the steady beat of marching footsteps kept in cadence by more than one officer who counted their footsteps off in Turkish: "*Bir! Iki! Üç!*" The jangle of bandoliers and scimitar hangers clattered up the mountainside, closer and closer, growing louder with each moment. And with each step of the march, Bozsok's militia became more aware of its precarious situation. The sergeant-at-arms, who had taken up a forward position behind a large embankment with a platoon of his troops, looked back uphill at Bohren. The soldier shook his head, his face grim, resigned to fate, ready to die a warrior's death, but without any false hopes of victory this day.

Bohren understood why. His ears betrayed to him the same circumstance that the sergeant could see directly as the Turks advanced. They were hopelessly outnumbered and hemmed in on three sides.

He drew his saber at nearly the same time as the sergeant. The enemy's noise covered the sound of the slithering blades coming free from their scabbards.

The sergeant raised his saber, his men took aim, and the sun glinted through the breaking clouds as the troops of the Holy Roman Empire shot off their first, and possibly last volley. The musket-smoke cloud obstructed the view of the enemy lines, but the eruption of battle cries and gunfire was conclusive.

Bohren wouldn't be troubled by his bad ankle for long.

CHAPTER 25

"I remember you," a voice says.

Pomp remembers the voice. She cannot see anything, nor does she remember how she came to be in this darkness, but none of it matters as soon as she hears the voice.

"You are resilient," Mowler says with a sense of perverse admiration. "You are strong. Therefore, I shall be saving you for a special sacrifice."

The jar thuds down onto a tabletop, Pomp guesses, unable as she is to see beyond the bag in which she is wrapped. Vertigo overtakes her as the jar falls on its side, spins, rolls. She hardly knows which way is up.

The jar lid opens and she feels herself completely disoriented as Mowler removes the bag with her in it and bangs it on the table once, twice, thrice. Something in her side breaks and she is helpless to resist as the sorcerer reaches into the bag and grabs her, pinning her arms to her sides and squeezing the breath out of her.

She can't see her surroundings, only rushing light as he throws her down on the table. She tries to fly, but something holds her down. Not Mowler, who is no longer touching her, not her injury, which, while extremely painful, is not completely debilitating. No, some force holds her there. She looks around her on the table and sees a circle of black symbols scrawled on the tabletop around her. She strains her wings against gravity, but to no avail. Her feet are rooted to the place, as if they had been doused with a quick-drying glue. She is not going anywhere, not now.

"You're not going anywhere," Mowler affirms.

She can move her head, so she looks around, as much to avoid having to look at Mowler as to assess her situation.

He is as hideous as ever. But there is something different about him now. Something has changed since the last time she saw him die. Burn scars in the shapes of writhing tentacles line his neck, spine, both jaw lines, and his chin—as if a fiery octopus had swallowed him up to the shoulders, then tried to pull the rest of him into its beak before he managed to free himself from its grasp with one last, desperate effort. He walks now with a gait that defies gravity, as if he is always about to fall flat on his face until some spectral puppet master violently pulls him upright. Pure evil ambition animates him in a perpetual Saint Vitus dance, a mockery of nature that makes death itself turn away in ashamed impotence. His limbs bend, jerk, and snap with such suddenness and at such awkward angles that Pomp wonders if his bones have been completely shattered.

Still, he moves swiftly, snatching up supplies from around the room with spastic accuracy. Pomp feels a cold chill, followed by a deep aching in her belly as she watches him grab a long, slender, curved knife that seems very familiar to her. After picking up a piece of chalk, he plucks a jar from a table other than the one to which Pomp is frozen.

This jar speaks. Screams, really.

She knows the voices.

"Doribell! Ilsie!" Pomp calls out.

But they are too busy screaming to hear.

Mowler shakes the jar so violently that Pomp can hear the ring of the metal lid and glass bottom as the fairies' bodies bounce around inside. He then pours the pair out of the container and on to the floor. Their wings have been plucked off, and their backs are bleeding from the cavities where their wings used to be. One of them—Pomp thinks it's Ilsie—shakes off her dizzies and tries to run away only to be grabbed by the teetering sorcerer who grasps one of her legs in both hands and snaps her knee backwards with a sickening crunch. Doribell is in too much shock to help her injured sister. She just sits up and stares at a wall.

"No!" Pomp screams. "Leave them alone!"

"Or what?" The madman turns to look at Pomp with a baleful glare. "You have no say in the matter," he says, picking up Doribell and ripping the hair from her head like a spiteful child with a broken doll. Doribell screams, then stops as the stunning pain leaves her gasping and voiceless. "However, as a favor, you will get a foretaste of what is to come. But you will do so in silence!"

He thrusts a crooked arm at her, as if throwing something across the room. She finds her lips instantly sewn shut with some kind of rough, itchy thread that irritates the new puncture wounds that perforate her lips. She is helpless, able only to weep and watch.

Mowler lopes over to a corner of the room and wheels over a full-length mirror, positioning it so that Pomp can see herself standing on the table. He takes a piece of chalk and scrawls something on the floor halfway between her and the mirror. Then he writes across the mirror with a piece of soap. The flowing script resembles that which she has become accustomed to seeing: the language of devils and sorcerers, Hell's alphabet. Next he retrieves Doribell and Ilsie, dangling them by their raw head and broken leg, respectively. He drops them, unresisting, onto a matrix of symbols on the floor, sets the knife down on the perimeter of the magic square, and kneels down with his back to Pomp. She can still see his every move in the mirror.

The old man's eyes roll up and back into his head as he repeatedly chants the words "Kek kek agl agl nathrak". He raises his hands toward the ceiling, palms up, then pulls his fingers to his palms, beckoning.

The mirror ripples, distorting the room's reflection, then returns to normal. It ripples again, bulges from the flat glass, then roils, sending out glass bubbles that gently float through the air before touching the floor or some nearby object and shattering into a miniature shower of glass. Bubbles soon pour out of the mirror, and the room becomes a scintillating orchestra of popping globes and tinkling glass.

A hand emerges from the mirror. At the tip of each finger and on the back and palm of the hand are eyeballs. Each orb darts about, scanning the surroundings from every possible angle. Then another hand, also studded with eyes, emerges. The hands part the bubbles like a curtain.

The thing that issues forth from the face of the mirror is shaped like the headless body of a very fat man. Its entire body is littered with eyes—some brown, some green, some hazel, and some ice blue. Pomp wonders how it protects the eyes on the soles of its feet, which Pomp spots as it steps down onto the floor.

"Panopticus!" Mowler says. "What news from below?"

A voice sounds, but Pomp sees no mouth on the devil, only eyes.

"Archaentus, Pollyx, and Cant report that all is in position. Vespit nearly betrayed us to him, but we discovered the subterfuge and dealt with him accordingly. It will be a long time before he regains enough wherewithal to pose a threat."

"And by then," Mowler says, "I will have consolidated my rule. He will have no place to hide but under the scattered remains of Beelzebub himself. I should like to feed them both to the worms for several thousand years, bite by agonizing bite."

"It would only be appropriate, my liege," Panopticus says.

"In the meantime, though, I have a sacrifice to arrange. Are our other agents in position?"

"The Sultan's head eunuch is prepared to open the floodgates at your command."

"I trust that he hasn't yet shown his hand?"

"No one suspects a thing, my master. Only you and he know the end game."

"And what a glorious game, Panopticus. The greatest sacrifice ever to take place on the face of the Earth. The souls of tens of thousands freed from their mortal coil, almost all at once. Can you imagine the power that will be unleashed?"

"I can, my master, yes."

"And I shall harness it all. No one will stop me, man or devil, from ruling the dominions of Hell!"

"The devils crave order more than anything else, master," Panopticus says. "We are helpless to overcome the entropy within and around us, the entropy that the Lord of Flies seems to embrace, unless you come to instill order."

"Then it is critical that you heed my commands, Panopticus. You will have your king when I snatch the Crown of Hell from the defeated Beelzebub. But our preparations must be carried out. You will go to the Pasha Mustafa Il-Ibrahim in disguise as a traitor to the Holy Roman Empire. I'm sure you will impress him with your keen observations. Tell him something that he thinks only he knows. He will let you into his good graces. Then tell him that Emperor Joseph is building a secret weapon that will surely defeat the Ottoman Empire if it isn't destroyed. He'll want to consult with the sultan, but you must convince him that the sultan will take all credit for having discovered the threat and rooting it out. It's in Pasha Mustafa's best interest to take the matter into his own hands and capture the weapon with his own army. If the sultan is impressed with his pasha's ingenuity and bravery, it is well. If the sultan takes exception to his brash actions, Mustafa will have, in the weapon itself, the greatest bargaining chip possible. The sultan will have no choice but to praise and publicly reward his pasha."

Panopticus bows. "What shall I tell him this secret weapon is?"

"A cannon capable of destroying a city quarter or an entire village in one shot, hidden beneath Schonbrunn Palace."

"Yes, master." Panopticus bows and begins to slowly back away toward the mirror, maintaining his obeisant posture.

"Before you go," Mowler says, "you will perform one more task for me. I'm sure you'll find it enjoyable."

"What is your will, master?"

"I am in need of a little makeover. My disguise takes more and more energy to maintain. I need to be able to keep Edelweir's face without so much effort. You will do this for me."

"Yes, master."

Mowler holds up Doribell in one hand, the nasty curved dagger in the other.

"Then prepare to receive the sacrifice," Mowler says.

Pomp watches as he draws the knife along Doribell's length.

"Doribell!" Ilsie cries out, then sobs.

Panopticus makes a sound like a man who has just risen from a restful sleep and is stretching out, refreshed, a sound of gratification, of needs fulfilled.

"Ah!" the devil says. Pomp can only imagine him smiling. "Her death, seasoned with your malice, tastes good. But her sister's sorrow is delicious to me. Delectable!"

"You shall have the second course when you have done as I have ordered. If you do *not* . . . ." Mowler smiles a rickety-toothed grimace, ". . . well, you know what I did to Tawdragari."

Panopticus bows. "Hell will never forget such punishment as that, master. I willingly give you all."

The devil holds his hand out toward Mowler's face. Rays fan out from the eyes at the ends of his fingers, shattering the remaining glass bubbles between it and Mowler. The rays engulf the over-aged sorcerer, and Pomp watches with morbid curiosity as Mowler's stooped back and limbs, all akimbo, straighten with the sound of snapping bone and tearing muscle. His face puffs out from skeletal thinness to some semblance of normalcy in mere seconds. A thin black mustache grows over his newly reddened lips. His teeth straighten with a series of snapping and crunching sounds. This transformation elicits from him a series of high-pitched shrieks that subside into low groans. Eventually a new voice emerges from a new body, both those of Graf Viktor Von Edelweir.

"Ah, much better!" he admires himself in the mirror. "I shall have to think carefully about how I wish to appear when I take over as ruler of Hell. I fancy a curly, blond-haired Lucifer would look quite handsome under the Crown of Hell. We shall see."

"We shall, my master."

"Then go with this, Panopticus!" Mowler says before slipping his knife's fang into the hapless Ilsie, who mercifully faints away at the issue of blood. "Take the energy of this dying sprite and use it for the convincing of Pasha Mustafa Il-Ibrahim! Go quickly and do my bidding!"

The eye-studded devil walks backward into the mirror and pulls the bubbling glass veil closed with its hands. The face of the mirror flattens and cracks as the remaining bubbles in the air fall to the ground all at once, spraying the room with crystalline dust.

Mowler drops Ilsie's limp body to the floor. A stream of blood trails out from beneath her.

The sorcerer-cum-Viktor turns to face Pomp.

"What you have seen is only a tiny view of what is to come. Think not of merely two sacrifices or two hundred or even two thousand. Entire armies, whole cities will fuel my rise to power over the regions of the damned. You see, my little friend, I don't fear condemnation for my sins. I embrace it. I know my fate lies in Hell. So why not become the ruler of my own fate? You shall see the sacrifice not of two meaningless fairies, but of two empires at once! And my dominion shall be greater than them both! Greater than the entire Earth!"

Pomp strains against the twine that holds her lips sewn shut.

"Amusing. I like your spirit! In fact, I shall save you for last. You shall watch your friends die first, then yours will be the final bit of energy needed to take me beyond the veil in a triumphal procession where I will snatch up Beelzebub's crown and sit on the Eternal Throne!

"But I don't want to squelch that fire of yours before its time." He makes a grasping motion toward her, as if grabbing something out of the air, "So I will rescind my declaration of silence."

The twine vanishes, and the needle-wounds in her lips heal in an instant.

She screams a stream of vindictive obscenity at him.

Mowler . . . Viktor laughs heartily. "You should speak more kindly to royalty, little one," he says. "Ha! In any case, carry on. No one can hear you here."

He turns away and exits through a side door, mumbling and under his breath as he goes.

Pomp surveys the room, but no matter how hard she strains, she cannot break free of the spell that binds her.

"Help!" she screams, but the words echo off the walls and fade into silence.

But then, a sound! A tiny sound coming from where? The floor. But that can't be, unless . . .

"Ilsie!" Pomp cries out.

The little body on the floor moves slightly.

"Ilsie! It's Pomp! Up here!"

Ilsie turns over onto her side and looks up through blurry eyes at Pomp.

"Ilsie! You're alive!"

But Ilsie's side is perforated with a slit from hip to rib. The knife has pierced all the way through her and out the opposite shoulder.

Still, she fights to crawl, using only her hands and her one unbroken leg, pulling herself through her own gore toward Pomp.

"Ilsie, come here!" Pomp encourages her.

The wounded fairy is determined to get to her cousin. Ilsie fades in and out of consciousness, barely able to pull herself up after each time she passes out.

"Ilsie, keep coming!" Pomp urges her.

And Ilsie pushes, or pulls on. It seems like forever, or however these mortals say it, but Ilsie makes progress, though her face and body have turned bone white from loss of blood. Still she draws closer and closer until she comes to the foot of the table, below which Pomp cannot see. All she can do now is, what is the word? Hope! And she can talk!

"Come on, Ilsie. I need you. You must live. You can do this thing. We can do this. We must. So much is at stake. We must *hope*!"

Pomp waits. Silence overtakes her. Hope fades. She doesn't think she will see Heraclix or Lady Adelaide or Von Graeb ever again. Not now. Ilsie was her last hope to have a chance to stop Mowler from committing an atrocity, the likes of which hasn't not been seen in . . . forever. Yes, she can't remember such an evil act, and she has lived since before man measured time, back when the whole world was pure and unspoiled. Before evil entered the heart of man. Before Mowler. And now it seems that evil will dominate the . . . what's it called? The future? All is done for now. Ilsie was her last hope, and now Ilsie is . . .

. . . climbing up over the edge of the table? How is it possible?

"Ilsie, I'm here!"

Ilsie is blind, following instinct and Pomp's voice. She pulls her broken, punctured body closer and closer, blood smearing across the tabletop.

"Ilsie, come to me! I cannot come to you. You have to come to me, Ilsie! Come, my cousin! My family! My love!" Pomp sobs.

Ilsie cannot speak. Her body makes strange gurgling noises as she breathes in through one good lung. But she can move, just barely. So she does. She moves, inch by agonizing inch, until her body simply stops just short of the circle that holds Pomp captive. So close, but just short.

"Ilsie, no!" Pomp screams, then cries in anguish. "Ilsie, no . . ." her voice fades.

Ilsie's blood flows out of her soul-fled body, a red river coursing out of her abdominal cavity, trickling towards the destination she had hoped to reach before she died, to be with her cousin, her family, before she departed, to be with blood of her blood.

Pomp's eyes are too full of tears to see Ilsie's blood cross the circle, breaking the perimeter line.

And she is free of the magical manacles that held her. She can move!

"Ilsie!" she yells, exultant, "you did it!"

Pomp runs over to her cousin's side, but her cousin cannot hear her, will not hear her again.

"Ilsie, my love!" Pomp cradles the dead fairy in her arms, weeping without restraint. She soon remembers Doribell and flies down to her other cousin, but Ilsie's twin is cold, lifeless, dead.

And so many more will be if she doesn't stop Mowler. She knows that the despot won't be satisfied with merely ruling Earth and Hell. He will enter her realm and rule there, too. His greed for power knows no bounds.

She checks her back. Her bow and arrows are still there. Good. She might need them. She flies over to the door and squeezes herself under the crack. Then she is off to warn her sisters, Heraclix, and Von Graeb of the dangers they face.

Or is it too late? How long has she been here? How long was she in the jar, unconscious? There is no way to know. There is only one thing to do, and that is to hurry!

CHAPTER 26

Her horse, so many miles back, was dead. It was a good horse. The steed had carried her in a few months farther than any of her ancestors had walked in years. Of course when the wanderlust had struck her forefathers, they traveled on foot, being too poor to afford horses. Now that her horse had died, she joined the ancestors, in spirit, on the ground.

But unlike her kin, she wasn't hounded from place to place, not condemned to vagrancy, to begging. What she lacked in resourcefulness, she made up for in simple intuitive cunning. She wasn't, like them, the hunted, but the hunter.

On a night like this, though, she was hard-pressed to keep her prey in her sights. The mountains just northwest of Bozsok seemed possessed with an undying need for tumult that conflicted directly with her aims. The sky itself had seemed to open to the elements of chaos as soon as the sun set. Waterfalls of rain now cascaded down, then whipped sidelong in the whistling wind. Here the furies danced unashamed of their wanton nakedness, like her great aunts and grandmothers had done by the light of the moon many years ago, when she was a child. But that all seemed trivial now— the odes to the earth mother and wild prancing around the dying fires of night. That was silliness.

This was serious business. She knew it. The one she hunted knew it. And the one her prey hunted knew it as well. Only she saw every link in the chain of pursuit.

She had almost lost sight of the one ahead of her.

He had slipped into the night, crawling up rain-swollen ravines, concealing himself behind trees, under giant boulders. He was trying hard not to be seen. And he was good at what he did.

But not good enough.

Were it not for the glinting visual echo of a lightning flash off of her quarry's scimitar, she might have lost him in the storm. She was pleased to confirm his location, but more perplexed by his intent in drawing the weapon. He had traveled with it sheathed for many long miles, for days. Even when his horse had been hounded by wolves, and when he had narrowly avoided a wandering band of Cossacks, he had kept the blade clothed. Now he bared it in a rampaging storm in the dead of night. Why?

She used the noise of the rain and the cover of darkness to close the gap between her and her target. She drew her dagger, though the little blade held faint chance against the curved scimitar, if it came to that. She had observed the man enough to know of his prowess, whether his sword was drawn or not. The occasional body of a traveler, neck broken and wearing a final, startled expression, left clear evidence that this man was a trained killer, a skilled assassin. For this reason she had kept her distance, until now.

Another bolt of lightning flashed ahead of the pair, casting an immense blink-of-an-eye shadow before the thunder rumbled through the air. It took a moment for her to realize that they were stalking, both she and the assassin, toward a looming tower, a tall castle surrounded by a clearing whose circumference was ringed with fire-blackened trees that made the night seem even darker. Lightning struck again, and she saw a huge shape—not the assassin, but another nearly twice the little killer's size, entering a door at the foot of the tower. The giant had to stoop to avoid hitting its head on the top of the stone-arched doorway. She waited for the lightning again. It struck nearby, barely allowing her to see the hind foot of the assassin disappearing into the same doorway before the resounding crash of a shattering tree shook through her body. She dashed for the doorway.

The tower reeked of old smoke. A faint light shone up above her as she entered the doorway. The door itself lay in pieces on the floor. She slowly, carefully ascended the open spiral staircase that hugged the outside wall. It was slow going. Halfway up her foot slipped off of a slick step, and it took all of her effort to keep her balance. She prayed that her startled gasp wouldn't draw the assassin's attention. One leg hung off the precipice above the castle's empty center shaft.

She gathered herself up and climbed higher. The feeble light from above grew stronger. Finally, she reached the final bend of the stairs, where she could clearly see an open trapdoor that led into the upper reaches of the tower. It was from there that the light came. Still, it was a weak light—that of a few small candles, at most.

She peeked up through the trapdoor only enough to expose her eyes.

The giant knelt before a great pile of ashes. She thought she could hear him crying.

Behind him, the assassin stood. The killer's sword arm was wound up across his chest, ready to uncoil and decapitate the kneeling giant.

Instead, the assassin grasped at his throat with a gurgle. He was shocked to find a dagger's point protruding out through his trachea.

The giant, startled, stood up at the sound of the scimitar clattering on the floor.

The assassin, assassinated, fell face first to the wooden floor with a thump.

Heraclix looked past the body to the cloaked woman who stood a good fifteen feet behind the would-be killer.

"Who are you?" Heraclix asked.

"It looks like I arrived just in time," the woman said.

"You haven't answered my question," Heraclix said, holding his fists up as if readying himself for a fight.

The woman removed her hood.

"Vadoma!" Heraclix said, incredulous. "Vadoma. I had hoped you hadn't . . ."

"Been killed by the rabble? No. I haven't lived so long by being overly careless and not having a backup plan for every situation. My grandmother taught me many things about taking care of myself."

Heraclix looked at the body on the floor. "Obviously." He flipped the lifeless figure over onto its back with his foot. "And who is he?"

"His name, I don't know."

He studied the dead man's features. He was a man of middle age, perhaps forty, dressed in well-worn, nondescript travel clothes. A bushy mustache extended well beyond the sides of his face. It had become entangled with his curly black hair when he had collapsed on the floor.

"But I do know that he's been following you for a long, long time."

Heraclix looked at Vadoma with a quizzical expression. Her comment finally registered with him.

"How could you know . . ." Then it dawned on him. "Ah! I see he hasn't been the only one hunting me, eh?"

"Hunting you? Me? No. Following, yes, but not hunting."

"And why have you been following me? When did you pick up my trail, anyway?"

"I have been observing you off and on since not long after I learned that you had been found floating on the Danube. There have been delays, however. There is a lot of commotion going on in these parts, and I lost you when you headed south and east. So did he." She indicated the body on the floor. "But he evidently picked up your trail again before I did. Thankfully, I never lost his trail."

"How . . ." he said.

"I told you. My mother taught me many things. But these are family secrets. They will die with me."

She turned her back on him and walked the perimeter of the room, looking at anything that remained on the walls or in the ashen pile in the middle of the floor. She ascended the left stairs to the half-crescent level above, then, finding nothing of interest there, descended the right stairs.

"I suppose you will next ask me why, no?"

"Yes. Why?"

"He has been looking for you since you left Vienna. Seeking revenge, no doubt."

"For what?"

"He is Romani. A newer member of our community, I'm guessing, since I did not really know him well. He blames you for the appearance of the Imperial soldiers. He, like many, lost much."

"How did he find me?"

"He probably heard the same rumor I did, that a hideous giant had been found floating in the Danube."

"And why are *you* following me?"

"I think I might be able to explain now that we are here."

"What do *you* know of this place?" he asked.

"This place may be the answer to why I have followed you so far." The words were directed at Heraclix, but the tone was introspective. Her eyes were on her surroundings, her thoughts elsewhere. She was, in a word, diffuse.

Heraclix looked at the blackened pile in the middle of the room. The center was mostly ash, with the occasional piece of charred but not fully consumed furniture. A chair leg here, a small section of board there. A few pieces of mirrored glass caught the candlelight.

Vadoma produced a few more candles from one of the satchels she carried. She lit them from the flames of the already-burning candles. The added light permitted closer investigation by both gypsy and giant, both of who circled the pile of refuse.

"Why were you weeping when I found you?" Vadoma asked.

"Because I knew who lived here, and I thought the worst for one I considered a friend."

"Friend?" Vadoma says with a bit of surprise. "Well, I will tell you that I knew him long before I ever met you, if my suspicions are . . . Ha!"

She knelt down at the edge of the pile and began digging with her hands. She examined each handful, casting some behind her, setting others aside. After sorting through several handfuls, she slowed, putting her face down close to the refuse. She carefully cleared soot and debris with the tip of a finger. Suddenly, she thrust a hand down into the pile and, with a triumphant yelp, wrenched something free and held it aloft with a broad smile.

"Ha! I'm right! It's him!"

The object at first appeared to be a simple stick. But, drawing closer, Heraclix saw the thing's smooth surface and the lightness of it in Vadoma's hands. She scrubbed at the black surface to reveal a patch of white bone under soot.

"You can see the cut marks, here at the wrist!" she exclaimed. "this is him!"

"Vladimir Porchenskivik," Heraclix said flatly, unsure of how to read her tone.

"That was his name?"

"Yes," Heraclix said with deep sadness. He didn't care whether or not she approved at this point. "That was his name. Tell me, how did you know him? Then, please explain why you have been following me this long time."

"I have already told you the answer to your second question. I followed you *here* to *be* here. I had an old debt to settle, but it appears I am too late now."

"And since you have led me here and given me his name, I will answer your first question."

"We Romani move. It is in our blood. We are an independent people. We value our liberty and don't like to be tied down to any one place. Every land is our homeland. We are a nation—or nations—of vagabonds.

"My family was no exception. Some time ago, when I was much younger, we were uprooted from our admittedly temporary home halfway between here and Sofia. This was an unfortunate time to have to move. I sensed forebodings about our journey as we loaded up our belongings. Not that I would miss the place we were leaving. We were never really welcome there, though we kept to ourselves and lived peaceably for several years. No, it wasn't any sense of forthcoming homesickness. It was just a sick feeling, like something was bound to go wrong.

"We discovered early on that there was much tumult in the regions round about. An irregular army of Serbs had the notion that there was something for the taking there. But it was a poor region, and it remains so. The Serbs found little by way of wealth, but they were already mobilized, so they took all that was left: dignity, virtue, and life, usually in that order.

"The Serbs had set up checkpoints along many of the major roads, so we crept along back roads and mountain paths, hoping to avoid them until we could find refuge in a more civilized area, in a city. But in the mountains, not far south of this place, we found trouble. Or, rather, trouble found us.

"My parents heard the horses approaching and told us to run into the woods off the pathway. We did, but didn't go far. We watched. We saw what they did to our father, then to our mother. I don't remember the men's faces. I only remember their taunting voices, their laughter, their grunts." Vadoma held up the bone: "And their hands." She looked at Heraclix's left hand, the hand that was once the Serb's.

"One of them was that hand, Heraclix. '*Osvetnik,*' 'Avenger.'"

"I . . . I am truly sorry," he said.

"There is no need for sorrow. You are a victim as much as my parents. Besides, I have had enough of sorrow and pain.

"That day, he saw me. He was one of the last to leave my parents' violated, murdered bodies on the road. My sister or I had made some kind of noise, I suppose, so he looked over into the woods where we thought we were hidden. We were *not* so well hidden. He saw me directly, looked straight into my eyes. At first, I was terrified. Then a strange numbness came over me. My parents were dead. We had nothing. I felt nothing. This was my way of dealing with the moment. When he finally tore his gaze from my own, he walked away with a puzzled look on his face. I wept. We wept, my sister and I, into the night until the wolves howled and we huddled around a small fire, protecting our parents' remains from the scavengers."

"I am truly sad for your loss," Heraclix said.

Vadoma looked hard into his eyes. "Yes. I think you are genuinely sad for me. That big chest of yours is full of compassion."

"I am finding that it was not always so."

"No one remains the same, Heraclix. People are more complex than that. People change over time. That is why I'm here."

"Because you changed?"

"Partly. But mostly because *he* changed." She held up the bone again, running her fingers along the squared-off edge where the hand had been removed.

"The man I knew," Heraclix said, "wasn't the man you knew."

"No, the man you knew was the man that had grown out of the one I first knew. Not a different man, a changed man.

"Many years later I had the chance to meet him again. We were traveling through Bozsok. My sister was very sick. I thought she might die. None of the cures my grandmother had taught me could help her. While in the village, we overheard some of the villagers talking about the hermit who lived in the mountains. Some said he was a madman. Others said he was a miracle man. I thought we might as well seek out this person, which we did. We found him both a madman and a miracle worker."

"You recognized him?" Heraclix asked.

"Not at first. As I said, I didn't remember the faces of my parents' killers. But when he laid his one hand on my sister, I recognized that hand. It all came back to me full force, the memory did. But he healed my sister. It was as if he drew the very sickness out of her body. She fully recovered in a matter of minutes.

"Curiously, he never recognized me. Or, if he did, he didn't let on about it."

"My sister thanked him, and we left. She hadn't seen the man when our parents had been killed. She had no idea who he was. But she was cured. I didn't feel the need to tell her the truth of the matter."

"So when you examined my palm . . ." Heraclix said.

"Yes, I recognized Porchenskivik's hand. The overwritten tattoo didn't fool me. I would have known it anywhere."

Heraclix became aware that he had involuntarily moved the hand behind him. The sense of shame that he felt indicated that the hand wasn't acting autonomously. He had hidden it, even if semiconsciously. He tested the indication by forcing the hand out from behind his back. It came naturally, a willing part of him. But the shame remained. He felt he should keep the hand visible, however, as a sort of penance.

"You don't have to hide that," Vadoma said.

"But it must be as painful for you to see as it is for me to show it. More so, even."

"When I read your palm, Heraclix, I saw that the hand no longer belonged to Porchenskivik. The lines on the palm are distinctive. Past and future were radically different."

"Then the lines determine my fate?" Heraclix asked.

"No. You make choices that determine the lines, my friend. Fate has little to do with it."

"You don't think it was fate that brought us here?"

"No. I followed you, remember? Now I . . . wait a moment."

She knelt down again and examined a corner of unburnt paper that was sticking out of the very edge of the ash heap. She carefully pulled the paper out of the ashes. She discovered that it was actually a pair of papers, loosely rolled together. The outer paper was surprisingly intact, browned from heat but not consumed. It adhered to the other page slightly, until Vadoma peeled them apart. The mirror image of some hastily scrawled, illegible writing showed on the inner paper, where the two were stuck together. The author had been in a hurry to wrap one paper inside the other, so much so that the ink had not even dried on the outer manuscript.

The outside document looked very familiar. It was a rough diagram of Porchenskivik's hand. Not as detailed as the one that Pomp had discovered at Mowler's apartment, but very similar to it.

The inner document was made of sturdy parchment with handwriting in a florid script, carefully crafted in a formal manner. The words were faint, but Heraclix and Vadoma could make them out, just barely. Heraclix read the words out loud over Vadoma's shoulder:

> Most honorable Pasha,
> I gratefully received news regarding your acceptance of the terms set forth in my previous communication. You should be prepared to act in full force by next winter. This will give you more than adequate time to be ready, though events have been progressing more swiftly than I could have ever hoped. Soon, sooner than you expect, you will be called a hero by the subjects of the Ottoman throne. Remember our agreement. We are confederate.
> *Truly,*
> *Graf Viktor Von Edelweir.*

"Fate or chance, this letter makes my arrival in Vienna even more urgent. I must be swift! Vadoma, farewell!"

"Wait!" she called out. "I want to help. How can I help?"

Heraclix thought for a moment. "Go toward Istanbul. Ask until you find the Agha Beyruit Al Mahdr. Tell him of what we have discovered here. He will know what to do next, I'm sure."

"I will make haste," she said.

On his way toward the trapdoor, Heraclix stopped. "I had all but forgotten about him," he said, looking at the assassin's body. He bent down and picked up the scimitar, turning it in the candlelight.

"It's coated with silver," he said. He removed the sheath from the man's body, sheathed the sword, and slid it under his belt. "He knew what he was doing."

"And we know what we must do, friend Heraclix. Make haste!"

CHAPTER 27

Pomp has to go home to warn them of what's coming. Her falsified "Mowler attacks!" is not false anymore. He will attack, and she must raise the alarm!

The city shimmers, folds, gives way to the flower-painted hillsides of Faerie. Nothing has changed, except for the absence of Doribell and Ilsie, who will never return to these fair meadows.

Gloranda is there, as beautiful on the outside as she is ugly on the inside. Pomp doesn't much like her anymore. Gloranda is, after all, an ignorant, possibly uncaring fairy. But she is family, and that is why Pomp is here now.

"Gloranda!" Pomp says with as much enthusiasm as she can muster.

"It's me, Pomp. I have come to warn you of danger."

Gloranda looks at her sister, then starts to laugh almost uncontrollably, rolling on the ground, holding her sides. Even the mirth has become painful, Pomp thinks. "Oh stop, my sister," Gloranda begs, "That was a very funny joke!"

"It's no joke," Pomp says.

Now Gloranda doesn't make a sound. Not because she is taking Pomp seriously. Because she is laughing so hard and so suddenly that she can hardly breathe.

Finally, she gasps her words out. "Ah, such good fun. Where are the twins?"

"The twins won't be coming back, Gloranda."

"Did they go to find another bat?"

"No, Gloranda. They are dead."

This is too much for Gloranda, who flies up into the air and cries out: "Come see Pomp! She is funny!" She then floats down and sits beside Pomp. "What is 'dead?'"

But Pomp doesn't respond. She is silent, waiting for something.

And something comes. It is big, like an ocean, but comes in many small parts, like drops of water. A buzz of wings sounds out here, then there, then here again. The buzz becomes a low throbbing as a few small groups of fairies appear over the hills all around her.

"Tell us a joke, Pomp!" one yells.

"Do some tricks!" shouts another.

"Dance! Dance!" orders a small group.

"This is *not* going to be easy," Pomp says.

"Sure it is!" Gloranda says. "You're funny!"

"But this is serious, coz'," Pomp says to Gloranda. Gloranda falls on the ground again, laughing.

"Tell us more!" jibes a silver-haired, freckle-faced sprite.

"I am telling you, this isn't funny!"

Which is funny to the fairies. Some of them laugh so hard they fall from the air into a heap of giggles.

"Oooo!" Pomp shakes her fists in frustration.

The fairies shake with laughter.

Pomp knows it is hopeless to talk. Words will only make things worse. She needs action.

She looks at Gloranda, still on the ground, holding her sides, barely able to breathe through her smile.

Then Pomp knows what to do.

Quickly, with a series of intentionally clumsy movements to keep them laughing, she traces a circle in the dirt around Gloranda. Gloranda stops laughing long enough to see what Pomp is doing. She reaches out to touch one of the sigils, but Pomp slaps her hand. Gloranda falls again on her back in hysterics.

Pomp draws. Pomp remembers. Not everything, but maybe enough. She feels something in the air, an unpleasant tingling that makes the hairs of her neck stand up, like flying through a ghost.

She draws some more, remembers more, again feels the sorrow of losing Doribell, the pain of Ilsie's absence.

Then, the circle is complete. Or almost complete. She isn't completely sure. Only Gloranda's actions will tell if she got it right. And Gloranda will stay on the floor laughing if Pomp continues to draw.

So she sits. And waits.

The laughter dies down. A few bored fairies at the edge of the crowd fly off. Some punch each other in the shoulder for no good reason. Others make fun of Pomp.

Pomp simply waits.

Eventually, Gloranda recovers from her fit and stands up in the middle of the circle. She takes a step toward Pomp, but her left leg is stuck. It is rooted to the floor so securely that she thinks Pomp has pulled a trick on her, which she has. Gloranda pulls and yanks and almost spins in a circle, but her ankle doesn't go that way. She tries to fly, but her wings won't work. She jerks against gravity and gravity jerks back.

Now it's Pomp's turn to giggle. Then she remembers why she is here, that she has serious business.

"I told you," Pomp says to Gloranda, "Doribell and Ilsie are dead! Mowler killed them!"

Gloranda thinks her cousin is still joking. "Dory and Ilsie are away to play, back another day!" A few of the remaining fairies respond with laughter.

Pomp paces, it's so hard to think sometimes, think of what to do, what to say!

"Gloranda. You are stuck, right?"

Gloranda tries again to free herself.

"Stuck, all right."

"Mowler's spell stuck you there!" Pomp says.

"No, Pomp's spell stuck me here."

Pomp pulls at her own hair in frustration. There seems to be very little left to try. How will she ever get through to them?

"Remember Cimbri!" she calls out to the crowd. "Remember Cimbri!"

"Huh?" says one fairy after another.

"What is remember?" one calls out.

"Remember is . . . no, never mind . . . I can't explain . . ."

She paces even more frantically, fluttering her wings in worry. Time is running out!

She thinks she has one last chance.

"Cimbri is saving us! Pomp is saving us! Mowler attacks! Fight Mowler!"

The crowd, somewhat agitated, looks around for the miscreant wizard. They have heard of him, heard that he is unhappy and angry since he left Faerie. He likes to snatch fairies away from their home.

But Gloranda isn't believing it.

"Pomp isn't saving us," Gloranda says. "Pomp is talking. I'm bored of talking."

"Me too!" someone says in the crowd.

"Let's go find some fun," says another.

"No, wait!" Pomp yells in her tiny voice. It is lost among the buzzing of wings as the fairies, all except Pomp and Gloranda, begin to take off.

"Wait!" Pomp says in a little voice.

"Wait!" she squeaks.

"WAIT!" she booms louder than any noise she thought she could make. Her voice sounds different now, too.

"WAIT!" the voice booms again. It isn't her voice. Many voices, actually. Many loud voices falling on them from above.

Like a shadowy wheel, something dark made of twelve flying somethings circles overhead.

"Whoo, whoo, wait!" the many voices call out.

The Armory owls are descending on the fairies.

"Well, that's interesting," says one fairy.

"And fun!" says another.

"No fun!" the quorum of three-faced owls bellows below. "Pomp is saving us! We must fight Mowler! To arms!"

"To arms!" the mustered fairies respond to the call, "To arms!"

Pomp, mission accomplished, flies on.

She navigates herself to the Armory, now empty of owls, who were too busy marshaling troops to guard an empty grove of trees. She prepares to make the transition to the mortals' world. She

266

remembers, all too well, the smoke and confusion that met her last time. She holds her breath and plunges forward.

Pomp flitted through the shredded veil between worlds, first catching mere glimpses of the mortal realms, like windows into the world of men, then emerging fully into it. She had to find Heraclix as quickly as possible. She knew that he wasn't at Vienna, but supposed that he would be coming back before too long. So she headed back along the road toward Bozsok, intending to return to Szentendre, where she had left him.

The fires had extinguished themselves a long time ago, but the place still reeked of smoke. A recent rain exaggerated the stench even more, swelling the air with ashen memory. The trail leading up to the Serb's castle was quiet. The ghosts had all burned up. The only sound came from a single raven cawing high above among the scorched tree limbs.

Pomp would have ignored the bird outright if it weren't for the glint of something caught in the dim sunlight. It shimmered near or *on* the bird; Pomp couldn't quite tell which. She had never heard of a shiny raven before, and she found it odd enough to distract her, momentarily, from her quest to find Heraclix.

It was small for a raven. On close examination it proved not much bigger than a common crow. But this bird was far from common. Its thick beak was made of pure silver, as were its eyes, and it wore a crown—a very familiar looking crown, one Pomp had seen in a much larger size in a much more Hellish place.

"You're an ugly bird!" Pomp said.

It turned to her with fiery eyes blazing.

"Go, go away!" it said.

"Why should I?" Pomp said.

"Kill, kill, die!" the bird-demon warned.

"But you're just a bird!" Pomp taunted.

"No!"

"Not a bird?" Pomp asked.

"No!"

"Do you have a name then, un-bird?" Pomp mocks the creature.

"Caw, caw, phony!"

"Cacophony?"

"Caw, caw, phony!"

"How appropriate."

The bird-that-is-not-a-bird's attention suddenly turned away from Pomp. Something was moving below. Something large. There was no secret to its arrival. Branches snapped, then fell to the ground in its wake.

Caw-Caw-Phony pushed off its perch, gliding momentarily, then diving almost straight down.

That breathing from below, the raspy intake of air, Pomp knew that rasp.

"Heraclix!" she yelled.

"Kill! Kill! Die!" Caw-Caw-Phony squawked.

Pomp dove after the bird, which was diving straight for the golem below.

"Heraclix!" Pomp yelled again. She hoped her friend could hear her.

"Caw! Caw! Ph—" the devil-raven stopped short.

Pomp nearly flew into the creature's back, it had stopped so suddenly. She also nearly skewered herself on the scimitar blade that protruded from the bird's back. A glowing yellow-green ichor dripped from the tip of the blade.

Heraclix brought the sword down, Caw-Caw-Phony still skewered on the curved instrument.

"It is . . . dead?" Pomp asked.

"Devils don't die, Pomp," Heraclix said. "They just go back to the bottom of the worm-pile to recirculate through eternity."

She hovered there with a puzzled look on her face.

"And it's good to see you, too," Heraclix smiled.

"Huh?"

"Never mind. Mortal humor." He flipped the raven's carcass off the blade. Somehow, the crown stayed attached to the bird's head.

"Pomp, my friend," he said, wiping the blade off on a patch of grass. "We need to get back to Vienna. And on the way, you and I have much to discuss."

"More talking?" Pomp said, exasperated.

"More talking," Heraclix said.

Chapter 28

A map of the Holy Roman Empire lay spread out on a desk between Major Von Graeb and Emperor Joseph. The northern edge of the map sagged over the precipice of the too-small desk's edge. Several wooden chits, each signifying a military unit, were scattered across the map, the largest clump near the precarious northern edge. Von Graeb moved a small group of chits from the hanging edge, on his left, to the far right corner opposite him, where the emperor stood.

"That's what we need." He slid the majority of the pieces back to their original location, then pointed to the meager remainders at the southeastern edge of the map, "And that's what we have."

"It does seem a rather disparate concentration," the emperor agreed with him. "but our spies in Prussia have noted a threat."

"I'd call it a desperate concentration myself. And isn't it odd that we have never, not once, heard from our spies in the Ottoman lands?"

"They have been rather quiet," the emperor said.

"Excuse my boldness, your Majesty, but they have been utterly silent. They have not reported back in . . ." Von Graeb paused ". . . months."

"In any case," the emperor said, "there's no sense discussing what has or hasn't happened. You have an immediate need."

"A need," a third voice said from a shadowy doorway, "that I intend to fulfill."

"Viktor!" the emperor said in surprise. "I thought you were in Saxony . . ."

Othman and Fahtma were both sick of marching. Othman, being as large as he was, felt the burn in his legs even more. His Agha had ordered him to lose weight many times. Now that they were on the march toward the borders of the empire, he had no choice but to shed the pounds.

Fahtma, in better condition, had no better of an attitude. "Ptah! What ever happened to the crusades, when the infidels came to *us* to be slaughtered?"

"Times have changed, my friend."

"And you have not. Pagh! March downwind of me if you are truly my friend."

"But then I fall behind."

"Better you get a taste of the agha's crop, rather than the both of us."

"Quiet you two!" shouted the agha. "We're about to enter enemy territory."

"How is that even possible?" Fahtma asked in a hoarse whisper.

The agha heard him. "You question the word of the pasha? He himself has declared it."

"He is an idiot," Othman whispered. He was not heard by the Agha. Perhaps the plump soldier couldn't keep up with his companion. At least he could keep his voice down.

Their unit, of which Othman and Fahtma were but a hundredth between the two of them, obeyed orders, putting one foot in front of the other. But as he watched his feet plod, Othman noticed that something was changing. The sky here seemed bluer, the air sweeter, and the clovers had teeth.

Teeth?!

"Aah!" yelled Othman, unable to keep his voice down.

This time the agha heard. Wheeling his horse around, he—his horse, really—pranced back down the line to the spot where Othman stood screaming.

"I thought I told you to be quiet!" the agha whispered with such harshness that Othman felt the agha's spit in his own mouth.

Othman stopped screaming, but his face was still stricken with terror. He pointed to the ground, shaking.

Some of the other men also looked down to the ground. What they saw there caused them to jump back and lift their feet as if avoiding a poisonous snake.

It wasn't just Othman's clover that had teeth. They all had teeth. And the troops were in the center of the clover field.

The men began jumping, pirouetting, practically dancing around to avoid the tiny mouths that nipped at their soles and bootlaces.

"Have you all gone mad?" asked the agha.

A few of the soldiers shook their heads and screamed "No!" not understanding that it was a rhetorical question.

The agha set about beating his men with his scabbarded sword, forcing them back into something like a marching line, only crooked and broken, nothing like a marching line. Well, at least his horse obeyed him.

Momentarily.

The horse executed his assigned duties with great precision until something sharp stabbed him in the flank. This would normally have had little effect on an Arabian stallion. Horses such as this were bred for war. They were disciplined and knew little of fear.

And even less about dancing.

But he felt first a desire, then an urge, then an outright compulsion to do just that: dance!

"What are you doing? the agha yelled, bucking in the saddle. "Settle down!"

But this was the last thing the horse wanted to do. No, its blood was up, it heard the call of the music, and its shoes went from metal tools to taps in a matter of seconds.

"No! Turn, I say, turn!" the agha yelled, quite forgetting his earlier orders to keep quiet.

The horse turned, just not in the direction or at the pace the agha would have preferred. The horse kept turning, whirling, really, like a dervish in trance. He spun and pranced, carefree and wild, touched by some musical ur-horse spirit (actually, he had been touched by a particular fairy's arrow, but such things can't be explained to horses). The agha, who had ceded control over his beast, simply held on to the saddle horn for dear life while his men screamed at the tiny teeth beneath them, only to be silenced on the unlucky occasion where man's fear and horse's dance came into conflict.

Physics dictated that the more massive object win.

Then there was the matter of the winged shadows overhead, hooting in chorus as they dove down from the sky toward the moil of humanity beneath.

"Word of the southern invasion came, and I thought it best to return quickly."

"Your timing is excellent," the emperor said. "Felix is in need of soldiers—"

"Which I have sent!" Von Edelweir interrupted the monarch. "They should be here in two days."

"Herr Graf," Von Graeb said, "the force is too small."

"Three hundred men and two pieces of artillery are quite enough to hold out until more help can be sent," Von Edelweir said in a voice full of condescension. "How long until further reinforcements arrive?"

"Three more days."

Von Graeb's jaw dropped. "Three more days? How can we possibly defend the city? The emperor? The empire itself?"

"You are a good soldier," Von Edelweir said. "You will, I am confident, keep the enemy at bay."

"By myself? Pardon my frustration, but we cannot defend the city with so few! We need more men in less time!"

"I cannot recall my orders. Events are already in motion," Von Edelweir said with an inflection of finality that made Von Graeb uneasy. "The orders stand."

The major stood in stunned silence.

The emperor looked back and forth at the two men, waiting for one or the other to speak. Just as he inhaled to begin talking, a shout erupted outside the door. The door opened, and in stumbled Lescher, clothes in disarray, sweating and panting for air.

"Milord," he bowed to Von Graeb, "Milord, your majesty," he bowed to Von Edelweir and the emperor. "Terrible news. Bozsok is in flames."

"Bozsok! Von Graeb said. "How?"

"The Ottomans have overrun it."

"The Ottomans," the emperor said, confused. "But last we heard they were marching from Sofia."

"There is no doubt," Lescher said, finally catching his breath. "A handful of survivors have reported it. One of the enemy was captured and interrogated. He divulged little, except that the force is led by Pasha Mustafa Il-Ibrahim and is coming to destroy some kind of super-weapon, though details on what exactly the weapon is or does were scanty."

"But no army can march that fast," the emperor said. "What kind of sorcery is this?"

"I think I can answer that," Von Graeb said.

"Answer what?" Lescher asked.

"The emperor's question: 'what kind of sorcery is this?'"

Emperor Joseph urged Von Graeb to go on, anxious to hear his reasoning.

"I have no direct evidence, I must admit. All I have is my intuition and a couple of observations."

"Scant argument, Major," Von Edelweir said with a hint of derision.

Von Graeb ignored the comment.

"I think that the same kind of sorcery that could bring an army from the center of one empire to the border of another in such supernaturally short order might also bring one man from the northern end of an empire to its southern end just as quickly."

The emperor turned toward Von Edelweir, then back toward Von Graeb. "Are you saying . . ."

"Careful, boy!" Von Edelweir said. "Your implication is subordinate, possibly even treasonous."

"As treasonous as slowly poisoning the minister of defense in order to place another in his stead?"

"What are you saying, boy?" Von Edelweir could hardly contain his anger.

"I'm saying that the mysterious death of one minister of defense, so swiftly followed by the arrival of a long-lost noble who conveniently fits the need to fill the vacated position, one with such intimate knowledge of the Ottomans, and this followed by the unwarranted redistribution of troops that leaves the empire's flank barely protected from an unprovoked attack at the same time—I say 'unwarranted' distribution because our spies in Prussia became very talkative and influenced the focus of our military at the same time that our spies in the Ottoman Empire seemingly disappeared. This was, as you know, not long after Graf Von Helmutter passed away a sickly and depleted man, though he had been a man of great vigor to that point . . ." Von Graeb stopped mid-sentence. He knew he needn't say more. He waited for their reactions.

The emperor spoke first. "Are you saying that Graf Von Edelweir engineered these events?"

"I am saying no such thing. I am saying that Graf Viktor Von Edelweir is not all that he appears."

"Not all that he appears?" the emperor asked.

"No. In fact, this Graf Viktor Von Edelweir is not the graf at all. This, your majesty, is a charlatan."

"But how can these accusations be proven?" the emperor asked.

"They cannot!" said Von Edelweir.

"Oh, but they can, your Majesty. By producing the *real* Graf Viktor Von Edelweir. In fact, I believe he should be arriving at any moment."

Through the doorway, a babble of voices arose into a crescendo of shouts. The voices, barking with authority, had to be those of the imperial guards who were charged with securing the room.

"Halt!"

"You can't just go in there without authorization."

"No, wait! Herr Graf? But . . ."

"It can't be him. He's up in Saxony."

"A Turk with him?! He must be an imposter."

"You two, stop!"

A look of rage rippled across Von Edelweir's face as a pair of men walked in. One was young, not much more than a boy, obviously Turkish, dressed in well-worn traveler's clothes. The other man wore long, black flowing robes of exquisite workmanship. A white skull was embroidered on each sleeve, reflecting the skulls on Graf Von Edelweir's and Von Graeb's fezzes. His face, much to the emperor's shock, was an exact replica of the Graf Von Edelweir that stood nearer the emperor and Von Graeb.

Graf Von Edelweir, the one dressed in the death's head-surmounted uniform, laughed so hard that his voice cracked. It continued to crack as he spoke, as if his vocal cords were shared by two men separated by wide gulfs of age and attitude.

"Ah, so a doppelganger! But your so-called disguise is imbecilic in its simplicity. You wear the robes of a necromancer."

"A very specific necromancer," said the second Von Edelweir. He held his arms up to display the garment. "These are the robes of one who died long ago. One named Octavius Heilliger. Does the name sound familiar to you, minister?"

The laughter stopped. "I don't know who you are referring to, necromancer." His voice took on more and more the tone of the bitter, aged man. "And who let you in, anyway?"

"I did!" a voice, deep and gravely, echoed through the hall, the sheer volume of the bellowing causing all in the room to startle.

The emperor watched, wide eyed, stepping behind Von Graeb, who had drawn his saber, as a gigantic mangled man stooped through the doorway. He turned sideways to let his bulging, scar-stitched form through the portal. When he stood to his full height, he almost entirely blocked the doorway.

The uniformed Von Edelweir visibly shrank. "You!" he said in what was now clearly *not* the young graf's voice.

"Your old student, Master Mowler. You told me once that my name was Heraclix, but I've learned otherwise. I've learned a great many things about you and about myself, not the least of which is my true name. I am Octavius Heilliger."

Von Edelweir, the Minister of Defense, seemed to age on the spot. His face became splotchy and crows' feet began to show at the edges of his eyes.

"What proof do you have that *he* is not the deceiver?" the minister said, pointing toward the graf in the necromancer's robes.

"I think it's becoming quite clear," Heraclix said.

The crow's feet were joined by other lines that spread across and creased the minister's face. His mustache grayed, then fell away, as did his hair. Like a wilting flower, his skin withered, hands curled, and back hunched. He spit teeth out from the puckered rictus that was once the graf's charismatic smile. There was no doubt of the deception. From the youthful bloom of Graf Viktor

Von Edelweir's false form, the core of the infamous wizard had emerged in all its decrepitude.

"So it's me. What harm have I done, playing a little chess? Surely this was all a game. No less, no more."

"More than a game," Al'ghul finally spoke. He drew out a small scroll from beneath his vest and held the document aloft. "Your intent was far from harmless," the youth declared in a heavy accent. He unrolled the scroll and read aloud: "Most Eminent Pasha Il-Ibrahim, of course our agreement shall be honored once control is assumed. You shall have the Lady Adelaide for your harem, still a virgin, in adherence to your own high moral standards. Sincerely, Graf Viktor Von Edelweir."

Von Graeb turned and swung his saber at Mowler. In a move far too quick for his aged frame, the necromancer deflected the blade with his bare hand. Von Graeb fell off balance as the weight of the blade was scattered into a thousand tiny shards that harmlessly rained down on the floor. He stood in an attempt to grapple the old man, but a circular wall of black flame sprang up around Mowler.

"Ah! So cold it burns!" Von Graeb shouted, withdrawing from the black fire. He put his burnt hand into his jacket and withdrew.

Viktor and Al'ghul both sprang toward the sorcerer, but they were likewise repulsed by the eldritch fire.

Lescher, infuriated, yelled "You used me! I thought you were the graf! My dedication is to the empire, not to a devil-lover. I'll have you, old man!"

The servant hefted a nearby wooden chair and threw it at Mowler, but it bounced harmlessly off the flickering ebony wall.

The sorcerer still stood, so Heraclix, determined to rid the world of his curse, drew the silvered scimitar and approached.

Mowler held one hand up, then the other, as if to defend himself from the golem's imminent attack.

Suddenly, Heraclix stopped still, frozen to the floor, unable to move.

"He has the marks!" Shouted Al'ghul, "the marks of binding on his hands!"

Those who could see his upheld palms through the black flame beheld two glowing yellow sigils there, as if hot coals had been embedded in the old man's flesh. Indeed, smoke writhed up past his fingertips and into the air before him.

"You know you *could* actually do me harm with that sword," Mowler taunted, "if only you could move . . . boy!

"As for the rest of you. I will hear no more of you. Silence!" he yelled, his voice magically amplified to the point that the chandelier in the room shook and all in the room covered their ears, momentarily deafened. Each tried to cry out, but their voices were mute.

If they could have heard, they would have heard a strange noise, a voice, but not a completely human voice, croaking its way through the air and into the chamber.

"Caw! Caw! Phony!" it said, circling overhead.

"Cacophony, my old friend," Mowler said. "Good. I was afraid I was at a momentary stalemate. Now the tide turns in my favor yet again. Come to me, my friend."

Caw-Caw-Phony flew down in an ever-tightening spiral, well within the circle of flame by the time the raven-demon glided beneath the topmost black tongues.

Mowler turned toward the emperor, whose hearing, as with the others, had now returned.

"Your majesty, perhaps you should save everyone here a great deal of pain by voluntarily surrendering to the Ottomans. It would be most judicious of you. They are, by now, through Bozsok and approaching the city gates. So much destruction is avoidable, if you make it so. So much sorrow. Such a waste."

The sound of running boots preceded the entry of Sergeant Herzog into the chamber. At first all he could manage was "What in . . ." Then, seeing the emperor, Herzog bowed, after hastily acknowledging the others in what appeared to be a rather chaotic matter of state in which he didn't want to become involved, and gave this report: "Your majesty, the enemy army is on its way from Bozsok followed by another Ottoman force ten times larger marching in its wake! There is little hope . . ."

"There is *no* hope!" Mowler shouted, delighted.

"Now you shall witness the greatest sacrifice the world has ever known! And I, I shall wrest the crown of Hell from the decapitated head of Beelzebub himself!"

He smiled a wide, gap filled smile, then turned to Caw-Caw-Phony, who had perched itself on his shoulder. "Come, my friend, we will go open the gates of the city and invite the first of our sacrificial host. They will soon be joined in battle with the forces to the north, whom I shall rush here for the special occasion. Then I will offer them all up to the very powers of darkness and open the gates of Hell on Earth. It shall be a glorious entry that will lead to the coronation of the new King of the Underworld! Now, we must go . . ."

Mowler paused for a moment, straining to hear something.

"What was that? Do speak up, you stupid bird. I can't hear what it is you are trying to tell me."

He moved his head to the side, closer to Caw-Caw-Phony.

"I said speak . . . Ow!" Mowler yelped and recoiled. "Ah! Stop! What are you doing, foul fowl?"

He winced, reached up to grab the bird, who pecked again and again at the sorcerer's head. Soon, a light stream of blood trickled from the silver beak.

"Get off of me!" Mowler yelled, swinging wildly at the bird. Caw-Caw-Phony deftly pecked at the sorcerer's pate until the old lich connected with a lucky swipe that sent the bird sprawling to the ground, seemingly dead.

"Even you are against me, but why . . ."

He stopped as he saw the bird's carcass flutter, lift up from the floor, and fall again. Its gut had been split, and from the hole emerged a diminutive figure who drew a bow back to its full strain.

"Pomp hates to do this," she said.

Pomp let the arrow fly. It struck Mowler full in the face, causing him to jerk backward and take two staggering steps back to maintain his balance.

As he steadied himself, his features softened. The evil grin that had smeared his countenance relaxed into a pleasant smile. His eyes grew wide and soft.

"My, but you are beautiful," he said.

The wall of black flame disappeared.

Pomp stifled a gag.

"Pomp really hates to do this."

"But I, Mowler, no, call me Mattatheus, I Mattatheus, well, I don't know if I have the words to express my admiration for you, my . . . yes, it's true . . . my love!"

"Hurry up!" Pomp called out.

"Oh, but let's not rush in, let's enjoy the time . . ."

"Not you!" Pomp said sternly, "Viktor, hurry up!"

"Right away," the real Graf Von Edelweir said, surprised that his voice had returned to him once the wizard was distracted. "But I was so enjoying . . ."

"Now!" Pomp yelled.

"All right," he said, pulling a round object from his robes.

Von Edelweir uttered some words that Mowler might have understood if he wasn't, at that moment, completely enamored of little Pomp.

Mowler didn't see that the object that the graf cast toward the ground at his feet was a painted ceramic eyeball that burst open in a flash and a puff of smoke. He didn't see the man-shaped headless figure that emerged from the smoke. Mowler only had eyes for Pomp, and he realized too late that Panopticus had eyes only for Mowler. Hundreds and hundreds of eyes.

When he felt his soul slipping from his body he began to understand that he was being killed by the demon.

"Pomp, my love! Help me! I only want to be with you, my life shall be a torment without you!"

Panopticus laughed and all in the room shuddered.

"Oh, you shall know torment," said the demon with no mouth, "I'll see to that. And as for life, you won't need to worry about that any more!"

And as the ghost slipped from Mowler's dying body, Panopticus grabbed the screeching ectoplasmic entity and packed it with his hands as if he were forming a snowball, cramming it in on itself until Mowler's screams grew more and more quiet—until it cried in a very, very tiny voice, it's final word: "Pomp!"

Panopticus laughed, holding up a barbed-tail larva by its hook, the wrinkled face of Mattatheus Mowler the only characteristic left to distinguish it from every other newly lost soul in Hell.

"His Majesty, Beelzebub, King of Hell, shall have a devil of a time with you, my little pet!"

"Pztkzx!" the worm replied.

Panopticus vanished in a blinding flash leaving only the smell of sulfurous smoke behind.

The agha and his men stumbled up into the foothills south of Bozsok, bruised and bitten. The town's location was easily seen as a plume of smoke atop the mountain. They quickly ascended the hill, as much to flee the strange place through which they had just traveled as to meet up with the rest of the pasha's army. The agha's horse had to be put down, as his dancing had killed three men and broken twice as many limbs before the men came to their senses long enough to kill the beast. To add insult to injury, the supernatural forces that had terrorized his men and entranced his horse saw fit not only to force his horse to dance into his men, but to do it in the form of a most undignified and embarrassing Germanic Polka.

But now the agha led his troops on foot up to the burning village and there reported to the pasha.

"Most exalted pasha," the agha reported, "I am here with my men, though we lost three men and my horse to some strange phenomena a few miles back."

"You need not make up stories for why you are late, agha," the pasha said. "Today will be ours. I can understand your giddiness at the prospect of victory."

"Victory, so soon?" the agha asked.

"Very soon. Look back whence you came."

A cloud of dust ascended from the foothills.

"The sultan has heard of my genius and has sent his army to join the fray! I shall be rewarded handsomely, I suspect."

The hooves of the approaching cavalry became a deafening roar. The air choked with dust.

But it wasn't dust that caused the pasha to wrinkle his brow. Though his own ego inflated with the thought of rich reward, it didn't fully overshadow his reason. He recognized the sultan's guard, the swordmaster at the head, a pair of janissaries behind him, and a cadre of viziers, at the center of which rode the sultan himself. Surely the entourage was meant to show the importance that the sultan had put on his meeting with Pasha Mustafa Il-Ibrahim.

One question nagged at him. "How did they get here so quickly?" he said aloud.

"Probably the same way we came," the agha replied.

"But that was not in the plan . . ."

"Pasha Il-Ibrahim!" the sultan called out. "Come forth!" The sultan's entourage parted to allow the pasha to dismount, bow, and crawl toward the Sultan's horse.

Il-Ibrahim expected to lift his eyes to a vision of grandeur: the sultan, fat and smiling, his gold tooth sparkling in the sun, hand extended to the pasha with a bag full of precious gems, a pair of shapely virgins to whom the sultan would nod, signaling the women to take their place by the pasha's side to be wed right there on the spot.

"Pasha!" the sultan's voice called him out of the dream.

He looked up and was sorely disappointed.

A circle of lance points converged on the area around his head like a sharp iron halo.

"Pasha. I did not authorize this incursion."

"Ah . . ." Il-Ibrahim began.

"Silence dog! Do not speak. You shall never again speak as a pasha."

The sultan gestured to the side.

"This," he motioned for someone to come nearer, "is your replacement, the new pasha, Beyruit Al Mahdr."

Al Mahdr ceremoniously stooped down and removed the fez from Il-Ibrahim's head.

"He won't be needing that any more," the sultan joked.

The shadow of an ax made its way through the crowd.

Epilogue

Heraclix and Pomp walked and flew, respectively, down a long, flat road lined with broad canals, sun to their right as evening approached. Behind them, Vienna was lit up with candles in celebration of the marriage of the new Viennese Ambassador to the Ottoman Empire, Graf Felix Von Graeb, to the emperor's cousin, the Lady Adelaide. Across the canals, vast fields of tulips swayed in the spring breeze, the cool, salty wind of the North Sea gently blowing in their faces. An old man in a green boat waved without looking, then retracted the gesture when he saw the enormity of the lone traveler. Of course, Pomp couldn't be seen.

"Another hour or so, and we'll be there," the giant says.

"Tell Pomp again, before we get there." She was quite proud to be the only one in Faerie to understand "before." "Tell Pomp why you must go."

"Think back"—Heraclix was amused and quite proud that Pomp was, perhaps, the only fairy who *could* understand these words—"to what happened after Pasha Beyruit Al Mahdr met Graf Viktor Von Edelweir, the *real* Von Edelweir, at the borders of Bozsok."

"They both smiled much."

"Yes?"

"They shook hands, talked, and wrote together."

"That was a treaty they were signing, Pomp."

"Treaty?"

"They were agreeing not to fight each other."

"By writing their names down?"

"In a way, yes—each representing their empire."

Some things Pomp would never understand.

"But wouldn't their people still be mad at each other?"

"Of course. But Von Edelweir and Al Mahdr explained it to the people so they wouldn't be mad."

"All the people? But how?"

"Al Mahdr sent his messenger, Al'ghul, to the Ottomans to spread the word. And Von Edelweir sent Von Graeb to Vienna, Prague, and other parts of our empire."

"Spread the word?"

"That a sorcerer had come among the people of the Holy Roman Empire and tricked them. So the Ottomans came to their aid. Together, they killed the sorcerer."

"But Panopticus killed Mowler."

"The people wouldn't understand. Not quickly enough, anyway, if they were told the whole story. It would be like you trying to explain what 'yet' means to all the fairies at once."

"That would be hard. I think I understand. And what will they do yet?"

"Who?"

"Al Mahdr, Von Graeb, everyone!"

"Those are three different matters, Pomp. And there are many more than that. But I'll try to explain as best I can."

Pomp landed on his shoulder to be able to concentrate better.

"Von Graeb and Al Mahdr will continue to talk to keep the peace between their countries. They will use reason and logic to try to make good decisions."

"But will they?"

"Make good decisions? I hope so. I suppose everyone makes mistakes, but these are good men. They'll do the best they can."

"Will Von Graeb *fight*?" Pomp said the word with some excitement.

"No!" Heraclix said.

Pomp felt sorry for what she said, though she couldn't figure out why she felt that way.

"No, his is a mission of peace. He refused to become minister of defense when the position was offered to him by Emperor Joseph."

"Then who will do it?"

"Apparently a cousin of your Polish friend Yrzmowski."

"Really? But he—"

"He is not his cousin. I am assured that the new minister of defense will be just that, a minister of *defense*, not a minister of offense. Besides, Von Graeb asked and received a favor of the emperor that should ensure that the new minister administer his duties properly. At Von Graeb's request, Lescher is the new minister's right hand man. He'll behave."

"Lescher or the Minister?"

"Both!" Heraclix laughed.

"Then what does Von Graeb do yet?"

"Lady Adelaide wants to move to the country, and Von Graeb has promised that they will do so once he has filled his duty to visit the edges of the empire to deliver news of the treaty."

"And Al'ghul?"

"Al'ghul has a long road, many long roads, ahead of him. He is young now, but he might be old by the time he has finished delivering his message to the ends of the Ottoman lands. They are a little more elaborate in their meetings and a little more deliberate in giving news."

Ahead of them they could see a small port city and, beyond, the sea. Sails like white butterflies caught the wind and pulled their ships off toward the horizon. They could see the sunlight reflecting off the buildings as they walked closer. Heraclix was struck silent by the beauty of it all. Pomp was also quiet for a long time. Then she spoke.

"Heraclix, am I good?"

The golem smiled. "Yes, Pomp, you are good."

"I'm glad. Because I've seen Hell, and I don't like it. There's no one there that I like."

"I can understand that," Heraclix said with a hint of remorse.

"The Serb wasn't there. And your Elsie and Rhoda weren't there, either."

Heraclix simply continued walking, watching the ships come and go. He wondered to where and whence and how long the seas would be there to sail upon.

"Will we go back . . ." Pomp asked with trepidation ". . . there?"

"I don't know, Pomp. I am working with the Shadow Divan now, and my work may take me there. We are going to cut off the entrances to Hell, or at least to ensure that they can be used only one way: in."

"So, no more Panopticus?"

"No. No more Panopticus, no more Bozkovitch, no more Beelzebub. They will not come here again, we will see to it."

"Why?" Pomp could hardly believe she had asked the question. It seemed to come out of her mouth at its own wish.

"Now is a new age, Pomp. An age of reason. An enlightened age. Devils, sorcerers, even golems and fairies don't make much sense here."

"But you're still here."

"Until my task is complete, yes. Then I shall close the door on this age and, likely, on this world, behind me."

Pomp thought about this for a long time as they wove their way through the streets of the city. She spoke up as they approached the docks.

"Friend Heraclix, if there is a Hell, then there might also be a Heaven."

"I hope, someday, to find out. But not today."

"Today you will find your 'yet.'"

"Yes, friend Pomp. But not without you. This is *our* 'yet.'"

They ascended the ramp of a large, three-masted clipper and boarded. The sails caught a stiff breeze and snapped in the wind, enticing the ship toward new horizons, beneath new stars, under a new sky.

ACKNOWLEDGMENTS

Thanks first and foremost to my wife, Natalie, and my kids, Issaka, Kaiser, Hayden, and Oakleigh (and even Loki), for tolerating their dad's long hermitic stretches at the writing desk. And special thanks to Kaiser, my best first reader. Heraclix & Pomp wouldn't be what they are without you. To Mom, thanks for the gift of the creative spirit and, Dad, thanks for corrupting my young mind with a love of science fiction and fantasy. Thanks to Kris O'Higgins, for believing in my work and your persistence in the face of my persistence; to Mark Teppo and Darin Bradley on the start of this new publishing adventure; and to Claudia Noble for the most beautiful cover I could have asked for. Heraclix would like to thank The Kilimanjaro Darkjazz Ensemble and Nick Cave for his soundtrack, while Pomp thanks Big Bad Voodoo Daddy and They Might Be Giants for hers. Mowler could not be contacted to ask his musical preferences, but I think he was rather fond of Blood Ceremony, Opeth, and Jess and the Ancient Ones. My thanks also to all else who lent any kind of help to this team endeavor. Most of all, thank you, reader, for taking this adventure with Heraclix, Pomp, and me. We hope you've enjoyed the ride!